THE THREADS OF TIME ARE UNRAVELING . . .

Neil gazed into The Separate Collection and recalled how frightened he had been when he first moved to the Wyrd Museum. He remembered how the building had almost seemed to be tricking him, leading him around and around until finally he was delivered to this very place, where the exhibits were eerie and sinister.

"Are you saying that the building is alive?" he finally ventured. "Watching and listening to us?"

The ghost hunter gave a brisk shake of his head. "Not in the sense that we understand. I do believe, however, that there is a presence that permeates every brick and tile—an awareness, if you like. Call it a mass accumulation of history and anguish recorded onto the ether that operates on some very basic and primitive level. That is what we are up against."

WYRD MUSEUM

The Woven Path
The Raven's Knot
The Fatal Strand

WYRD MUSEUM

The Fatal Strand

Robin Jarvis

Troll

Visit the author's website at www.robinjarvis.com

This paperback edition published in 2001.

Copyright © 1998 by Robin Jarvis.

Published by Troll Communications L.L.C.

Published by arrangement with HarperCollins Publishers Ltd.

Cover illustration by Shi Chen.

Printed in the United States of America.

10 9 8 7 6 5 4 3 2 1

CONTENTS

Many thanks to Ann-Janine Murtagh for guiding me along The Woven Path, then to Stella Paskins for helping me tie up The Raven's Knot and ensuring I wasn't left Fatally Stranded.

1:30 AM

Shrill screams, raging with grief, echoed throughout the Wyrd Museum. From the rambling attics, where frightened pigeons shuffled uneasily on their perches, the hideous shrieking blistered. Down into the shadow-filled rooms it poured, an incessant flood of anguish, streaming from chamber to chamber—until finally it seeped beneath the foundations and babbled through the subterranean caverns.

Miss Veronica Webster—she who was Verdandi, youngest of the immortal Fates—was dead. She who had once measured out the lives of men; she who had sat at the ensnaring Loom upon which every strand of existence was woven; she who wielded the ultimate tyranny of Doom and Destiny was no more.

A darkness more profound than the pressing night smothered the museum, and the incessant lament endured.

Outside, one of the bronze figures that flanked the main entrance lay shattered on the ground. The shadows within the Wyrd Museum deepened, swelling the rooms with a solid suffocation of light.

To every neglected niche of the ancient building the chilling dirge eventually penetrated, ripping through the previously inviolate night. Wretched and racked with pain the dismal chorus tolled, filling every invisible corner with the agony of loss.

Then it happened.

In that choking gloom appeared a delicate pulse of light, and a new sound was born. Softly at first, a gentle creaking began, like floorboards easing and groaning after a long day underfoot. Gradually the noise grew louder. Creaks became snaps, and the troubled dark rang with the frenzy of splintering wood.

Suddenly another noise joined the increasing clamor: a panting, rattling breath that rasped and heaved when the rupturing of timber escalated to its height. Then a yelping, piglike squeal spiked through the black gloom.

With one last, straining effort, the unseen creature was free. A hiss of exultation steamed from its wide mouth, and it dropped to the floor.

Clawed feet clattered on the ground as the small imp landed. For a moment it paused, a pair of large eyes blinking in the eternal dark, its tail switching from side to side. Then, with a gargling gasp upon its lips, the creature leaped forward, gnashing out a constant cacophony of barks and grunts. Through the ebon shadows it scurried, and in that jumble of guttural chattering, it repeated a single word over and over again.

"Gogus . . . Gogus . . . Gogus . . ."

CHAPTER 1

THE HOMECOMING

The chill night airs that encircled Glastonbury Tor sliced through the barren trees, crowding its lower slopes and gusting with icy vigor up the narrow track that climbed the shoulders of that steep, ancient hill. The desperate conflict between the hideous forces of Woden and the small group from the Wyrd Museum was over. A horrible battle had been fought on the Tor, and now, for those few who remained, this was a grief-filled time.

Standing there in the cold, his school uniform providing meager protection against the biting breeze, Neil Chapman felt his flesh tremble—but the boy made no other movement.

On his shoulder the feathers of a mangy-looking raven stirred as the bird considered his young master with its single beady eye.

"Gelid doth the blood flow thick and laggard," Quoth cawed faintly. "Cold as a frog art thou, yet the icy breath of the northern wind is blameless in this."

Lifting his head, the raven gazed on the dreadful scene that lay before them and clicked his tongue sorrowfully.

There, lying across the muddy path, was the body of Miss Veronica Webster. By the old woman's side eight-year-old Edie Dorkins knelt in the crimson pool that had formed around her, weeping hopelessly. In the macabre mire lay a rusted spearhead, steeped in blood.

Quoth sniffed and wiped his beak across one wing. It was a terrible moment, and although he racked his decayed brain he could find no words of comfort to offer.

Beyond Edie's sobbing figure several small fires burned on the hillside, and the raven stared at them thoughtfully. There the last of the enemy's servants, the *Valkyrja*, were burning. The small crow dolls that had taken possession of twelve local women were utterly consumed in the greedy flames, and their reviled existence in this world was finally banished forever.

It had been a terrifying contest, and Quoth pulled his head into his shoulders as he counted the cost of this unhappy victory. His brother, Thought, and many others had been lost in the horrendous violence. Aidan, the mysterious gypsy who had brought Neil to Glastonbury, now lay dead upon Wearyall Hill, which reared into the darkness across the valley.

Almost drowned out by the dejected cries of Edie Dorkins were faint whimpers from the few lucky survivors, and the raven shook his feathers in readiness to seek them out. But before he could unfurl his wings, a wail of sirens joined the common grief, and the night began to strobe with harsh blue lights.

Turning, Quoth peered down the track. Through the screening trees he saw many vehicles gathering in Wellhouse Lane. He heard the voices of men raised in wonder and dread amid the confused blare of alarm and engine.

"Squire Neil," the bird croaked into the boy's ear, "the reckoning hath come. We art besieged, and guards toil up the mountain's side to seize us."

Slowly, Neil Chapman wrenched his eyes away from the desolate sight of Edie and Miss Veronica and moved like one roused from a fathomless sleep, gradually surfacing back into the grim, waking world.

At first he was only vaguely conscious of the frantic sweeps the flashlight beams made as they blazed through twigs and branches, dazzling in the muddy puddles and searing the shadowy night. Then one of the lights shone directly in his face, and he threw up his hands to ward off the blinding glare.

Suddenly he was aware of everything: the angry, bewildered yells and the urgent progress of the figures hastening up the track.

"There's a kid up here!" someone bawled.

"This is the police," another barked with authority. "Stay right where you are."

Captured in the accusing glare of a dozen dazzling beams, Neil squinted and automatically raised his hands while Quoth gave a frightened squawk and buried his beak in his wing.

"We haven't done anything!" Neil protested, his mind racing. How could he possibly explain what had really happened and expect anyone to believe it?

Then the bright lights fell upon Edie and Miss Veronica.

"Another two behind him!" one of the officers cried. "Get the medics up here—quick."

Edie Dorkins tossed her head at the intrusive light, and she curled her mouth into a ferocious snarl. If one of those men so much as touched Miss Veronica she was ready to fly at him, biting and clawing as rabidly as any wild creature.

"God almighty," someone muttered, seeing the rivulets of blood streaming from the old woman's body. "Explosion or somethin', they said. She's been knifed—look at the state of her!"

The first of the policemen drew level with Neil, and the confused man stared at the boy questioningly.

"Don't you do nothing," he snapped as others pushed by him. "What 'appened 'ere?"

Before Neil could reply, one of the policemen ventured too close to Edie, and there followed a savage struggle as he fell backward into the mud, with the feral girl scratching and kicking him.

It took two of the astonished officer's colleagues to drag the fierce child away. Although they kept a firm grip of her arms, their shins suffered vicious blows from a barrage of kicks.

"We're not going to hurt you," they assured her through gritted teeth. "Let the doctors by to 'ave a look at her."

"She's dead!" Edie screeched in a thin, shrill voice.

"Let her 'lone. Don't you touch her. Veronica! Veronica!"

Neil gently tugged the sleeve of the distracted superintendent, and the man started nervously.

"Keep your hands where I can see them!" he ordered, but Neil could tell that the policeman was almost afraid of him. Did he think that Neil had murdered Miss Veronica? The whole town must be wondering what had happened on the Tor. Tremendous rumbles had shaken the earth, and angelic fires had raged on the summit, spreading a blistering light across the surrounding countryside. Perhaps the officer thought that he and Edie were responsible.

Watching the man's expression, Neil was certain of it. Yet there were more immediate concerns.

"There are others," he said, nodding toward the dark hillside where the small, scattered fires still crackled. "People—up there. Some might still be alive."

The superintendent stared at him for a moment, then gave a shout to the police officers nearby. A group of them hurried up the track, their flashlights thrashing the night as they searched the surrounding slope.

Feeling helpless, Neil looked on as a team of paramedics from one of the ambulances clustered around the body of Miss Veronica. Then he saw a fat sergeant carefully place the blood-covered spearhead into a plastic bag.

"Looks like this is what did it," the man said, unable to hide his ghoulish glee at having been the one to bag the murder weapon.

"Who did this?" the superintendent demanded sharply. "Did you see? Was there someone else up here?"

Neil shook his head. The raven on his shoulder shifted his weight from one foot to the other while ogling the man with the utmost displeasure.

Before anything further could be said, a new, abrupt voice called out, "Willis, get your lads out of the way! I'll deal with this."

The policeman turned and shone his light straight into the face of a man who had quickly pushed his way up the track.

Neil looked at the stranger. He was a tall, big-boned man whose graying beard framed a hollow-cheeked face that was corrugated with irritation.

"Turn that damn thing off!" he rapped severely.

"Chief Inspector!" the superintendent exclaimed, fumbling with the flashlight. "We've got a mess here. I was just—"

"I said, get your lads out of the way," his superior insisted. "Those damn reporters'll be here before you know it. Set up a cordon around the Tor and one over at Wearyall Hill. Hurry up, man—I mean now, not some time next week!"

Cowed by Chief Inspector Hargreaves's unusually curt directives, Superintendent Willis set about organizing what had to be done and left him alone with Neil.

Staring at the stretcher that now bore Miss Veronica's body, Hargreaves's face looked more sunken than ever, and he gripped hold of Neil's shoulders to steady himself. Then in a rush of anguished words, just low enough to prevent anyone else from overhearing, he implored, "Is it true? Can Verdandi really be dead? How can the deathless die?"

Neil stared up at him. "Who are you?" he asked in an astonished whisper.

It was Quoth who answered. "Canst thou not perceive it, my master?" the raven cawed. "'Tis another scion of Askar who standeth afore thee. That fairest of cities doth glimmer dim yet steady in his eyes. As Aidan was, so too is this spindle-shanked beanpole—a servant of the Loom Maidens is he."

The chief inspector lowered his eyes, murmuring, "To the descendants of Askar, the world's first civilization, Aidan was our leader. I've just come from Wearyall Hill. I . . . I saw him there. It's up to the rest of us now to continue his work."

Setting aside his consternation and sorrow, he cast a wary glance over his shoulder before hastily continuing. "There's not much time. You've got to trust me. Can you get the girl to come with us without a fight?"

"Where are we going?"

"Back to the museum. The sooner Verdandi is returned to that sacred place, the safer we'll all be. The Cessation of the Three has begun. Anything may happen now. The order of Destiny has been interrupted. Go calm the girl. If we don't leave soon, it'll be too late."

With that, Hargreaves directed the two officers holding Edie to release her, and at once the girl sprang forward to hare after the stretcher.

Neil caught up with her and spun her around.

"Lay off!" she squealed, brandishing her woolen pixie hat in the boy's face. "You an' your crow stay 'way from me."

"Listen!" he hissed back. "Keep quiet and do as you're told for a change or we'll never get home. That man wants to help us. He's the same as Aidan—do you understand what that means?"

The girl ceased her struggles and swept the hair from her eyes to regard the chief inspector more keenly. "Then he must take Veronica to Ursula," she demanded. "An' the spear—that has to come as well."

To the surprise of his men, Chief Inspector Hargreaves announced that he was personally taking charge of the children and would drive them to the police station at Wells. Any awkward questions were abruptly swept aside when a shout sounded on the Tor, and Neil guessed that yet another mutilated body had been discovered.

In the ensuing confusion, Hargreaves led the children down the narrow track to where his car was waiting. A private ambulance with dark, tinted windows was already moving off with Miss Veronica on board, and Edie glared up at the chief inspector, suspecting treachery.

"Don't worry," he assured her. "The driver is one of us. He's going to wait on the Wells Road, then you can sit by Verdandi's side all the way to the museum. The weapon is with her also. I know just how dangerous it is."

Presently Hargreaves's car pulled away. Perched in the back, his feathery face pressed against the cold rear window, Quoth watched the vast black shape of the Tor recede into the distance.

In a small dejected voice he croaked a final farewell to his deceased brother, and soon the lights of Glastonbury were left far behind.

*   *   *

Still wet from the previous day's downpour, the roads of London's East End reflected a dun-colored sky. The night had grown old, and a dim, gray dawn was beginning to reach over the irregular horizon of ramshackle rooftops. At Bethnal Green, the many turrets and spikes that crowned the Wyrd Museum were mirrored in the countless dirty pools surrounding it. When viewed from the corner of the alleyway, the dark, forbidding building appeared to become a sinister moated castle.

At the rear of the museum, within the drab cemented courtyard, a solitary figure stood in the reservoir of shadow that gathered deep beneath the high encircling walls.

Wearing only an old T-shirt and a pair of ragged pajama bottoms, Neil's father, Brian Chapman, was staring up into the fading night. Even the brightest stars had fled from the brimming heavens, yet still he gazed at the realm of diminishing darkness high above.

A cloud of vapor streamed from his lips as, slowly, he lowered his eyes. The unlovely shape of the museum filled his vision, and he shuddered involuntarily.

"There was a crooked man," he muttered under his breath, "lived in a crooked house . . ."

Gooseflesh prickled his bare, scrawny arms, and he

looked down with surprise at his naked feet, now purple with cold. Just how long he had been standing out there he had no idea, and he could not recall what had drawn him from his makeshift bed in the first place. All he remembered was the shrieking that had awakened him. But there had been something else too—a compelling urge to venture outside and be wrapped in the embracing cold.

That might have been hours ago. Under the blank gaze of the museum's darkened windows he had remained. The violent weeping had ceased, but what had happened in the meantime? Surely he could not have fallen asleep out here in the yard?

"Blood and sand!" he scolded himself, pattering toward the caretaker's small apartment once more. "This lousy place'll drive us all nuts."

Clambering back onto the couch, he wriggled inside the sleeping bag beneath his comforter—but the memory of the cold lingered with him and refused to thaw.

* * *

Even as the caretaker tried to get warm, the tall, gaunt shape of an elderly woman stood silhouetted within the grand Victorian entrance of the Wyrd Museum, silently watching the last dregs of night melt into glimmering day.

On the topmost of the three steps she waited: Miss Ursula Webster, Urdr of the Royal House, the eldest of the Fates. She, who throughout the long tale of time had been feared far more than her sisters, appeared drawn and defeated. In former ages it was she who had severed the threads of life, determining that irrevocable ending that sundered families and lovers with a single, merciless cut. Now a similar parting had been visited upon her, and the pain of that loss was something she had not felt since the first days of the world.

Over her delicately boned features a fine dew sparkled, perfectly matching the glitter of the jet beads that bordered her black evening gown.

A cauldron of emotions seethed and boiled within her. Rage and guilt battled with her grief, but she remained erect and alert, steeling herself against the contest she knew was to come.

At the bottom of the steps, scattered in a disjointed snarl of twisted bronze, lay the fragmented image of Verdandi. The sightless eyes of the broken, upturned face seemed to stare at her sister, but the old woman avoided meeting that steady gaze and maintained her unwavering vigil, glaring out into the alleyway.

She knew exactly what had transpired on Glastonbury Tor and who was responsible for this heinous tragedy. His unseen hand had driven that enchanted blade through her sister's immortal flesh as surely as if he had gripped the spear himself. In some dank corner her great enemy waited, weaving his evil designs just as she and her sisters had spun the Cloth of Doom.

Perhaps even now he was watching her, savoring the full extent of his abhorrent crime.

"Do you hear me?" she asked, abruptly snapping

the silence, her clipped voice charged with contempt and condemnation. "Is this what you have yearned for? Is this the triumphant victory you have sought these many centuries? How pitiable you have become, mighty Woden! Is this the same god of war who hung for nine nights upon the World-Tree? Is this He who fought with axe and sword against the ogres of the first frost? Has the Captain of Askar been reduced to this—murdering a woman too old and too witless to defend herself?"

Miss Ursula's pale eyelids drooped closed as she fought to control her anger, fiercely pressing her thin lips together before attempting to speak again.

"What sweetness can there be in my sister's death?" she eventually continued in as level a voice as she could maintain. "Wallow well in this, the vilest of deeds. If it is still your avowed intent to destroy the remaining daughters of Askar, then you will never succeed. Against the powers that are mine to command you can only fail. The fortress of my museum has, in its keeping, defenses beyond either your strength or your comprehension. Neither you nor your agents shall ever set foot over this threshold.

"Do you mark my warning? If you desire this war, then so be it. The challenge is accepted. But know this—to the death shall the campaign be waged. The Mistresses of Doom and Destiny will conquer even you in the end."

No answer came to Miss Ursula as she stood dignified and grave upon the step. Before she had time to wonder if her adversary had heard her censorial words, she became aware of a forlorn sniveling behind her, and she turned archly.

Into the main hall a bundle of dirty wash seemed to be making its clumsy, faltering way down the wide staircase. It paused next to a rusted suit of armor. The pale light that flickered from a small oil lamp lapped over the ragged form for a moment before the hobbling gait continued.

Swaddled in a grubby nightgown that was fringed with filthy lace, Miss Celandine Webster stumbled on. She who was once Skuld of the Royal House of Askar was now an old woman. Her face, which normally resembled an overripe apple, was wrung into a wizened prune, and in her large hands she clutched a mildew-speckled handkerchief.

"Oh, Ursula!" she blubbered. "Don't leave me all on my own. I can't bear it—I can't!"

The figure in the entrance regarded her coldly, her face betraying none of the emotions that churned within her.

"Control yourself," she instructed. "Histrionics won't bring her back."

Miss Celandine staggered forward, her grimy feet slapping over the polished parquet floor. "Make it better!" she beseeched. "Bring Veronica back to us. How can she be killed? We don't die—we can't! I won't believe it—I won't, I won't!"

The eldest of the Websters recoiled from this infantile display and returned her attention to the alleyway outside, completely ignoring her sister's heart-rending pleas.

"Oh, help me, Ursula!" Celandine wept, dragging the handkerchief over her face and twisting it into her wrinkled eyes. "I'm frightened. What's happening to us? Why did Veronica run away? My heart hurts me so. Please hold me. Make me feel safe."

But Miss Ursula had no comfort to spare for her sister. Like a house of cards demolished in the draft, Miss Celandine crumpled to the floor. There she stayed, weeping and sobbing until her voice cracked and the spring of her tears ran dry.

For an hour they held their positions, one rigid and silent, the other a quivering heap of choking despair, and neither of them could give solace to the other.

Eventually the sound of an approaching engine roused Miss Celandine from her pit of grief. Raising her head from the crook of her elbow, where she had sniffed and whimpered away the dawn, she saw her sister move onto the middle step as the sound grew closer. Throwing her two braids of corn-colored hair over her shoulders, she rose and crept forward, her dry bones crackling in complaint.

"What is it, Ursula?" she cooed with a fearful voice. "Who is it?"

Pressing close to her sister, she tried to venture onto the topmost step to peer out, but Miss Ursula barred the way and propelled her back into the museum.

"Stay in there," she rapped severely. "Veronica is returned to us."

Rumbling into the alley came an unmarked ambulance with dark tinted windows. Lumbering as close to the entrance as possible, the vehicle braked in front of the iron posts that barricaded one end of the alleyway, and the doors opened slowly.

Clambering from the passenger seat, Neil stepped onto the cobbles, with Quoth in his usual place on the boy's shoulder.

It had been a dismal journey in which few words had been exchanged. Neil had given Chief Inspector Hargreaves a sketchy account of all that had happened on Glastonbury Tor, but he soon lapsed into weary silence, snatching occasional moments of much-needed sleep. The eyes he turned to the Wyrd Museum were ringed with gray, and he ached for his bed. There was, however, one more duty to be done before then, and he gazed at the man who was already closing the driver's door.

Chief Inspector Hargreaves stood solemnly before that ugly building to which he and the other remaining descendants of Askar made their annual pilgrimage. For as long as he could remember he had come to this place to lay an offering of flowers at the drinking fountain in the yard. It was a demonstration of fealty to those who lived within, yet never once had he or any of the others caught so much as a glimpse of the three undying Fates.

In all his imaginings he had not dreamed that he would ever meet the Handmaidens of the Loom. Now here he was, burdened with this most dreadful of errands—delivering the corpse of the youngest to her sisters, and his soul quailed inside him.

In somber silence, he stared across to where Miss Ursula waited on the steps, and he bowed reverently. The woman's thin lips twitched with agitation, but she inclined her head in acknowledgment and gestured for the man to complete the grim task he had undertaken.

Turning on his heel, Hargreaves led Neil to the rear of the ambulance and pulled open the large double doors. Presently they emerged, bearing between them the stretcher upon which lay the body of Miss Veronica Webster.

Throughout the journey, Edie Dorkins had clung to the dead woman's hand. Now, as she walked alongside this melancholy procession, she held it still.

A blanket had been wrapped about the girl's shoulders during the long drive from Somerset, but it fell to the ground as she traipsed alongside the stretcher. Distractedly, she wiped her nose on the sleeve of her coat.

Seeing the frail body of her sister looking so shriveled and old, Miss Ursula drew herself up to her full height and bit the inside of her cheek. She must not allow herself to weaken now. There must be no betrayal.

"Take her within," she uttered thickly, standing back to allow them entry. "Place her over there, on the floor."

With bulging eyes, Miss Celandine watched as the litter carrying her younger sister passed under the archway, and she yelped shrilly at the awful sight.

Miss Ursula knew it was pointless to try to stop her, and so, with Miss Celandine's ghastly squeals echoing in the hallway, she patiently waited until the stretcher had been gently placed where she had directed.

"My family is in your debt," she informed the chief inspector. "I thank you for returning our sister to us."

Hargreaves could only stare at his feet, suddenly speechless at this meeting.

"You have risked everything to bring her here," Miss Ursula continued. "Your career, possibly even your freedom. If there was anything in my power to give you, it would be yours. The children of Askar are loyal, indeed."

The chief inspector shook his head and found his voice at last. "It is enough to have served," he muttered.

"Then leave us now," she told him. "But do not stray far. In the dark days to come, Urdr may have need of you again."

Hargreaves returned to the entrance, and with her taffeta gown rustling like dry grass as it swept across the floor, Miss Ursula Webster brushed him outside, closing the door in his face.

Upon the steps the chief inspector drew his breath and shook his head. The death of Miss Veronica had altered everything. His thoughts in turmoil, he hurried from the alleyway with a hideous dread gnawing at his spirit.

Something terrible was about to befall the world, and as he climbed back into the ambulance, he determined to summon as many of the descendants of Askar as possible.

"The children of they who were there at the beginning," he told himself darkly, "should be here to witness the end."

CHAPTER 2

VIGIL FOR THE DEATHLESS DEAD

"You!" Miss Ursula snapped at Neil. "Remove that accursed bird of ill omen from my sight before I wring his wretched neck."

Tickling Quoth reassuringly under the chin, Neil returned the old woman's imperious glare yet did not answer. Normally he would have shouted right back at her, but that morning he made allowances for her grief—and besides, he was too tired.

"Come on," he told the raven. "We'll grab something to eat, then I honestly think I could sleep for the rest of the day." With the scraggy-looking bird casting a fretful glance over his shoulder, they made their way through the many rooms and galleries toward the caretaker's apartment.

When they reached a dreary passageway ending at a door covered in peeling green paint, Neil hesitated and turned to his faithful companion.

"Listen," he began. "My dad can be a bit funny sometimes."

Quoth gave a hearty cluck and hopped up and down with excitement. "Thou art the son of a jester!" he chirruped. "That is well, for this sorry chick is melancholy as a gallows cat. 'Tis most surely a great truth that the memory of joy doth make misery thrice times awful. Haste, haste, Squire Neil, let us to this worthy fool. I wouldst be made merrie!"

Neil groaned. "I don't mean it that way. My dad can be a bit strange, that's all."

The raven nodded sagely. "Ah!" he croaked. "Thy father is mad."

"Very likely." Neil couldn't help smiling. "So don't make it any worse. Try and keep quiet. He doesn't like stuff he can't understand, and there's enough going on in here to last him a lifetime."

Trying to make as little sound as possible, Neil opened the door and crept inside the apartment.

To his surprise he found that his father was already awake. Half-submerged in the padded blue nylon of his sleeping bag, Brian Chapman was sitting up on the shabby sofa, his face turned toward the window.

He did not seem to hear his son enter, and Neil eyed him quizzically. "Dad?" he ventured.

The man continued to stare fixedly out of the window.

"Dad," Neil repeated, "I'm back."

Quoth craned forward to peer at the boy's father more closely.

"'Tis most certain an affliction of the moon," he

cawed. "Never hath this poor knave espied such a muggins."

At that moment, Brian Chapman gave a violent shiver, and he whipped around, startled.

Taken aback by the sudden movement, the raven squawked in surprise and flapped his wings to steady himself.

"What's that?" Neil's father cried, scowling at the bird in revulsion. "Take it out of here, Neil. It's vermin! Full of germs. You'll catch your death!"

"Don't worry," Neil said hurriedly, seeing that Quoth was already clearing his throat to let loose a fitting retort. "He's very clean, and he doesn't bite."

"You can't keep him."

"I don't have to—he's my friend."

Brian pinched the bridge of his nose, a sure sign that he was growing impatient.

"I hate this place," he grumbled, extricating himself from the sleeping bag while snatching his glasses from the nearby shelf. "Always something peculiar happening. Never stops. Couldn't sleep a wink last night. An absolute madhouse! One of those crazy women was screeching her head off till all hours."

"One of them has died," Neil said simply.

But his father wasn't listening. He glared at the raven and shook his head resolutely.

"Disgusting!" he declared. "It's bald and mangy. What's happened to its other eye? Might have rabies or worse. You've got to get it out of here. I don't want it anywhere near your brother."

Unable to remain silent any longer, Quoth finally defended himself against these unwarranted insults.

"Woe to thee, most ill-favored malapert!" he quacked. "Verily dost thou show how abject be the poverty of thine wits! No ornament nor flower may this morsel be, yet mine eye findeth no delectation in thine own straggled visage! Thou hast the semblance of a wormy turnip which yea, even the famined wild hog wouldst snub."

Brian gaped at the bird, but anger swiftly overcame his astonishment. Lurching forward, he grabbed the raven, and Quoth bleated in fright as he tried to escape. Neil's father, however, held him firmly and marched to the door, holding the wildly flapping bird at arm's length.

"It's come from upstairs, hasn't it?" the man shouted. "For heaven's sake, Neil—isn't it bad enough having to live in this asylum without you fetching the freaks down here?"

"Let him go!" Neil protested, trying to grab his father's outstretched arm.

But it was no use. Quoth was flung out of the apartment and ejected into the corridor.

For a brief instant, the raven found himself tumbling helplessly through the air. Then he crashed into an oil painting, slid down the canvas, and fell to the floor with a loud squawk of dismay.

Sprawled on the cold wooden boards, he glared at the now firmly closed door, looking like a tangled clump of half-chewed feathers that an idle cat might have abandoned. He puffed out his chest indignantly.

"Toad-frighter and donkey-wit!" he mumbled to the expanse of peeling green paint. "Clodpole and besom steward!"

Picking himself up, the bird shook his tail and inspected his wings before waddling closer to the door, where he waited for it to open again.

"Master Neil?" the raven cawed expectantly. "Master Neil?"

Within the caretaker's apartment, Neil Chapman struggled to barge past his father, but Brian pushed him backward.

"If he can't stay, then I won't either!" the boy fumed.

"Go to your room!"

"You haven't even asked where I've been or what happened!"

"I'm not interested!" came the cruel reply. "I'm sick to death of having to live in this looney bin with that old bag upstairs bossing me around all day. Well, it won't be for much longer."

Neil stared at him. "What's that supposed to mean?"

"Time we left," Brian said with uncharacteristic resolve. "I'll find another job."

"You can't do that!" his son cried. "Not now!"

Running a hand through his lank hair, the man grunted with exasperation. "Blood and sand!"

Neil turned away from him and stomped toward the bedroom he shared with his younger brother, Josh. "You never stick with anything," he muttered resentfully.

Barging into the room, the boy threw himself onto the bed and miserably wondered what he would do if his father tried to make him leave the Wyrd Museum.

"I can't go now," he told himself. "This place hasn't finished with me yet. I just know it. And what about poor old Quoth?"

But his wretched reflections would have to wait, for all his energies were utterly spent and the softness of the bed proved to be too potent a force to resist. In a moment, his eyes were closed and he felt himself drifting off to sleep.

In the living room, Brian slumped back into the armchair and gazed fixedly up at the ceiling, insensible to the dejected chirrups sounding from the corridor outside.

"Not long now," he whispered to himself. "Then I'll be free."

* * *

In the main hallway, still clasping Miss Veronica's hand, Edie Dorkins knelt on the hard floor, arranging the dead woman's dyed black hair about her shoulders while brushing the mud flecks from her shriveled face. Miss Celandine was still yowling, but she had buried her head into her spadelike hands and so the shrillness was muffled and less unbearable than before.

At her side was Miss Ursula with a countenance that was fixed and immovable as any stone. Edie had placed the Miss Veronica's cane upon her breast, and at her side was the plastic bag containing the rusted spearhead.

"It is well that you brought it here," Miss Ursula observed, her flinty aspect vanishing when she saw the gobs of blood that smeared the vicious-looking weapon.

Visibly wincing, she cleared her throat. "In all creation there are few artifacts that can do us injury. This, the Roman blade that pierced the side of He who perished upon the cross, is one of the most lethal. I ought to have accepted it within the confines of the museum long ago, when first it was offered unto my keeping. Veronica is the price I have paid for that folly, and most bitterly do I accept it now."

Clasping her hands in front of her, Miss Ursula bowed her head, and the jet beads that hung in loops about her ears gave an agitated rattle.

"We gonna bury 'er?" Edie asked. "I'm good at digging 'oles."

Miss Ursula straightened. "No need," she said. "Celandine and I shall take her down to the cavern. In the Chamber of Nirinel, beneath the surviving root of Yggdrasill, Veronica will sit out the remaining span of the world. That hallowed place shall be her tomb, and no corruption will touch her. Now come."

Striding to a section of paneled wall, the woman held up her hand and gave the wood three sharp raps.

With a clicking whir, the wall shuddered and slid aside, revealing a low stone archway and a steep, winding staircase beyond.

"Edith, dear," Miss Ursula began, "take up Veronica's cane and the oil lamp if you will, and bring the spearhead also."

Inhaling great, gulping breaths, Edie hurried to obey. The stale air that flooded out of the darkness into the hallway was perfumed with a hauntingly sweet decay. Holding the lamp in one hand and the ivory-handled cane under her arm, she picked up the bag that contained the hideous weapon and carried it warily. When she accidentally touched the metal, the power within it prickled and hurt her, even through the plastic.

"Celandine," Miss Ursula said tersely. "You must aid me in this."

The woman in the grubby nightgown peeped out at her elder sister through a chink between her fingers. Then she blew her nose on the nightgown's large collar and shuffled reluctantly closer to the stretcher.

"I want to be nearest her pretty little head," Miss Celandine muttered. "I shan't be able to talk to her if you make me carry the feet."

Miss Ursula indulged her. "Very well," she sighed. "Grip the handles soundly. I don't want you to let go."

"Oh, Ursula!" her sister objected. "I wouldn't— you know that, you do, you do!"

She pulled a face as if she was about to cry once more, but Ursula was already lifting, and so Miss Celandine quickly forgot the offending remark and assisted her in hoisting their dead sister off the ground.

"Why, the dear darling's no weight at all!" she exclaimed.

"Come," Miss Ursula said. "We must bear her down the great stair."

With Edie Dorkins treading solemnly at their heels, the despondent pair were quickly swallowed by the intense and stagnant dark as they began their descent, deep beneath the museum's foundations.

Down into the severe blackness that filled the underground stairway and mocked the pitiful flame of the oil lamp they slowly made their way. The plummeting path was perilous, and progress was painfully slow. Inch by inch they bore Veronica's body, avoiding the slippery patches where dripping water and the tread of countless ages had worn the steps treacherously smooth. Beneath lengths of moldy pipework they ducked, until Edie suddenly called out and pressed her ear to the crumbling stone wall.

"There's somethin' behind it!" she cried. "Listen— it's gettin' closer."

Miss Ursula tilted her head to one side and tutted with irritation. "Remember what I told you, Edith, dear," she began. "How near this secret stair brushes against the advances of mankind? A meager few inches beyond this very wall runs one of their subterranean railways. Brace yourselves, both of you—the engine approaches."

All three could now hear the faint roaring noise that vibrated within the shaft, causing a tremor to ripple through the steps beneath their feet. Swiftly the sound soared, mounting to a trumpeting clamor that blared up the stairway. Edie fell back from the wall, expecting it to explode at any moment before the unstoppable force of the train that was surely about to cannon its way through.

The steps were shuddering violently now, and the body of Miss Veronica swayed unsteadily on the stretcher as her sisters endeavored to remain standing. The din was deafening, a screaming rumble that reverberated through Edie's chest, and she opened her mouth to yell amid this clangorous thunder.

Then it was over. Beyond the narrow barrier of stone the Underground train had passed, and all that remained was a juddering echo that flew up the spiraling stairs and vanished in the winding gloom above.

Catching her breath, Edie lifted the oil lamp to peer around her. The surrounding masonry was crazed and fractured, and from the still-quivering cracks, fine rivers of dust were pouring.

"One day our sanctuary shall be unearthed, and all our secrets laid bare—but not yet," Miss Ursula assured her. "Come, Celandine, there is still some distance to travel before we can lay our sister to rest."

In the wake of the train's tumult, the ensuing silence was horribly oppressive. It made the pool of darkness seem resentful and full of invisible, unfriendly eyes.

The overwhelming hush made Edie uneasy; she did not like silence. She had only recently been plucked from the time of the Blitz, with its constant din of exploding bombs and the crackle of the anti-aircraft guns. Not since the time when she had been imprisoned under the ruins of her home, with the bodies of her mortal family around her, had she known such deathly quiet. She started to make small noises to fend off this unwelcome absence of sound.

At first she hummed tunelessly then, true to her feral nature, she tried a gentle, droning growl. After a short while, Edie was amused to find that her echoes sounded as though some little animal really was in there with them. Once she was almost certain that a snuffling bark had not stemmed from her at all, and she flourished the lamp behind her to check that nothing was hiding in the shadows. But before she could prove her suspicions, the descent was over. The staircase came to an abrupt halt, and the space opened up around them, changing the nature of the echoes completely.

"Edith," Miss Ursula instructed, "you must proceed in front and light the way. Nirinel is at hand."

Through a network of caverns the girl led the Websters, until at last they came to a large metal gateway that swung open before them.

Immediately the golden radiance of many flaming torches flared up to greet their straining sight. Edie ran forward to gaze up at the magnificent spectacle of the last surviving root of the World-Tree—astounded afresh by its titanic majesty.

Up into the lofty, vaulted shadows the massive shape stretched, where no leaping lights could reach. The child's eyes traced an imagined arch down to where the momentous root plunged back into the flame glow and thrust through the chamber's far wall. It was a monumental vision of permanence, the oldest of all living things, the most wondrous of secrets hidden in the forgotten depths of the earth—Nirinel.

From history's cradle the Webster sisters had tended it, guarding their sacred charge against the relentless corruption of the marching years. It was only fitting that Miss Veronica would remain beneath its enchanted bulk for the rest of eternity.

"Careful," Miss Ursula scolded Miss Celandine as they approached a large circular dais built in the center of the cavern. "Lay her down gently."

The ancient wellhead, from which divine waters were once drawn to anoint the ravages of age afflicting the great root, was now choked with moss and a haylike growth of dead weeds. Upon their dry, cushioning layers the stretcher was laid, and Edie placed the ebony cane in Miss Veronica's lifeless hands.

"And the blade," Miss Ursula directed. "It should be beside her."

The girl obeyed, carefully removing the deadly weapon from the bag. Then she caressed the dead woman's cheek with her fingertips and whispered, "You can rest now."

Miss Ursula regarded the child keenly, a curious light glittered in her eyes, and she returned her attention to her dead sister.

"Are you in truth at peace?" she asked, intently scanning the lined face. "Is your soul finally free? You were never content, Veronica. In our youth I denied you your happiness, and to this unending existence you were irrevocably fettered."

Edie kissed the dead woman's forehead then gave Miss Ursula a conciliatory smile. "At the end," she told her, "Veronica said as how she were sorry and didn't blame you for what happened."

On hearing this, the eldest of the Fates squeezed her eyes shut. Then, when she had mastered herself, she took the oil lamp from Edie and leaned forward, holding it over that cold, expressionless face as if the answer to what troubled her could be found among the countless wrinkles that mapped its aged contours.

How different those familiar features now appeared. Without the inner spark to kindle that mottled flesh and fire it into life, it was like viewing some poorly executed sculpture of her sister. No trace of the character that had once burned within her could be glimpsed or guessed at. The absolute stillness was hideous to see, and the pallid skin reflected the lamplight in a cadaverous ghastliness.

Still searching that beloved face, Miss Ursula muttered in a voice that at times cracked with despair.

"Of this world there is little I do not understand," she said huskily. "But to this plane alone, and of those who are bound unto it, does my wisdom extend. Beyond the frontiers of life, Urdr has no knowledge. Outside the immutable confines of this strangling reality, is there an end to care and suffering? Can there indeed be a paradise? Is that where you are now, my dearest little Verdandi? Is all your hurt now healed?"

Listening to this, Miss Celandine sniveled into her handkerchief once more. It frightened her to hear Ursula so uncertain and questioning.

"Is Veronica with Mother now, do you think?" she spluttered.

Her elder sister lowered the lamp and let out a long breath. "I do not know," she replied with a bitter edge in her voice. "And I doubt whether I shall ever discover the answer. For how may the immortals ever know the truth of that, the most hidden secret of all?"

The woman lapsed into silence as she continued to survey the wizened corpse lying upon the dried weeds.

"How small she seems, and how ignominious her journey to this place. Verdandi, princess of the Royal House, and yet she was carted here as though she were of no more import than a sack of coal."

Spreading her hands wide, Miss Ursula lifted her eyes to the towering vastness of Nirinel as she contemplated the pomp and dignity that her late sister truly deserved.

"In the forgotten past, the funeral of this daughter of Askar would have been effected with the highest ceremony. A legion of horns and trumpets would have sounded in the heavens, and banners of sable would have flown from the city walls to mourn her passing. What solemn elegies the poets would have composed, what glorious outrage to inspire the balladeers' songs.

"In every window a candle would burn in memory of her. Across the land, monuments would rise, and the brightest star in the firmament would be named anew."

The woman's voice trailed into nothing, and she looked again at the wasted body upon the wellhead. "I regret that such ceremony is forever behind us," she admitted, "but still we will do what we can. Verdandi may indeed have to remain in this blessed place until the end of all things, but not for a moment shall she be alone. In this, her tomb, we shall take turns to sit beside her. However, on this grievous day, we shall all keep watch."

"Oh, yes!" Miss Celandine cooed. "And when it's just her and myself, I shall bring down a plate of jam and pancakes to put at her side and tell her everything that happens—I shall, I shall."

Under Miss Ursula's instruction, they each took a torch from the carved walls and fixed them into the soil around the wellhead. Then, together, they knelt before Miss Veronica's body, and the long vigil commenced.

With her head to one side, and the torchlight sparkling in her bright eyes, Miss Celandine rocked backward and forward on her knees, murmuring the snatches of old rhymes and songs she remembered from the ancient city of Askar and the days of her youth.

"Oh, see within that sylvan shade
the fairest city that e'er was made.
A mighty tower roofed with gold,
where dwells the Lady, so I'm told.
Queen of that ash land she may be,
with daughters one, two, and three."

Turning to the old woman in the nightgown, Edie saw that large tears were trickling down her walnut-like face as she recited. But Miss Celandine's memory soon failed her, and the words trailed into nothing. Humming to herself, she twisted the ends of her braids around her knobbly fingers while she slowly began to whisper another half-remembered rhyme:

". . . thus spurred by need she wove her doom.
Then all were caught within that weave,
and from its threads none could cleave.
The root was saved, but by the Loom
all things are destined, from womb to tomb . . ."

At Edie's side, the girl thought she saw Miss Ursula flinch when these words were uttered and wondered what she was thinking.

". . . How fierce He roared, she cheated him
of the ruling power hid within . . ."

Again the poem faltered, but Miss Celandine continued to drone the rhythm until a sad smile suddenly smoothed her crabbed lips as a different thought illuminated her muddled mind. Clumsily she rose to her feet and, assuming a dramatic pose, pointed a big, grime-encrusted toe. Then, very carefully, she started to dance.

Edie shifted around to watch her. Swathed in her ragged nightgown, the old woman, moving less than gracefully, was a peculiar sight. In other circumstances Edie would have laughed, but here in the midst of their grief, Miss Celandine's shambling performance possessed an aching poignancy.

Around the Chamber of Nirinel Miss Celandine waltzed, twirling and revolving with her arms flung wide. At times she looked like a collection of tattered sheets torn from a clothesline and caught in a buffeting gale, but there were moments when the crackling torch flames clothed her in an enchanted light, and the endless years fell from her shoulders. In those brief moments Miss Celandine was beautiful; her hair burned golden and her supple limbs skipped the steps with dainty precision.

Then the vision was lost as she sailed out of the torchlight and reeled toward the entrance, where the metal gates formed a perfect backdrop for the rest of her display.

"Oh, what heavenly dancing there used to be," she pined, temporarily interrupting her tune. "What darling parties we had back then. Terpsichore, the gallants called me—Terpsichore, Terpsichore."

Flitting behind Miss Celandine, a dozen shadows stretched high into the darkness above, magnifying her every move. Edie stared, enthralled by their grotesquely distorted, whirling shapes.

Even Miss Ursula had turned to watch her sister, yet the eyes that regarded her clumsy cavorting were filled with pity.

All their attention was diverted from the corpse that lay upon the wellhead, so not one of them noticed when the withered hand of Miss Veronica began to move.

With painful slowness the arthritic fingers twitched and flexed, creeping across the blood-stained robe like the legs of a great, gnarled spider. Down to her side the hand inched, until the groping fingers closed about something metal, and in that instant the old woman's eyes snapped open.

"Such is the demented doom that awaits me," Miss Ursula breathed, still following Miss Celandine's ungainly prances. "As Nirinel rots, so too does my sister's mind. That is the measure of how closely we are bound to it. Veronica was the first to fall victim. Then, piece by piece, Celandine followed until she became this witless fool. How many years are left unto me, I wonder, before I too hitch up my skirts and join her in that abandoned madness?"

Edie chewed her bottom lip thoughtfully. "I'll look after both of you," she pledged.

"I know, child. To you I entrust the care of the museum and the many secrets it holds."

Over the carved beasts that crowded the chamber's walls Miss Celandine's wild shadows continued to leap, and Edie narrowed her almond-shaped eyes as she watched them. Something was wrong.

Among those gyrating shapes was a disharmony she could not place. Across that stone menagerie the fleeting silhouettes licked and bounced with the same deranged vigor as before, but now a new element mingled with them—an extra shadow that did not belong there.

At first it was difficult to distinguish this additional outline from the rest of the frenetic show. Confused, Edie peered at the strangely stilted shade with a puzzled expression on her face. Then a sudden terror clutched her stomach as the awful truth dawned on her.

Spinning around, the girl let out a yell of fright. The stretcher was empty. There—standing directly behind Miss Ursula, her raised hand clutching the rusted blade and ready to strike—was Miss Veronica Webster.

CHAPTER 3

AN UNHOLY ABOMINATION

Down stabbed the spear, slicing a savage arc through the stagnant air. But Edie's shout had been enough, and Miss Ursula moved aside a moment before the weapon plunged through the space where she had just been sitting.

Springing up, Edie pulled the eldest of the Fates to her feet, and both stared in horror at the decrepit figure before them.

Orbs of darkness glared out from Miss Veronica's haggard face in place of eyes. Like mirrors of polished ebony they reflected the surrounding torchlight, but no hint of life gleamed within their inky depths. About her hunched shoulders her long, coal-colored hair snaked and streamed as though an infernal breeze blew upon it. Taking a lurching step forward, the apparition once again slashed the scarlet-steeped weapon in front of her. Edie managed to drag Miss Ursula clear of the sweeping blade. But then those dark eyes bent their power on her, and the girl shuddered, caught in the malevolence of their glance.

With jerking spasms, the lifeless limbs lashed out, and Miss Ursula covered the stricken child's sight as she hauled her out of range.

"Do not look at her!" she cried. "That is not my sister. A foulness is in possession of her body. Edith, come quickly!"

Avoiding the spiking blows they fled, but the animated cadaver darted in pursuit, furiously ripping and tearing the air behind them.

Around the well Edie and Miss Ursula ran, barely dodging the vicious thrusts. Suddenly Miss Veronica's shriveled mouth gaped open, and the malice-filled spirit that drove her let loose an unearthly, echoing howl.

At the gateway, Miss Celandine staggered to a standstill. With the folds of her nightgown swishing about her, she stared at the scene incredulously.

"Veronica!" she exclaimed, a wide grin splitting her face. "Veronica!"

Overcome with joy, she bounded across the earthen floor toward the horror that awaited.

"No!" Miss Ursula shouted. "Celandine—that is not Veronica!"

But Miss Celandine did not heed her. All she saw was her younger sister, alive once more, and she flung herself forward, squealing with wondrous exultation.

A hideous snarl twisted the dead lips as the corpse

wheeled to meet her and the spear glinted ruddily in the firelight.

"Celandine!" Edie bawled. "Stop!"

Too late Miss Celandine beheld those black, soulless eyes. She could not halt her blundering gait and went slithering to the ground, at the very feet of her departed sister.

Screaming shrilly, she frantically rolled aside just as the spear came plummeting toward her chest.

Deep into the soil the weapon bit, but the creature immediately tore it loose. Already Miss Celandine was scrambling away, but she was no match for the adamantine will that propelled that repellent carcass. From the bloodstained robe a cold hand came raking. Grasping fingers clawed at her hair, seizing one of the wildly swinging braids.

In despair, Miss Celandine felt the violent wrenching of her scalp, and she buckled backward, torn off balance. Down she fell, and up flew the spear once more. This time there was no escaping; the fingers that yanked her head to the floor owned an unnatural strength, and no amount of squirming would loosen their malignant, murderous grip.

Up into Veronica's withered face Miss Celandine was compelled to stare, and from that dead mouth came a rasping breath that filled her shrinking nostrils with the reek of lifeless lungs.

Miss Celandine wailed in terror, and her exposed throat quivered and trembled. Then the slaughtering strike came rushing down.

"Get away from her!" a furious voice shrieked.

Before the blade could drink yet more Webster

blood, Miss Ursula came running up and threw herself upon that scything arm, using all her might to shove it aside.

By a hair's breadth, the killing blow missed Miss Celandine's neck, and at last she wriggled free.

A repugnant hiss issued from the corpse's mouth as it leaped after her, but Miss Ursula jumped forward. Just as Edie scurried to the nightmare's heels on her hands and knees, the woman gave an almighty push.

Backward the abomination blundered, tumbling over the obstacle that lay in wait behind. A hellish screech ricocheted about the cavern, and the creature fell heavily against the weed-wrapped stone of the wellhead.

In a second it had rallied and risen once more. Brandishing the lethal blade, it darted greedy glances at the waiting prey, selecting which would be its first victim.

"We can't stop her!" Miss Celandine wept, scampering toward the gateway. "She'll kill us all!"

It was then that Edie discovered she was completely alone. Miss Celandine's mewling wails were already echoing through the adjoining chambers, and with a shock, she realized that Miss Ursula had also disappeared. With those glittering black eyes turned full upon her, the girl saw the corpse's sepulchral flesh come prowling closer.

"Get back, you!" the girl growled. "I warns yer!"

Yet her threats sounded feeble and unfounded, for the unclean darkness that beat from those venomous eyes rooted the child to the spot. There was nothing she could do; her limbs were locked, and still the monster advanced. The hairs on the back of Edie's neck prickled when she saw how sharp the rusted blade now appeared, and she swallowed helplessly.

Then it lunged.

Yet in that moment, Edie was whisked off the ground, and a glimmering light streaked past her.

With unerring accuracy, Miss Ursula hurled the oil lamp at her dead sister, and it exploded at the corpse's feet with a blinding burst of glass and liquid flame.

Onto Veronica's bloodstained robe the fuel fires splashed, and an instant later the garment was ablaze.

"Begone and burn!" Miss Ursula commanded, setting Edie back down.

Vivid, crackling flames were now leaping over the possessed creature, wreathing it in bright, lapping tongues. A hollow, squalling screech boiled out from the blackening lips.

The long dark hair that had been Miss Veronica's pride crinkled, burning away in the devouring heat while the wrinkled skin began to roast and smoke.

Yet still the eyes glared out at Ursula and Edie, and though the flames raged about its face, it could see them well enough.

As a writhing pillar of fire, the fiend tottered a wavering zigzag toward the woman and child, fiercely flailing its wasted, fiery arms.

"Quickly!" Miss Ursula told the girl. "Back this way."

To the wellhead they stumbled, with the burning body chasing after, like a pursuing demon cloaked in flame. From this roaring terror they fled, and shining brighter than ever in that scorching grasp, the spear slashed a broad crimson web of hellish light.

Columns of twisting, fuliginous smoke poured from the lumbering lantern that had once been Veronica, coiling high into the upper darkness, giving it a turgid, churning density and substance. Within the inferno of that blistering furnace only a charred outline could now be glimpsed. The old woman's bones were tinder dry, and the rapacious fires eagerly consumed them.

Glancing backward, Edie suddenly stopped running.

The fiend's steps were beginning to falter. Its sinews withered, and the marrow fluxed from cracked bones, spitting and sizzling in the flames.

"Edith!" Miss Ursula called anxiously.

But the child grinned impishly at her. "It's finished!" she cried. "Frazzled—all crispy like!"

The flaring glare in the cavern began to diminish. Like dying candles the bright, licking tongues sputtered as they were quenched. Yet the power that steered that cindered skeleton was not quite beaten.

Swaying from side to side, as though the very effort of binding those blackened bones together was a tremendous strain, the smoking remains reached out a sizzling arm toward the young girl and flung itself forward.

Edie squealed and leaped onto the stone dais to escape the unexpected onslaught. Over the tangled weeds she ran, and the nightmare bolted after her, screeching for her death. Through the woody growth the horror lunged, but the guttering flames that still sparked about those misshapen limbs leaped into the moss, and immediately the wellhead ignited.

Her clothes singed and smoldering, Edie Dorkins jumped clear as this new blaze roared into existence, sending a sheet of searing, tumultuous fire high into the curling smoke above.

Every dry stem burst into livid life, forming a dazzling pinnacle of flame. High into the age-old darkness the flaring light blasted, banishing the ancient shadows. For the first time in many years the entire straddling shape of Nirinel could be glimpsed above the towering beacon.

Shielding her face from that blistering funnel of fire, Edie saw, within its seething heart, the animated cadaver stumble and lurch as the mind that drove those charred bones finally wrenched itself free.

Caught in the cremating maelstrom, the blackened form teetered for a moment near the wellhead, then toppled down into the gaping shaft at its center.

Into the chasm fell the clattering bones, down into the empty deep.

Suddenly a violent quaking shook the chamber, and from the echoing regions of that immeasurable gulf, a gigantic ball of boiling flame exploded. Up to the arching height of the World-Tree's last surviving root the rumbling cloud rushed, erupting with an ear-splitting discharge of scorching heat and fire-dripping vapor as it stormed against that massive bulk.

Then, abruptly, it was over.

The exiled shadows quickly engulfed their old realm, and a hot, squalling wind gusted about the cavern, dispersing the curdling clouds. The air became a blizzard of ash.

Only two of the torches remained alight, and a thick

layer of soot obscured the wide stone ring of the well.

Moistening her parched lips, Edie darted forward.

A few cherry-glowing embers still hissed and snapped, but the child clambered back onto the dais and plowed through the choking mantle of fine powder. The heated stone scalded her knees as she crawled over to the broad round hole, where she stared down into the empty darkness.

"It's gone." Her morose voice resounded from the void's brim.

Behind her, Miss Ursula steepled her forefingers and tried to quell the anguish and panic that had overthrown her usual cold, collected bearing.

"How dare He invade this hallowed place and make a puppet of my sister!" she spat with passion.

Edie wrinkled her nose. "Smells 'orrid in 'ere now," she stated, swiveling around to disclose a soot-smeared face. "Like burned sausages—only worser!"

"Ursula!" a timid voice called as Miss Celandine padded back into the cavern, looking warily about her. "I can't go up the stairs in the dark, not on my own. Is Veronica gone? Why was she being so beastly?"

It was Edie who answered. "It were that Woden," she guessed.

Surveying the wreckage, Miss Ursula nodded tersely. "Indeed," she uttered in a voice quivering with barely checked anger. "The age-old enemy of the Fates was the force behind the peril we have just faced. Did He not manipulate her enough when she was living? At least the shell of her being is out of reach now. Poor Veronica—how we all used her."

"He'll try again though, won't He?" Edie murmured.

The woman gave an affirming nod. "Of that there can be no doubt. This was merely His calling card, to let me know His endeavors are only beginning. None, save He and I, know just how long this contest has endured. He will balk at nothing to destroy us. That is His only wish."

Edie gazed back down the ponderous well mouth. "In Glassenbury, Veronica an' me found a undine. I thought he might've come here to be with us—I asked 'im to, so as the water'd fill up again. Do you think he'll ever show?"

"An undine!" Miss Ursula snorted in disbelief. "I doubt that, Edith. Their like have long since departed this world."

"I did find him!" the child asserted. But Miss Ursula was looking beyond her, to a mound of ash and cinders a little distance away.

"Even if you had," she conceded, "it would not avail us. The well is dry, Edith, and will always remain so. The time of the sacred waters has passed into memory only. We must find other sources of protection to defend us from our enemy."

Striding around the wellhead, she lifted a familiar object from the soot, only to drop it almost immediately. Edie stared at the thing and shivered. The spear blade had not fallen into the abyss with Veronica's bones, and the girl drew her breath sharply.

"Should I throw it in?" she suggested.

Miss Ursula shook her head. "It would do no good. Woden will still try to find a way of using it against us. I would feel more secure if this perfidious object were under my scrutiny in The Separate Collection."

The old woman wrung her hands. "I have been careless," she said. "I had thought the defenses of my museum could withstand all assaults. Yet His base arts were able to creep through my barriers and seize control of Veronica. How vain and stupid I have been. Better to have left Celandine in charge. What use are all those exhibits in The Separate Collection? Powerful and dangerous I have always thought them, but look at this—see what He has done. My fortress is weaker than I ever . . ."

Her despairing voice fell silent as her gaze turned to Miss Celandine, who was still standing by the gateway and yawning widely. Suddenly, Miss Ursula's face lost all trace of her discouraged melancholy, and she pulled herself up sharply.

"Of course!" she said with renewed hope. "After all these years locked away in the museum, the exhibits have become sluggish and inert. Their forces are sleeping. This ennui must cease and the stagnation must be purged. The enchantments that were once so vigilant must be roused and made strong once more."

Infected by the old woman's sudden excitement, Edie bounced to her feet. "How do we do that?" she demanded.

Miss Ursula turned a secretive smile upon her. "We do not have to *do* anything, my dear. You shall see. Now come, bring the spear and let us return to the museum. I have a further commission for your obliging policeman."

With Edie and Miss Celandine hurrying after, Miss Ursula Webster strode from the Chamber of Nirinel, and the metal gateway clanged shut behind them.

* * *

Outside the Wyrd Museum, a river of gray mist poured into the alleyway. The early morning light was weak, and the squat building seemed flat and shapeless beneath the pale sun that hung low in the dim sky.

Over the cobbles the thick fog flowed, filling the narrow way with a dense, swirling cloud. Suddenly the smoking sea divided as a hooded figure, wrapped in a moldering black cloak, drifted toward the entrance.

A thin, whispering laugh issued from the blank shadows beneath the heavy cowl as that hidden face looked on the remaining bronze figures around the ornate doorway.

"Oh, Urdr," Woden's mellifluous voice murmured. "This time I shall be the victor. The war will not cease until you and those you harbor are utterly defeated. Do what little you think you can. Woden will not be bested by your paltry tricks and somnolent enchantments."

With ropes of mist winding tightly about him, the enemy of the Nornir sank back into the fog. But, before the blanketing vapor engulfed him, his foot dragged against a fragment of shattered bronze, and his laughter sounded once more.

Upon the upturned face of the sculpted Verdandi he brought his heel crashing down, and the metal cracked, snapping in two beneath the callous violence. Then into the smoke his low chuckles melted, and he was gone.

CHAPTER 4

AN EARLY SUMMONING

Mrs. Gloria Rosina focused a bleary eye on her alarm clock and snorted in disgust to learn that it was only twenty to six in the morning. An impatient ringing had awoken her, but the little clock was not to blame.

Someone was incessantly pressing her doorbell, and brutal thoughts whisked through her mind as she hauled herself out of bed. Swearing, she thrust her pudgy feet into an icy pair of slippers.

"All right, all right!" her gravelly voice ranted as she heaved herself into her worn bathrobe and bundled out of the bedroom, snatching up her cigarettes and lighter en route.

The landlady of The Bella Vista boarding house was a slovenly, overbearing, fifty-three-year-old widow who suffered no one gladly.

Still the bell rang its urgent summons, and the woman's overgenerous bosom heaved with annoyance as she regarded the wobbly outline showing through the frosted glass of the front door. Pulling the belt of her bathrobe so tight that her ample figure ballooned around it, she padded down the shabby hallway with her arms formidably folded, an unlit cigarette twitching between her lips.

"I hear you! I hear you!" she bawled angrily. "You'll break the bell in a minute."

The ringing ceased, and the landlady grunted as she stooped to unbolt the door, wisely keeping the chain on.

"Better have a mighty good reason to wake decent people up at this godforsaken—"

She left the sentence unfinished as she opened the door a fraction and saw the tall chief inspector upon the step.

"Sorry if I woke you, Madam," Hargreaves apologized, "but it is important."

Mrs. Rosina shut the door again to slide the chain off, then opened it fully.

"What is this?" she asked, folding her arms once again. "A dawn raid?"

The chief inspector cleared his throat. "Nothing like that," he assured her. "I understand you have a Mr. Pickering lodging with you. Is that so?"

The woman bristled visibly, and she raised her dark eyebrows. "I see," she drawled with tart disdain. "What's he done?"

"Nothing. I'd just like to have a few words with him, that's all."

"Look, love, I know it's early, but I don't look that green, do I?"

"Is Mr. Pickering here or isn't he?"

Mrs. Rosina pursed her thin lips, and the cigarette waggled insolently as though it were a substitute tongue.

"You'd better come in, then," she finally invited.

Removing his cap, the chief inspector stepped inside the hall and gazed mildly about him.

"Well, he's not down here," the landlady was quick to point out. "Only me and me old mother have those rooms. What sort of a place do you think this is? That Pickering's in Room Four, upstairs. This way."

Leading the policeman up to the landing, the woman gave a wheezing breath. "So what do you want him for?" she insisted, blocking the chief inspector's progress with her substantial form. "Got a right to know, ain't I? I don't want to be murdered in my bed."

The chief inspector eyed her restlessly. He did not have time for this tedious woman. "I have already said that I only wish to speak to your boarder, Madam," he repeated, a note of impatience creeping into his voice. "I guarantee that you have nothing to worry about."

"So you've only come to have a cozy little chat with him—at this time of the morning? You must think I've just got off the boat. Hoping he can help you with your inquiries? We all know what that means."

"I'm sorry, Madam," Hargreaves interrupted, unsuccessfully attempting to squeeze by her. "It really is urgent."

Mrs. Rosina sniffed belligerently, then she trotted to the door marked with a plastic number four.

Using the butt of her lighter, she vented some of her irritation by rapping loudly and calling for the occupant of the room to wake up.

"Yes?" a muffled, sleepy-sounding voice answered. "What is it?"

"Visitor for you."

"If you could give me a minute or two to get dressed. . . ."

The woman threw the chief inspector a sullen look. "Hope you've got some of your men out back—in case he jumps through the window."

The corners of Hargreaves's mouth curled into a humoring smile that infuriated her more than ever.

"Wouldn't put anything past him, anyway," she said sulkily. "Bit too quiet, if you know what I mean. Doesn't talk much—gives nothing away. Been here a couple of months now, on and off. Right through Christmas an' everything, which I thought was downright peculiar."

Before she could unleash any further spite in the hope of startling some hint or disclosure from the policeman, the door opened. Since she'd been leaning on it, Mrs. Rosina nearly fell into the room.

"Austen Pickering?" the chief inspector inquired.

A short man with a high forehead encompassed by an uncombed margin of grizzled hair looked up at him in drowsy astonishment.

"Inspector Clouseau here wants a word with you," Mrs. Rosina chipped in.

Her lodger blinked at her behind his large glasses.

"With me?" he asked in surprise. "Is something the matter?"

"You'd know, I'm sure," she rejoined in a voice that positively fizzed with acid.

Hargreaves coughed politely. "It's all right, sir," he said. "I merely wanted a word with you—in private."

The landlady ground her teeth together, but she was prevented from speaking her mind on this matter by a voice that called to her from downstairs.

"Glor?" came the anxious cry. "Is that you, Glor?"

Mrs. Rosina scrunched up her face in exasperation and hurried to the landing banister, where she leaned over and shouted down, "Quiet, Mother! Go back to bed."

"I heard voices, Glor."

"We got the police in."

"Right, I'll put the tea on."

"No, just get back in your room."

Returning from the banister, the landlady pouted with pique, for the door to Room Four was now firmly shut, and the policeman was already inside. Not knowing whether to demand entry or try to overhear what was being said, she crept closer.

However, just when she had decided on the latter course and was pressing her ear to the grubby paintwork, the door was yanked open again, and both her guest and the chief inspector bumped right into her.

"And you say that I can start immediately?" Austen Pickering asked, pulling on his raincoat and taking no notice of the large woman in his excitement.

Already striding down the stairs, Hargreaves

nodded briskly. "They want to see you at once, sir," he said. "Made that point very clear when I got the message."

"Why now, I wonder?" the little man gabbled. "I've written scores of letters but never received any reply. Has something happened? I mean, why should you come and tell me this? Why the police? I don't understand. There's not been an . . . incident, has there?"

Pausing at the foot of the stairs, Hargreaves stared up at him. "*She'll* tell you everything you need to know, sir," he said. "But don't worry, this isn't police business."

"Then why—"

"Just come with me, please."

And so Austen Pickering was bundled out of The Bella Vista, and the frosted glass of the front door rattled as he slammed it after him.

Standing in the hallway, an elderly, kindly looking woman gazed after the departing pair, then turned her attention to the staircase to see her daughter Gloria come stomping down.

"I'm not having this!" Mrs. Rosina stormed. "Cops turning up at all hours. What'll the neighbors think?"

"But you don't speak to any of them, Glor," her mother put in. "You don't like them. Nothin' but thieves and spongers, you said."

Fumbling with the lighter, her daughter finally lit the cigarette and drew a long, dependent breath. "Go an' watch the news," she said, exhaling.

"Don't you want that cup of tea, then?"

"What I want," Mrs. Rosina snapped between

puffs, "is to know what's been going on in my own house! Well, I'm going to find out. No snotty policeman's going to tell me what I can and can't know about my lodgers. Where's them spare keys?"

With her glowing cigarette bobbing before her face, she stamped back up the stairs, and her elderly mother tutted after her.

"I don't think you should go through that man's things, Glor," she advised. "'Tain't right."

But Mrs. Rosina was too vexed and curious to listen. Besides, it wouldn't be the first time she had rifled through the private belongings of one of her guests. It really was fascinating, not to say revealing, to pry into what some of these people lugged around with them.

In the hallway, the landlady's mother gave one final shake of her head and ambled back to her own little bedroom. "Blood will tell," she lamented. "Glor's just as bad as *she* ever was."

CHAPTER 5

AWAITING THE CATALYST

Kneeling in front of a large open cupboard in the Websters' cramped attic apartment, Edie Dorkins sucked her teeth and surveyed the cluttered, dusty bric-a-brac of Miss Veronica's belongings.

Among the neglected jumble were some interesting odds and ends culled from every age of the Wyrd Museum's existence. A rolled-up bundle of parchments tied up with a lavender ribbon revealed a collection of sonnets, letters, and poems written by the finest poets and playwrights. There were tiny framed miniatures of all three sisters; the women still appeared old, even though they had posed for the portraits centuries ago. A purse of moth-eaten velvet contained diverse and sumptuous pieces of jewelry, from plain and chunky lumps of twisted gold to single earrings or broken bracelets that sparkled with finely cut gems.

Edie coveted this fabulous treasure and stuffed many of the shiny trinkets into her coat pocket before crawling a little deeper into the cupboard to see what else she could discover in this fascinating hoard. To her annoyance, her progress was impaired by countless stone jars and bottles that Veronica had squeezed into every conceivable space. Edie resented all of them; they were maddeningly in the way and did not contain anything that appealed to her poaching piracy.

Among those many pots were the late Miss Veronica's innumerable aids to beauty. There were the tins of flour and chalk that she had applied to her face; she had thought that the dramatically bloodless effect granted her a much younger appearance. This grotesquerie was always heightened by a great daubing stripe of garish red from a tub of vermilion ooze, which the old woman had spread thickly across her lips, making her look like a nightmarish clown.

In another vessel, Edie found the lumps of charcoal Miss Veronica had used to highlight her eyebrows, and a green glass bottle contained an unctuous, tarry mixture with which she had dyed her long hair. Carelessly piled on top of each other, these receptacles were every shape and size and maintained a brittle balance that Edie's foraging threatened to capsize with each fresh incursion.

Sitting in the armchair next to the cold hearth, latticed by the gray early morning light that shone weak and pale through the one diamond-crossed window, Miss Ursula tapped her fingers on the worn upholstery, patiently counting out each slow second.

No expression modeled her pinched, camel-like features, but her raw eyes were a testament to the suffering she had endured during the recent hours.

A clattering avalanche of pots and jars caused the woman to jerk her head back and look across at the young girl half hidden inside her dead sister's cupboard.

"You will find nothing of note in there, Edith," she told her.

Edie rolled backward and lay on her side, playfully flicking a dead, dusty mouse she had found across the threadbare carpet.

"Where's Celandine?" she asked.

"I allowed her free movement through the museum. I think it best for her. You know how she likes to wander, talking to the exhibits. It may help her come to terms with . . . what has occurred."

Miss Ursula's eyes fell on the empty grate by the armchair, and she gave a slight shudder as she stared at those cold ashes and cinders. "Not since that day when we first came to the forest clearing have I known such distress."

Chewing the inside of her cheek, Edie regarded the black-gowned woman and said, "Tell me about the Loom."

The faintest of creases furrowed Miss Ursula's forehead. "You already know everything. The Loom was made from the first bough hewn from the World-Tree by the Lord of the Frost Giants."

"But what was it like?" the child persisted.

Miss Ursula sank back into the chair. "There are no adequate words to explain," she said. "From the moment I set it in motion and the glittering threads ran through the warp, everything was enslaved, including myself. Many have cursed my name since that day, but had I balked at the deed, then the lords of the ice would have destroyed the last vestige of Yggdrasill, and the end would have come before there had barely been a beginning. What choice had I?"

Edie reached for a small, unglazed ceramic jar that fit pleasantly in her palm and toyed with the idea of dropping the dead mouse inside it.

"Was you scared?" she asked, irked to find that the lid of the jar was stuck in place.

"Terrified," Miss Ursula confessed. "I had taken it upon myself and my sisters to become Mistresses of Destiny. Yet I was exhilarated also, and when the first glimmering strands began to weave the untold history of the world, it was the most entrancing sight I had ever beheld, outshining even the spectacle of Askar beneath the dappling sky of the great ash's leaves."

The old woman lifted her face to the ceiling, where deserted cobwebs festooned the chandelier, and her stern countenance melted.

"What ravishing beauty the fabric of the Fates possessed," she murmured. "Every stitch was an unseen moment in time, and the threads of life shone with an intensity according to the nature of who they belonged to. How that shimmering splendor captivated me and my sisters, and how easily we accepted our roles—even Veronica.

"You cannot imagine how bewitching that tapestry became—a rippling expanse of color and movement that burned with a light like no other. Patterns of joy and creation glowed within its fabric in an ever-shifting performance of lustrous delight."

Rising from the seat, the woman fetched Edie's woolen pixie hat down from the mantelpiece, where she had placed it to dry after washing the blood and dirt of the girl's adventures from its fibers.

"The glittering strands that course through this hat are an impoverished representation of the glorious wonders that once stretched upon the Loom. Yet the garment is a symbol of your bond with us, Edith, dear. A joining of your life to that of Nirinel."

Edie came to stand next to her. "Is it dry?" she demanded. "Give it to me."

The old woman placed the small pointed hat on the girl's head and, with a slender finger, traced the interwoven streaks of silver tinsel.

"Celandine knitted this from a single thread taken from the patterns of our own woven doom," she explained. "Through it passes the unstoppable might of Destiny, and your life is tied to it."

"What did the Loom look like?" the child asked.

Miss Ursula walked across the room to where a damask curtain hung across a doorway. "Come, child," she instructed.

The old woman led the girl down the narrow flight of stairs that led to the third floor of the Wyrd Museum, only to pause when they reached halfway. A huge oil painting hung on the near wall, and Miss Ursula regarded it with satisfaction.

"I remember that I was a trifle harsh with the artist when he delivered the work to me," she said. "I thought he had taken my description a little too literally, but on reflection, it is a fine enough depiction of those far-off days."

Edie stared dutifully at the great canvas.

The borders of a vast forest crowded the edges of the frame, but rearing from the ground in the center was a representation of a titanic ash tree. The figures of three young maidens stood beside a wide pool by the roots. Edie guessed that they were supposed to be the Websters, and she smiled to note that, even here, Miss Celandine was dancing.

"I do not recall if I ever congratulated the artist on his capturing of my sisters," Miss Ursula muttered. "I know that I was irritated by the veil he had painted across my face. But, now that I look closely, that nymph robed in white is unmistakably Veronica. An unbounded beauty and tenderness, more so than the others. Veronica was like that; none could outshine her."

Lifting her hand, she pointed at the measuring rod in the figure's hand. "There is her cane," she said regretfully. "Alas for its loss in the burning—it is another power gone from this place, and I wish we still had it in our keeping."

The old woman's jaw tightened, and an expression that was drenched in dread settled over her gaunt face. "I must not anticipate the days ahead," she cautioned herself. "The ordeal will be severe enough without wishing it any closer."

"But the Loom," Edie prompted.

Miss Ursula's caressing hand traveled across the varnished oils to where violet shadows were cast over her own, younger counterpart, and she directed the girl's scrutiny toward a large structure fashioned from great timbers.

"There it is," she breathed. "That which yoked us all and made us slaves to the lives we were allotted."

"Don't look like much," Edie grumbled with disappointment.

Miss Ursula straightened. "I was deliberately vague in the description I presented to the artist," she explained. "There were certain . . . details I had reason to leave out. But, in essence, that is the controlling device that dominated us all.

"The span and tale of all things was entwined in that cloth, Edith. Yet within its bitter beauty were also large, ugly patches of fathomless shadow, where hate and war were destined to occur. Sometimes those conflicts were bidden to prove so violent that the horror and cruelty fated to transpire in the world would rip and tear through the fabric, causing vicious rents to mar the surrounding pattern. Dangerous and ungovernable are those fissures in the web of Fate. Although we did our best to repair them—poor Celandine toiled so hard, so often—many lovely things and brave souls were lost forever within those hollow voids, and there was naught we could do."

"I came from one of them," Edie chirped.

Miss Ursula inclined her head and bestowed one of her rare smiles upon the child. "Indeed you did, Edith," she said. "When war rages and the cloth rips wide, my sisters and I are blind. We could see nothing beneath the banner of death that obscured those years, and so we missed you—the very one we had waited for all this time. Still, once we realized our error, we were able to perform a little belated repair and pluck you through to join us."

Her eyes still riveted on the indistinct portrait of the Loom, Edie asked, "What happened to it?"

Miss Ursula smoothed out the creases of her taffeta gown. "I believe I told you before you went to Glastonbury, Edith. The Loom was broken many years ago and cannot be remade. The tapestry of the world's destiny was never completed, and thus our futures remain uncertain."

Edie lowered her gaze and fiddled with the jar she still held in her hand. Miss Ursula seemed to forget her young charge and was following her own train of thought.

"Without the Cloth of Doom to guide me, how can I be sure that the path I have chosen is the right one? Is there still time to turn back and steer away from this course? Too long have I spent foretelling the pages of the world to act blindfolded now. Halt this, Ursula!"

Not listening to her, Edie gave the lid another twist and at last the wretched jar was opened. Bringing it close to her face, the girl inspected the contents to see if there was room for a dead mouse inside. But a foul-smelling, ochre-colored ointment filled the small vessel, and she groaned inwardly at having unearthed yet more of Miss Veronica's wrinkle cream.

At her side Miss Ursula looked up sharply as though she had heard something.

"It is too late!" she cried, expelling her indecision with a clap of her hands. "He is here! Come, Edith, the one I have sent for, our catalyst—he arrives. We must greet him."

Edie had not heard anything, but she knew that the eldest of the Websters was more attuned to the vibrations of this mysterious building than herself.

As Miss Ursula descended the stairs, the girl hesitated. She gave the ointment within the jar one final sniff, then stuck out her tongue to lick it experimentally. Retching and coughing, the girl hurriedly followed Miss Ursula into the main part of the museum, shoving the jar into her pocket with the rest of her magpie finds.

* * *

Neil Chapman had slept deeply for a couple of hours, but he woke suddenly at quarter past six. His little brother, Josh, was still fast asleep, and Neil looked at his watch in disbelief. After all that had happened, after his complete exhaustion, he was now wide awake for some unknown reason, and no amount of burying his head under the warm blankets could make him doze off again.

Climbing out of bed, he dragged on some clean clothes and crept out to the living room. To his relief, he found that his father was finally sleeping, and the boy silently left the apartment to look for Quoth.

He did not have to roam far to find him. The raven was roosting in The Fossil Room across the hallway. With his head tucked under one wing, the bird sat on one of the display cabinets, making faint purling noises in his sleep. In fact, his slumber was so profound that Neil managed to walk straight up to him without the raven waking.

The boy did not have the heart to disturb his rest. Quoth looked so content there, in his dim little corner, that Neil almost tiptoed away again.

At that moment, however, a sudden pounding resounded within the museum, and the raven was startled awake. With his scruffy feathers askew and his head wiggling drunkenly up and down, the bird stretched open his beak and fixed his eye upon his surroundings.

"Good morning," Neil greeted him.

"Fie!" Quoth squawked in alarm. "The hammers of the underworld doth strike! Alarum! Alarum!"

"I think it's just someone at the door," the boy chuckled.

The bird rubbed the sleep from his eye and stared at Neil with dozy happiness.

"Squire Neil!" he croaked, slithering across the glass in his haste to salute him. "The argent stars of heaven's country are but barely snuffed in their daily dowsing, yet already thou art astir! Good morrow, good morrow, O spurner of Morpheus!"

Neil laughed and stroked the bird's featherless head. "I'm sorry about what happened last night," he apologized. "Were you okay out here?"

"This lack-a-bed sparrow hath nested in more danksome grots than this."

"Once an idea gets into Dad's head there's nothing anyone can do," Neil explained. "With any luck he'll have calmed down by tonight."

Again the knocking sounded, and Neil held out his arm for Quoth to climb up to his shoulder.

"We'd better see who that is."

"Good tidings ne'er rose with the dawn," the raven warned in his ear.

They hurried through the collections until they came to the main hallway, and Neil pulled the great oaken door open. To his surprise, he found the chief inspector waiting on the step.

"What's happened?" the boy asked, instantly fearing the worst.

"Nothing yet," Hargreaves reassured him. "I've come on an errand—Urdr commanded me."

Neil peered past him and saw, standing in the alleyway, the fidgeting figure of Austen Pickering. The boy recognized him immediately. The man had stopped him in the street after school a few days before and warned him of the dangers of living in the Wyrd Museum. Neil had not forgotten those forbidding words, and it made him uneasy to see this little man again.

"A plainer pudding this nidyard ne'er chanced to espy," Quoth reflected, regarding the man with his beady, yet critical, eye. "'Twas a poorly craft which didst shape yonder lumpen clay."

The chief inspector coughed awkwardly but added in a whisper, "I brought him as soon as I received the message from Urdr. I was to bring Mr. Pickering here. It's not my place to ask why."

"But that's the ghost hunter," Neil muttered. "I don't understand. What can she want with him?"

"If you would be civil enough to allow the gentleman inside," a clipped voice rang out from the hallway, "you might be able to learn."

Neil turned and Quoth chirped morosely. Upon the

stairs, looking as regal and supreme as any empress, Miss Ursula Webster stood gazing down on them. At her side, in contrast to the old woman's tall, stately figure, Edie Dorkins looked like a river-scavenging mudlark. Her oval face was smudged with dirt, her clothes were torn, and wide holes gaped in her woolen stockings.

Hargreaves lowered his eyes in reverence and bowed to both the woman and the child. "I have done what was asked of me—"

"Is there an outbreak of deafness?" Miss Ursula demanded. "I said for you to let the man inside!"

Hastily leaving the entrance steps, the chief inspector permitted Austen Pickering to take his place, and Neil looked at him keenly.

It was obvious the man was fighting to remain calm, but he was so excited that his breaths were shallow and gasping. With his already large-seeming eyes widening behind the thick lenses of his glasses he came to the arched doorway and placed his stubby fingers on the bronze figure at his left.

Timidly, he stared in at the museum's gloom-laden interior and took another gulp of air, as if he were swigging a measure of whiskey for courage. Then, with an acknowledging glance at Neil, the man calmed himself. He had been longing for this moment for so long that he wanted to cherish it in his memory ever afterward.

"First impressions," Neil heard him mumble to himself. "I must be free to receive all I can. Come on Austen, old lad—be the blank paper, the empty jug, the untrodden snow."

"What are you waiting for?" Miss Ursula called. "Be quick to enter."

Half-closing his eyes, Austen Pickering stepped purposefully over the threshold and drew a deep, rapturous breath. For several moments he stood quite still with his head tilted back, and Neil began to wonder if the old man had gone into a trance.

But the peculiar silence did not last, for Mr. Pickering presently opened his eyes and looked gravely about him.

"Yes!" He sighed. "I was right. But so many— hundreds upon hundreds. I never dreamed!"

"What is it?" Neil asked.

"Most incredible!" the man exclaimed. "I never expected so staggering a number. Quite astounding."

Neil exchanged looks with the chief inspector, but Hargreaves's hollow-cheeked face was solemn, and the boy couldn't guess what he was thinking.

Her chin resting on the banister, Edie grimaced and took an instant dislike to the strange newcomer. Everything about the man's bearing and attire suggested the strict military discipline with which he ordered his life. What was left of his tightly waved hair was too neatly combed, a crisp knot secured his regimental tie in place, and his brown shoes shone like chestnuts freshly popped from their casings.

During her untamed life in the bomb sites Edie had spent too long distrusting and evading the figures of authority who had tried to catch her to abandon those natural suspicions now. To her, this fastidious little man was no different from the countless air-raid wardens she had hated. Austen Pickering wore his clothes like a uniform, and she despised him for that fact alone.

Forsaking him in revolt, she looked to see what Miss Ursula made of him and was intrigued to read in the old woman's face a considerable degree of approval.

"You admire my museum?" Miss Ursula said.

Mr. Pickering turned to her and peered over the rim of his glasses. "'Admire' is not the word I would have chosen, Madam."

"That is to be expected," she said. "From the many letters I have received from you, I would have been sorely disappointed if you had not felt the pulse of life that courses through this building."

"Pulse of life!" the man spluttered in disbelief. "I assure you, Madam, that it is the pain of the anguished dead that I feel—and that most deeply."

The taffeta of Miss Ursula's black gown rustled faintly as she stirred and gripped the banister a little tighter. "Tell me what it is that you sense," she commanded. "When you walked through that door— what was it like?"

The ghost hunter knitted his brows, and in the grave tone he reserved for these matters said, "The atmosphere is electric—charged like a battery. No, more like a dam that is close to bursting. If nothing is done to release the pressure then I cannot begin to imagine what will occur. The tension is unbearable."

Casting his gaze about the dim entrance hall, from the small window of the ticket booth to the drab watercolors that mobbed the paneled walls, he tapped his fingertips together and nodded grimly.

"I've never been in so ancient a place. It's staggering. How many trapped souls are locked in here? How many poor unfortunates have never been able to break free of its jealous clutch?"

But Miss Ursula had heard and seen enough for the time being. "That will be for you to discover," she told him. "I wish your investigations to commence at once. The caretaker's son shall guide you around the museum. If there are tormented souls locked in here, you have my permission to do whatever you please with them. Now, close the door—the draft is intolerable."

Neil glanced apologetically at the chief inspector, who was still waiting outside, but Hargreaves was not in the least bit offended.

"Close it, I say!" Miss Ursula commanded.

Hargreaves moved away from the entrance. "I'll be around should you need me," he called to Neil as the boy reluctantly pushed the door shut. "Urdr knows, those of us who are left will be here."

The oaken door shuddered in its frame, and Neil glared up at the imperious figure on the stairs.

"There's no need to be so rude!" he shouted.

But Miss Ursula had her back to him and was already ascending to the second floor. Giving the stranger a final suspicious glance, Edie Dorkins pulled an impudent face and capered after her.

Austen Pickering could only shake his head in disappointment. "Awful manners," he murmured.

"Ignore them," Neil began. "They're both bats."

The old man regarded him for a moment. "I've come across worse. There's no escaping it in my field of study. When you talk about phantoms and the unquiet dead to people, it seems to bring out the worst in them. I've been called more names than I can remember, but so long as the job gets done, they can call me twice as many again."

Pausing, he looked at the raven sitting on the boy's shoulder and winked at him in amusement. "That's a dandy specimen you've got there, lad," he said, peering at the bird with interest. "However did you come by him?"

Quoth held his head up proudly while the man viewed him, and the raven turned so that his best side showed.

"Vain little fellow, too," Mr. Pickering observed.

"He that be a foe of beauty is an enemy of nature," the raven retorted.

The man started and looked at Neil, as though suspecting him of ventriloquism. Then he laughed and removed his glasses to polish the lenses. "A long time I've been waiting to get inside this place," he declared. "I told myself I'd have to expect all kinds, but I wasn't counting on a talking raven to be my first surprise."

Returning his glasses to their rightful place on his nose, Austen Pickering smiled happily. "This is birthdays and Christmas all rolled into one," he explained to Neil. "I hardly know where to start. It's like being given one enormous present, but I'm too excited to peep inside the wrapping paper."

He walked toward the door that led to the first floor collections and rubbed his hands together with an almost childlike glee. "You don't have to show me around if you don't want to. I'd be perfectly content to wander about on my own."

"No," Neil replied. "I'd like to. What you said about there being trapped souls in here . . . do you mean it's haunted?"

At once Mr. Pickering grew serious again. "Can you doubt it?" he cried. "You who live in this revolting building?"

"I believe you—honestly I do," Neil assured him, and his thoughts flew to his friend, Angelo Signorelli.

When the Chapmans had first come to stay at the Wyrd Museum, Neil had encountered the soul of that unfortunate American airman in The Separate Collection. There, in one of the display cabinets, Angelo's spirit had been imprisoned for over fifty years, locked within the wooly form of a shabby old teddy bear. Together, they had journeyed back into the past to save the life of Jean Evans, the woman Angelo had loved. But "Ted," which had been his nickname, had chosen to remain in that time, and Neil still missed him.

Addressing Austen Pickering again, Neil asked, "When I saw you that time, out on the street, you said this place was like a psychic sponge—that it trapped souls and kept them. What you did just then, when you came in—are you psychic?"

The man stared at him. It was unusual for anyone to accept the things he said, but this boy was doing his best—even trying to understand. "I'm blessed with a very modest gift," he murmured. "From the moment I stepped inside this horror, I felt the unending torture of those who should have crossed over but are still bound to this world. This place has known untold deaths during its different roles throughout the ages."

"I know that it used to be an insane asylum."

"Oh, it's been a lot more than that, lad. I've done my homework on this miserable pile of bricks, researching back as far as the scant records allow. Orphanage, a workhouse for the poverty-stricken silk weavers, before that a quarantine house, and going even further back—a hospital for lepers. Think of all the suffering and anguish these walls have absorbed. No one can imagine the number of hapless victims that this monstrous structure keeps locked within its rooms, condemned to wander these floors for eternity. The poor wretches have been ignored for far too long."

Clapping his hands together, he announced in a loud voice that boomed out like that of a drill sergeant, "Well, I'm here now—Austen Pickering, ghost hunter. Here to listen to their cries, and no matter what it takes, I'm going to help them."

CHAPTER 6

TWEAKING THE CORK

The rest of Neil's morning was taken up showing Austen Pickering around the Wyrd Museum. The man marveled at every room and at each new display. He was a very methodical individual who took great pains to ensure that no exhibit was overlooked, reading each faded label. Therefore, the tour took longer than Neil had anticipated, for the old man found everything to be of interest and had an opinion about all that he saw.

Quoth found this a particularly tiring trait and yawned many times, nodding off on several occasions, almost falling from Neil's shoulder.

While they were in The Roman Gallery, Miss Celandine came romping in, dressed in her gown of faded ruby velvet and chattering away to herself. The old woman was giggling shrilly, as if in response to some marvelous joke, but as soon as she saw Neil and the old man she froze and a hunted look flashed across her walnut-wrinkled face.

"Don't leave me!" she squealed to her invisible companions. "You said we might go dancing. You did! You did! Come back—wait for me! Wait!" And with her braids swinging behind her, she fled back the way she had come.

Austen Pickering raised his eyebrows questioningly, and Neil shrugged. "She's not all there, either," he explained.

"The vessel of her mind hast set sail, yet she didst remain ashore," Quoth added.

Their snail-like progress through the museum was delayed even further by the ghost hunter's habit of pausing at odd moments while he jotted down his impressions in a neat little notebook.

"You never know what may turn out to be important," he told Neil. "A trifling detail seen here, but forgotten later, might just be the key I'll be looking for in my work. The investigator must be alert at all times and record what he can. It might seem daft and over-meticulous, but you have to be thorough and not leave any holes for the skeptics to pick at. I pride myself that no one could accuse me of being slipshod. Everything is written up and filed. No half measures for me. I've got a whole room filled with dossiers and indexes back home up north, accounts and news clippings of each case I've had a hand in. It was the *Northern Echo* that first called me a ghost hunter, although—blimey! Would you look at this!"

They had climbed the stairs to the second floor

where great glass cases, like huge fish tanks, covered the walls of a long passage, making the way unpleasantly narrow. Neil did not like this corridor, for every cabinet contained a forlorn-looking specimen of the taxidermist's macabre art.

They were the sad remnants of the once fabulous menagerie of Mr. Charles Jamrach, the eccentric purveyor of imported beasts, whose emporium in the East End of London had housed a veritable ark of animals during Victorian times. After both he and his son died, the last of the livestock was sold off and a portion of it eventually found its way to the Wyrd Museum.

Stuffed baboons and spider monkeys swung from aesthetically arranged branches. A pair of hyenas with frozen snarls looked menacing before an African diorama, incongruous next to an overstuffed whiskery walrus gazing out with large doe eyes. In the largest case of all, a mangy tiger peered from an artificial jungle.

In spite of the fact that the cases were securely sealed, a fine film of dust coated each specimen, and the tiger's fur crawled with an infestation of moths.

Shuddering upon Neil's shoulder, Quoth stared woefully at the crystal domes that housed exotic, flame-colored birds and whimpered with sorrow at the sight of a glorious peacock, the sapphires and emeralds of its tail dimmed by an obscuring mesh of filthy cobwebs.

"Alack!" he croaked. "How sorry is thy situation— most keenly doth this erstwhile captive know the despond of thine circumstance."

"Your raven isn't comfortable here," Mr. Pickering commented. "I don't blame him. The Victorians had a perverse passion for displaying the creatures they had slaughtered. Disgusting, isn't it? Beautiful animals reduced to nothing more than trophies and conversation pieces. You might as well stick a lampshade on them or use them as toilet-paper holders."

"I don't like these exhibits either," Neil agreed, pushing open a door. "If we go through here we can walk around them. There are more galleries this way—even an Egyptian one."

Leaving the glass cases and their silent, staring occupants behind them, they continued with the tour. It was nearly lunchtime and Neil was ravenous, remembering he hadn't eaten anything since the previous day. But the boy wanted to show Mr. Pickering one room in particular.

Eventually they arrived at the dark interior of The Egyptian Suite, and the old man gazed at the three sarcophagi it contained. "Not satisfied with parrots and monkeys," he mumbled in revulsion. "Even people are put on display. Is it any wonder the atmosphere is filled with so much pain?"

But Neil was anxious for the ghost hunter to enter the adjoining room, for here was The Separate Collection.

Moving away from the hieroglyphs and mummies Mr. Pickering followed his young guide, but the moment he stepped beneath the lintel of the doorway that opened into The Separate Collection he gave a strangled shriek and fell back.

"What is it?" Neil cried. The man looked as though he was going to faint.

Mr. Pickering shooed him away with a waggle of his small hands and staggered from the door, returning to the gloom of The Egyptian Suite.

"Can't . . . can't go in there!" he choked.

Neil stared at him in dismay. He hadn't been expecting such an extreme reaction. The man's face was pricked with sweat, and his eyes bulged as though his regimental tie had become a strangling noose.

As Austen Pickering blundered against the far wall, his gasping breaths began to ease, and he leaned on one of the sarcophagi until his strength was restored.

"My, my," he spluttered at length. "How stupid. Austen, old lad, you should've expected it. You told yourself there had to be one somewhere. Oh, but I never dreamed it would be so . . . well, there it is."

Quoth fidgeted uncertainly. "Squire Neil," he muttered, "methinks yon fellow may prove a swizzling tippler. The ale hath malted and mazed his mind."

"Are you all right?" Neil asked the old man. "You look awful. What happened?"

Mr. Pickering mopped his forehead and stared past the boy into the room beyond. "A fine old fool I am," he wheezed. "I'm sorry if I startled you, lad. It's that room. I can't enter—at least not yet."

"How sayest the jiggety jobbernut?" Quoth clucked.

"What stopped you?" the boy asked, ignoring the raven. "Is it one of the exhibits?"

The ghost hunter shook his head. He had recovered from the shock, and an exhilarated grin now lit his face.

"All the classic case studies tell of them," he gabbled, more to himself than for Neil's benefit. "Though I've come across the more usual cold spots before, I've never experienced this phenomenon. This really is a red-letter day."

"What is?" Neil demanded.

Mr. Pickering clicked his fingers, as though expecting the action to organize and set his thoughts in order.

"Occasionally," he explained excitedly, "a haunted site will have a nucleus—a center of operations, if you like, where all the negative forces and paranormal activity begin and flow out from."

"And you think it's The Separate Collection?" Neil murmured. "I suppose it would make sense. There's a lot of strange stuff in there."

"I'm quite certain of it. But the intensity—it's incredible. Oh no, it didn't want me to go in, that it didn't. It knows why I'm here and doesn't want to let its precious specters go. Well, we'll see about that."

Neil gazed into the large, shadow-filled room that lay beyond The Egyptian Suite and recalled how frightened he had been when he first moved to the Wyrd Museum. He remembered how the building had seemed to be almost tricking him, deceiving his sense of direction, leading him around and around until finally he was delivered to this very place, where the eclectic jumble of exhibits was eerie and sinister.

A shout from Ted had put a stop to it back then,

but the spirit of the airman who had possessed the stuffed toy was finally at rest.

"Are you saying that the building is alive?" he finally ventured. "Watching and listening to us?"

The ghost hunter gave a brisk shake of his head. "Not alive, no, not in the sense that we understand. That would imply intelligence, and I wouldn't go so far as to say that. I do believe, however, that there is a presence that permeates every brick and tile—an awareness, if you like. Call it a mass accumulation of history and anguish, recorded onto the ether, that operates on some very basic and primitive level. That is what we are up against. It is a force that feeds on the energies of both the living and the deceased and binds them to itself."

Gingerly moving toward the doorway once more, the ghost hunter considered The Separate Collection, and a gratified smile beamed across his craggy face. "This is amazing," he declared. "Absolutely amazing. There mustn't be any more delay; the investigation proper will have to commence at once. But first things first. I'll have to go back and fetch my equipment."

Infected by Mr. Pickering's delight, Neil laughed. "What are you going to do?" he asked. "An exorcism?"

The ghost hunter calmed himself. "Don't be silly," he replied. "I can't do that. Besides, I don't want to make any rash judgments. I'll work through the museum systematically, room by room and floor by floor. That Separate Collection is the supernatural heart of this place, and I'm not ready for the surprises it might throw at me—not yet, at any rate."

* * *

When Austen Pickering left the Wyrd Museum to return to his lodgings, Neil hastened back to the caretaker's apartment, taking care to leave Quoth in The Fossil Room once again. It proved to be a wise precaution, for Brian Chapman was in a terrible mood. He had been awake for only half an hour and it was now nearly two o'clock.

When he realized the time, he had looked into his sons' bedroom but found it empty. Hurrying to the kitchen, he discovered a pool of spilled milk near the refrigerator and a bowl of half-eaten cereal in the sink. Tutting, he left the apartment to search for the boys.

Josh was playing in the walled yard, his coat pulled on over his pajamas and a pair of rain boots covering his bare feet. The little boy told him that he hadn't seen his brother all day and that he'd tried to shake his father awake. When his efforts had failed, he had made his own breakfast.

Brian ran his hands through his greasy hair and pinched the bridge of his nose. He'd had an awful night and was now even more determined to look for another job. Anything. To get out of this hideous place was all he craved, and nothing anyone could say would change his mind. It wasn't like him to sleep so late, and he was more angry at himself than anyone else.

Neil hated when his father was like this. He decided against mentioning Austen Pickering, for that would certainly make matters worse. The only course to take was to give Brian some time to calm down. So, shutting himself away from the squall of his father's temper, the boy calmly began to make sandwiches for them all.

Miss Ursula had not set any new work for Brian to do, so in the afternoon he slipped out, hoping that she wouldn't notice. Entrusted with looking after Josh, Neil took the four-year-old to find Quoth. The child was scared of the raven at first, but he was soon tickling him under the beak, feeding him ham sandwiches, and laughing at his absurd speech.

At four o'clock, a morose jingling announced Austen Pickering's return, and Neil ran to the entrance to admit him. Three large, much-battered suitcases surrounded the grizzle-haired man as he waited on the steps, and he grumbled to Neil about the exorbitant cost of cabs in London while the boy helped him haul the luggage inside.

"You've certainly brought enough!" Neil said. "What sort of equipment have you got in here?"

"That witch of a landlady told me to leave! Got a terrible tongue on her, that cat has," the man puffed, dragging a heavy suitcase under the sculpted archway. "She's chucked me out. This is everything I had with me. You know, lad, it's the living that scare me most. The dead I can deal with."

Neil contemplated the suitcases thoughtfully. "So, you're staying here then?"

"Makes sense really," the ghost hunter replied. "I'd have to be spending the nights here anyway, so I might as well stay. No point shelling out for a new room when I won't even be there. The Websters won't mind, I'm sure."

But Neil was not thinking about them. He was

wondering what his father would have to say about this.

"You know," Mr. Pickering said, "I'm sure that nosy woman was going through my stuff. She better not have messed with any of my apparatus. It's already getting dark, and I want to get started right away."

When Brian Chapman returned to the museum he discovered, to his consternation, that Austen Pickering had taken over one corner of The Fossil Room and was busily setting up his equipment in the rest of the available space. Several of the connecting rooms also contained one or two experiments: lengths of twine were strung across windows and doorways, and a dusting of flour was sprinkled over certain areas of the floor.

Neil's father regarded the man with irritation. He had certainly made himself at home. His raincoat was hanging from a segment of vertebrae jutting conveniently from a fine example of an ichthyosaur skeleton set into the far wall. His highly polished shoes had been placed neatly beneath a cabinet, and his feet were now cozily snug in a pair of slippers.

That disease-ridden raven was playing in one of the suitcases, tugging at a spare pair of suspenders he had unearthed among a pile of T-shirts, and the newcomer himself was talking to Brian's sons about haunted houses.

"Blood and sand!" Brian mumbled. "It's one thing after another in here."

There was, of course, nothing he could do about it. If his eccentric employers wanted to have seances that was their choice, but he wasn't going to permit Josh to remain and listen to this nonsense.

Brian had spent the afternoon trawling the local markets and pubs, asking after casual work, and he had eventually ended up in the job center. His searches had not been successful, but he had brought a bundle of newspapers and leaflets home with him. Leaving the ghost hunter to his own business, he returned to the caretaker's apartment, with his four-year-old son trailing reluctantly behind.

Neil heaved a sigh of relief. For a moment he had thought his father would demand that he join them, but Mr. Chapman's mood had mellowed in the time he had been out, and he was obviously too anxious to hunt through the papers to begin an argument.

"Doesn't say much, your dad," Austen Pickering commented. "Now, where did I pack my pullover? It'll be drafty in here tonight—already turned a mite chilly."

Neil glanced at him. Mr. Pickering was busy putting new batteries inside an old tape recorder, and the boy cast his eyes over the apparatus the old man had arranged on the glass surface of the display cabinets.

The ghost hunter's paraphernalia was disappointingly mundane. Neil had envisaged sophisticated electronic gadgets that bleeped and flashed at a phantom's approach. But the most advanced piece of technology was an ordinary camera loaded with infrared film.

The tape recorder and the camera were the extent of Mr. Pickering's scientific instruments for studying specters. The rest of the so-called equipment was hardly impressive: a flashlight, at least a dozen balls of twine, a carrier bag filled with candles, several thermometers, a tape measure, and a packet of chalk.

The familiar notebook had joined forces with a clipboard, a bag of flour, and a small brown glass bottle.

"Smelling salts," Mr. Pickering explained, seeing the boy's curious expression. "It has been known for people to swoon with fright when they come in contact with the spirit world. Always pays to be prepared."

Neil began to suspect that the old man had never before actually seen anything ghostly at all, and that the smelling salts were for himself. Perhaps he was just a harmless crank who had let his hobby turn into an obsession. At the moment, anyone looking at him could mistake Mr. Pickering for a lonely old senior citizen settling himself down for a quiet night in front of his stamp collection, rather than a ghost hunter keeping watch for the supernatural.

"Do you think you'll see anything?" Neil asked.

The old man peered at him over his glasses. "Who can tell?" he answered. "I might be here a week before I hear so much as a creaking floorboard."

Neil groaned inwardly and realized how much he had been looking forward to what might never materialize.

"Then again," the old man added, "there's so much bottled up in here, I think it'll be more a case of what *won't* I see. Soon as I tweak the cork that's holding it all in place, just stand back is all I'll say."

Neil brightened up—perhaps he wasn't a fraud after all.

"You wouldn't believe some of the things I've seen," the ghost hunter continued. "Misty shapes drifting over the ground, blurred figures melting into walls—investigated the lot, I have."

"What was the most frightening?" Neil asked ghoulishly.

Mr. Pickering reached into a case for his pullover. "The dead can't hurt the living," he declared, his voice a little muffled as he dragged the olive green sweater over his head. "Like I said, all I want to do is help them and see that they pass over. Besides, I've got the most powerful defense I could wish for."

From another case he brought out a small black-bound book, the pages of which were gilded about the edges, and he brandished it with great solemnity. "My Bible!" he proclaimed. "That's the first and most important safeguard. No harm can come to me with this as protection."

Evening was closing in. Darkness pressed against the blank windows of the Wyrd Museum, and the old man moved through the rooms, measuring distances and drawing diagrams of the layouts in his notebook.

"Would your dad mind if I filled my thermos with hot water?" he asked. "Three large mugs of strong black coffee should see me through and stave off the drowse."

Neil thought that if his father was still in his relatively good mood then there was no harm in trying, so he led the old man to their apartment.

Brian Chapman was sitting at the small table, surrounded by a sea of open newspapers. Josh had been put to bed, and the caretaker scowled at the interruption when the door opened.

"What is it?" he snapped.

Neil guessed correctly that his father's job hunting was proving more difficult than he had anticipated, and he was glad that he had not brought Quoth along.

"I said Mr. Pickering could have some hot water for his thermos."

His father grunted and irritably flapped the paper he was reading. "You know where the kettle is."

"This way," the boy began.

Austen Pickering followed him inside the apartment, then drew a sharp, astonished breath. "Tremendous!" he exclaimed, blowing on his hands and shivering uncontrollably.

"What's the matter with him?" Brian asked.

"Can't you feel it?" the old man cried.

Neil shook his head, but glanced warily at his father.

"It's *freezing* in here!" the ghost hunter declared. "This room is a definite cold spot. Something quite dreadful must have happened here in the past. Let me get my thermometer—I must see if it registers."

Brian Chapman rose from the chair and slammed the newspaper on the table. "That's it!" he snapped. "You and your crackpot notions can get out of here. For God's sake, I've got a four-year-old boy trying to sleep in the next room. I don't want him scared by this mumbo-jumbo claptrap. Go on—I said leave!"

Still shivering, a crestfallen Austen Pickering looked away, embarrassed. "I didn't mean to alarm you," he uttered. "I sometimes get carried away. I'm sorry. I'll get back to The Fossil Room. It doesn't matter about the hot water."

"Oh, well done, Dad," Neil shouted when the old

man had departed. "There was no need to be so nasty. He isn't doing any harm."

The boy's father sat down once more and rested his head in his hands. "I've had it up to here for today," he groaned. "On top of everything else, I don't want a loser like him telling me that this apartment is haunted."

"This place must be a magnet for losers, then," Neil snapped, heading for the door.

"Where do you think you're going?"

"To apologize! Though I don't see why I should— but I know you wouldn't dream of it."

Neil slammed the door behind him, and with a yell of frustration, Brian Chapman threw the newspapers across the room.

* * *

In The Fossil Room, Neil found Austen Pickering sorting through the many candles he had brought with him. Quoth nibbled at the wax and pecked at the tantalizing, wormlike wicks.

"Sorry about Dad," Neil said. "He's been a complete pain lately."

The old man brushed the incident aside. "I told you some people don't like what I do," he reminded the boy. "I'm used to it by now. A solitary vocation, that's what this is."

"I could go back and fill your thermos for you."

"Don't trouble yourself," Mr. Pickering replied with a wave of his hand. He walked over to his raincoat and pulled a silver hip flask from one of the pockets. "A nip of brandy will do just as well. I said I was prepared."

Gathering up a handful of candles, he placed one in each corner of the room then threw Neil a cigarette lighter. "If you could light those for me, I'll just put two more in the center here and jot down the direction of the drafts."

In the bright glare of the electric lights, the candle flames looked cold and pale. Quoth amused himself by dancing around trying to blow them out—until Neil saw what he was doing and scolded him.

"There." The ghost hunter finally nodded with satisfaction. "Now, if you could flick the switch, lad."

Neil obeyed, and the room was immediately engulfed in shadows that leaped about the walls. The huge black bones of the fossils appeared to twitch as great hollows of darkness yawned between the massive ribs, and prehistoric nightmares flew through the dark above their heads.

Beneath them, however, the six cheery candle flames were reflected in the glass of the cabinets, and the cases that contained mineral samples glinted and winked as the faceted crystals and pyrites threw back trembling fires.

"Such glistering gaudery!" Quoth cawed, hopping across to spread his wings and let the shimmering light play over his ragged feathers. "Fie, how this sorry vagabond doth put the lustrous phoenix to shame."

Neil grinned, but Austen Pickering was already heading toward the next room. "Much more conducive," the ghost hunter remarked. "This kind of investigation always works better in the soft glow of candlelight. It's all to do with light waves and atmospheric vibrations. Electricity is a terrible obstacle for some of the weaker souls of the departed."

The boy followed him, and dragging himself away from the sparkling cabinets, Quoth came waddling after.

"Put the rest in the other galleries, I think," Mr. Pickering decided, handing Neil a dozen more candles. "Then I'll settle down and wait. I've got high hopes for this night. Once the usual noises of an old building settling onto its foundation have subsided, who knows? Perhaps there'll even be a manifestation. I've never been so excited, not even in the Wigan case."

"What was that about?" Neil asked.

The old man set another candle down and marked its position in his notebook. "Up till now it was my most rewarding investigation," he announced, "and an object lesson that proves that not all hauntings occur in churchyards or ancient buildings. Just an ordinary house that a young family had moved into. Wasn't long before they noticed strange things were happening, so I was called in."

Wandering into the next room, he paused and lit another candle before continuing. "Five nights I was there before the poor soul made his appearance," he chuckled. "Except for the baby, we were all downstairs, and I was beginning to wonder if the young couple had imagined it all. But sometimes the departed don't want to let go of their ties with this world, and they can get a bit wily. That's what was happening there. The old chap who'd lived there originally didn't want to leave, and he was hiding from me. If it wasn't for modern technology, I might still be there trying to find him."

"How do you mean?" Neil broke in. "Did the ghost show up in one of your photographs?"

The old man laughed. "Nothing like that," he chuckled. "No, as I said, we were all downstairs when we heard a voice over the baby monitor. He was up there in the nursery, talking to the littl'un in her crib!"

"That's creepy."

"Oh, he didn't want to hurt her," Mr. Pickering asserted. "Just sad and lonely, that's all. People don't change just because they die, you know. He was a kindly soul, old Cyril."

"What about those who were nasty when they were alive?"

"Luckily, there's more good in the world than television would have us believe," the ghost hunter replied.

In each of the first floor rooms they had placed four candles, and the winding, connecting corridor was lit with another fifteen at five-foot intervals. All the electric lights were switched off, and now only those small flames pricked and illuminated the momentous dark.

When they reached the main hallway, where the stairs rose into the impenetrable, prevailing blackness of the upper stories, the old man clicked his fingers in the manner that Neil already recognized as the sign that he was marshaling his thoughts.

"There," he muttered, gazing back at the

glimmering trail they had left behind. "I'm ready. I propose to begin here and work my way back to The Fossil Room. Thanks for your help, lad."

The boy smiled at him. The lenses of the ghost hunter's glasses mirrored the candle he held in his hand, and two squares of bright yellow flame shone out from his lined face. Yet behind those reflections, Mr. Pickering's eyes burned just as keenly. Neil wished he could stay and see what would happen, but he sensed that tonight the eager newcomer would rather work alone.

"Good luck," he said.

Mr. Pickering raised his hand in a slight wave, then took a deep breath to prepare himself.

"Come on, you," Neil told Quoth, lifting the bird onto his shoulder. "Let's see if I can sneak you past Dad."

Walking through the collections, the boy looked back to catch a last glimpse of the ghost hunter. He was cocooned in a golden, glowing aura, the cavernous night dwarfing and besieging his stout form as he began his lonely vigil.

"Hope he finds what he came for," Neil said. "This place could do with a psychic spring cleaning."

In the entrance hall, Austen Pickering took out his Bible and held it tightly as he lowered his eyes and murmured a heartfelt prayer. The candle in his other hand fizzed and crackled as particles of the Wyrd Museum's ever-present floating dust drifted into the heat, and presently, the man lifted his head. He was ready.

"I know you can hear me," the ghost hunter called

in a firm but friendly voice. "I don't want to frighten any of you. There's nothing to be afraid of. My name's Austen. I'm here to help. Now is the time you have waited for. Listen to me. I can feel your torment. Don't let this place keep you any longer. Come forward, I beseech you. In the name of all that is good, I call you to me."

The ghost hunter's words echoed through the hall and out into the collections. Passing through The Roman Gallery, Neil and Quoth heard his compassionate appeals, the sonorous tones ringing through the still emptiness of the vacillating dark that surrounded them.

"Make yourselves known to me. Let me guide you to the peace you have been denied."

Quoth's single eye gleamed small and sharp in the shadows as he cocked his head to listen, and Neil felt a sudden tremor of apprehension judder through the raven's body.

"Is something the matter?" the boy asked.

"Yea," Quoth answered in a hoarse whisper filled with dread. "The lumpen one knows not what is moving. From the stygian mirk it cometh. Mine very quills doth rise at its approach. Tarry no longer, Master Neil. To thy father and the light we must away and flee this ray-chidden dankness."

"There's nothing to be scared of."

Yet the urge to leave that place was mounting within the boy, too, and he quickened his pace. About the walls, the shadows of the countless terracotta pots and jars that crammed the shelves seemed to move independently of the candle flames. Neil forced himself not to look at them, for it was easy to see any number of imagined horrors in that crowding dark.

"I should have taken the quick way through the corridor," he muttered.

"Come to me!" he could hear the ghost hunter calling. "Show yourselves!"

Quoth let out a bleating yelp and clung tightly to his master's shoulder. "Canst thou not sense the terror?" he wailed. "The wall of night doth quake and crack. Make haste afore the barricade is riven!"

Into The Neolithic Collection Neil hurried, running past cases that housed fragments of Stone Age skulls and avoiding the gaze of the reconstructed Neanderthals.

"Squire Neil!" the raven yammered, glancing behind them. "Behold the flames!"

Whirling around, the boy saw that the candle flames in the rooms they had passed through were guttering.

"Lo!" Quoth uttered miserably. "The nocturn breath of the unquiet dead doth blow upon them."

As though caught in a gusting draft, the small flames sputtered. To his dismay, Neil saw in the distance an engulfing darkness creep closer as, one by one, the candles were extinguished.

"Midnight as an ice lord's gullet," the raven cawed.

Through the galleries the blackness moved, pouncing from corner to corner as each flame died. Neil could no longer hear Austen Pickering's voice, and when he spun around again, he saw the lights ahead were also dwindling and beginning to fail.

"Too late!" Quoth shrieked. "We are captured!"

With a rush of stale, swirling air, every light in The Neolithic Collection was suddenly snuffed out. Neil and the raven were plunged into a blackness that seemed almost solid.

"The doom hath descended!" Quoth cheeped forlornly.

Neil rubbed his eyes, but the darkness was absolute. This room had no windows, so there was not even a pale glow from outside to guide him. "Stop panicking," he reproached the raven crossly. "You're not afraid of the dark, are you?"

"Alas, yes!" the bird replied. "'Neath night's mantle all manner of fell frights may stalketh—with gangrel limbs to drag the ground, clustering eyes, and dribble-drenched snouts a-questing our hiding places. Oh, how the fetor steameth from their fangs! Aroint this umbral broth; 'tis the unseen fancy which inspireth the horrors tenfold."

"This is stupid," the boy answered, trying to sound calm. "It was only the wind that put the candles out. But if it was a ghost, then I've seen them before and I'm not scared. Edie used to keep loads of them in the bomb sites during the Blitz, the same as other people keep goldfish."

"Doughty and of the halest oak is thine heart fashioned," Quoth whimpered in admiration. "Yet, what sayest thou if the shades who dwell herein doth prove to be fiends most bloody and angersome? No wish hath I to be plucked untimely and robbed of mine gizzards. Spare this frail flower from the greed of the unclean eclipse!"

Neil rummaged in his pockets for the lighter but

remembered that he had given it back to Austen Pickering. Then, unexpectedly, he let out a cheerful laugh. "Why don't I just switch the lights back on?"

Groping through the dark, he felt his way around invisible cabinets until he came to a wall and walked alongside it, picturing their progress in his mind.

"The door to the passage should be near here," he muttered. "The switches are right next to it."

As he fumbled beside a long glass case, Neil felt the ridges of the doorjamb abruptly meet his fingertips, and at that same moment an anxious voice called out to him.

"Are you all right, lad?" Austen Pickering's concerned cry came echoing through the museum. "All the candles have gone out. Stay where you are and I'll come find you. Blast it! The lighter won't work, and I've left the flashlight back with the fossils."

"Don't worry!" the boy shouted back. "I'm going to put the——"

A frantic dab at his cheek caused his reply to falter. "What's the matter now?" he demanded of the raven.

"Hush!" Quoth urged, his rasping voice now charged with genuine terror. "We are not alone in this chamber. Hark—something hath stolen within!"

Neil held his breath, and his skin crawled when he heard faint scrabbling sounds coming from the direction of the far wall. It was a small and furtive scuttling noise that seemed to keep close to the baseboards, traveling the boundaries of the large room as though shy of the open space within.

"What did you say?" the ghost hunter called. "I didn't catch it."

But Neil was too afraid to answer. Whatever had joined Quoth and himself in The Neolithic Collection had overcome its reticence and given a sudden, pig-like grunt. Even now they could hear it snuffling across the floor, scampering under the cabinets, and growling softly to itself.

"'Tis a beast of the ancient wild!" the raven whispered fretfully. "Or some frightsome bogle crawled from its brimstone grot. Master Neil, the great lights—command them!"

With the guttural breaths now sounding from the center of the room, the boy hunted feverishly for the switches on the wall but found only a blank expanse, and his heart beat faster in his chest.

"They're not here!" he hissed. "Quoth! I can't find them. I must have got it wrong. This is the door to The Norman Hall—I thought we were on the other side of the room!"

At the sound of their frightened voices, the bestial snorts ceased and a foul, exulting gurgle issued from the blackness.

"The fiend hath detected us!" Quoth yowled. "We are discovered! Fly, Master Neil!"

A triumphant chattering whooped from the deep shadows as the creature bounded from beneath the cabinets with a gnashing and champing of teeth.

Unable to contain his panic, Neil scrabbled with the door handle and cried out in despair. "It's locked!" he wailed.

"Then flee another way!" Quoth implored, hopping up and down in terror. "The demon is upon us!"

Blundering sideways, Neil ran blindly across the room, but the snapping horror veered around in pursuit, its claws clattering over the polished floorboards.

"More speed!" the raven shrieked.

Neil flung himself through the gloom, and the gargling snorts of the unseen beast rose to a horrible squeal.

Suddenly, the boy yelled in pain as he crashed into a table. Unable to check his momentum, he vaulted head over heels through the darkness, landing in a crumpled heap on the other side.

Screeching, Quoth toppled from his shoulder and went tumbling backward, straight into path of the oncoming nightmare.

CHAPTER 7

MARY-ANNE BRINDLE

For an instant, the raven lay on the ground, wings outstretched and beak askew. Then the raucous shrieks of the marauding beast brought him to his feet, and the bird bolted across the floor in search of his master.

Tormented with panic and terror, Quoth scurried in completely the wrong direction, quite forgetting in his fear that he could fly. Garbled cries howled from his throat, for his jaw had locked open and he could not move it. Behind, he could hear the fangs of the pursuing creature grind together as it lunged after him, and he swung his head from side to side, despairing for his life.

Then, with a painful thud, he ran headlong into the leg of a cabinet. The collision stunned him for a second, but his stringy legs continued to gallop and lurch onward despite his confusion. Thankfully, the aching blow clicked his beak back into place, and when the raven could direct any thoughts beyond the immediate throbbing of his skull, he let out a shrill squawk.

"Squire Neil!" he honked. "Run whilst thou may. The scourge is biting at mine tail. Aiyee! Aiyee!"

Spreading his tattered wings wide, the raven darted forward, careering clear across the room until he raced into The Roman Gallery. Huge dim squares reared up on the bird's right, and he stumbled toward them, skittering through the patches of melancholy light that fanned from those grimy Georgian windows.

After him the nightmare came, and dithering with terror, Quoth did not know which way to run.

Then he saw it.

Wheeling around, his breast heaving, the bird stared back into the dismal gloom, and his puny legs dissolved under him. Catching his wheezing breaths, Quoth sank to the ground as, up to the brink of the dismal light, the creature came prowling.

Faint with fear, the bird saw a squat, outlandish silhouette, no taller than his master's knees. It lowered a mane-crowned head, and Quoth's feathers prickled when he heard a grating babble issue from its unseen mouth.

"Gogus . . ." the imp-like figure panted. "Gogus . . ."

Quoth could only stare while the alarming aberration hesitated, and he wondered what it was waiting for. Was it taunting him, wringing out every last morsel of fright, before it leaped in for the kill?

"Quoth?" Neil's scared voice shouted from the other room. "Where are you? Quoth? Are you okay?"

Shuffling backward over the floorboards and shrinking against the wall, the raven shook his head vehemently, too petrified to cry out. But, at the sound of the boy's voice, the menacing apparition jerked its unwieldy head aside. With a furious chittering, the creature slapped the ground with its splayed claws and bounded back into The Neolithic Room.

"Quoth?" Neil cried again.

Staggering to his feet, the raven spluttered, then shrieked. "Squire Neil! 'Ware the demon—'tis thou it seeks! Save thyself!"

Nursing his bruised shins, Neil felt horribly vulnerable. Hearing that warning, he hobbled through the darkness, his flailing hands striking the cabinets and cases as he battled his way across the room.

Suddenly, the veiled shadows on his left were filled with a loathsome yapping, causing the boy to forget his injuries, and he pelted forward. The doorway to the passage could not be far off; already he could feel a current of air blowing on his face, and he charged recklessly toward its source, slithering and skidding in his haste to escape. But the fiend was closing in, and its jabbering cries became outraged barks as it scooted toward the boy.

Even in that unmeasurable dark, Neil could sense the open doorway as he got closer to it. He did not think to reach for the light switches, and he threw all his strength into one last sprint.

Too late—the berserking creature was at his heels.

Launching its squat form from the ground, the small misshapen figure leaped. Wrapping its arms around the boy's legs, it clung to him fiercely.

Neil howled in fright as powerful claws pinched and squeezed. He toppled sideways, slamming into the wall. Squealing and snapping, his attacker held him with an iron grasp and would not let go.

"Gogus!" it raged. "Gogus . . . Gogus!"

"Get off!" the boy cried. "Let go!"

"Gogus . . ." was his only reply, and the vise-like clutch tightened all the more.

"Help!" Neil bawled. "Help!"

At that moment, the night was filled with ferocious screeches as Quoth came swooping through the air, shooting to his aid. "Afright not, my master!" he crowed. "Yon runted minikin shalt bear the mark of the raven afore thy boggling serf is slain."

With talons outstretched, Quoth plummeted down. Toward the feverish barks and grunts he flew, his master's cries jangling loud in his mind. His one thought: to do all that he could to save Neil, whatever the cost to himself. Across the beast's large, ill-proportioned face the raven's claws gouged long scars, and the enemy yowled in fury.

"Avaunt ye!" Quoth commanded. "Creep back to thy venomous lurks. Begone!"

Incensed by the bird's harrying onslaught, the small figure loosened its grasp around the boy's legs and retaliated. Before he realized what was happening, Quoth was plucked from the air, and his squawks were throttled in his scrawny throat as those mighty claws hooked about him.

"Gogus!" the monster gargled madly, shaking Quoth as though he were a mouse in a cat's jaws. The raven jiggled and flapped hopelessly, coughing and choking as he fought to breathe.

"Quoth!" Neil called, finally able to move his legs. "What's happening? Quoth?"

The grunting horror let out a frustrated hiss and discarded the annoying bird, hurling him into the darkness as it swung back to pounce on the boy once more. Mewling piteously, Quoth rocketed across the room.

"Run, Master Neil!" he wailed, before his head smashed into a Neanderthal display and the dazed raven slid down the cracked glass, burbling a warbled chirrup as he dropped to the ground.

Framed in the open doorway, Neil heard Quoth's collision and prayed he was unharmed. Yet there was nothing he could do, for in that instant the pigmy-sized creature jumped up at him again, and Neil let out a yell of fright as he tumbled backward into the passage.

* * *

Immediately the clamoring barks ceased.

Neil sat up in consternation. The stupefying dark was gone and the passage was lit with a dim light. He let out a long, grateful sigh.

"Be still!" a breathless voice hissed in his ear, and a filthy hand was clapped over the boy's mouth before he could make any further sound.

"This way!" he was told. "They'll be here in a minute. Don't let them find us."

With rough, hauling movements, the owner of that frightened voice dragged the struggling boy away from the doorway and pulled him into a shadowy alcove, where he was thrust into the corner and forced to crouch on his haunches.

"Stay put and do as I say."

His face was pushed against the wall, and the weight of his captor was pressing against his back to keep him there, but Neil managed to twist his head around and glare at the person who had seized him. Anger and resentment ebbed away to be replaced by an uproar of confusion and bewilderment, for he was staring up into the face of a young woman.

The gas lamp in the passage burned so low the feeble flame barely flickered, and the resulting phosphorescence bathed everything in a deathly, dappled pallor. The woman's skin was painted cold and gray under this chill radiance. Beneath those crinkling brows, her small eyes darted this way and that, glimmering like an owl's in the ghastly illumination. A cloud of dark, matted hair fell about her tensed shoulders in an unkempt, twining tangle, and snarled hanks fringed her high, furrowed forehead.

Scouring the gloom, she cringed deeper into the alcove, bunching herself into as small a shape as possible. The crisply starched linen of her nightgown crackled faintly.

Neil's mind surged with questions. He had no idea who she was. Had she broken into the museum? Did the vicious animal in the other room belong to her? Peering past her into the shadowy passage, the boy realized with a jolt that something else was not right. Mounted on the paneled wall, enclosed in a globe of frosted glass, was the gas lamp that saturated the corridor in its pallid glow. But Neil was certain that all the lighting in the Wyrd Museum was electric. There were no gas lamps.

"You'll do it, won't you, boy?" the woman spat, bringing her face close to his. "Mary-Anne can make you, and she will if you force her!"

Neil wormed around a little more, his nose edging clear of the woman's stifling palm. A sickly, antiseptic smell hung heavily in the air, but a sharp jab at his throat concentrated his mind on a new danger. In her other hand, the woman was holding a knife.

"You'll know the way out, won't you?" she said in a threatening whisper. "Nice clean boy like you. Come a-visiting, have we? Been shown what they wanted you to see? No one gets to come down this way. It's not agreeable, not refined. Offend the paying relatives, it would."

The woman pressed the flat of the cold steel blade against his skin, and the dim gas flame reflected an anemic sliver of light up into her eyes. Neil looked into them and swallowed uneasily. Those small, shifting pupils were filled with a wild, dancing desolation, and he knew that she would not shrink from slitting his throat.

"You want to live, boy?" she demanded. "Then take Mary-Anne out of this. She'll spike you if you don't. Already killed once this night, she has. Can't endure it no more."

The woman rocked forward to glance down the

passage once more, and as she moved, Neil saw that her nightgown was sprayed with large, spattered stains. In the somber light the ugly marks and blotches were a purplish black, but they glistened wetly and the boy knew that he was looking at blood, freshly spilled from the vein.

"Peace, now!" Mary-Anne entreated, her voice rising with panic. "They're coming. Rokeby's been found. Josiah Rokeby, you devil!"

Gripping the knife so tightly that the blade sliced into the skin of her forefinger, the woman shivered, and Neil could feel that her every sinew was hideously taut and strained. Suddenly, she whipped the blade away from the boy's throat and wrenched her hand from his mouth as she swept the matted tresses from her ears, pushing herself against the alcove wall.

"No!" she whimpered, her mouth dry with horror. "*He* is with them. Oh, sweet heaven! Save Mary-Anne Brindle from that one."

Wailing, she shook her head violently, banging her skull on the paneling and beating her temples with her fists. Then, abruptly, the tantrum was over and she sat there, panting feverishly. Her face half-hidden behind an untidy curtain of hair, Mary-Anne peeped out at the passage and nodded slowly.

"Tick-Tock Jack has found him," the woman murmured. "It's that one she should've stuck. No time for hiding now, not with Tick-Tock after her. Oh, Lord, Jack Timms will knock the life out of her this time. Hers won't be the first head he's broken."

Still crouched in the corner, Neil heard the sound of running footsteps approaching down the corridor, and the noise caused Mary-Anne to spring to her feet. "Let them pass!" the woman cried, hugging herself in distraction. "Rokeby had earned it. All the wardens warrant the same, but he and Tick-Tock the most. Dear Jesus, let them run by her!"

Only a few minutes ago, when he had faced that gurgling fiend in The Neolithic Room, Neil had thought he had been afraid. But now, gazing up at this petrified, insane woman, he truly understood the meaning of real fear. Like a fountain of despair the terror flowed out from her, breaking in wave after hopeless wave from her blighted, tortured form.

The noise in the passage was louder now. Heavy boots were pounding over the floorboards, and Neil felt an overwhelming desire not to be found. Squeezing himself as far into the corner as he could, he waited, not daring to look up.

"There!" a rough male voice yelled. "She's there!"

The woman screamed, and angry shouts boomed within the corridor as her enemies thundered forward. Leaping from the alcove, she hared away, and Neil heard her high, fluting shrieks as she disappeared from sight. He shrank further into the gloom, anxiously holding his breath.

Suddenly three dark, burly figures hurtled past his hiding place, momentarily obliterating the feeble gaslight, and the boy knew that Mary-Anne would not escape them. Foul curses blared in his ears, but all sounds were instantly drowned when another fierce, bellowing voice roared through the building.

"Get back here! I'll teach you to kill old Joe!"

It was a repellent, contemptible pronouncement,

and Neil's scalp crept with the inexhaustible hate and malice that fueled it. Then there came a shrill screech, accompanied by a frantic scuffling. The woman had been caught.

"I'll learn you!" the spite-charged voice snapped. "Pin her still, lads!"

Deafening screams tore the gloom, and as savage, battering thuds shook the walls, vile jeers galed from the darkness.

Neil clapped his hands over his ears, but the brutality jolted through his bones, and nothing could shield him from the woman's howls.

"Stop it!" he yelled. "Leave her alone!"

And then, it was over.

The evil din ended. The final, piercing notes of Mary-Anne's suffering lingered briefly upon the ether, until they were quenched by an ominous silence more horrible than anything he had yet experienced.

A nauseated burning bubbled in Neil's stomach, and he felt the bile rise to the back of his throat. At that moment, a deep shadow was cast over the alcove when a figure stepped in front of the gaslight. Neil scrambled to his bruised knees, cradling his head in his arms.

"Get off!" he cried. "Don't you touch me!"

Looming over the huddled boy, the black shape reached toward him.

"What's this, then?" a gruff voice demanded.

CHAPTER 8

AWAKENING

Hearing those words, Neil jerked his head back and blurted out a great, glad cry. Standing over him, with the flame of his cigarette lighter bowing in the draft that coursed through the passageway, was Austen Pickering.

"What happened, lad?" the ghost hunter cried, seeing the fear graven in the boy's face. "Are you all right? Did you fall and hurt yourself in the dark?"

"Mary-Anne!" Neil shouted, staggering to his feet and lunging from the alcove. "How is she? Where are the others?"

Stumbling up the corridor, he whisked around but could see nothing in the darkness that had returned. Snatching the lighter from the old man's hand, he hastened forward, then halted and came running back.

"Others?" Mr. Pickering repeated. "Who do you mean? Who's this Mary-Anne?"

Neil rushed to the wall opposite his hiding place and held the wavering flame above his head while he ran his fingers over the worm-ridden wooden panels. But the gas lamp was not there, and all he found was a tarnished brass fitting that had not been used for many years.

"It was here," he murmured faintly. "She was here—Mary-Anne Brindle."

An envious smile formed on the old man's face. "You've seen something, haven't you?" he marveled. "What was it? Tell me everything—I have to know each detail."

The boy stared at him blankly. "But you must have heard them!" he exclaimed. "They were just here, they chased her down . . ."

His protestations trailed into silence, and he took a nervous, sampling breath. "That disinfectant smell," he muttered. "It's gone as well."

"An olfactory emanation!" Mr. Pickering declared. "Of all the luck!"

Neil scowled at him. "It was nothing to be jealous of, I promise you."

"Even better!" the ghost hunter exclaimed, rubbing his hands together. "Let's get back to The Fossil Room. I want to record this."

Neil drew a hand over his face. "But it was real," he whispered.

"I'm not suggesting you imagined it."

"No. I mean they weren't ghosts. They were actually here. And back there, in The Neo—"

The boy's insides lurched as he suddenly remembered and went charging back to The Neolithic Room.

"Quoth!" he yelled.

Bursting in, he swung around and slapped his hand across the light switches. The sudden flaring of the electric bulbs was blinding, and the boy screwed up his face as he rampaged inside, jumping over the table he had crashed into in the dark.

"Quoth!" he called again. "Where are you?"

Neil threw himself on his hands and knees and scuttled through the room, searching under the cabinets until he heard a frail, bleating cry.

"Fie, sir!" the familiar tones trilled in a delirious, hiccupping prattle. "Ne'er hath this riddled bucket met with such a boggling—a tree-nesting milch cow! What prodigious eggs thou must be blessed with."

The raven lay at the foot of the tallest display case, blearily gazing up at the ceiling. His bald head was lolling to one side, his legs split beneath him, one wing raised in the air and the other twitching erratically.

"Alas, this goodly knight cannot sup with thee. A feast of running cheese and malmsey awaits him. Good Sir Geoffrey, see to mine steed. The rose-cheeked damsel beckons."

Neil hurried to his side and glanced worriedly at the large crack in the glass where the bird had struck the case. "Quoth . . ." he ventured.

The raven wagged his head as though he was drunk, and Neil touched him gingerly.

"M'Lady!" Quoth objected. "'Tis most unseemly amid the crocks and dishpots!"

"Is the poor thing injured?" Austen Pickering spoke up as he joined them.

"I don't think anything's broken," Neil answered. "He's got a huge bump on his head, but—he doesn't seem to know me."

The boy lifted the raven's limp body off the ground and held him in his arms, while the bird's one eye rolled in its socket.

"Does look a bit dazed," the ghost hunter agreed.

Neil bit his lip nervously. "Will it be permanent, do you think?"

"Dunno, lad. I'm no vet, and I've never kept so much as a parakeet before. Hang on, this might do the trick."

From his pocket, the old man pulled the small bottle of smelling salts and wafted the pungent vapor under the raven's beak.

The result was swift and startling. Quoth bolted upright, spluttering and squawking. "Pickled toad stink and squeezings of sourmost mordant fish!" he gasped. Blowing down his bill to dispel the noxious fumes, he stared accusingly around him until he caught sight of Neil's face, and his belligerent expression transformed to one of joy.

"Master Neil! There is a remedy for all hurts, save death, and its name is thine."

The boy laughed. "You're back to normal," he said.

Quoth nuzzled against him, then tugged his head aside to glare and squint down at the floor.

"The imp!" he cawed, remembering the fiend that had attacked them. "Hath it fled hence? Didst thou dispatch it?"

"What's he talking about?" Mr. Pickering asked. "He's still rambling."

Neil turned to him. "No," he replied gravely. "When the candles went out, something came after us in here. I don't know what it was, but it was definitely no ghost. Couldn't you hear us?"

"I thought you'd tripped, that's all," the old man answered. "I know I did when I came to find you."

"So you didn't see anything?"

"Not a thing. Was it some kind of animal?"

Before Neil could reply, Quoth uttered a mortified croak, and they lowered their eyes to where the raven pointed with his beak. Lifting one foot in the air, the bird flexed his talons, and a splintered shaving of wood dropped onto Neil's outstretched hand.

"Behold!" Quoth announced in a quavering voice. "'Tis a token gouged of the demon's brow."

Mr. Pickering eyed him doubtfully. "What's he saying?"

Neil stared at the evidence in his palm. "No animal was in here tonight," he said, hardly believing his own words. "Whatever it was that attacked us wasn't flesh and blood."

* * *

A little while later they were sitting in The Fossil Room, discussing all that had happened from the moment the candle flames were extinguished. Not content with recording Neil's experience on tape, Austen Pickering also took pages of notes, then went back to the scene of the visitation to see if any clues had been left behind in his scatterings of flour.

"What a pity," he sighed on his return. "The

marks were too confused to tell me anything. The only clear tracks I could find were a neat little set of raven footprints."

Quoth gave a mournful cluck, but the ghost hunter was not disheartened. "Better luck next time," he assured them. "I'll put some more flour down later."

"I don't think I want to see the next time," Neil put in.

Mr. Pickering took out his handkerchief and polished his glasses. Peering at the blurred boy in front of him, he tutted and said, "Don't say that. I'm counting on you, Private Chapman. I know you were scared, but there really was no need. I've never heard of a case where the departed harmed the living. Fear alone does that."

"You don't understand!" Neil insisted, smacking the glass counter he was leaning on. "That thing back there and those people I saw, they weren't ghosts. They were as solid as I am."

"They might have *seemed* solid . . ."

"Listen to me, they were! How else do you account for that splinter of wood?"

The ghost hunter replaced his spectacles and browsed through his notes. "Your little friend could have scratched one of the tables by mistake. It was pitch black in there. As for the woman in the passage, how *could* she be real? Your confusion between this world and the next is very common, lad. Those who witness such events are often so caught up in the tragedies unfolding before them that their perspective on reality is altered, and they believe that what they are seeing has substance, when in fact it does not."

Neil scowled and folded his arms. "She dragged me halfway down the corridor," he said emphatically. "I'd call that pretty substantial, wouldn't you?"

"You *thought* that she did," Mr. Pickering persisted. "I'm a trained observer of this kind of phenomenon, lad, trust me."

"So what do you think it was then?" the boy asked.

The ghost hunter put down his clipboard and leaned forward across the counter. "Most definitely an incident that happened way back in this building's past. Judging from what you've told me, my first guess would be that it occurred in the time of the lunatic asylum, but we must wait until we have all the facts before we can be certain."

"That would explain the awful smell," Neil agreed.

"Think of this place as a vast camera, and the air that fills it a photographic plate. Just like a camera, that plate is very sensitive—not to light in this case, but to certain actions and emotions. What you saw was a moving projection of some horrible, violent act that was so severe it imprinted itself on the atmosphere within that corridor. And, unless someone can release that unfortunate lady's suffering, that scene will be replayed over and over forever."

Neil wasn't so sure. "But it wasn't like that," he protested one final time. "It was more like I had slipped back in time, gone back to the past."

Austen Pickering gave a humoring chortle. "Now, that *is* preposterous! I'm sorry, lad, but when I write this up for the psychic journal I can't put that down. I'd never be taken seriously again. Time travel, indeed."

The boy realized it sounded ridiculous, but he also knew that within the Wyrd Museum anything was possible. He could not help smiling at the thought that Austen Pickering would undoubtedly have to eat a great many of his words before his investigations were over.

"Master Neil!" Quoth interrupted, pulling the boy's sleeve to get his attention. Still grinning, Neil turned to him and saw that the raven was jerking his head toward the doorway. Before he could swivel around on his chair, there came an awkward cough.

Standing behind them, looking embarrassed and abashed, was Brian Chapman. "It's nine o'clock," he muttered in a small voice. "There's a bit of supper left. It's a school day tomorrow."

Neil realized that his father was trying his best to make up for what had happened earlier. "So was today," he admitted.

"Well, you got back late last night, and I got up late. One day won't matter."

Austen Pickering regarded the lanky, disheveled man with mild interest. The boy's father was the opposite of Neil. He didn't appear to be capable of looking after himself, let alone two children. The ghost hunter's critical, observing eyes flicked over the gangly figure before him and made a quick mental appraisal.

Brian had not shaved that day. His greasy hair curled over the collar of his unironed shirt, and wiry bunches spiked from his nostrils. A wide gap between the tops of his scuffed shoes and the bottom of his ill-fitting trousers betrayed the fact he was wearing mismatched socks, and his slouching stance suggested that he was trying to pretend he wasn't there. Mr. Pickering had never encountered anyone who was so uncomfortable in his own skin before, and he pitied the boy for being afflicted with such a parent.

"I brought you this," the caretaker said, shyly bringing his hand from behind his back to reveal a thermos filled with hot water. "Didn't mean to snap before. Been a bad few days."

Austen Pickering smiled disarmingly. "Don't mention it," he said, and he meant it. "Thank you for this. I could do with a cup of coffee right now."

"You . . . you could come and have something to eat if you like," Brian offered, not meeting the other man's eyes.

The ghost hunter grinned, but he declined with a polite wave of his hand. "Appreciated, but no thanks. I have some fruit and an instant soup if I get peckish later. I might take you up on it tomorrow, though, if the invite still stands. Lot to do tonight, got to get to work."

"Not found any spooks yet, then?" Brian inquired, forcing a strained laugh.

Neil shot the ghost hunter a look that was loaded with meaning. Mr. Pickering understood, and a difficult silence followed that was broken only when

Quoth shook his wings and cawed softly.

"Haven't made a proper start yet," the old man said evasively.

Brian nodded and backed clumsily to the doorway. "Well, see you in the morning, then," he mumbled. "See if your hair's turned white."

"Not enough of it left for that," Mr. Pickering joked.

Neil hesitated before following his father. "Dad," he called. "What about Quoth?"

At the mention of his name, the raven flew to his place at the boy's shoulder and let out a sorrowful croak.

"Oh, well—bring him along then," Brian relented, seeing how downcast and forlorn the mangy bird appeared. "But he's not to sleep in your room."

"Zooks hurrah!" Quoth sang.

Neil thanked his father and said good night to Mr. Pickering. "Be careful," the boy warned him.

When he was alone in The Fossil Room, the ghost hunter shivered slightly and inspected one of the thermometers.

"Down five degrees," he commented aloud, adding the information to his notebook.

The next half hour was spent sprinkling more flour in the adjoining rooms, relighting all the candles, and switching off the electric lights again. When everything was done, the old man made himself a mug of strong black coffee and eased himself into his chair.

A brooding silence had descended over the Wyrd Museum, and Mr. Pickering took time to gaze around him. Like a dark sea, profound shadows lapped the walls and ceiling above him, and he lightly closed his eyes, trying to assess the building's mood.

"Nothing," he murmured. "Having a bit of a rest are we, or is it the sulks? Well, let's see what else you've got up your sleeve, or should I say drainpipe?"

His voice echoed hollowly into the empty gloom, and he shrugged. "Maybe you prefer frightening children. You'll not upset me so easily."

Placing his Bible upon the counter, he took a swig of coffee and chose a book from one of the suitcases.

"*Billy Bunter!*" he proclaimed to the watching night. "A perfect read for the small hours. You'll love it."

Turning the pages, he moved the two central candles a little closer and started to read aloud. The beetle-black canopy enclosed around him, and the ghost hunter reflected that it was going to be a long, but hopefully eventful, night.

* * *

Obscured behind thick, impenetrable cloud, the moon imparted little light on the unlovely shape of the Wyrd Museum. Yet what drizzled through the large square windows was far brighter than the hoard of shadow with which the building clothed its galleries.

Those rooms facing out onto Well Lane benefited from the extra glare of the street lamps. Their stark, sodium glow diffused through the cluttered spaces in an unnatural, sulphurous daubing, and up on the second floor Edie Dorkins meandered through The Separate Collection, the silver tinsel in her pixie hat glittering with small green sparks.

After the Chamber of Nirinel, this was her favorite place. She loved to stare at the exhibits, wondering what they were for and, in some cases, who they had been. The headstrong little girl reveled in the delicious oblivion the dark afforded and relished the musty, decaying smells of the museum that were always stronger in the lonely, shadowy murk.

Standing on a box, she pressed her nose against one of the glass lids, and her mouth watered at what she saw inside. A large golden locket, bigger than her fist and curiously shaped, lay on a cushion of faded purple velvet. Edie traced the snaking loop of the fabulous chain with the tip of her tongue.

Staring at the accompanying label, she almost wished that she was able to read what it said, for who could have worn such a heavy, prodigious pendant?

"It contains the heel bone of Achilles," Miss Ursula's voice sounded at the entrance to The Egyptian Suite.

Without taking her tongue from the glass, Edie raised her eyes. The eldest of the Websters was standing in the semi-darkness of the threshold to that midnight, windowless room, but the girl could only make out a black shadow shape that glinted when the jet beads of the woman's evening gown caught the glow of the street lamp.

"You can remove it from the case if you wish, Edith."

With an impertinent toss of her head, the girl jumped from the box. The lumpy locket had lost some of its appeal now that she had been given permission to wear it, and she ambled over to another cabinet.

The figure in the doorway remained in the masking gloom. "Soon you will know the history of each exhibit," she promised. "Remember that you are to succeed my sister and me as custodian of these precious and perilous objects. Ask of me what you will, before my mind collapses into the dementia of Celandine and Veronica before her."

Peering into the recess of this larger case, Edie inspected the contents. Balanced on a roughly carved granite plinth was a great globe of worn and crackled leather. Over the irregular bumps of its scarred and weathered surface the mustard-colored light curved softly, making the pummeled and dented sphere look like a giant, moldering apricot.

"Big soccer ball?" the girl speculated. "Break yer toes kicking that around the park."

"You know very well it is nothing of the kind," Miss Ursula's floating voice upbraided her. "It is the Eye of Balor."

Edie studied the huge, swollen globe anew. "A real eye?" she breathed, misting up the glass. "It's massive."

"The Fomorians were monsters who plagued Ireland in ancient times," the old woman began in a whispering chant. "Yet even among their hideous company, Balor, the son of Buarainech, was as a mountain. All feared him, for one of his eyes had the power to wither and kill at a single glance. Such was its dreaded strength that he was compelled to keep it firmly closed and covered. But when the Fomorians rode across the plain to meet their enemies, the attendants of Balor would raise his eyelid with a great hook, and entire armies fell before its destroying gaze."

"Cool!" Edie mouthed.

The dim silhouette in The Egyptian Suite let the girl stare in fascination for a while longer before concluding the tale.

"Balor was eventually slain by the hero Lugh," the voice recounted, "who hurled a great stone at the Fomorian's head, even as the lid was being lifted. The ogre's skull exploded and the eye catapulted clean through the other side. But, even in death, the Eye of Balor lost none of its slaughtering might and was wielded as a merciless weapon. Today, out there in the modern world, its memory lives on. When the ignorant gesticulate to defend themselves from the evil eye, it is to that they are referring."

The old woman's dark figure stirred, and her Victorian gown swished with the movement.

"Yet there is no protection," Miss Ursula declared, her voice harsh and censorious. "That is why the Eye was entrusted into my care. Sealed within that orb of gnarled hide and rigid vellum, it is still as deadly as ever."

Edie gave a wicked cackle and flung her arms around the cabinet as far as they could reach—to hug it.

"Better 'n all the bombs and air raids!" she rejoiced.

"The museum is host to many dangers," the old woman intoned. "When my wits have crumbled, it will be your duty to ensure that nothing leaks from these confines."

Edie stepped away from the Eye and darted across the room to where a column adorned with gilded, scrolling ferns formed the pedestal of a shapely foot sculpted in ivory.

"Where's the rest of it?" she demanded.

The darkness of The Egyptian Suite rustled, and a sudden, sharp breath caused Edie to forget her question.

Into the faint light Miss Ursula stole, leaving the extreme shadows behind her. Wonder glimmered over her features, and she turned her face toward the surrounding paneled walls, as if listening to what they might tell her.

"Can you sense it, Edith?" she gasped, her voice trembling with excitement. "It is beginning. The museum awakes!"

Whirling around on her heels, the old woman let out a peal of giddy laughter, then hastened toward the other doorway.

"Quickly!" she urged. "Let us return and share this with Celandine."

Edie Dorkins gaped at her. She had never seen Miss Ursula behave like this but, even as she stared in bemusement, an almost imperceptible tingling sensation prickled down the back of her neck. Swiftly it grew within her until an electric thrill buzzed inside the child's head, and she squealed with a bubbling excitement.

Miss Ursula was right—the atmosphere within the Wyrd Museum was changing. It was as though the vast, slumbering building was starting to rouse itself, and the girl raced after her, boisterously firing a string of questions.

"My head feels like there's stars in it, and there's bees in my feet!" she cried. "What'll happen? Does this mean Woden can't get at us? Will it last?"

Hurrying down the corridor past the fixed, glassy stares of the stuffed menagerie, Miss Ursula could only shake her head at the girl's impatient cries.

"Silence, Edith," she commanded when they reached the end of the passage and stepped out onto the landing. "Listen."

Clapping her mouth shut, the girl obeyed. From the first floor, flowing through the flame-flickering collections, an indistinct, disembodied voice rose into the heights, melting into the invisible space above the heads of those two figures who listened by the banister.

Edie strained to catch the words, but the echoing distance made them impossible to decipher. "Is it ghosts?" she whispered, jumping eagerly down from the top step. "I want to go see!"

Miss Ursula caught her by the arm and pulled the child back. "No, dear," she instructed. "It is the sound of our new guest, reading aloud."

"That old geezer!" Edie groaned, unable to prevent a sneer from stealing over her face.

The eldest of the Websters laid a tapering hand on the banister rail and gazed down into the black void below. "His is the force that pricks and goads this realm from its lethargy," she told the child. "You must learn to use every instrument in your gift, Edith."

Pausing a moment longer, Miss Ursula breathed deeply. "I was right," she uttered in relief, "and tonight is but the start. The museum's defenses will soon be revived and vigilant once more, and we shall have nothing further to fear."

Lifting the skirt of her gown, the old woman began to climb the stairs. "There is nothing more we can do this night," she said. "The pettifogging wraith seeker is performing his role perfectly, as I hoped he would. Will you retire with me?"

"I'll stay up for a bit more," Edie answered, lingering as Miss Ursula disappeared into the gloom above.

The night was charged with marvelous possibilities, and Edie ached to go scampering through every room to experience this euphoric awakening to its utmost. She giggled at the dizzy lightness that inspired her.

"Good night, Edith, dear," Miss Ursula called from above.

Resting her head against the banister, Edie continued to listen to Austen Pickering's droning tones, and she wondered how long it would take for the museum to become an unassailable fortress. Her capricious nature demanded the answer immediately, and she decided to chase after Miss Ursula and ask.

Tearing herself from the landing, she headed for the Websters' apartment, scrambling up the stairs to the third floor and throwing herself through the door that led to a long gallery called The Tiring Salon.

Thronging this spacious, night-drenched room, a multitude of headless mannequins stood massed in an eerily frozen gathering, crowding the way to the small door that led to the attic rooms. Edie had to duck under an outstretched wooden arm when she entered.

Miss Celandine had a passion for this place, although it was too close to the Websters' apartment and her sister's watchful eye for her to enjoy its delights to the full. Today, however, having been given the liberty to roam where she wished, she had played with the dummies and positioned them in appropriate attitudes, as if they were attending a ball.

Naturally, she had not returned her motionless partners to their rightful places when she had finished her frolicking play, and now they stood in an inert assembly, as if waiting for their enchantress to return and waltz with them again.

A jumbled pageant of costumes and garments from many different ages surrounded Edie as the child pushed into their midst, passing medieval nobles and tripping over their cloaks. Grunting in annoyance, she plowed into the fixed embrace of a flamboyantly tasseled flapper from the Twenties, then kicked the legs from under it in irritation.

At the far side of the gallery, above the severed necks and between the hats and bonnets that were propped on poles and stands, she could just make out Miss Ursula's retreating figure. The girl shoved the motionless crowd aside as she surged forward. A minute later, a wake of stricken, richly robed figures lay toppled and overturned behind her, as though some terrible tragedy had decimated a formal dinner party, and Edie wiped her nose on her sleeve.

The door before her was decorated with a skillful carving of the World-Tree and its three roots. Edie could not resist touching the golden circle framing the inlay of lapis lazuli that represented the sacred well beneath Nirinel, then she turned the handle and hurried inside.

Miss Ursula had already ascended the narrow staircase that rose up past the great oil painting of the three sisters, to where a damask curtain was draped over the entrance to their apartment. Taking the steps two at a time, Edie capered after her.

* * *

In the Websters' apartment, six tall candles burned in the ornate candelabra that stood on the round, central table. Admiring herself in the mottled mirror, Miss Celandine had arranged a green sequined shawl around her sagging shoulders. A toothy grin smoothed the old woman's crabbed lips as she tilted her head from left to right, assessing the effect that the spangling cloth had upon her reflection.

"Do you like it, Veronica?" she addressed the empty room. "Such a day I've had. So many handsome gallants wishing to dance with me. I declare I shall have to look my very best tomorrow, dear. You will, too. They asked where you were—they did."

Bundling the shawl about her head so that only her dark, bright eyes peeped out through a twinkling gash, she thought how mysterious and alluring she looked and twittered girlishly.

"What a party it will be," she rattled on, unwrapping the fabric and tying the corners under her chin like a glamorous headscarf. "You mustn't be jealous if I get asked to dance more often than you. It's not my fault I'm popular—it isn't, it isn't."

Framed by the green glinting sequins, Miss Celandine's brown, wrinkled face was speckled in lustrous dots, and she was pleased to see how well they detracted from the upturned, bulbous blob of her nose.

Just then Edie Dorkins burst in, and Miss Celandine struck a wobbling pose so that the girl could praise and flatter her. But Edie barely looked at the old woman. The incorrigible child was staring about the poky little room as though searching for something and not paying her any attention at all.

"Where's Ursula?" the impudent girl demanded.

Miss Celandine decided to give her a second chance and revolved prettily to give Edie that extra nudge of encouragement.

"Where is she?" the waif snapped. "Stand still, Celandine, an' take that daftness off yer 'ead."

"Well!" the old woman cried, her grace and poise deflating as she tore the shawl away and threw it at the little savage. "Oh, you're so rude and spiteful! I shan't talk to you ever again—I won't, I won't!"

Edie ignored her wounded ramblings and ran around the attic room, looking behind the armchairs and in the cupboards. Miss Celandine plopped herself down onto a cushion that exploded with dust at the violence of her descent, then she folded her arms and pouted peevishly.

"Where did she go when she came in?" Edie pressed, when it became obvious that there was nowhere Ursula could be hiding.

Miss Celandine turned her face to the wall. "Not talking to you," she said petulantly.

Edie scowled and gave one of the old woman's braids a sharp tug. A shrill howl blasted through the attic, and Miss Celandine buried her head in the mildewed velvet of her dress.

"Not fair!" her muffled voice whined. "That hurt. It's not fair—it isn't, it isn't. Ursula hasn't been in here, she hasn't—has she, Veronica?"

Edie's forehead creased all the more, and she ran back to the doorway. Yanking its damask curtain aside, she glared out suspiciously. The narrow flight of stairs leading down to The Tiring Salon was deserted.

"Not a sign of her," Edie murmured.

CHAPTER 9

TICK-TOCK JACK

The countless spires that jabbed up from the turreted roofs of the Wyrd Museum seemed to puncture the low, oppressive clouds. Cold air flooded down to whisk the weather vanes and tousle the feathers of the raven who perched on the topmost spike.

With his head pulled into his hunched shoulders, Quoth trilled despondently and gave a dispirited sniff. Forbidden to sleep in the children's bedroom, the living room, or the kitchen, only the bathroom of the caretaker's apartment had remained for him in which to rest his weary wings.

A contented hour had passed when everyone snuggled into their beds. Quoth had made himself more than comfortable on a large towel he dragged down into the trough of the bathtub, and he was soon fast asleep.

Yet Brian Chapman could find no peace, for the bird's slight snoring was amplified by the bathtub. When he could endure no more of those uncanny, echoing peeps, he opened a window and jostled the startled raven outside.

Stupefied and baffled by this brusque awakening, Quoth found himself expelled into the walled courtyard at the rear of the museum. Fluttering forlornly at the windows, like a huge ragged moth tapping against a lantern, he pecked at the panes, but Brian Chapman refused to let him back in.

Quoth flew to Neil's bedroom window, but his master was sound asleep, and so the raven tried to nestle upon the sill. But the ledge was too narrow, and after a few teetering minutes he judged that not even a starved sparrow could be comfortable there.

Up to the roof of the Wyrd Museum he soared in a wide, climbing spiral and cawed his unhappiness across the chimneys of Bethnal Green. Feeling sorry for himself, the raven swooped through the slate-covered canyons and gullies, seeking a roost. But all the best perches, which were shielded from the wind, were already taken by a swarm of dirty pigeons.

Quoth circled up around the turrets and spikes until he finally alighted on the highest spire. The bump on his head stung in the cold, and his tattered feathers were scant insulation against the cutting breeze. Shivering, he told himself that if he could only wait until the morning, then his beloved master would call for him and all would be well.

All around, Bethnal Green glittered in its rest. Tower blocks checkered the night with small, bright squares, and the noise of the late traffic was borne to the raven on the chill breeze. Glancing at the ground far below, Quoth wondered what would happen if he fell while sleeping, then he stiffened, and his eye opened wide.

Down in the lane, a river of mist was moving.

Directed by some guiding power, the curdling vapor poured into the litter-strewn alleyway in front of the museum, where it mounted into a swirling cloud.

"Memory . . ." came a sibilant hiss inside the raven's head.

The bird trembled. That voice reached deep inside his decayed brain, to those vague, remote images he preferred to leave buried with his former existence.

A hooded shape began to form within the rolling smoke, and Quoth whimpered piteously.

"Behold!" he croaked in a small, fear-cracked voice. "The God of the Gallows hath come."

From the thick, heaving fog the shrouded figure of Woden stepped, and the dark shadows beneath his concealing hood stared up at the roof where the raven quivered and shook.

"Will you harken to me, my true, trusted companion?" he called.

Quoth gripped the spire more fiercely than before, and although he felt faint at heart, he gritted his beak and made no reply.

"Your master is here to receive you back into his service," the commanding whisper told him. "When I attempted to recall you and your brother from the corruption of death, I had not the power to restore both. The Witches of the Wood completed the task I had commenced. But at what cost to your sanity, my faithful adviser? I know the war that rages in your damaged mind."

Quoth squeezed his eye shut and tucked his head underneath his wing. But he could not evade those insistent, compelling words that drummed inside him.

"Thought, your brother, is dead once more, and from that gulf I cannot deliver him again. But you, Memory, I can bring peace to your divided reason. My arts will repair the cunning intellect you once possessed."

Flustered and frightened, the raven fanned his feathers and peeped through the spaces of his outspread wing. "Verily, this white-livered rascal doth lack the menseful load," he called wretchedly. "Yet I wouldst rather a small fire to warm me than a great one to burn me."

A laugh of recognition issued from the shadows beneath Woden's cowl, but the sound was unpleasant and needling.

"So!" he declared. "Not all is forgotten. Still you speak in those ridiculous mottoes that so infuriated your brother. Assume your rightful place by my side, Memory, and united we shall vanquish the Nornir."

Quoth clicked his tongue while his impaired mind strove for something to say. "'Tis better to live in low degree than high disdain," he managed at last.

"And better to bow than break?" the hooded figure retaliated sharply. "Don't fire those absurdities at me. Better alone than in bad company, is that what you would tell me? I, who raised you from a fledgling. Can you reject your Captain so easily? Would you spurn your true lord?"

Quoth projected his beak through the scruffy feathers and nodded feebly. "This pot-headed marplot hath a fresh, magnolious master," he announced. "Memory, thy felonious vassal, didst perish and shalt ne'er take wing no more. Hurroosh for that!"

"I warn you, Memory," came the severe, cautioning hiss, "be not hasty in this. Are you so mad you would side with the Spinners of the Wood against me—I who hung for nine nights upon Yggdrasill?"

Shuddering in his quills, the raven squawked miserably. "Depart this world, O jargoozling shade! This cockalorum, craven cove hath no desire to heed thy honeyed distorts."

Alarmed by the brash insolence of his own words, Quoth withdrew his beak, and in the alleyway, the mist curled about the dark folds of the figure's cloak.

"Because of the great love I bore you," Woden uttered coldly, "I forgive you this once. Three times I swore I would appeal for your return. This has been the first."

Raising a wizened hand, the cloaked figure pointed an accusing, bony finger at the woe-filled bird and, in a chilling whisper, pronounced a terrible warning.

"Twice more will I visit you," he vowed. "If my lieutenant returns to me, then he shall be all that he was and more. Yet if you flout my invitation a second time, Memory, then my clemency will be sorely strained. On that occasion, if you persist in this imbecilic attachment to your new master, then a forfeit must be paid."

Quoth nearly dropped from the perch in fright, for Woden's voice growled with menace, and the raven knew that the threat would indeed be carried out if he refused again. Shifting uneasily, he gazed down, and the sinister figure continued his decree.

"Should there be a third instance," he snarled, "you will be at the brink. If your ingratitude and folly deny me then, you will pay the ultimate price. Do your rusted wits understand my meaning?"

The raven gave a hopeless cheep, and his wings drooped at his side.

"Quail and think on my words," Woden declaimed, the fog creeping up around him again. "Though I would rejoice in your company, there are others only too eager to obey my bidding. Already there is one I have chosen, and I go now to recruit him into my service."

Into the ever-shifting vapor the hooded figure melted, and as the banking mist flowed steadily out of the alleyway, his final, doom-laden words floated on the wind to the raven.

"Consider my warning well. It is the time of deciding—beware and choose with wisdom."

Into the sable streets the gray vapor vanished, and a petrified Quoth was left to weep at his plight.

"Squire Neil!" he cried in a purling whine. "This miching mallecho is beset with doubt and qualm. Spare me this evil judging—what may a labbering juggins do in such a trial?"

It was a hideous decision to make, but the outcome was assured: abandon Neil—or perish.

"Neil!" a small voice urged. "Neil!"

Josh's brother mumbled in his sleep and turned over. "Go back to sleep," he groaned.

Joshua Chapman lay on his back, the blankets pulled up to his nose. He held Groofles, his stuffed polar bear, tightly to his chest.

"Neil!" he whispered again. This time, the four-year-old gave his brother a frantic kick, and Neil rolled over crossly.

"Look," he growled, "if you want to go, you're old enough to do it on your own. If you don't, shut—"

The older boy lapsed into silence as the toddler clung to him, and he realized that Josh was terrified.

"What's the matter?" Neil said, adopting a kinder tone. "Bad dream? Do you want the light on?"

The youngster's head shook against Neil's shoulder. "No!" his smothered voice cried. "They'll come and get us."

"Who will?" Neil asked, putting his arms around him.

"Out there—the bad men."

Neil cuddled his brother a little tighter, then he too heard what had frightened Josh. From the living room there suddenly came the sound of rough, ugly voices raised in dirty laughter, and Neil sat up in surprise.

Under the door a slice of light glimmered, and the boy immediately knew that something was dreadfully wrong. As he listened, he counted at least three voices, but not one of them belonged to his father. Sitting there, in the dark, with his brother trembling beside him, Neil could sense the air growing stale, and the reek of tobacco smoke gradually permeated the children's bedroom.

"Spill us some gin in there!" a wheedling male voice spat. "I'll drink to him what's gone."

"More than he would for us," retorted another. "And that's the last you'll be having of my bottle, Harry Naggers."

"Josiah Rokeby wuz a villain right enough," agreed a third in a hoarse, rattling rasp. "Too handy wiv his knuckles, wuz Old Joe. All us warders've been boxed by 'em more'n once."

A horrible understanding washed over Neil as the voices continued. Josiah Rokeby was the man Mary-Anne Brindle had claimed to have killed. The phantom shapes he had seen charging after her were now in the living room.

"Just lie still," he hissed to Josh, desperately wondering where their father was. "They'll go away."

But the voices on the other side of the door showed no sign of ceasing, and a forbidding thought crept into Neil's mind. What if, like the corridor before, the caretaker's living room had slipped back into the past?

A chair leg scraped against bare boards, and Neil's suspicion was confirmed, for the entire floor of that room was normally covered in worn, swirly carpet.

"Gasper's not wrong there," weasel-voiced Harry agreed. "All the same, I'd rather have Old Joe's fists a-whacking me and deckin' me out than be whipped by Mr. Timms."

There followed an uncouth babble of fellowship at this sentiment, broken only by a parched interjection from Gasper. "'Course, be all the worserer fer us now," he complained huskily. "Wiv Cauliflower Joe gone, it's us who'll get it more oftener from him."

"I ain't afeared of Jack Timms."

Neil heard someone slap a table, and Harry Naggers snorted with nasal laughter. "You say that when Tick-Tock's standing here, Mr. Mawdle," he goaded. "Then we'll believe you. You don't know him as we does. Need to be 'ere longer than you've been."

"What's he doing, anyways? Why ain't he 'ere?"

"Tuckin' his favorites up for the night," Gasper cackled. "Ever so considerating is Mr. Timms. Makes sure they drop off a-thinkin' on him and how hard he'll whack 'em in the mornin'. Loves to taunt 'em, he does, and keep 'em jitterin'."

Harry snickered callously. "Tick-Tock's not doing his rounds," he corrected the others. "Paying his last respects to Fisticuff Joe while he's laid out on the slab, that's what he's doing."

"Goin' through his pockets, more like," Gasper chuckled.

"Or givin' him one last beating," Harry guffawed. "Likes it when they don't fight back, does Mr. Timms."

The warders' disgusting talk stopped suddenly, and Neil heard a new sound echoing from somewhere deep within the museum. A slow, almost mechanical tapping was moving through the galleries, and the men grew agitated as the noise drew closer.

"You'd best've saved him a drop or two, Mr. Mawdle," Gasper croaked. "He'll be wanting a tipple after all his sweat."

The rhythmic knocking was now very near, and in the bedroom, Josh was on the verge of bursting into loud, inconsolable tears. Soaked in the cold perspiration of panic, Neil pushed Groofles against his brother's mouth and pleaded with him to keep quiet.

"Take out the cards, Naggers," Mr. Mawdle said rapidly. "He might fancy a hand or two to soften that temper of his."

"Pull that stool out!" Gasper prompted. "Likes to rest his heels, he does."

The tapping was almost in the room with them, and the men's feverish preparations halted when, abruptly, the regular pulse stopped.

Neil heard the door from the passage creak open, and the others greeted their fellow warder with a fawning welcome.

"Mr. Timms!" Harry Naggers hailed, mealy-mouthed. "How's about joinin' us in a game of braggers?"

"Your seat's a-waiting," Gasper coughed nervously. "We wuz jus' a-sayin' as how poor Joe'll be missed."

"Let me fill your tankard," Mr. Mawdle toadied.

Their anxious reception was met with a surly grunt, and Neil held Josh a little closer as heavy boots clumped into the room. A shrill squeal vibrated through the floor as a chair was dragged roughly aside, before squeaking in protest as the newcomer sat down heavily.

"Would you like me to put your stick over here, Mr. Timms?" Mr. Mawdle offered. A resounding crash, which caused the bedroom door to shiver in its frame, thundered within the room.

"You lay your thievin' hands on my cane, and you'll be pickin' your fingers up with your teeth!" bawled a ferocious, malice-swilling roar.

Neil's stomach convulsed inside him, and the nausea he had felt in the corridor burned at the back of his throat again. That was the man who had so terrified Mary-Anne Brindle.

"No one touches Mr. Timms's cane, 'ceptin' hisself," Gasper scolded Mr. Mawdle.

"You should know that by now," Jack Timms snarled, and the menacing tap-tap-tap commenced once more. "The shepherd has his crook, and Tick-Tock has his Tormentor."

"Have you been spending time with anyone special tonight, Mr. Timms?" Gasper continued, trying to appease him.

"On my way back from attending to our dearest chum, Rokeby," he began with mock piety—"him who didn't have so much as a shilling nor a watch on him when that vixen pricked him, by the way—I acquainted myself with that bedlamite clerk what came in yesterday."

"You must be awful tired by now, Mr. Timms," consoled Mr. Mawdle.

"Aw, you're not at that, are you?" Gasper scoffed at the suggestion. "Mr. Timms don't start the fun right away. It's his Tormentor what gets 'em going first."

Jack Timms gargled his amusement. "'Tick-Tock,' said I as my cane went drumming along the walls. 'Tick-Tock, Tick-Tock.'"

"He likes to let 'em know he's getting near," Gasper explained.

"They've got to learn," the repugnant voice declared. "They've got to know that I'm here, measurin' out their time with the Tormentor, lettin' them know how long and drawn out the days are in this place."

"Most obliging of you it is, Mr. Timms," Gasper put in.

"Gives the barmies something to look forward to," Harry Naggers added. "Should see their faces when they hear the rod a-knocking in the wards. Seen it send many of them into screamin' fits, I have."

There was a pause as Jack Timms guzzled his gin, then he smashed the pint pot down on the table and emitted a loud, rippling belch.

"Where's my game of brag, Harry Naggers? Dole us three cards, and if I catch you sharping me, I'll slice that pinched mouth of yours a bit wider."

In the unlit bedroom, Josh could contain his fear no longer. Pulling Groofles away from his lips, he let out a juddering howl. At once, the commotion behind the door was stilled.

"Quiet, Josh!" Neil wept fearfully.

"There's someone in the blanket store," Gasper muttered.

Four chairs scuffed across the floor as the brutal warders jumped to their feet.

"One of the lunatics?" Mr. Mawdle asked.

"Have to be completely mad to think they could get out that way," Harry told him.

Then Jack Timms spoke. "Stand back, lads," he ordered in a low, intimidating hiss. "If there's one thing I doesn't like, it's being vexed when I've got good cards. Tick-Tock doesn't like being made unhappy. Looks like he's going to have to have himself a jamboree to buck his spirits up."

To Neil's horror, the tapping noise began, and with deliberate, unnerving slowness, it started to pound its way toward their bedroom. Josh was wailing now, and Neil saw the narrow chink of light under the door waver as shadowy figures moved before it.

Tap-tap-tap drummed the Tormentor.

"Can you hear that?" Jack Timms teased. "Tick-Tock's counting out the time you got left. Not long now, it isn't."

Tap-tap-tap.

"Don't let him in!" Josh screamed.

Revolting laughter burst from the other side, and to the boys' horror, the brass handle of the bedroom door began to turn.

"Tick-Tock!" the appalling voice spoke through the keyhole. "I've got you now."

"No!" Neil yelled. Wrenching himself free of his brother, he cleared the space from the bed to the doorway in one single, frantic leap. The handle twisted sharply, and Neil hurled all his weight against the entrance as it gave a jerk inward.

"Get out!" he shrieked. "Go back—go back!"

An angry shout erupted behind the shuddering barrier as the brass doorknob rattled furiously. Clenching his teeth, Neil rammed his shoulder against the wood and reached out to seize control of the wildly swiveling handle. Desperately, his fingers closed about the brass, and immediately, the boy howled in shock.

Snatching his hand away, he tumbled backward, while on the bed, Josh continued to scream.

The door was thrust open.

"Blood and sand!" Brian Chapman snapped, flicking on the light and staring at his elder son, who lay sprawled on the floor.

"For God's sake, Neil!" he stormed. "What do you think you're doing? It sounded like . . . well, I don't know what it sounded like. Blue murder, mostly!"

His eyes still round with terror, Neil stared apprehensively past his father's lanky figure and into the living room beyond. It was just the same as he had always known it. Not a sign that Jack Timms and the others had ever been there.

"Nasty men, Dad!" Josh piped up from the bed.

"What?" Brian demanded.

Not moving, Neil tried to explain. "We heard voices coming from in there," he said shakily. "Only it was different. Four men, they were murderers. I—we thought they were going to burst in."

"I told you!" his father fumed, smacking the doorjamb. "Didn't I warn you this would happen? All this rubbish from that Pickering nutcase has given you nightmares. I can understand Josh, but Neil—I'm surprised at you."

The boy shook his head fervently. "I didn't dream it," he asserted. "They were there. Why didn't you hear them?"

"All I heard was you two screaming to wake the dead."

"That's not funny, Dad."

"Well, you woke me, and that's all I'm bothered

about," Brian told him. "I don't want to hear another word tonight, is that understood?"

Neil closed his eyes. What was the use?

"Perfectly," he answered.

"Right!" his father cried. "And before you do anything tomorrow, you can clean that mess off!"

Not understanding what his father was talking about, Neil turned to follow his angry glare. "I didn't do that," the boy uttered faintly.

"I don't care who did it—just make sure you get rid of it." With that, Brian returned to the living room, slamming the door behind him.

Alone with Josh once more, Neil picked himself up from the floor and stared at the wall just inches above his pillow. There, written in a clumsy, crayoned scrawl, were the words:

Help me

Neil sat on the bed and stared blankly at the graffiti, confused and afraid. "Did you do this?" he asked Josh. "I won't be angry if you did."

His brother shook his head dumbly, and Neil knew that he was telling the truth. Shivering, he wrested his eyes away from the jagged writing and stared down at his hand.

"Does it hurt?" Josh asked.

Neil blew on the fingers that had touched the door handle. They were numb with cold and bitten by frost.

Raising his eyes, he looked at the doorway and, in a determined voice, told his brother, "We'll keep the light on in here tonight."

Chapter 10

White and Black Pieces

Only five minutes remained before the dusty collection of timepieces that ticked and whirred in The Horology Room on the second floor would commence chiming the strokes of midnight.

Edie Dorkins sprinted down the stairs. She had now searched all the upper floors of the museum for Miss Ursula but had not found her. As she descended to the main hallway, the girl could hear Austen Pickering's voice drifting through the galleries as he continued to read aloud to the darkness.

The entrance hall quivered in the tremulous glow of the candles. The frail flames were mirrored in the glass of the frames that obliterated the walls, so that the space resembled the interior of a vast, grubby jewel. Even the suit of armor, silently on guard by the tall weeping fig, glinted in the rare patches that had not rusted.

Edie jumped the few remaining stairs and ran across the parquet floor, where rivers of molten wax had formed snaking ridges that ended in ever-widening pools. Over these the child hurried, to the wall where the entrance to the deep caverns beneath the museum was concealed amid the paneling.

Edie was sure she would find Miss Ursula down in the Chamber of Nirinel. The girl stretched up on her tiptoes to locate the place where the old woman had knocked upon the wood in order to set the secret mechanism in motion.

"Open up!" she ordered, banging her small fists against the wall. "Let me in. I want to see Ursula."

But the panel remained obstinately closed, and no amount of pushing or pulling would budge it.

"Ursula!" the child shouted. "Tell it to open." Impatiently, Edie hopped back and gave the wood a sharp kick. Still the hidden entrance did not reveal itself, and the girl dragged herself away, feeling more perplexed and crotchety than ever.

Suddenly she paused and pushed a flap of her pixie hat away from one ear. From the umber shadows that lay beyond the doorway of the first collection there came a peculiar snuffling sound—a faint, grunting snort accompanied by the clattering of claws.

An exultant grin flashed across the child's grubby face as she spun around, seeking for somewhere to hide.

The piglike gabbling grew closer, and Edie scooted back to the stairs, only to realize that they were useless as a place to conceal herself if she wanted to spy on the unknown creature that was pattering toward the hallway.

Hurrying to the tarnished suit of armor she wondered if she could squeeze herself behind it and remain undetected. But one glance at that rickety assortment of pauldrons, jambes, vambraces, and cuisses warned her not to do anything that might upset their fragile equilibrium.

Hastening to the grand entrance, Edie thought that if she could curl herself up in the corner of the doorway, then perhaps the creature would not notice. It was a futile hope, but there was nowhere else to go, for the gurgling chatter was almost inside the hallway with her.

At the last moment, even as she squashed herself against the oak door, Edie caught sight of the perfect hiding place.

Above her, cut into the panels, was an arch-shaped hole over which peeling golden letters announced: TICKETS FOR ADMITTANCE.

In a flash, Edie sprang up and hauled herself through the opening, dropping headfirst into the cramped, cupboard-sized space beyond. Swiftly, she righted herself, and with her nose resting on a narrow counter, she peeped out at the glimmering hallway—just in time to see a small, squat shape come swaggering inside.

Edie almost cried out in excitement at the sight of the astounding creature. She had never seen anything like it in her young life, and she sank her teeth into the wooden ledge to stop herself from squealing with pleasure.

Into the hallway the outlandish figure scampered, its short, bowed legs waddling with a comical, straddling stride. Three hooked claws at the end of each arm dragged across the floor as it scurried along in a hunching gait. Lashing behind, slapping against the door frame, was a powerful, prehensile tail.

Edie bit the ledge a little harder, struggling to contain the exhilaration that volcanoed inside her when the strange beast finally emerged into the candlelight.

The head, which sat on round, sloping shoulders, was too large and unwieldy for the deformed, stunted body. A thicket of spiky tongues bristled between the waggling, pointed ears. But it was the face that Edie marveled at most.

As the creature edged closer to the flame glow, the gentle flickering illuminated a pair of large eyes with sharp corners that pointed down to a small, flaring snout. Beneath those questing nostrils was a gibbering mouth, so wide that it practically divided the weird face in two, filled with rows of peglike teeth.

Shaggy fur frilled the unnatural beast's outline, but as it entered deeper into the radiant realm of the candlelight, the final, fabulous secret was disclosed, and Edie almost choked as she stifled a yell.

The mysterious imp was made completely of wood.

Every detail of the face, from the untame jungle of hair to the inquisitive, inscrutable eyes, had been chiseled and carved from a single piece of timber. It was as if a graven, medieval nightmare had somehow escaped from the gothic decoration inside a cathedral, and in her hiding place, Edie was beside herself with joy at the sight of this miraculous being. If only she could befriend it—how ecstatic she would be.

Turning away from the candles, the creature blinked its wooden eyelids, and the lower lip quivered as it unleashed a continuous stream of unintelligible yaps. The imp stole farther into the hallway, keeping close to the wall.

Up into the lofty blackness that hung over the staircase it cast its curious eyes, sniffing and tasting the air as though aware that another presence was close by. Suspiciously it glared at the imposing entrance, then directed its accusing gaze at the ticket office window. Edie ducked from sight just in time, but the creature gargled and growled uncertainly.

Her face still wreathed in smiles, Edie Dorkins waited in the confined dark of the ticket booth while a succession of foraging grunts warily inspected the space directly outside.

Presently there came a restless, relinquishing bark, and the girl heard the wooden claws clatter back into the main part of the hallway. Cautiously she raised her eyes over the ledge once more and watched as the creature pranced across to the wall that concealed the hidden entrance. It sniffed along the baseboard, like a dog hunting for a scent.

Then, jabbering softly to itself, the living carving raised its pugnacious head to stare up at the panels and, with infinite ceremony, took three steps backward.

Silent now, except for its wheezing breaths, the bizarre figure put its arms down by its sides and bowed low until the forest of its hair brushed the ground. Remaining in that prostrate, venerating position, with great solemnity and in a gravel, guttural voice, it barked one proclaiming word.

"Gogus . . ."

In response, and to Edie's amazement, a grating whirr vibrated behind the paneling, and a section of wall slid aside. The hidden entrance to the secret winding stair was revealed, and in the stone archway beyond, the stout door swung open.

Muttering to itself in a grating gargle, the wooden creature reared its large head and skipped to the opening, its tail swishing after it.

Into the dark, plunging deep the imp melted, and its excitable, echoing snorts went spiraling down into the earth. Her mouth gaping, Edie Dorkins clambered from the ticket window and set off in pursuit.

"Gogus! Gogus!" she cried in elated imitation. "Come back, Gogus!" But even as she reached the entrance, where the fragrant, stagnant airs breezed up from the subterranean caverns far below, a different, alarming sound reached her ears, and she hesitated on the threshold.

From some far region down the steep stairway there issued a ferocious baying, a trumpeting roar that stopped the girl in her chase and sent her scurrying backward. Louder the tremendous clamor grew, booming and blasting up from the confounding shadows that filled the plummeting path, and the child chewed her lip uneasily.

Over the steps some colossal beast was charging. She could hear its mighty hooves smiting and splintering the ancient stones in its furious, rampaging ascent. The blaring challenge was deafening now. The very air trembled, and Edie could feel the floor begin to quake as the monster stampeded up the remaining distance.

Beside her, the leaves of the weeping fig shook madly, and the suit of armor went toppling to the ground with a clanking crash of collapsing metal.

Breathing hard, her almond-shaped eyes glittering, Edie hugged herself and waited anxiously for the mighty tempest to erupt from the darkness. In a moment she would see it. The roars blasted inside her head, and the pictures on the walls swung on their wires. Even the candle flames yielded to that pounding gallop, and the light leaped in a chaotic frenzy about the hallway.

Then, as the floorboards buckled and frames smashed from their fixtures, it burst through the entrance. Like a savage, supreme storm it exploded into the persecuted gloom, and Edie's field of vision was filled with a solid tower of rippling muscle. Pawing the dark, silver hooves bruised the ruptured air, and a great, worshipful stag snorted its awesome presence.

The ailing light licked over the splendor of its snow-white coat, and fierce flames blazed in its huge, amber eyes. Tossing its gargantuan head, it defied the surrounding, constricting walls. Into the wooden panels the argent spurs of immense, branching antlers tore, and a torrent of splintered oak came raining down.

Edie Dorkins could only stare at the glorious creation that bayed above her. Never had she imagined such perilous, absolute majesty. Here, stamping and rearing before her, was the God of the first forest, and an insane giggle sailed from the girl's lips.

With that, the father of stags became aware of her. Like a piercing horn blast that raged with the power of the forgotten world, it bellowed once more and lowered its antler-crowned head. The Lord of the Wild Wood raced over the fracturing floor to gore and rend. Edie screamed, throwing her hands before her face. Hot, steaming breath gusted around her, and she waited for those terrible antlers to hurl her shattered body aside.

Then, at the last possible moment, the divine beast gave a bass, bone-jangling roar, and the ground in front of the girl was trampled and trounced to splinters. With a shake of those ornate, thrusting antlers the stag reeled, and kicking its glimmering hooves, it thundered off—plunging down the corridor.

Breathless and close to fainting, Edie opened her eyes, then clapped her hands in delight. A delicious, mossy musk laced the air, and she darted to the doorway to see the ghostly shape of the mammoth beast go hurtling into the first of the collections.

Enraptured, the girl watched the titanic, milky shape leap over the cabinets and tables before it veered off into the connecting corridor, and she raced after it, shrieking with demented glee.

* * *

In The Fossil Room, at the first rumble of the stag's approach, Austen Pickering lowered the book he was reading and took up his Bible. Pushing his glasses high up on his nose, he left the chair to fumble with the "Record" button of the tape machine. Then, snatching up his camera, he hastened over to the open doorway.

"I'm impressed," he murmured, listening to the uproar that resounded from the main hall. "Pulled all the stops out on the first night."

Before him, the candles he had positioned along the twisting corridor were guttering, and the ghost hunter's blustering bravado abated rapidly as the snorting maelstrom cannoned from the collections.

Gripping his Bible to his chest, he saw a horned, horrendous shadow engulf the walls, and then, around the corner, the apparition of a vast white stag came charging.

"Impossible!" Mr. Pickering cried, aghast and afraid.

Into The Fossil Room the calamitous creature crashed. Austen Pickering staggered back, tripping and falling, his Bible flying from his hand.

The beast's great eyes blazed with wrath, and it reared up on its mighty hind legs, baying an ear-shredding note of defiance and thrashing the air above the old man's head with its pulverizing hooves.

Every display case rattled as the contents jumped and bounced in the violence of that racketing blast. The hoary mountain twisted its huge head, the silver antlers sparking with fire as they crunched into the large fossils on the wall.

The ghost hunter called out in terror as the destroying hooves came hammering down. And then, without warning, the stag vanished.

The air within The Fossil Room whisked and eddied for a moment, and then the place seeped back to its former silence.

Incredulous, the ghost hunter stared at the empty space above him. Stumbling to his feet, he gazed in stupefied shock at the broken floorboards, crushed by those unstoppable hooves, and he shook his head in disbelief at the chipped and shattered ichthyosaur bones that lay scattered over the ground.

"It's gone." A sorrowful voice spoke suddenly, and the old man leaped in fright.

"Oh!" he stammered. "You . . . you startled me."

Standing in the doorway, Edie Dorkins tilted her head and pouted sullenly. "The 'orse with 'orns," she said longingly and with aching disappointment.

"You saw it, then?" Mr. Pickering asked. "I can hardly believe it. I don't know what to . . ."

But he discovered that he was talking to himself, for the child had already scampered back down the passageway.

Edie raced to the main hall but, when she reached it, she saw that the secret entrance had closed once more, leaving only a blank expanse of paneling.

"Open up!" she demanded.

No answering click responded to her angry command, and she gave the wooden wall a second, irritated kick.

Alone in The Fossil Room once more, Austen Pickering reached for his hip flask and took a long, comforting gulp.

"What have you taken on, old lad?" he asked himself.

* * *

The long night crawled into the early hours, and in the walled courtyard outside the caretaker's apartment, a dense fog flowed through the gaps in the boarded gateway. Steadily the vapor flooded in, covering the cheerless expanse of cement until a lake of turgid smoke filled that dim, dark place. In the sooty gloom, enveloped in the shadows that skulked behind the tall, wooden gate, the cloaked figure of Woden gazed up at the square ugliness of the Wyrd Museum, and a soft, purling chuckle issued from beneath the concealing cowl.

"Her defenses are waking," he whispered, his thoughts probing the bricks and mortar of the darkened building to sense the forces stirring within. "Yet no matter. In her haste Urdr has opened the way for me. Her squalid abode is beginning to remember its former existences. Thus is the key to the downfall of the Nornir delivered unto my hand and the method of their destruction made plain."

The hidden face turned away from the unlovely building and stared up at the overcast heavens, where the lurid glare of the city could be glimpsed above the high, glass-fanged wall.

"Urdr has permitted the binding years to be unraveled," he cackled. "She has chosen both the board upon which the battle will be fought and the pieces. Thus shall I choose mine, the one who will serve me and bring about her lasting doom."

A sharp, compelling hiss escaped from his unseen lips, and he raked a withered hand through the chill air. Ribbons of mist rose in a high, coiling arc around him, and at once the courtyard in which he stood began to flicker and change.

Overhead, the orange glow of the modern age dwindled and dimmed, and the endless, distant din of the lumbering trucks that traveled through Bethnal Green grew faint and abated.

Beneath the curling fog the cement evaporated, exposing an area of uneven flagstones, and beyond the screening wall the street lamps of Well Lane were quenched, their towering posts winking from sight.

The boards that covered the battered gateway dropped off their nails, revealing the tall rails and scrolling flourishes of the robust wrought iron beneath. Through that ornate barrier, only a few feet away, the Victorian gas lamp, whose lantern had been smashed for over fifty years but had not worked in eighty, abruptly flared into life.

Somewhere in the grimy streets a horse's hooves rang off the cobbles, and Woden withdrew into the fusty shadow of that earlier time as heavy, booted footsteps came stomping down the lane.

Into the lantern light a corpulent, burly figure lumbered. He carried a gnarled, club-ended stick tucked under one of his trunk-like arms, and a large hoop of keys jangled at his belt. A shabby black greatcoat, hanging in heavy creases about his knees, worn shiny at the elbows and sploshed with stains down the front, could not obscure the gross barrel shape of the man within.

A rumpled top hat, smeared with grease and bitten at the brim, cast a band of night across his features as he leaned drunkenly against the lantern post to drain the dregs of porter from the pewter pot in his hand. A trickle of the black brew drizzled down his stubbled jowls and over the rolls of his fat neck, and a tarry, swollen tongue slithered out in search of those precious escaping drops. Then a sour, rancorous belch blossomed in the shade of his hat as he consigned the empty tankard to a hook on his belt.

The keen, chill air blew cold on his spit-soaked skin, and he cursed as he wiped his chin with the ends of his grubby green scarf.

"Tick-Tock likes a drop of the heavy wet," his phlegm-slurring voice gargled.

Still propped against the post, Jack Timms shifted his gaze down to the hoop of keys and fetched them into the light.

"I'll school it to them crazies tonight," he promised himself as he turned the key in the lock and heaved the squealing gate open. Raising his stick, he clattered it over the ironwork and smithied a clanging tattoo to rouse the unfortunate inmates of the Well Lane Infirmary.

"Wake up, you dribblers!" his menacing voice called. "Time's come for one of you."

Honking with evil mirth, he kicked the gate shut and staggered through the waist-deep mist of the courtyard, lurching from side to side.

"Who'll it be, Tick-Tock?" he asked himself. "Whose mad skull are we going to crack some learnin' into tonight? Can't be that clerk, he ain't had nearly enough tormentin' yet."

Tottering toward the rear door of the museum, he

grasped his Tormentor as though it were a conductor's baton, and he tapped lightly on the brick wall.

"Soon they'll know," he said biliously. "They'll hear Jack Timms a-Tick-Tockin' down the wards, and they'll pray their time ain't up just yet."

Holding up the circle of keys once more, he squinted at them, but they swam before his intoxicated vision, and as he fumbled, they fell from his fingers and dropped, jingling, into the fog.

A bestial oath sprang from the man's mouth, and he prodded his stick into the veiling vapor to search for them.

"Jack Timms," called a soft voice.

Immediately Jack reeled about, his greatcoat whirling as he thrashed the Tormentor, viciously swiping it through the shredding mist.

"Who's back there?" he bawled, keeping the Tormentor raised and ready. "Sneaking up, is it? Well, I've found you and hiding won't save you. It's in the river they'll find you, come morning."

"Lay your weapon aside," the whispering voice instructed in a persuasive, mellifluous chant.

Tick-Tock snorted, then blew a nugget of brown spit at those shielding shadows in which the stranger hid.

"Old Jack warned you," he snarled, taking a cocksure step forward and slapping the club end of his stick into the palm of his hand.

Through the smoke he strutted, back to where the gaslight shone through the iron bars of the gate, and their long shadows striped his brutal face. Beneath the chewed brim of his hat two sly rat eyes were set deep in a mire of florid, pockmarked skin. In the center of that liquor-bloated face a squashed drinker's nose, like a clump of ripe raspberries, burgeoned and bloomed. A puckered crescent scar traced a perfect "C" down from his right temple to the scabby corner of his leering mouth.

It was a repellent countenance, stamped with only a fraction of the unmined resources of sadistic cruelty and overwhelming hatred that pervaded his abhorrent being.

Striding a little closer to the gateway, Jack Timms switched the Tormentor before him, and his small eyes squinted into the shadows.

"I come only to invite you into my employ," the voice assured him.

The scar on Tick-Tock's face twitched uncertainly. "'Ere!" he warned. "Stop that clownin'."

The fog rolled thickly in the darkness. Then, with the tendrils of mist twining about him, a tall, cloaked figure stepped out into the gaslight.

"Who's hiding under that hood?" Jack Timms demanded.

"The one who can give you what you crave."

"And what's that, then?"

"Whatever you wish it to be."

Jack Timms's fat red lips parted, and he growled impatiently through the blackened stumps of his teeth.

"What I want right now is to see you split an' spurtin'!" he cried, charging forward.

The robed stranger lifted a withered hand, and immediately the Tormentor flew from the brute's fist.

High into the air it soared, spinning and twirling in the night. Tick-Tock Jack spluttered in confusion, stumbling back to catch his cherished possession when it returned to earth.

But the stick did not return. Far above the courtyard it continued to wheel and turn, and he gawked at it in slobbering amazement.

"What you done?" he asked, not taking his eyes from the whirling cane in the sky.

"It is but a paltry testament of my strength," Woden whispered menacingly. "Will you now not listen to me?"

Jack Timms dragged the hat from his head and lowered his gaze, nodding profusely.

"This is my offer," Woden began in coercive tones. "If you consent to be directed by me, then you shall name your own reward."

An unpleasant smirk sneaked over the warder's repugnant face. "I know the work you're speaking of," he snickered. "You should've said so sooner, without the theatricals. I'll see the job's done an' keep my mouth shut. Tick-Tock don't mind a bit o' honest thuggery. You just tell him who you'd be rid of."

"Then we understand one another," Woden murmured. "That is all to the good. With your help, Jack Timms, I can invade the very heart of the Nornir's domain. No time nor place shall be safe for them."

Tick-Tock sniffed, his vile wits still clouded by the drink. "What's that you say?" he asked.

A cold laugh needled from the cowl, puncturing even the larded hide of Jack Timms. "You will learn," the shrouded figure told him. "I will instruct and guide you."

From the swathing robe the wizened hand reached out toward Jack Timms, and the warder stared at it skeptically.

"To seal the contract," Woden told him.

Tick-Tock wiped a palm on his coat, then wrapped an enormous fist about the proffered hand.

"If you cross me," he threatened, "I'll rip your head off, and you won't need no hood no more."

Woden said nothing, but his fragile-looking fingers suddenly gripped the warder's giant mitten and pressed with such force that Tick-Tock yelled and tried to pull himself free.

"And I warn you, Jack Timms," the Gallows God made his vow, but his voice showed not the slightest tremor of exertion as the evil lout in his grasp cried in pain, his knees buckling beneath him. "Fail me, and you shall be consigned into the darkness from which there is no redemption."

"I won't!" the man blurted, dropping to the ground as the bony fingers squeezed and crushed.

"Do you accept my terms—whatever they may prove to be?"

"Anythin'! You're mashin' my hand, damn you!"

With an exultant hiss, Woden released him and Tick-Tock fell back.

"Crippled fist ain't no good to no one!" he cursed.

The cloaked figure chuckled with scorn. "I broke no bones," he said. "That task is for you alone. Rise, Jack Timms. The time has come for you to commence your assassin's work."

As Tick-Tock Jack lurched to his feet, high above his cudgeling cane ceased its uncanny tumbling and plunged back to the ground, clattering over the flagstones.

Woden's cold laughter rang out over the courtyard. "The doom of the Loom Maidens is approaching," he called. "Let us depart this place."

Retrieving his Tormentor, Tick-Tock stared about him. The dense gray fog was rising, swelling and churning until it was up to his chest.

"Hey!" he bawled. "What's this—more tricks?"

The shadow-filled hood gazed blankly back at him. "You have a long journey ahead of you, Jack Timms," he muttered. "The first of many. You are my agent now, my creature, and you will be sent whither I will it."

Over the warder's ugly head the mist flowed, and his great bulk was soon only a dark, writhing blur deep within an ocean of swirling vapor that suffocated his filthy protests.

Gradually, the glare of the city reappeared in the heavens, and as the cement flooded back over the flagstones, the courtyard returned to the present.

By the boarded gateway, the figure of Woden remained. The last threads of smoke were gone, and he regarded the great black shape of the Wyrd Museum once more.

"It is done," he murmured contentedly. "The sisters and their allies have no hope now."

Then he melted into the darkness.

CHAPTER 11

TREADING DESERTED PATHWAYS

It was a bitterly cold morning that Neil and Josh awoke to. Neither of them had slept very well with the harsh electric light on throughout the night, and the memory of those hideous voices had colored their dreams.

With dark circles under their eyes, the boys shambled into the living room where Brian Chapman was already up and preparing breakfast.

"Has Quoth had something to eat?" Neil asked, wiping the drowse from his eyes.

His father took an extra large swig of tea to wash his toast down. "It's not here," he mumbled.

"Oh, has he gone into the museum already?"

"No, well . . . look, Neil, that germ-ridden thing was making such a racket in the bathroom that I put him outside."

Neil slammed the spoon into his cereal bowl. "You did what?" he cried. "So where is he now?"

"With any luck it'll have flown off."

The boy ran to the window. A sharp frost had ferned the glass with ice. "He might've frozen to death out there!" he shouted, his anger charged with anxious concern. "How could you?"

Without pausing to pull on his bathrobe, Neil ran to the back door and out into the courtyard. The cold air bit into his lungs. The walls of the museum were stippled with a white, wintry rime, and slender icicles spindled down from the gutters.

"Quoth!" the boy called. "Quoth, where are you?" There was no response, so he yelled a little louder, and presently he heard a mournful croaking in the sky.

Over the pinnacled rooftop of the Wyrd Museum he saw the black, ragged shape of the raven tumble through the air. Down Quoth flew, but it was an artless, clumsy descent. The tattered wings were flapping in stiff, sporadic jerks, and the bird pitched alarmingly.

Below him, a worried Neil watched as the raven overshot the yard, narrowly avoiding the broken glass on top of the high surrounding walls. Squawking in frustration, Quoth began beating his wings with furious determination, and he swerved back toward the museum. Like an erring missile he came charging through the biting cold, and Neil held out his arm as the raven came swooping down. But the bird could not check his speed; his wings brushed the boy's face and he zoomed past, heading straight for the wall.

At once, Neil spun around and tore after him. Just inches before Quoth crashed into the bricks, Neil reached out and caught hold of the bird. In a tangle of feathers and pajamas, they rolled over the ground, and the raven crowed in gratitude.

"Squire Neil," he cheeped, gazing up adoringly, "thou didst deliver this unlicked cub from a bruisome calamity. A thousandfold thanks."

Holding the raven in both hands, Neil clambered to his feet. Quoth was icy to the touch, his primary feathers edged with frost. His scalp was almost purple, and his beak chattered uncontrollably.

"No wonder you couldn't fly properly," the boy said, hurrying to the door. "Let's get you inside."

"What of thy parent?" the bird asked with a shiver. "His charity is more cold than aught in the wild."

"Leave him to me," Neil reassured him. "Dad won't touch you again."

A little later, while Neil changed into his school uniform, a pampered Quoth ate a hearty sausage breakfast. He was now finishing the last drops of some warm milk under the disdainful gaze of Brian Chapman.

"I still think it's unhygienic," the caretaker grumbled.

Quoth fixed him with his eye, but before he could furnish a satisfying retort, Neil butted in. "You can't talk," he said, glancing at his father's scruffy appearance. "You've been wearing the same clothes for two days, and when was the last time you had a shave?"

Brian made no answer, and Neil slung his schoolbag over his shoulder. "Do I have to go today?" he asked. "After what happened last night, I really don't feel—"

Brian kicked one of the chairs aside and jabbed his

son with his finger. "Don't give me any of that!" he argued. "I won't hear it! Just get ready and go."

"I am ready," the boy answered.

Taking the raven with him, he left the caretaker's apartment. "Just keep out of Dad's way today," Neil advised the bird as they made their way down the passage toward The Fossil Room. "I'll be back this afternoon. Think you can stay out of trouble till then?"

Quoth nodded, and in a strangely melancholic tone, he answered, "This knave shalt not trouble trouble till trouble troubles he."

A slight frown scored Neil's forehead. The raven was unusually quiet today. It was not surprising, really, after suffering outside all night. But the boy wondered if there was something else—something his friend wasn't telling him.

"I'm sorry you had to sleep out in the cold," he said. "It must have been horrible for you."

Quoth lowered his head. He remembered the condemning words of Woden, and a shudder of fear rifled down his body.

"Haven't you thawed out yet?" Neil asked.

"Yea!" Quoth responded. "'Twas but the memory." And he sank into a languishing silence.

In The Fossil Room, Neil found Austen Pickering poring over a fusty-looking book, the pages of which were yellow and brittle with age. Beside him, forming a teetering tower on the glass counter, were ten other volumes of differing sizes.

"Records and registers," he announced when he heard the boy approach him. "Miss Ursula Webster brought them to me first thing. Said they might be instructive and that they will, no bones about it—completely absorbing and utterly fascinating."

Adjusting his glasses, the old man looked up abruptly and grinned like a child with a new toy. "Good morning!" he greeted. "What a treat you missed last night!"

Not giving Neil a chance to speak, he pressed the "Play" button on the tape recorder, and the room suddenly blared with the tremendous bellowing of the huge white stag.

"This is where it came bursting in," he shouted above the distorted din, pointing at the doorway. "And this is where you can see it smashed the floorboards. There are similar marks all the way to the main hall, and up there, look—the fossil bones are shattered."

Excitedly, he explained what had happened. So great was the ghost hunter's delight that his words collided with one another, and he had to calm himself down more than once before he finished the story.

"There now!" he cried at length. "What do you think of that?"

Neil could only stare at the damage and shrug. "Looks like that ghost was pretty substantial as well," he eventually said.

The old man jiggled his eyebrows. "Exactly! I can't begin to understand the phenomenon. We can only record what has happened."

Mr. Pickering returned to the prodigious heap of books. "The significance of the stag has me stumped for the present," he conceded, "although it was quite common for large houses to keep wild game in their parkland. I did wonder if perhaps the beast might be linked with those poor stuffed specimens upstairs, but I've already been to check and they're all most definitely of the exotic variety. Still, there must be some mention of it somewhere. I'm going to spend the whole day reading through as many of these as I can."

"You'd better research someone called Jack Timms as well," Neil told him.

The strain in the boy's voice caused another wide smile to light the ghost hunter's face.

"You've seen something again, haven't you?" he cried. "I knew this place was fit to burst, but I didn't expect all this so quickly. At this rate I won't have time to write up any notes."

Neil gave him a brief account of the diabolic conversation he and Josh had overheard, and the old man's eyes shone brighter than ever.

"Excellent!" he declared. "Jack Timms at least we can check up on. There must be a record of accounts in here somewhere. He's bound to get a mention. Well, I call that an amazing first night's work."

"That's not all," Neil began, not sure whether to mention it or not. "Some writing appeared on the wall by my bed."

Mr. Pickering reached for his camera. "What does it say?" he demanded. "I must get a picture. I wish I'd had the presence of mind to take one of that magnificent apparition."

"I wiped it off," the boy confessed, cutting through his enthusiasm. "It wasn't much, just written in crayon. 'Help me' it said. That's all, and it was more of a scribble really. Josh said he didn't do it, but I'm beginning to think he might've, in his sleep."

"Bit advanced for a four-year-old," Mr. Pickering remarked.

"Maybe I don't like the thought of the alternative."

"Of course," the old man noted, "*you* could have written it in your sleep."

"I hope I did," Neil admitted.

Austen Pickering gave a benign grin, then dabbed a finger at the raven on the boy's shoulder. "He seems a mite downcast this morning," he observed. "I was just about to ask if the cat had got his tongue, but maybe that's not the most tactful remark to make."

Quoth gave a morose sniff. "Thinking be furthest from knowing," he muttered.

"My dad threw him outside last night," Neil explained. "Been in a bit of a sulk since he got back in."

"Your feathery friend is more than welcome to keep me company tonight if your father's of the same mind," the old man offered. "He can stay with me today as well, if he likes."

Neil scratched the raven under his beak, and Quoth closed his eye mournfully as he pressed against him.

"Best the new friend than the old foe," he cawed under his breath.

"I'd better get going," Neil announced. "I'll be back about four."

The raven accompanied him to the main entrance, where Neil had to tug and pull at the stout oaken door to wrench it open. Hopping onto the ledge of the ticket window, Quoth stared at his master miserably.

"Sluggardly shalt the hours leech by," he croaked.

"Just remember what I said," Neil warned him. "Keep out of Dad's way."

The door to the Wyrd Museum shuddered in its frame, and the boy set off through the bleak cold. Alone in the hallway, Quoth hunched himself into his furled wings, and morning in the Wyrd Museum stole by.

* * *

The windows of The Separate Collection were crusted with ice, more so than anywhere else in the building because of a broken pane. The weak daylight that glowed over the delicate latticework of frost did little to disturb the shadows that still lay heavy within that room.

Gaunt in her faded finery, a portrait of regal composure, Miss Ursula Webster stood by one of the glass cases, slight breaths escaping from her thin lips in wisps of steam.

The elderly woman's near translucent eyelids were half closed, and only slices of white showed between her lashes. Over her sharp features her pale skin was stretched taut, but that morning her face possessed none of its usual acid austerity. There was an air of resignation and acceptance about her that leavened those severe lines around the mouth and banished the age-old scars of distress and care.

"Not long," she whispered. "Let my mind be mine till then." Very gingerly, she began to lift the lid of the cabinet and, with a timidity alien to her, reached inside.

"Ursula!" a young voice called.

At once the old woman snapped the lid shut and turned archly.

"Edith!" she exclaimed, her face suddenly stern and strict once more. "What are you thinking of, slinking and creeping about the place like a thief?"

"Where did you go last night?" the child asked, undaunted by the woman's scathing outrage. "I looked all over. How did you get past me?"

Miss Ursula moved away from the cabinet and became absorbed in picking a stray thread from her evening dress.

"I'm sure I don't know to what you are referring," she replied curtly. "You could not have searched so very hard. I was there to be found."

"Where?" the girl demanded.

A secretive smile flickered about Miss Ursula's mouth. "You shall have to discover that for yourself, Edith, dear," she said cryptically.

Edie pouted, then the excitement of the previous night bubbled up within her again. "I saw a big 'orse with a tree on his 'ead," she babbled.

As she glided between the exhibits, Miss Ursula's measured tread faltered. "You saw the stag?" she murmured. "I did not presume that the prying powers of our dilettante phantom catcher were so strong."

"Tell me about it," Edie urged. "And about the Gogus as well."

But Miss Ursula's face had assumed an implacable, obstinate reticence, and nothing Edie could say would goad or provoke her into disclosing any more.

"I really must be more stringent and firm with the caretaker," she began, avoiding the child's questions. "There is still much to be done in here. That broken window must be repaired without delay. I shall go and give him my instructions at once. Good day, Edith."

Her arms folded, Edie watched the old woman depart, then darted across the room to look at the case Miss Ursula had been taking such an interest in before the girl had disturbed her.

Standing on the same box she had used the night before, Edie stared in at the large golden locket and sucked the inside of her cheek, ruminating thoughtfully.

"Has Ursula gone?" whispered a meek voice.

The child turned. Peeping around the entrance to The Egyptian Suite was Miss Celandine.

"I wanted to ask if I may go dancing again," the old woman simpered. "Veronica wants to come, too. I said she might, but only if she lets me choose her partners. Do you think Ursula will allow it? She can be so cross and mean sometimes—she can, she can."

Edie jumped from the box and led Miss Celandine into The Separate Collection.

"*I'll* let you go dancin'," she promised. "An' if Ursula don't like it, she can lump it."

A happy, toothy grin flashed across Miss Celandine's ripe, ruddy face, and she cooed with pleasure. "Oh, you're not such a horrid little ruffian after all," she cried, clapping her hands. "You are a darling! If you were jam and pancakes, Veronica would eat you up—she would, she would."

The old woman paused, and her button-bright eyes disappeared in her rouged wrinkles. "But Veronica . . ." she muttered in distraction. "She isn't here, is she? Something awful happened to her. Where is she? Where's my sister?"

Like a great, galumphing goose, she spun around and stomped through the room, flapping her arms and shaking her head so that her long braids whisked madly about her face.

"Burning!" she shrieked. "There was fire! Flames and cinders, that's where she is. Ashes and death! My sister is dead—Veronica is dead."

"Celandine!" Edie called, running after her. "Veronica's waiting to dance with you upstairs."

The old woman halted suddenly, and her decayed mind relinquished its one lucid thought.

"I must go to her," she gabbled. "Veronica will steal all the gallants and leave me with no one—she will, she will."

"Not yet," Edie said forcefully. "They won't start without you."

"Are you sure?"

"I told 'em not to."

Miss Celandine sighed with relief. "I do so hate to miss the first waltz or galliard," she declared. "Ursula always wants to be late and Veronica doesn't care either way, but it's so important."

"Tell me about the stag," Edie prompted, taking hold of the old woman's large, leathery hands. Miss Celandine stared down at the girl and screwed her walnut face into a crumpled ball as she foraged inside the deserted pathways of her memory.

"There were four of them," she eventually uttered. "Four beautiful, snowy-white creatures. Oh, how lovely they were, but fierce and noble, too. Veronica was quite scared of them, especially the largest. But I wasn't—I wasn't, I tell you."

"What else?" Edie encouraged.

Miss Celandine drifted to the windows and blew absently on the ice. "I don't think even Ursula knows what they really were," she breathed. "But they were with Nirinel long before us. They'd guarded it for simply ages and were filled with wild magic. I used to love them so very dearly. It was they who carried the Loom from the court, and when that dreadful day came, when the ogres of the cold destroyed the poor World-Tree, it was the handsome great stag who led us through the forest."

Staring at the branching pattern of frost on the glass, she hugged herself and looked away.

"What happened to the Loom?" Edie persisted. "Do you remember?"

A vacant, faraway look had settled over Miss Celandine's face, and she began chewing the end of one corn-colored braid. "Ursula said it was broken," she mumbled.

"When?"

"Ask Veronica. I can't remember. We never saw it again."

"Where did Ursula put the pieces? Are they down in the caves?"

The old woman sucked her bottom lip as she considered. "There was such a commotion . . ." she began, plundering the vague, crumbled store of her thoughts. "Veronica was so cross—or was it me? I know we both looked but we didn't find it, and Ursula would never tell."

As she lowered her face so that it was close to Edie's, a faint gleam shone in her eyes, and in a confiding whisper, she said, "If you ask me, I always thought—"

Suddenly, Miss Celandine drew a sharp breath and sealed her lips with a quick, zipping mime.

"I was told to fix the window," a man's voice intruded.

Edie whipped around and saw, to her annoyance, Brian Chapman standing in the doorway with his tool kit in his hand and Josh at his side.

"I must go!" Miss Celandine cried, lifting up the skirt of her velvet gown and revealing her hole-ridden petticoats beneath. "Veronica will claim all the dances if I don't stop her—I must, I must!"

In a sprightly dash, the old woman fled from The Separate Collection, leaving a bellicose Edie Dorkins to glare at the scruffy man.

Brian gave her a clumsy smile. "I'll put a board across it," he said, nodding at the window.

Edie watched him as he advanced to the broken pane. "It's mine, all this," she told him flatly. "Not yours."

"You're welcome to it," Neil's father answered.

Keeping her eyes upon him, Edie paced across the room, pretending to peer into the cabinets. That man didn't belong here as she did; this was her home.

Sitting on the floor by his father, Joshua Chapman stared at the girl shyly. He longed to run over and play, but she ignored him. Covering his face with his hands, the little boy decided that he would take no notice of her either and rolled backward, kicking his legs in the air.

Leaning on an empty wooden crate a short distance away, Edie saw Josh rocking on his back and scrutinized him curiously. The boy sat up again and caught her looking. With a squeal, he darted beneath one of the cabinets and peeped out again. Forgetting herself, Edie laughed, and Josh scuttled under another display case, a little closer this time.

Brian Chapman began to hammer a square of wood in place, but the girl was oblivious to him now and ducked down to see his young son go scudding along the floor.

From the room beyond The Egyptian Suite, the faintest of noises began, yet no one in The Separate Collection noticed. Josh was squeaking happily like a mouse under the cabinets, and Edie was now on her hands and knees pretending to be a cat.

With three nails still clenched in his teeth, the caretaker finished the task and surveyed the work critically.

Then he heard it.

The sound had risen to a rhythmic, clicking whirr, and even Josh crawled out from beneath the cases to listen.

Leaping to her feet, Edie held her breath as the monotonous, mechanical beat grew ever louder.

"Don't say the heat's acting up," Brian prayed. "I haven't a clue about that old boiler." Spitting out the unused nails, he picked up his tool kit and strode toward The Egyptian Suite, calling for Josh to follow him. The four-year-old gave Edie one last, playful glance then ran after his father.

But Brian never reached that windowless room.

Even as he approached the entrance to The Egyptian Suite, there came a grunting snarl, and the man let the tool kit fall to the ground with a crash.

"For heaven's sake!" he mouthed.

Inside the gloom of The Egyptian Suite a short, squat figure was creeping, a threatening growl gargling in its throat.

"Gogus . . ." it gibbered. "Gogus . . . Gogus."

Onto one of the sarcophagi the wooden imp leaped, its claws raking the air. The peglike teeth champed and gnashed in its wide, chattering mouth, and behind it, the long tail switched in agitation. With those large eyes trained on the caretaker, the creature started to bark ferociously.

Hearing those familiar sounds, Edie ran forward. "Hello, Gogus!" she cried.

But the imp ignored her and snapped all the more savagely.

"Stop it!" Edie ordered.

At that, the carving clamored even more loudly, drumming its claws on the side of the sarcophagus and bobbing up and down on its bow legs.

"What . . . what is it?" Brian asked in fearful disbelief.

The sound of the man's voice seemed to incense and enrage the creature even more. Yammering and shrieking, it threw up its arms and then, without warning, it sprang.

Too horrified to cry out, Brian Chapman blundered

back as the Gogus leaped into The Separate Collection and pounced on him. Onto the man's chest the stunted terror threw itself, its claws thrashing in a barbarous frenzy of scratching and tearing.

"Dad!" Josh screamed.

Recoiling beneath the vicious onslaught, Brian Chapman went crashing into a display counter, and the glass exploded around him. Gogus's tail lashed madly as the caretaker battled to break free, and its unwieldy head lunged and darted between his panicking blows, nipping and biting with its teeth.

"Get off!" Edie demanded, stamping her feet.

But the creature only fought more rabidly, and the girl jumped up at it. Catching hold of the churning tail, she pulled hard. A discordant yowl issued from the wooden throat, and Gogus glared down at her.

The distraction was enough for Brian. Using all his strength, he ripped the hooked claws from around his neck, and before the imp could stop him, Brian hurled it across the room.

Wriggling helplessly in the air, his assailant yowled and went bouncing over the cabinets to land with a clatter on the floor. But at once it was up again, its troll-like legs scampering over the ground, wheezing and gurgling as it raced toward Brian Chapman.

"Gogus . . ." it cackled. "Gogus . . ."

Cut and bleeding, Neil's father gasped for breath, his eyes trained on the fiend's scuttling return. The Separate Collection rang with Josh's screams, and the caretaker motioned frantically for Edie to get the boy out of there.

"Quick!" he shouted.

Shuffling backward, the man stumbled, tripping over his tool kit. Then, giving a glad cry, he eagerly snatched up a hammer. "Now!" he shouted, feeling a shade braver as he brandished the weapon before him. "Come and have a bite of this!"

Gogus let out a hate-filled hiss as it watched the hammer swing to and fro, and the creature somersaulted with fury.

Taking hold of Josh's arm, Edie lingered by the entrance to The Egyptian Suite, anxiously watching what would happen.

"I said get Josh out of here!" Brian bawled.

The girl scrunched up her radish-shaped nose with displeasure, but Josh's face had turned an alarming scarlet so she hauled him into the darkness of the adjoining room.

Gogus's demented yammering escalated even further, and with its mouth gaping open, the creature shot forward, caterwauling at the top of its guttural voice.

Within The Egyptian Suite, the uproar of The Separate Collection faded swiftly, and above Josh's howls, Edie heard the racket of machinery. A putrid reek of sweat and squalor filled her nostrils, and she spun around in the darkness. The room had changed. The hieroglyphs had been replaced by moldy green wallpaper, and only sawdust covered the floor where the sarcophagi had been.

Not a murmur could be heard from The Separate Collection now, and when she stared at the entrance, an impenetrable murk met the girl's eyes.

"Where'd it go?" she muttered. "Where are we?"

At the girl's side, Josh could only shriek in reply.

CHAPTER 12

IN THE WELL LANE WORKHOUSE

Edie shook the boy and told him to be quiet, but it only made him worse. Letting go of his arm in disgust, she began to retrace her steps back to the doorway. The repetitive rumble thrummed through the air, and the shadows closed in around them.

Suddenly, from the blindness in front, a figure no taller than herself came barging into the small, unlit room.

The stranger ran stumbling into Edie Dorkins as he cast a feverish glance over his shoulder.

"Shift it!" a desperate voice cried out. "Now look! You made me go an' drop 'em all."

Edie jumped away, but the figure fell to his knees and scavenged over the floor, retrieving the precious food scraps he had lost.

"Didn't pilfer these jus' to fatten the rats," the

newcomer said hotly. "Muzzle that tyke, can't you?" he rapped, indicating Josh. "You want the beadle after me? If he tells Old Snotter, that's the end of Ned Billet!"

The girl watched in fascination as the boy continued to grub and scour the ground. Ned Billet was a scrawny stick of a boy. Scraps and shreds of filthy rags barely covered his rickety form, and whatever he redeemed from the sawdust he clutched tightly to himself. In the exposed gashes that slashed his torn shirt, Edie could clearly see the bones of his spine pushing up through his starved flesh like a long row of knuckles, and his chest rattled as he gasped and panted from his recent exertions.

"I said sew up his stocking!" he hissed, stumbling to his bare feet.

"He won't shut up," the girl answered. "I tried before."

Ned's eyes bulged from his skull like those of a famished frog. His skin was sallow and he was shaking. Anxiously, he looked around them. "Get you in here," he told her, hastening through the gloom and pushing open a door covered in dirt and crackled varnish.

"Sharpish!" he entreated. "He'll catch us for sure, he will!"

Taking hold of the wailing Josh once more, Edie followed Ned and found herself in a dingy, foul-reeking room. Drowned in a deafening, repeating din, she gazed around her, amazed. Even Josh ceased his shrieking, and through the blur of tears, he too stared.

Here, in the space where a collection of tapestries normally adorned the walls of The Dissolution

Gallery, and the cases displayed fragments of exquisite stained glass and gold plate, all was altered.

Plaster blackened with damp flaked off the barren walls, exposing the brick underneath, and threadbare, moth-eaten curtains, through which the dirty daylight streamed, were strung across the large windows. In place of the cabinets and gleaming abbots' treasure the frames of nine looms filled the room, each of them clattering wildly as the shuttles darted through the warps.

The poverty of the weavers who operated the back-jarring mechanisms was painfully apparent. Many of them were wraithlike in appearance, wavering between starvation and death. In a dazzling contrast to the sordid surroundings, the fabric strung on the frames of the looms shimmered richly with silken threads.

Gathered around a central table, like a group of standing corpses, eight emaciated girls between five and ten years old were engaged in making trimmings and covering buttons. Even from a distance, Edie could see that their fingers were pricked raw.

"I want my dad!" Josh whined.

Edie cocked her head to one side and contemplated the wooden frameworks. Her thoughts flitted to that other device, where the Websters had woven the Doom of the world, but according to Ursula, the Loom of Destiny had been broken for many years.

"We're too long aways back from your dad," she told the child mysteriously, "but not far enough fer me."

Closing the door behind Edie and Josh, Ned Billet hurried to the far corner where a haggard woman sat, jolting back and forth, slaved to her loom. The skinny boy offered up an armful of scraps to her.

"All I could collar without getting buckled," he said. "Hold off a while and eat a bite. You'll end up joinin' Father and our Meggie if you don't."

Coughing, the woman turned her stark, skull-like face to him, and gradually the tyrannical contraption clicked and smacked to a halt.

"Ned!" her cracked voice called above the noise of the other rattling frames. "Give some to Violet."

The boy shook his head stubbornly. "It's you what needs it more."

Mrs. Billet rested her head in her hand and tentatively stretched her tormented back. "I must finish this pattern today," she wept.

"It's you what'll be finished if you stay off your peck and don't touch a morsel," her son urged.

Relenting, the sunken-eyed woman took a small, bruised apple, but she hardly had the strength to break the skin with her teeth.

"I don't want you filching in the market no more," she told him. "It's 'prentice work I wants for you, not the life of a shivering jemmy."

Ned deposited the squashed remains of a pie, two soil-clogged potatoes, and a chunk of cheese upon the windowsill before he answered. "There's none such work for me!" He laughed mirthlessly. "There's only this workhouse and you know it. A fine little lineup the Billets'll be in the ground, the life shaked out of them—an' all to make dandy new waistcoats for them rich folk."

Moving farther into the squalid room, Edie drew

closer to Ned and his mother. The wasted, weary woman turned her tired eyes on the girl and Josh. "Who's this you've brought?" she asked her son.

Edie stared at the woman, muted and wary. She could see that her death was very close, and a horrible thought formed in the girl's mind. Her fey, fate-filled instincts told her that this was a scene from the museum's past. This had all happened before, but now she and Josh were bound up in it. The atmosphere inside the room was hideously oppressive and charged with a ponderous anticipation, as though it was waiting for some imminent drama—and she could only watch it unfold around them.

"Bumped into her out there," the boy piped up. "Must have gone a-wanderin'."

His mother smiled weakly. "Poor mites," she said. "Lost your family, have you? Not hard to do in this warren. Ned'll take you back, don't fret. He knows this unholy lair better than the rats themselves."

"I ain't steppin' outta this sweat den," Ned objected. "That little'un was making a devil of a stir. Old Snotty Hanky's already—"

Before he could finish, there came a thundering crash as the door was kicked open and into the festering, clanking room stormed a heavily built man.

Like quicksilver, Ned dived under his mother's loom and cowered there as she swiftly surrendered herself to the jolting cruelty of her labor once more. The cadaverous girls around the table suddenly applied themselves to their tasks with renewed vigor, and the operators of the other looms bent their heads over their crippling work.

Edie stared at the invading, arrogant man as he booted the door shut again and came stalking through the stinking room. It was plain that everyone was mortally afraid of him, and she despised him instantly.

His size and girth made him an imposing figure of towering menace. A revolting leer contorted his red, swollen face, and his small rodent eyes slid malignantly from one broken soul to another. He wore no jacket, but a brown waistcoat, festooned with a silver watch chain, spanned the bulging curves of his ample belly, and the sleeves of his shirt were rolled up to his fat elbows.

In one of his large hands he carried a brutal-looking stick, and on the right side of his face was a great, crescent-shaped scar.

"Where is he?" the lout roared, barging past the quailing girls and swaggering toward Ned's mother.

"I said where is he?" he demanded, striking the loom's wooden frame with his cudgel.

The frail woman brought her toil to a lurching halt and raised a distressed, imploring face to the foul, bullying man.

"Mr. Hankinson," she spluttered. "I'm sure I don't—"

"The devil you don't!" he raged, swiping his cane across the window ledge, splattering Ned's precious plunder.

"Your young dog's been out thievin' again!" he yelled. "He was seen, and this time Obediah Hankinson will whip him proper."

The woman cowered, coughing as she shook her

head. "I haven't seen our Ned all day," she lied piteously.

Obediah seized her fragile face in his powerful, grimy fingers and squeezed until the woman emitted a gasp of pain.

Beneath the loom, the silken fabric forming a gorgeous canopy above him, Ned heard his mother's whimpering cry, and his bulging eyes streamed with tears. Baring his teeth, the scrawny boy gave a yell and lashed out, kicking the despicable taskmaster hard in the shin.

"Get your filthy paws off her!" he shrieked.

Obediah Hankinson bawled in agony, then reached into Ned's crouching space with grasping, clutching hands. But Ned was too quick for him—he had already scampered clear and was dodging beneath another silken ceiling.

Like a charging bull, Obediah gave chase, hurling the weavers from their stools to jab his stick under the wooden frames and thrash it viciously.

"Run, Ned!" his mother called. "Run and never come back!"

Between the swinging arms of the looms the boy darted and ducked, but the overseer was never far behind. His murderous club stabbed and pounded into the cramped spaces, cracking against the upright timbers in a frantic onslaught as Ned slithered and sprinted through them.

"I'll beat the life out of you!" Obediah cursed, smashing the stick into the shadows and lashing out with his enormous boots. "I'll kick your ribs in and snap the twigs of your arms!"

Out of the corner of his eye, the boy saw the man's lumbering bulk gaining on him, and as he sprang across the gap between one loom and its neighbor, he felt the frame judder and tilt as the weapon thumped in behind. Only one more short dash and he would reach the door. Once through, he would flee from this hellish place and the overseer would never catch him.

Scrabbling under the final obstacle, Ned suddenly heard a violent tearing as the silk was ripped from the warp above. Before Ned could hare away, Obediah's brawny arms flashed inside, and a huge hand gripped one of the boy's spindly legs.

"Got you!" the man spat, hauling the lad up through the shredded fabric in one ferocious movement. "You'll be sorry you went a-thievin' today—but not for long."

Hanging upside down in the braggart's iron grasp, Ned kicked out with his free leg and swung his fists, but the evil man only let out a coarse, braying laugh at the puny struggles.

"A catcher of vermin," he guffawed. "That's what I am! Now one more rat's a-goin' to get its brains bashed in."

Hoisting Ned high in the air he shook the boy, and Ned squealed as the dim world wheeled around him. The other workers were too terrified of Obediah Hackinson to interfere, but Mrs. Billet rushed from the corner of the room, her watery eyes filled with dread and horror.

"No!" she wailed. "My son!"

With one callous, sweeping blow, Obediah knocked

her to the ground, where she sprawled, weeping grievously and gasping for breath.

"Devil take you, Snotter!" screeched Ned. "To the blazes with you!"

The taskmaster whirled him around his head like a sack of onions, and then, with a relishing sneer twisting his face, he raised his stick and took a practicing swipe at the boy's bony back.

In the farthest corner, Edie Dorkins had watched everything in grim and ghastly silence. Her heightened sense told her that here was the moment the room had been waiting for. Inside the Well Lane Workhouse, in this very chamber, young Ned Billet had been flogged to death by his overseer, and she felt the ether tingle with apprehension as that gruesome instant drew near.

Shrinking against the wall at her side, Joshua Chapman hid his face from the terrible sight, his cries swamped by the uproarious shouts of Obediah Hankinson as he flexed his bloated muscles.

Then the rod went whistling through the crackling air.

"NO!" Edie screamed.

Her eyes blazing and an angry heat burning in her face, the girl flung herself forward. She leaped over Mrs. Billet's foundered body and sprang up, wrapping herself around the overseer's trunklike arm.

Snarling, the odious man staggered under Edie's attack, but he recovered immediately and shook her off as he would a tick. Yet Edie launched herself at him again, this time clutching hold of his clammy hand, and sank her teeth deep into the flesh.

Swearing, the overseer threw Ned aside and rounded his slaughterous attention on Edie Dorkins. Grabbing the collar of her coat, he snatched her up. Leaving her stockinged legs squirming and dangling, he laughed in her face.

"Scarper!" she shrieked to Ned at the top of her voice. "This potbelly can't hurt me!"

A sly, almost triumphant gleam shone in the man's ratty eyes.

"Yes, I can," he gargled. "That's what old Tick-Tock was sent here for."

Such was the compelling certainty in the man's malevolent voice that Edie stopped her struggles and looked into his leering face.

"There's a clever one," he hissed, the scabby corners of his mouth pulling wide. "He said as how the hags' daughter'd know. She can feel it right enough, don't you, Duchess?"

A sharp prickling needled into Edie's scalp, and a cold fear washed over her. This was wrong; that foul man did not belong here in this time, and she was filled with doubt.

"Who are you?" she cried. "You don't fit in this place—not *now*."

Jack Timms sniggered. "Well, I'm here, ain't I?" he mocked her. "But only brief. Just enough time to do what I was sent for. Got the power to pop back and forward whenever he likes, has Jack now, an' more besides. Like the music hall, this is. Tick-Tock's only play-actin' in old clothes an' havin' his fun."

"Obediah!" Ned Billet hollered. "You drop her." Rising unsteadily from the floor, the skinny boy ran at

Tick-Tock Jack, but the repugnant man struck him across the head, sending him flying.

"If he don't stay down," he cackled heartlessly, "he'll wind up dead after all."

Edie's hands flashed out, and four deep scratches bled across Tick-Tock's burgeoning nose. Wrathfully, he swung the girl in a sickening, yawing jostle, and Edie dangled as though she were a rag doll in his great hands.

"Let's get this done, shall we?" he snapped. "This stinkin' room's waiting for a nipper to croak, and you've gone and took that lad's place!"

Roaring, he hurtled toward the wall and drove Edie's small form against it with all his colossal might. There was an eruption of blackened plaster and the wall shuddered under the impact, but to Tick-Tock Jack's irritation, the girl in his hands simply threw back her head and giggled.

"Told you you couldn't 'urt me!" she taunted.

"I ain't finished!" he promised. "The guv'nor an' me, we got a surprise waitin'. Real special it is, but you won't like it, oh, no!"

The girl kicked out at him, but it was Jack's turn to laugh now.

"Never earned so easy a crust," he snickered. "First you, then the two old crones. Doddle work this is."

From somewhere deep in the workhouse there suddenly came an echoing bellow, and the warder flinched uncertainly. "What were that?" he asked.

Edie's eyes sparkled and she grinned joyously.

Then the rumor of galloping hooves vibrated through the building, and Jack Timms turned his sweat-glistening face to shout at the shadowy corners of the workroom. "What's out there?" he cried. "I don't like it. He never said nothin' about this!"

Stricken with fright at this unknown terror, the weavers rose from their looms and crowded into the dark corner, holding on to the skeletal young girls, who bleated in misery.

The frightful trumpeting was closer now. Down the hallways some immense beast was charging, and the agent of Woden wavered in doubt.

Edie Dorkins hooted to see him so confounded. "It's the stag!" she sang. "He's come to get you!"

"Call it off!" Jack Timms demanded, shaking the girl by her coat.

Edie waggled her head from side to side. "You should see its 'orns!" she teased. "Pop your great guts in a jiffy, they will."

The crashing of hooves was almost outside the workroom now, and the air trembled as the bass, blaring roars became an agony to hear.

"I'll kill you first!" Tick-Tock vowed, wrenching her from the wall. "There's a new Tormentor for Jack to use on your kind."

But as he carried the girl across the room, the warder's giant knuckles brushed against the wool of Edie's pixie hat. At once the silver tinsel woven into the knitting flared with glittering sparks, and Jack Timms let out a screech of pain as the fires of Fate scorched his skin. Yowling, he flung the child from him.

"Little witch!" he yelled, clutching his smoking hand. "Cost you dear, that will!"

Suddenly the door buckled as terrifying blows rained down upon it. Tick-Tock backed away fearfully.

His lip bleeding, Ned Billet ran over to Edie and helped her up. "Get out!" he shouted. "Get gone, quick!"

Not waiting to argue, Edie pushed past him and dashed over to Josh, who still had his face buried in his hands. Yanking him by the arm, she dragged the boy across the room and headed for the splintering door.

One of the panels was already breached, and a silver, hammering hoof could be glimpsed through the shattered wood. Wrath-filled amber eyes burned in the darkness beyond, and standing as close to that quivering, convulsing barrier as she dared, Edie reached for the handle.

"Don't let it in!" Jack Timms shrieked.

The girl turned a merciless grin on the frightened man, then beckoned urgently to Ned. "Come with us!" she ordered.

Ned Billet shook his head and threw himself at his mother's side.

A gray shadow flitted over them, and Edie wrested her eyes away. Then, even as the door snapped in two and the clamor of the stag thundered all around, she tore at the handle and flung it wide.

Hauling Josh after her, Edie Dorkins pelted forward, into the very heart of that primeval anger, and like a squall-crowned god of the wild, the beast pranced and reared above them.

In a moment the tumult faded, and the children found themselves standing in the dim gloom of The Egyptian Suite once again.

"Dad! Dad!" Josh squealed, bolting from Edie's side to tear into The Separate Collection.

Edie Dorkins remained where she was. Glancing back, she knew that the broken doorway had long since gone, even before she saw The Dissolution Gallery beyond, with its tapestries and abbey gold.

Narrowing her almond-shaped eyes, the girl expelled a regretful sigh. "Ned did die in there," she whispered. "They all did, in the end."

Jamming her hands into her pockets, she left The Egyptian Suite.

In The Separate Collection, Josh discovered his father kneeling on the floor, trembling with shock. His neck was scratched, and a dark bruise had already appeared on his face. When Josh approached, the man seemed to stare right through him.

"Where's Gogus?" Edie asked.

The caretaker winced and shook his head. "That . . . whatever it was, ran off when you went in there. Blood and sand! What sort of nightmare was it?"

Lumbering to his feet, he stared around the room as though expecting that growling voice to come racing from the shadows.

"That settles it," he muttered. "We're packing up and getting out of here as soon as possible."

CHAPTER 13

THE HORSE'S BRANSLE

In the late afternoon, Neil returned to the Wyrd Museum, heaving his full weight against the Victorian entrance to push it open. It had been a terrible day. His troubled mind was full of the previous night's horror, and his nerves were jangled and worn.

Yet, away from the museum's labyrinthine galleries and passageways, the boy felt an unaccountable sense of guilt. Perhaps it was the thought of not knowing what might be happening to Josh and Quoth, but there was also a vague sense that he was deserting a battlefield. Now he was almost glad to be back inside its enclosing walls, and he hurried through the echoing hallway to check on his family.

The Fossil Room was deserted when he reached it, and although a hundred awful possibilities flashed into his brain, he hoped that Austen Pickering and

Quoth were merely conducting investigations elsewhere in the building.

Running the remaining distance to the caretaker's apartment, Neil found it strewn with clothes and belongings while his father stuffed as much as he could into their suitcases and a large footlocker.

"What's going on?" the boy demanded.

"We're moving out of here tomorrow, first thing," Brian Chapman answered resolutely. "I called your Auntie Marion, and we can stay with her for a few weeks."

"But she lives in Scotland!" Neil objected.

"That's why we're not starting till the morning."

"What's the big rush all of a sudden?"

His father waved a quaking hand at him and turned his head to reveal the scratches. "You haven't seen what I have!" he shouted. "I always thought this place was crazy, but . . . I don't even have a word for what it really is! I wish we didn't have to spend another night here. If it wasn't so cold I'd sleep in the van. God knows what this has done to Josh. He hasn't stopped crying all day."

Neil started to protest, but his father would not listen. "There'll be no arguments!" he declared. "We're leaving, and that's final."

Flinging his schoolbag into the room, the boy turned on his heel and ran back down the passageway.

"Neil!" the caretaker's voice yelled. "Get back here and put your stuff away."

Through the museum Neil hurried, flushed and furious that the decision to leave was out of his control. He knew that if he remained in the apartment, a terrible argument like the one that had raged after his mother had walked out on them would ensue.

Pounding up the stairs, Neil felt his overflowing resentment turn toward Sheila Chapman. Neil had never before blamed his mother for abandoning Josh and himself, but he did now. "I won't go!" he told himself. "He can't force me. I've had enough of his stupid moods—he's useless! I hate him!"

A loud cawing broke through his rage, and Neil lifted his face to look up the stairwell. From the third-floor landing, Quoth flew down, rejoicing to see his master again.

"Squire Neil!" the raven hailed him. "'Tis a merrie meeting! Thine company doth shame the vaults of kings." Alighting upon his usual place, Quoth nibbled the boy's earlobe.

"You've perked up since this morning," Neil commented. "It's me who's in a stinking temper now."

The raven rested his head against him. "He is a fool who is not melancholy once a day."

"Maybe," Neil griped, "but Dad's set on going away tomorrow morning. I'm sick of him."

A hopeful glint kindled in the raven's eye. "Thou and I are to depart this grooly abode?" he chirruped.

Neil was positive there was no way his father would let Quoth come with them, but he said nothing and let the raven chatter happily.

From the landing above, the pink, craggy face of Austen Pickering appeared over the banister.

"There you are, lad!" he called. "Thought it was

about time you got back. Your raven's been pining for you all day. Come up here. I have news!"

Neil ran up the remaining stairs but, even before he reached the third floor, the ghost hunter began. "Listen to this," he rattled. "I came across it at lunchtime and almost choked on my sandwich!"

Mr. Pickering was sitting on a fold-up camp stool, wearing his raincoat to keep out the chill. Several ledgers and inventories were arranged in a neat, organized pile beside him, and he flicked through one of them to where a strip of notepaper marked a certain page.

"Did you find out about Jack Timms?" the boy asked.

The old man chuckled. "Did I?" he exclaimed with relish. "You would not believe what I have discovered about that man. To call him a villain would be an insult to criminals everywhere. He worked at the asylum for nearly four years, instilling fear into everyone. He taunted the patients, hounding many of them to suicide, and intimidated the other staff. He should have been behind bars himself. Shortly after he started work here there was, by no coincidence, a spate of violent cases that naturally needed a firm hand to quell them. At least five patients died as a direct result of his beatings, but a great many more perished in dubious circumstances. He was a drunken killer, no doubt about that."

Quoth croaked softly. "The aled man who doth murder shalt be hanged when sober."

"Ah, but I don't know what happened to him,"

Mr. Pickering added. "At least, I haven't discovered that yet. Jack Timms abruptly disappears from the records. He went out one night, to get a skinful no doubt, and never returned. No one knew what became of him."

"I hope he got what he deserved," Neil muttered.

The ghost hunter shrugged. "Probably died in a pub brawl," he said dismissively. "What I wanted to read you is this."

He slid a forefinger down a long list of entries written in a scratchy, copperplate script.

"*Seventh of June, nineteen hundred and five*," Mr. Pickering began. "In the admission's column for that day: one *Henry Mattock of Hatton Garden . . .*"

"What is that book?" Neil interrupted.

"Register of the Wyrd Infirmary," Mr. Pickering explained hastily without taking his eyes from the page. "Quite the home away from home for the mad middle class of the day it seems. None of your lowly dock workers or market porters allowed in here when they went off their rockers."

Tapping his finger on the paper he resumed his reading. "*Henry Mattock of Hatton Garden: condition—general paralysis of the insane.*"

"Who's he?" the boy asked.

The old man held up a silencing hand. "And on the same day," he continued, "there's this entry. *Mary-Anne Brindle of Stoke Newington: condition— unwedded with child.*"

"She can't have been put away just for that," Neil muttered.

Looking up from the register, Mr. Pickering

tutted at him. "She could, and she was," he said. "Only the very poor and the very rich got away with that sort of thing in those days. For those sandwiched in between, the shame and disgrace was unimaginable. The usual practice, if the baby was to be kept, would be for the girl to go on a long visit somewhere. But if there were no relations who lived at a sufficient distance, an infirmary did just as well. Can you imagine having a kiddy in a lunatic asylum?"

Leaning on the banister, Neil recalled the face of the terrified woman he had seen in the corridor.

"She *was* insane though," he told the ghost hunter.

"Ah, well," the old man began, clearing his throat as he laid the register aside to take up a smaller volume, "the person you saw was Mary-Anne, but a projection of how she appeared three years later in nineteen hundred and eight."

"Hang on. Why was she still here after all that time?"

"Oh, she was institutionalized by then. Her four-month incarceration waiting for the child was enough to do that. Don't forget that Jack Timms would have made her existence unbearable. No, she was driven right over the edge by his bullying torture."

"So what happened to the baby?"

Mr. Pickering browsed through the second book. "Stillborn," he said simply. "Now, *this* is a journal of Samuel Lawrence, a surgeon who ought to have been locked up with the inmates, whom he treated no better than laboratory animals. Queasy reading, this. It's an account in his own words."

In a low voice, the ghost hunter began to read aloud.

October twenty-second, nineteen hundred and eight.

. . . the wretched creature was strapped onto the table, but the laudanum had little effect on her and I forbade the use of chloral, so she squealed like a scalded cat throughout.

To the assembled gathering I had explained my intention. The experiment would prove my theory that the liver could be removed then replaced without deleterious injury to the subject. They were all most curious to witness this ambitious procedure, in particular Lord Darnling of the Surgical College in whom I set great store for advancement. I had conducted similar operations upon dogs, but the anesthetic had killed each one.

Perhaps it was the esteem in which I held my audience that caused my hand to tremble. My nerves were in such an agitated state that the first incision was no better than that which a novice might make. Notes of disapproval were whispered, and my mouth grew salty dry on hearing them.

Yet worse was still to come. In my anxious fervor, the blade turned and an artery was opened. At once the pumping blood spouted up into my face and I was blinded. By the time I had wiped it clear, Lord Darnling was already leading the company from the operating theater. He would not hear my apologies.

Sick at heart I returned to the subject and endeavored to seal up the wound. But she had expired for want of blood, and the attendants were laughing at my ill fortune. The furtherment of my career has met with a sad blow this day.

Austen Pickering closed the journal with a snap and Neil jumped.

"Mary-Anne Brindle died on that operating table," the ghost hunter declared. "In the room now called The Separate Collection."

"That was revolting," Neil uttered in disgust. "The madman murdered her."

"She would have been hanged anyway," Mr. Pickering reminded him, "because of the warder she'd killed. In the eyes of the law, she was only fodder for the noose and much more valuable to scientific investigation. Sad to say, she wasn't missed."

Hopping from Neil's shoulder onto that of the old man, Quoth croaked in a sepulchral tone, "Death dealeth himself unto all."

Pushing his sliding eyeglasses higher up his nose, the ghost hunter rose from his seat. "Is it any wonder she haunts this awful building?" he asked. "It is a bad place with an ugly past, riddled with guilt and horror."

"It is also my home," a clipped, censorial voice added as Miss Ursula Webster strode from the third-floor corridor and out onto the landing.

Quoth gave a startled squawk and returned to his master. "Forsooth!" he whispered hoarsely. "'Tis the Hecate in rustling skirts."

"I trust those records have been of use, Mr. Pickering?" she asked haughtily.

The old man fidgeted uncomfortably before her imperious stare. "They have," he replied. "I am now more certain than ever that my work here is of the utmost importance."

"And what exactly is it that you have discovered?" she pressed in a vaguely disdainful tone. "Did you learn much from the fossils and the samian ware? Were they truly implements of death and catastrophe, all of them? Did the bronze lamps illumine dire deeds, and were the coins an assassin's fee? What a busy time you'll have, to be sure."

Austen Pickering bristled before her caustic remarks. "Ridicule me all you like," he retorted. "It doesn't make the slightest difference. Whatever needs to be done to cleanse this foul place, I'll do it."

An appraising gleam shone coldly in the old woman's eyes. "Yes," she murmured, "I'm certain you will."

"Excuse me," the ghost hunter said. "I'm setting up my apparatus out here tonight. I must go and see to it before the light fails completely." Taking his notebook with him, Mr. Pickering left the landing and entered the passageway beyond.

A shrewd smile curled over Miss Ursula's mouth as she watched him depart. "I do believe I discomfort our spirit supervisor," she said querulously.

Neil turned to her. "Why did you invite him here?" he demanded. "What manipulating game are you up to this time? You're not interested in releasing trapped souls."

"Harsh words from such a lowly maggot as yourself," the old woman said. "Who I choose to allow into the portals of my museum is my own affair. You would condemn me because I use others. That is the role of Fate, Child."

"No," the boy refuted. "You use people because you enjoy it. Only a twisted mind could have allowed what has gone on in this building to happen. Why didn't you stop them? Why did you let monsters like Jack Timms in here? What about Mary-Anne Brindle?"

"Squire Neil!" Quoth clucked in his ear. "Thy tongue doth dig a ditch most deep."

Miss Ursula regarded the boy coldly. "My sisters and I are not responsible for the events you speak of," she told him with harsh severity. "The museum has always been a mirror for the ages in which it lives, and for long periods we took no interest in its daily running. There were other concerns. Whatever occurred within these walls was not our fault."

"I don't believe you!" Neil countered. "You stage-managed everything back then, just as you're doing now. Mr. Pickering's here to do your dirty work, isn't he? Something you can't do yourself."

A twinge of annoyance flickered momentarily over Miss Ursula's stony face. "I must check on Celandine," she said quickly. "I must keep her in the apartment if our good specter inspector is to conduct his important investigations up on this floor."

Striding to the doorway, the old woman paused when Neil called out to her. But this time the boy's voice was imploring, and when she turned to look at him, he felt as though she already knew the question he was about to ask.

"Please," he began. "When you wanted me to go to Glastonbury to bring back Veronica, you said that my thread was still caught up in the Web of Destiny."

Miss Ursula's arched eyebrows gave an almost imperceptible twitch. "I recall what I said then," she answered.

"What I mean is," Neil continued, thinking of his father and the enforced departure the following morning, "is it all over? Am I free now, or am I still a part of it?"

With deliberate slowness, the old woman spun on her heel and walked away. "Most certainly you are a part," her mocking voice rang out to him from the connecting corridor. "The strand of your life is bound to the weave more tightly than ever, Child. You could not escape me—even if you wanted to."

* * *

In the long, spacious gallery of The Tiring Salon, Austen Pickering had already maneuvered many of the costumed mannequins to one side of the room. The headless congregation huddled in a splendidly arrayed row in the gathering gloom opposite the windows, and catching them in the corner of his eye, the ghost hunter wished he had spared the time to alter the undignified positions that someone had enforced upon them.

"Like a paralyzed chorus line," he mumbled to himself.

He placed the last of eight candles on the far side of the room, and he made a note of the hour before setting his lighter to the first wick.

"Four fifty-seven," he said aloud, writing the figures in his book. "Turn the main lights out in eighteen minutes, Austen, old lad. See what happens."

Crossing to the middle of the gallery to a low table that bore his tape recorder and thermometer, the old man took his first temperature reading.

"Strange," he observed. "Must be at least four degrees lower inside than it is out. No wonder I thought it was chilly. Never heard of a whole building turning into one great cold spot."

Setting down that absorbing fact, he then checked on the lengths of twine he had fixed across the room and in front of the three doorways that opened into it, carefully stepping over those in his path.

"A couple more?" he asked himself, eyeing the small door decorated with the image of a tree. "Should stretch a few over there, really."

Taking a reel of twine from his pocket he advanced toward the entrance that led to the Websters' apartment, but before he reached it, the door was pulled open and a beaming Miss Celandine came barging out.

"Careful!" Mr. Pickering cried, pointing at the taut strings. "You'll break them if you're not—"

Three faint pings followed Miss Celandine's carefree, gamboling progress as the twine snapped around her.

"Is there to be more dancing?" she twittered in astonishment, staring in confusion at the assembled row of dummies. "What are they whispering about over there? Is it to decide who will have the honor of leading me into the first waltz?"

Austen Pickering groaned and attempted to steer the rambling woman away from the other strings. "Shall I call your sister?" he asked, trying to humor her.

Miss Celandine heaved a great sigh and flashed her

goofy teeth at him. "You don't want to bring Veronica," she crooned, coyly batting her lashes. "What a polite and gentle fellow you are. If you wish, you may dance with me and make those others jealous. Serve them right, it will, for skulking and having secrets."

The ghost hunter shambled away from her, inadvertently breaking another of his strings. "I . . . I don't dance," he hastily explained, mortified at the suggestion. "Never did like or learn it."

"Oh, poo!" Miss Celandine said, not to be thwarted. "Even Ursula enjoys a waltz when she starts, and I know steps that are ever so easy to pick up—they are, they are!"

"Well, not without music they're not," Mr. Pickering added with firm finality.

The old woman swung her arms sulkily. "Meany," she sniveled. "Wouldn't hurt, just one teeny waltz. Not much to ask."

Casting her eyes to the ceiling, she gazed at the empty air and let out a heartfelt sigh. "We had lovely parties in here," she reminisced dreamily. "They were such grand occasions with fine, gallant knights always ready to whirl you away. Once I wore out two pairs of dancing slippers in one evening—I did."

Her wistful expression faded, and she lowered her lost, lamenting eyes until they were level with those of the ghost hunter. A desperate sadness creased her age-old face, and she covered her bare, mottled shoulders with her large hands as though suddenly aware and ashamed of their nakedness.

"Where did the days go?" she asked forlornly.

"When did I grow old? Why can't it be as it always was, with music and laughter? I know I do silly things and upset Ursula, but I can't help it—really, I can't. Why must it be like this? I wasn't always foolish. I was clever once, when I was young . . . and there was dancing."

A great tear sprang from the old woman's eye, and she hung her head, sobbing.

As Austen Pickering watched this muddled elderly lady mourn for the vanished days of her youth and sanity, a mastering wave of compassion overcame his usual reserve. There was no awkwardness on his part, no self-conscious show of righteous pity. In his regimental, orderly fashion, he simply removed his raincoat, tugged at the cuffs of his pullover, and with his heels together drew himself up to his full height.

"Madam," he said, holding out his hand to her, "would you do me the honor?"

Miss Celandine looked up hesitantly. A large tear was dangling from her bulbous nose, and it fell to the floor with a splash. "You . . . you mean it?" she sniffed.

"Nothing would please me more," came the warm and genuine reply.

Her lips quivering with emotion, Miss Celandine reached out to the man and rested her nut-brown hand on his. A sudden, rosemary-scented draft blew into The Tiring Salon, and the electric light was quenched, leaving only the flickering candles to illuminate the room.

In the glow of the flaring flames, the dim interior

underwent a transformation. With the gentle, easing sound of relaxing timbers, the wooden panels on the walls constricted to become smaller rectangles of oak, and the ceiling lifted with a comforting creak, rising up to a lofty apex supported on sturdy, straddling beams.

The Georgian windows dwindled and diminished, the glass dissolving to be divided by leaden strips forming regular square and diamond panes. Beneath them, long settles emerged from the deep brown shadows that were dispelled when fifteen tall candlesticks spluttered into lambent life.

Garlands of greenery decorated the walls, and a great globe of wicker, interwoven with ivy and decorated with cherries and golden pears, was suspended from the rafters.

Staring open-mouthed at the wondrous changes, Austen Pickering gaped even more when the mannequins suddenly left their positions against the wall to roam into the center of the room. No longer were they headless dummies, but living, breathing people, whose merry company filled the air with a pleasant, chattering babble.

Gone was the motley assortment of diverse costumes, and a more uniform attire, reflecting the new surroundings, was worn by all.

The gentlemen sported doublets and jerkins, many of them following the fashion of "slashing," with intricate patterns cut into the cloth to show a richly contrasting garment beneath. All of them boasted broad-brimmed, beretlike hats perched on their close-cropped heads, ornamented with brooches and dyed feathers that bobbed and bounced when they moved.

The consorts of these strutting peacocks in their paned trunk hose were demure-looking ladies with downcast eyes. Their pale faces were framed in gabled hoods set with semiprecious gems around the edge. Tight bodices that flattened their chests were cut low to reveal expanses of creamy skin and were adorned with fine golden chains and jeweled pendants.

As their partners guided them to the middle of the chamber, their long skirts of velvet and silk brushed silently along the ground; forming two long lines, they all turned to face the end wall where a minstrel's gallery had pushed its way into the candlelight.

A look of enchanted bliss shone on Miss Celandine's enraptured face, and she wiped her dribbling nose on the lace of her ruby gown, utterly captivated by the scene before her.

"It's the seventh of September," she whispered in a choked, yearning voice. "The party to celebrate the princess's birth. Oh, what a glorious fortune Ursula had me weave for her. Said she would be so very much like her in lots of ways."

Blinking the tears away, the old woman dried her eyes and surveyed the finery of the guests. "The darling clothes," she pined. "And what colors; look at that sweet hat of popingay green! The orange-tawny robe and the lion's color kirtle—oh, that cloak of coleur de Roy!"

Bursting into sudden giggles, she pointed at a somber-looking woman clad in drab garments. "Goose-turd green and puke!" she squeaked. "Even

Ursula would never wear that. And see those frightful, dreary petticoats; why, that's dead Spaniard!"

With a sorrowful shake of the head, Miss Celandine murmured, "Even the names of colors were more beautiful then, weren't they? How tired and dull everything became." Austen Pickering was too dumbfounded to respond.

"This was the last party Ursula let us have," she breathed. "No one ever came to call again. Ursula said it grew too dangerous outside, and we had to be shut upstairs. Once I wrote out hundreds of invitations for a grand ball, but she put a stop to it, even burned my pretty dresses, she did."

From the minstrel's gallery a drum broke into a jaunty, beating rhythm, and Miss Celandine looked longingly at the awaiting guests. "Is it a pavane?" she cried. "I do hope not. They're so stuffy—they are, they are!"

The throaty notes of a recorder and tabor suddenly joined the tune, and the old woman jumped up and down with glee. "The Horse's Bransle! Oh, one of my very favorites. Do let's join them!" Before he knew what was happening, the ghost hunter was dragged into the throng with Miss Celandine telling him what to do.

"It's so easy!" she enthused. "Just hold my hands and watch me. Start with your left foot and sidestep. That's it."

Intoxicated by the spectacle around him, Austen Pickering could not resist. It was a peculiar, formal dance, where the couples took turns to paw the ground with their feet like horses, and in spite of her age, Miss Celandine did it beautifully. Maybe it was because she was truly in her element, for her impaired mind recalled every step, and among all the gathered noblewomen, her movements were the most graceful, her steps the most delicate.

Mr. Pickering was soon laughing with delight at the strangeness of it all, and although his prancing was a trifle clumsy, his partner more than compensated. Casting his gaze along the aisle of couples to see how poorly he compared with them, he saw three figures enter the room, and his broad grin was replaced with an expression of intense curiosity.

Standing by the door emblazoned with the image of the tree, the newcomers hung back from the dancing while the tallest of them exchanged a few sharp words with the others. A puzzled frown appeared on the ghost hunter's face, for he suddenly recognized two of those women.

There, standing erect and corseted in a bodice and skirt of sable silks, was a slightly younger version of Miss Ursula Webster. A pendant dripping with tear-shaped pearls hung around her neck and a silver belt encircled her waist. Her head was covered in a black peaked hood, also beaded with pearls.

The striking woman at her side, whom Mr. Pickering did not know, wore a simple, whey-colored gown. She alone amongst all the company had left her head uncovered, and her long raven tresses trailed down to her knees.

The third in the trio, peering around the room, anxious to partake of its delights—was Miss Celandine.

Austen Pickering stared at her, then swiftly reverted

his glance to his dancing partner. There was no doubt about it, they were the same. Yet the new arrival was a fresher-looking reproduction; the face was not ruddy and crabbed, and she was extravagantly dressed from head to toe in ravishing red velvet and cloth of gold.

At a signal from Miss Ursula, her sisters ran to the dance and were at once surrounded by admirers. With a gratified, matronly gaze, Miss Ursula considered them, nodding with approval at the revels. Then her eyes met those of the ghost hunter and she held him in her glance.

Pushing through the crowd of those who had declined to enter the lines of the Bransle, the eldest of the Fates moved toward him, taking two earthenware beakers from the tray of a serving maid along the way.

Austen Pickering dropped out of the dance and his place was taken immediately. "What the devil's going on?" he asked Miss Ursula.

The sable-garbed woman held out one of the drinking vessels to him, and they moved to the edge of the room, away from the merrymakers.

"Sup well, Sirrah," she instructed, lifting her two-handled beaker in a toast. "The daughter born to good King Hal this day shall be among the very great. Though her travails be many, Providence will smile upon her, of that you can be assured."

Mr. Pickering looked at the pot in his hand. The emblem of a white stag was painted under the glaze, and he touched it thoughtfully before taking a cautious sniff of the contents. The scent of nutmeg mingled with cloves, spices, and a deep brown ale filled his senses, and reflecting that there was nothing to lose, he quaffed down a great, gulping draft.

"You slake your thirst handsomely," Miss Ursula commented.

The old man smacked his lips and chortled to himself. "I don't understand any of this," he confessed. "In all my years . . ."

"Was the feast to your taste?" she questioned. "As mistress of Little Wyrd Hall, I would know that my guests hold my hospitality in esteem. Did the boiled meats and roasts find favor with you? No doubt you found the lack of venison unusual, but I will not permit its consumption. Of the tarts and curds, was there sufficient? Were you shown the quinces and orange fruits?"

Mr. Pickering considered the woman and wondered if she was purposely making fun of him. There was an ambiguous timber in her voice that he recognized as belonging to the other, older counterpart of Miss Ursula, and yet this markedly younger woman seemed to suit this Tudor age just as much, if not more so. Giving voice to his doubts, he said, "It is Miss Webster?"

A placid smile was his only answer, and she let her eyes wander to where the elderly aspect of Miss Celandine began a new dance that involved a procession of different partners kissing her hand in turn.

"How well your companion enjoys this celebration," she observed. "It gladdens me to see her so."

"But that's your sister!" he blurted. "And look at me in my old sweater and trousers. I don't belong in this time. Don't you think my clothes are odd?"

Miss Ursula returned his baffled gaze with one of her own. "I hope you do not consider me so ill-bred as to make adverse commentary on a country gentleman's russets, Sirrah," she replied. "Just as my guests do not raise an eyebrow at our flouting of the sumptuary laws, in particular Celandine and her cloth of gold. As to her, she and Veronica are both making a pretty show of themselves over yonder. I fail to see a semblance twixt either and your good associate."

"All right," Mr. Pickering yielded. "I'll just make the most of it while I'm here." And he took another swig from the beaker.

The mistress of the house clasped her own vessel in front of her and regarded him keenly. "Tell me something of yourself, Sirrah," she began.

"Why do you keep calling me that?"

"It is the fashion of the time," she rejoined. "It is as well to fit in."

"Ah, then you admit it! You are the Miss Webster I know."

"I admit that you have not answered my question," she said blithely.

The ghost hunter drained his spiced ale. "I come from the north, originally," he told her.

"As did we all," Miss Ursula remarked. "And what of your estates?"

Mr. Pickering gave a chuckle. "The only estate I ever owned had two rooms and a leaky roof. Are you playing games with me?"

"All of us play games," she said enigmatically.

"Do we not? How else can eternity be endured? And when the diversion is entered into, each role must be performed to the utmost. Would you not agree?"

"I wouldn't know. I prefer quieter pastimes, like Solitaire. I'm good at crosswords, too."

"Then what of your family?" she inquired. "Is there no Mrs. Pickering? Someone to share your interests, to hold your tape measure, and light your little candles?"

The old man scowled through his glasses at her. "It *is* you!" he snorted. "And no, I never married, not that it's any of your business."

Miss Ursula took the beaker from him and strode to the window, where she placed them both on the sill. "And I, like you," she told him, "have always been tied to my work. That has been my only binding passion."

"Then we have something in common," Austen Pickering said.

"Perhaps."

There was a strained pause between them as each strove to understand what the other was thinking.

Finally, Miss Ursula took a deep breath and assessed the festivities. "It was a fine celebration," she admitted, "surpassing all others we had before. A fitting way to mark the birth of one destined for greatness, but also to signal our withdrawal from the world. Tell me truthfully, Mr. Pickering, have you enjoyed this glimpse of our past?"

"I'm none the wiser," he said, smiling vaguely. "But yes, I have—very much."

The woman looked at the paneled walls around them. "Then that is good," she replied. "I wanted you to see that my home is not wholly filled with ugly memories. My sisters and I were very happy here for a long time."

"I'm sure you were, but I still have my work to do."

Miss Ursula nodded briskly. "That you have," she said. "And I recall that I was never that fond of parties. Celandine has had her treat, and now it, like all things, must end."

As she removed the peaked hood from her head, her impeccably coifed white curls sprang back into place and strings of jet beads entwined them. The sable silk of her garments shimmered briefly, then Miss Ursula Webster was dressed in her Victorian evening gown once more, and the intervening ages crept back into her face.

"Come," she declared.

Escorting Mr. Pickering through the assembled nobles, the old woman traversed the room to where Miss Celandine was still pointing her toes and parading in a circle, her spadelike hands joined with the suitors of the past.

"It is time," Miss Ursula gently informed her.

Her sister whirled around, a sad, regretful smile etched upon her old, wrinkled features. Reluctantly she made her apologies to her partners and curtsied daintily. The gallants bowed in return, and Miss Celandine came away, her heart fit to burst.

Taking hold of her sister's hands, she pressed them gratefully. "Thank you, Ursula," she whispered. "Thank you." And then the music slowly faded, the laughter died, and the candles were extinguished.

While Miss Ursula stood stiff and stern, the last glimpse she saw of that earlier time was the younger figures of her two sisters, Veronica and Celandine, as they both were before their reason rotted in tune with Nirinel. Then, suddenly, the electric lights snapped back on and the Tudor vision was gone.

"Not long now," she murmured. "Not long."

Austen Pickering rubbed his dazzled eyes. They were back in The Tiring Salon, and the mannequins in their sundry costumes were once more grouped against the wall.

Leaning heavily on her sister's arm for support, Miss Celandine refused to lift her head, her long braids screening her sight. The usually sprightly old woman finally appeared to have surrendered herself to the crushing ages, and in a small, husky voice, she said, "I'd like to go upstairs now, please. I'm tired."

Miss Ursula assisted her to the small door that led to the attic. Then, remembering Mr. Pickering, she halted and took their leave.

"Good night," she began, glancing back at the long gallery and the table upon which his thermometer and tape recorder lay. "I'm so sorry if Celandine broke your ghost strings. Do remember to reset them."

Then the ornate door closed behind the two sisters. Austen Pickering scratched his head and roared with giddy laughter.

CHAPTER 14

THE MENAGERIE OF MR. CHARLES JAMRACH

Balancing on the banister, Quoth paced up and down while Neil flicked through the register of the Wyrd Infirmary. "So many unexplained deaths," he murmured in revulsion.

Executing an ungainly pirouette, the raven gave his master a consoling croak. "Verily," he trilled, "this great, grotsome grave doth run over with the despond damned. Soonest we depart hence, the gladder this cockle shalt be."

Neil put the book down and groaned. "I've really got to talk to Dad about that," he decided. "No use putting it off. I just hope Miss Webster's right."

"Thou dost not wish to leave?" Quoth queried in surprise.

"We haven't got anywhere to go. As soon as Auntie Marion gets tired of Dad, and she will, what then?"

The raven shook his feathers uneasily. He wanted to put as much distance between the Wyrd Museum and himself as possible.

"Better get it over with," Neil announced, leaving the landing to descend the stairs. "Might as well let Dad do all his shouting tonight."

Spreading his wings to stabilize himself, Quoth sat down on the polished banister rail and slid down after his master.

The inadequate electric lamps that lit the stairwell could not expel every shadow. Where the steps opened onto each landing, pockets of puddling gloom remained steadfastly in the corners, and it was within one of these dim patches that Edie Dorkins waited on the second floor. Hearing Neil's descent, the girl retreated to the doorway and watched.

With their thoughts elsewhere, neither the boy nor his skating companion even knew she was there until they began the downward traipse to the main hallway.

"Don't your brother never stop blubberin'?" Edie called, suddenly springing out behind them.

Neil started, and Quoth gave a loud squawk of surprise as he slipped from the rail in fright and tumbled from view. In a moment he came fluttering back and shot straight to his master's shoulder. "How sorely is mine mettle tested at every turn!" he clucked woefully.

Neil stared at the girl, intrigued. "What do you mean?" he asked. "Were you with Dad and Josh when they were attacked today?"

Scuffing her shoes along the floor, Edie said nothing.

"What happened?" the boy persisted. "Do you know Dad's on the warpath and wants to leave?"

"Good!" she snapped, pulling open the door to the corridor. "He scared my Gogus off."

Then Neil understood what had so terrified his father. "Gogus . . ." he muttered. "So that's what it was. That thing in the dark."

"The imp of wood!" the raven interjected. "Thy parent's quarrel with this dire dungeon hath just cause."

Edie tossed her head, then dashed away through the door.

"What did she mean, *her* Gogus?" Neil asked. "Edie—wait!"

Hurrying after her, the boy ran through the doorway and into The Dissolution Gallery beyond. Within that large room, where Ned Billet had been beaten to death over a century ago, Edie Dorkins stared thoughtfully at the large hanging tapestries, lifting them to peep curiously at the wooden panels behind.

Hearing Neil enter, the girl frowned and stamped her foot.

"Tell me what happened," he asked. But Edie refused and ducked under the tapestry in front of her so that she would not have to see him. Her figure formed a large, obstinate bump behind the folds of dusty fabric.

"Your feet are sticking out," the boy said wearily.

"Get gone," her muffled voice demanded. "I'm busy."

Quoth scratched his scalp. "Yon maid maketh a fitting successor to the Sisters of the Well," he commented softly. "Her wits also hath leaked full empty."

"Edie," Neil said, bored with the whimsical child's tantrums. "I just want to know—"

Before he could finish, the raven clapped a wing over his mouth, and the boy spat out two feathers. "What's that for?" he cried.

"Peace, mine Master!" Quoth hissed, looking desperately around them. "Canst thou not sense it? Another presence hath joined us in this chamber of looted booty."

Neil caught his breath and listened. "I can't hear anything," he mouthed.

The raven's one eye darted around the room, glancing suspiciously at the treasure inside the cabinets, then fixing his attention to the darkened entrance of The Egyptian Suite at the far end.

"From thence it cometh," he cawed fretfully. "Let us flee afore the lightning bulbs be doused."

Hearing the bird's frightened warning, Edie emerged from beneath the tapestry, then she and Neil both became aware of faint, snuffling breaths.

"The imp," Quoth muttered.

"Gogus!" Edie gasped excitedly.

"Quick!" Neil hissed at the girl. "We've got to get out."

But Edie ignored him, sprawling on the floor to peer under the cabinets.

"What are you doing?" the boy cried as she reached out with her hand and tapped the ground encouragingly.

Lying on her stomach, Edie could see a pair of carved wooden legs prowling around the room. A long tail swished behind them, and she clicked her tongue to attract the creature's attention. "Gogus!" she called. "Come here, Gogus."

The guttural panting ceased, and two slanting eyes abruptly blinked under the cases to glare at her. "Don't be scared," Edie continued, beckoning with her fingers. "There's a good Gogus."

"Squire Neil," Quoth wailed. "The dunceling knows not what she doeth!"

"Edie!" Neil protested. "Leave it!"

A low, throaty rumble issued from the imp's wide mouth, and it took a cautious, stalking step forward.

"That's it," Edie enticed.

With another waddling step, Gogus cleared the cabinet, and Neil beheld its bowed and stunted form for the first time. The wooden eyes swiveled to glower at him and the raven. Then, its jaw quivering, the creature unleashed a warning bark in their direction.

"A gargoyle of the enchanted forest!" Quoth bleated. "Fly, Squire Neil, fly!"

"Edie!" the boy pleaded. "Get up, get away. It'll bite your hand off."

But Edie was fascinated by the imp and yapped back at it. At once Gogus stopped its clamor and whimpered fitfully, sniffing and snouting the air.

"Little bit more," the girl invited. Gurgling, the creature edged forward, closing the distance between them, its tail flicking hesitantly while the unwieldy head tilted from side to side.

"Gogus . . ." it grunted shyly. "Gogus . . ."

"There's a good, pretty pet," Edie continued. "Come on, that's right. Nothin' to be frighted of."

"You're crazy!" Neil whispered in desperation. "It's not some kind of dog."

The pointed ears flicked and twitched uncertainly, and the creature's alarming face turned to him as a threatening gargle sounded in its throat. Quickly, the noise grew into a menacing growl and Quoth trembled.

"Too late!" the raven warbled. "The tree wight shalt pounce and devour us all."

That was enough for Neil. Lunging forward, he snatched Edie from the floor and hauled the girl's struggling figure toward the door.

At once, Gogus flew into a fury. The hooked claws thumped and raked the ground, and it let loose a ferocious barking. Lashing its tail, it leaped after them, but Neil kicked out, and emitting a high, gibbering yowl, the imp was sent reeling.

"Hurry durry, Master!" Quoth beseeched him.

Hastily, Neil barged through the door, dragging Edie with him, then slammed it firmly behind. Trapped in The Dissolution Gallery, Gogus was beside itself with thwarted rage and cartwheeled across the ground. Flinging its body against the door, it hammered and scratched, jumping up to bite the handle with its peg teeth. But it was no use, and after a minute's frantic scrabbling, the carving pressed its snout against the keyhole to bark and shriek.

Suddenly it fell silent, and its ears waggled inquisitively. With a worried yelp, the creature dropped to the ground, slapping its head and jabbering, the expression upon its face a grotesque mask of dread.

"No . . . no . . . no!" it uttered. "No . . . Gogus . . . no."

Through the room the imp scuttled, its voice puling and crying in genuine distress as it scooted into The Egyptian Suite.

* * *

In the corridor outside, Edie Dorkins wriggled free of Neil's restraining arm and rounded on him fiercely. "Gertcha!" she yelled. "Nearly caught it then, I did! Keep your nose out!"

"That thing in there's vicious!" the boy snapped back. "It would've pulled your head off."

"No, it ain't!" the girl shouted, her hands on her hips. "Could've made friends with it then, I could. Lemme back in!"

His fingers closed tightly about the door handle, and Neil shook his head. "No chance," he refused.

"I'll go back another way then," she told him.

"Edie!" he warned. "It'll attack you."

But the child would not listen and walked huffily up the dimly lit corridor, her small shape dwarfed by the huge glass cabinets flanking the walls. "Keep out my way!" the girl called over her shoulder as she reached the first of the gloomy pools between the feeble lights.

Neil gave the nearest case a frustrated kick, and the stuffed bird of paradise it contained wobbled on its branch. "She's determined to get herself killed," the boy muttered.

At his shoulder, the raven turned his gaze from the

retreating girl and stared morosely at the taxidermied specimens surrounding them.

"I can't let her," Neil said, anxiously seeking for a solution. "Quoth, go and fetch Miss Ursula. She's the only one that daft girl listens to. I'll hold her back till she gets here."

The raven nodded his agreement. "'Twill be a pleasure to escape this hall of the gogglesome dead," he cawed, spreading his wings in readiness. But, before he could take to the air, a rhythmic tapping came echoing down the passage and Neil spluttered.

"I know that sound," he whispered.

Quoth jerked his head aside to listen while the slow, measured drumming steadily grew louder, vibrating upon the musty air.

"The imp hath put on boots of iron and advances with snail speed?" he suggested.

His master did not reply, and his fingers slipped from the door handle. "Tick-Tock Jack," he breathed in horror.

Halfway up the long corridor, Edie Dorkins paused to look around her, wondering what caused the insistent knocking.

"Gogus?" she called, peering into the shadows beyond the reach of the overhead lights. Only the tap-tap-tap answered, and all her senses told the girl that this sound had nothing to do with the wooden carving. "Who is it?" the girl demanded.

Neil swallowed nervously. "We've got to get her out of this," he said.

With Quoth flying apprehensively behind him, the boy ran up the passage toward Edie and caught hold of the girl's hand. This time she did not resist. The rapping was very loud now, and perceiving the malevolence behind it, Edie gasped.

"Somethin' bad's gonna happen," she predicted. "I can feel it."

At the end of the corridor, where African shields and tribal weapons decorated the wall, a shadow deeper than those around it began to move and take shape.

"God's blood!" Quoth cried.

Stepping from the darkness ahead, a tall, barrel-girthed figure emerged, tapping his cane against the wall and cackling in a thick, phlegm-drenched voice. Dressed now in a gaudy, dandelion-colored costume emblazoned with large mustard checks, a brown derby jammed on his florid head, and white spats wrapped around his boots, the forbidding form of Jack Timms swaggered into the passage.

His pox-pitted face was smeared with greasepaint. Red dots blobbed the corners of his ratty eyes, and circles of rouge daubed his waxy cheeks. Under his scratched, festering nose, a black, curling mustache had been drawn, and his eyebrows were broad lines of charcoal. But in spite of the showman's makeup and flamboyant carnival clothes, he was as repellent and malignant as Neil had imagined.

"Roll up, roll up!" Tick-Tock cried, pounding his stick on the ground. "Ladies and gentlemen, such a miraculous, mouth-stopping, maceratin', Machiavellian marvel you ain't never seen afore."

Not daring to take their eyes from him, the children backed away cautiously, and Quoth fluffed out his feathers as he hid in his wings.

"If it ain't the little witch," Jack Timms announced, touching the brim of his hat in scornful salutation. "And she done brought some playmates with her this time. That's all to the good. Wouldn't want anyone to miss this dazzly delight."

"You don't scare me!" Edie cried. "Couldn't hurt me last time, and you can't now, neither!"

Tick-Tock's red lips parted, and a repulsive snicker hissed through his blackened teeth. "Old Jack didn't get time to finish before in the workhouse," he told her. "But he will now. The guv'nor done gave him a new Tormentor—one that'll jab the last squeak out of you."

Flourishing his cane in the air, he made a clumsy bow then spread his fat arms wide.

"For your despairin' delectation!" he called. "From all the way out the darkest Congo, wrested from the hands of the heathen and making the second of its four performances . . ."

Reaching to the wall, he unhooked one of the African spears and brandished it tauntingly.

"That can't help yer!" Edie told him.

"Wait!" Neil gasped. "Don't you see what it is?"

The girl looked at the weapon again, and her hand squeezed Neil's tightly as she recognized the rusted blade now fixed to the shaft. "The spear!" she whispered, suddenly daunted as she realized her peril. "The one what killed Veronica."

Tick-Tock chuckled wickedly. "Fancy leavin' this ruddy thing lyin' about fer anyone to pick up," he mocked, reveling in the fear graven upon the children's faces. "Thought you was so safe locked in 'ere, dintcha? Well, not now Jack's let loose. There's nowhere and no time to hide in. Gut you all, he will, and the guv'nor'll be well pleased with him."

"Run!" Neil urged. "As fast as you can!" But the girl was paralyzed with fear. The ancient blade in the evil warder's hands froze Edie's thoughts, and her spirit quailed within her. Miss Veronica's face as she lay dying on Glastonbury Tor, impaled upon that lethal blade, reared in her mind, and she shook her head helplessly.

Clutching his blubbery sides, Jack Timms honked with laughter. "You can't get away this time! You won't reach the perishin' door. There's other things Tick-Tock can use against you. He belongs to this place just as much as you, and it listens to his voice as well as the old harpy's."

"What meaneth the suet-swollen rogue?" Quoth cheeped.

Neil didn't know, but he started to pull Edie down the corridor.

"The spear'll get me," the girl mumbled. "I know it will."

Letting go of her hand, Neil whisked her around. "Only if you let him catch you," he said angrily.

Tap-tap-tap.

The staccato rhythm commenced once more, but this time it was the tip of the rusted spear that beat on the wall, and Jack Timms chuckled to himself.

Hopping from one of Neil's shoulders to the other, Quoth eyed the brutal man and spoke in a quacking, alarm-filled prattle. "Yon scoundrelous cur is not in pursuit. Why doth he not come after?"

A dull thud sounded by Neil's left ear, and the boy glanced sideways. Next to him was a great glass dome filled with a display of stuffed hummingbirds.

"What made that noise?" he asked.

Quoth craned forward to look. "'Tis the brazen-vested sparrows!" he croaked with a degree of relief. "One of their number didst drop from its—"

The raven abruptly broke off, for as he stared, the fallen hummingbird righted itself and beat its tiny wings until they seemed invisible. Up into the large dome it darted, zigzagging through the branches, its long beak drilling against the curving glass.

"Squire Neil!" Quoth began to wail.

Neil and Edie looked at each other. Then, behind them, a web-enshrouded peacock filled the corridor with its ugly, bugling cry. As if that was a signal, the dome was suddenly filled with a frenzy of brilliant, scintillating color as the other hummingbirds flew from their perches to crash against the imprisoning crystal.

"Time's up for you," Jack Timms declaimed. "Jamrach's menagerie and my new Tormentor will see to that."

Edie whirled around. The case opposite was now alive with a flock of flame-feathered parrots who squawked and spread their garish wings. Their screeching cries were immediately taken up by the birds in the adjacent cabinets, and the narrow passageway was drowned in a shrieking, raucous din.

Neil stumbled backward, and with living specimens screaming on each side, his fear intensified. Beyond the parrots and birds of paradise he saw a new, larger movement, and the boy turned to run.

In the primate case, a howler monkey began swinging from its branch. With its lips peeled back over vicious teeth it added its shrill voice to the riotous cacophony. Abruptly, the long-faced baboons who shared the display jerked into life as, further down the corridor, the two spotted hyenas whooped and shrieked, feverishly clawing the sides of their confinement.

Within every cabinet Woden's power, directed by Jack Timms, animated the stuffed specimens, and the cases rocked and juddered as the creatures struggled to break free. Tick-Tock guffawed to see the frightening spectacle. The girl would never escape him.

A tremendous explosion suddenly flooded the passage with shivering fragments of glass as, from the primate case, two large adult baboons came charging. Lowering their maned heads, they yelled at the tops of their bestial voices.

Hearing the crash, Edie glanced back to see the apes dragging heavy branches from their cabinet and lifting them over their heads to smash the glass of their neighbors' confines. The howler monkey came flying after the fleeing children, bounding onto the cases and hurtling across the tops, inciting the occupants to a wild madness with its ghastly shrieking.

Losing his footing in shock, Quoth fell from Neil's shoulder. "The ape!" he cawed. "It chaseth us most hotly."

Along the cabinets the howler pelted after them. Its glass eyes were fixed on the sprinting children, but its lithe legs were the faster. In an instant it had overtaken them. Down the passage it sped, leaping from the cabinets and onto the floor in Neil and Edie's path, barring the way to the landing door.

"Jump over it!" Neil told Edie.

Yet even as they surged forward, the monkey snatched up a vase of dried flowers and hurled it at the nearest case. Another shower of shattered glass erupted into the corridor, and with high, nickering barks, the hyenas vaulted from captivity.

Their fearsome, doglike faces were contorted into murderous snarls, and confronted by this new terror, the children staggered to a halt. With their hump-backs bristling, the dust-coated hyenas prowled toward them, yipping and snapping. The glossy brown paint that covered their quivering lips was cracked and peeling, and one of the ravening creatures had chipped its snout, revealing the yellowing plaster beneath. Yet to them had been given the semblance of life, and they were more horrific and deadly than any animal of flesh and bone.

Neil didn't know what to do. Behind him a third case shattered, and a troop of spider monkeys flooded out, their long, curling tails erect. They swarmed over the displays and smacked the cabinets with their brown, wrinkled hands.

Groaning inside its snowy diorama, the overstuffed walrus gave a pathetic wave of its flippers and attempted to heave itself free, but the movement caused a great rip to crackle along its side, and a torrent of sawdust gushed out. Throwing back its head, the creature bellowed and another tear split across its neck.

Shepherded back up the corridor by the growling hyenas, Neil and Edie had nowhere to run. Jiggling in the air above and flapping his wings dementedly, Quoth looked around to see one more cabinet destroyed. He whined pitifully at the emergence of this new danger.

Screaming in hysterical shrieks, the golden spider monkeys hurtled over the broken cases. They leaped to and fro across the narrow gulf between the flanking displays, and the baboons came lumbering after. On the ground, Neil and Edie were driven back still further. Past the dome of buzzing hummingbirds they were compelled, while over their heads the primates went caterwauling.

Then, as yet unseen by the terrified children, an immense form slinked from the largest of the cabinets. As it left its artificial jungle, a tawny glass eye popped out of its head to go rolling across the floor.

Surrounded suddenly by the host of spider monkeys, Quoth was afflicted by a hail of missiles; sticks, pieces of glass, small stones—anything the creatures could get their hands on was flung at him, and the raven cried out in pain. "Master Neil!" he yelped. "Beware the terror behind thee!"

Tearing his eyes from the advancing hyenas, Neil turned. Stalking toward him and Edie, its powerful shape rippling as it padded through the shadows, was the massive bulk of the Bengal tiger.

A deep, hostile purr issued from its dry throat, and the hapless children huddled close to each other.

Even more terrifying in its advanced decay, the tiger's banded fur seethed with its crawling infestation of moths, and the stitches that held the skin together unraveled with each menacing step. A trail of trickling sawdust leaked from the rupturing wounds, but the strength and might of the animated creature was undeniable.

Then the whiskery jaws gaped open and a rattling roar blared out, to the exulting appreciation of the apes, who screamed and slapped the cabinets in response to goad on their horrific champion. With its remaining eye trained on the children, the tiger swayed from side to side, judging the distance between them, preparing to pounce.

Still standing at the far end of the passage, Jack Timms grinned malevolently. "Just the lad, pussycat," he called. "The little witch is mine."

Snarling, the tiger sprang.

Through the narrow hallway its honey-colored, rotting body flew. A cloud of moths discharged into the air in its wake, and Edie screamed as Neil was wrenched away from her. Huge claws seized the boy's torso as the full weight of the enormous cat battered him to the ground.

There was no time to think. Winded and choking for air as a fine rain of dust poured down onto his face, Neil stared up into the monster's jaws.

Squealing, Edie rushed to his aid, tugging at the tiger's filthy fur, but tufts of hair and hide ripped away in her hand, exposing the bleached bone of the tiger's skull underneath. Then the nightmare lowered its head to snap its teeth around the boy's exposed throat.

"Fie, foul feline!" Quoth crowed, plunging down, his talons outstretched. "Have at thee!"

The raven swooped low, and its claws ripped through the poorly preserved flesh and sliced deep gashes into the mangy skin across the massive snout. Then he soared upward with the second glass eye in his grasp. But no further help could he give, for a monkey's hand flashed out and snatched at the bird's wing. With a dismal yowl, Quoth was yanked from the air and the shrieking apes fell upon him.

Two blind holes now gaped in the tiger's head, and streams of sawdust poured from the empty spaces like a macabre parody of tears. Yet Quoth's attack had only enraged it further, and it was not deterred. Pinned beneath its colossal weight, his nostrils filled with the fetor of moldering skin, Neil saw the awful mouth come lunging down again.

Deep within the horrendous throat he saw the line where the painted plaster ended and the straw and stuffing began. The tiger's fur might have disintegrated, and now the beast was only an animated mass of aged wadding wrapped about a metal armature, but the teeth and claws were just as sharp and powerful as they had always been, and the boy howled helplessly.

Suddenly, instead of the expected death blow, a heap of pulp and sawdust dropped onto the boy's upturned face, filling his open mouth and burying his eyes and nose.

Shouting triumphantly, Edie Dorkins waved her hand, and her pixie hat glittered with green and silver fire in her grasp. In desperation, she had torn the garment that had been knitted with the strands of Destiny from her head. Binding it tightly about her fist, the girl had begun a furious attack on the monstrous beast.

A ghastly hole now yawned in the tiger's head. The savaging jaw hung limply from one side, and one by one, the cruel teeth dropped from its crumbling gums.

Laughing grimly, Edie plunged in for another assault. Onto the tiger's skull she pounded her fist, and where the pixie hat touched, the sparking threads ate into the flesh, dissolving the bone and stuffing beneath. Blow after blow the child hammered upon the enormous head while, above her, the monkeys screeched and smacked themselves in dismay.

Into straw and sawdust the tiger's head collapsed, leaving only a metal prong protruding from the mighty neck, at the end of which a ball of wire mesh twisted furiously on the steel spine.

Below it, Neil Chapman coughed and retched, spitting out the pulverized mulch. But even without its head, the tiger still held him firm, and the terrible claws pierced through his clothes to maul and rend.

Yelling fiercely, Edie began a fresh onslaught, this time driving her small fist deep into the creature's side. But the girl could not keep it up for long. Even as she smashed her sizzling hat against one of the powerful striped legs there came a defiant growl, and before she could whirl around to defend herself, the hyenas launched themselves on top of her.

Squealing, Edie Dorkins was thrown to the ground at the tiger's side. But, as she fell, the pixie hat was flung from her grasp. Burning a blistering path through the air, the gift of the Fates shot out of her reach and lay fizzing with emerald flames upon the floor.

Laughing in high, whinnying voices, the hyenas sniffed and pawed at the girl, but they leaped away when, from above, two hairy arms came grasping.

On either side of the corridor, each sprawled upon the top of a cabinet, two baboons stretched their long arms to her, hooting and grunting at one another. Edie felt the apes' strong fingers close about her arms, and she was hoisted into the air to dangle between the cases.

Chattering and gabbling across the divide, the baboons rose to their feet, lifting the struggling girl still higher. Then they began lumbering up the passageway, swinging Edie between their outstretched limbs, to where Jack Timms was waiting.

In his circus barker's costume, Tick-Tock Jack chuckled vilely, and Edie Dorkins wailed in despair. Moistening his fat lips and relishing his victory, Jack Timms watched the helpless girl being brought to her death. Delighting in the murderous urge that tickled and thrilled him, he lifted the Spear of Longinus and sucked a delicious breath through his crooked teeth. With steady, practiced hands, the agent of Woden brought the rusted blade in line to where he gauged Edie would be thrust upon it and snorted with pleasure.

Her arms felt as if they were being torn from their sockets as the baboons raced and bounced along, and the girl wept when she saw the deadly spear pointing straight at her heart. This was the end. Her thread would leave the web, just as Veronica's had, and

Ursula would have to find another to take her place. All around her the wild beasts' rioting clamor inspired and fed her terror as the lethal blade swept ever closer.

"No!" she cried. "No-o-o!"

Suddenly, the tumultuous uproar escalated as a tremendous crash blasted into the passage and the apes screamed in fury. Unable to drag her eyes from her imminent doom, Edie did not see a milk-white tempest come raging from the landing, hurling down the door and thundering into the corridor behind her.

Through the entrance, trumpeting and baying, its eyes blazing with unquenchable fires, the white stag of Nirinel came charging. Up the narrow way it stampeded, its magnificent head lowered, and sitting in the midst of the glorious branching antlers, yammering at the top of its piggy voice—was Gogus.

Snorting furious challenges, the wondrous beast blasted between the cabinets, and the spider monkeys threw up their hands at the harrowing sight. The stag fiercely tossed its head, which set Gogus jolting wildly as the silver antlers smashed and scraped along the walls above the great glass cases. The monkeys screeched in panic.

Trapped beneath the headless tiger's shredding claws, a bloody rent torn in his side, Neil Chapman felt the ground judder and quake. Rolling his eyes, he saw the gigantic stag's pulverizing hooves come galloping on top of him.

Bouncing up and down in his lofty perch, Gogus seized hold of his mount's right ear and jabbered quickly into it. At the last skull-crushing second, the god of the forests leaped. Over the length of Neil's pinioned body the creature jumped, and with a ferocious backward kick of its hooves, it destroyed the tiger utterly. The headless nightmare was dashed into its sawdust, and Neil was interred in a suffocating pile of pulp and crawling moths.

Overhead the spider monkeys fled, but the stag was too swift, and its antlers came sweeping after them. Shrieking and howling, they were mown down, and their internal wires buckled as their hairy hides flew apart, rent by the silver horns.

The avenging commotion was too much for the baboons that held Edie in their grasp. Screeching, they threw their captive down—to the fury of Jack Timms— and still the momentous stag came rampaging.

His face distorted with fear and anger, Tick-Tock Jack darted forward, lifting the spear above his head. "You'll not cheat me this time!" he fumed.

Wiping the sawdust from his eyes, Neil sat up, wincing from the pain in his side, to see Jack Timms lurch forward with a murderous thrust. Lying on the ground where the apes had thrown her, all Edie Dorkins saw was the rusted blade come slicing down in the fat warder's hands.

Then the harrowing darkness was dispelled by a glimmering light as the largest of the four ancient stags reared above her, and from its perch within the bright antlers, Gogus launched itself at Jack Timms's face.

The horrendous man stumbled backward, with the wooden imp clawing and biting him. The Spear of Longinus fell from his cruel fingers, and the worshipful stag stepped over Edie, planting its hooves protectively around her. Shaking its head, the Lord of the Wild Wood bellowed until the walls shuddered, and the remaining crystal display domes fractured into a thousand diamond splinters.

Peering out through its sturdy legs, the girl watched breathlessly as Tick-Tock Jack recoiled into the shadows, cursing and bawling.

"It's not over!" he yelled. "Next time the reckoning will come!"

Swearing, Jack Timms tore the wooden imp from his face and fled into the gloom, becoming one with the dark. Only dust-swirling shadows remained.

At once, the animated animals that had escaped the stag's decimating blows had the unnatural life ripped out of them. Up on the cabinets, the baboons petrified and toppled where they stood, pitching to the ground where they split apart. The birds ceased beating their wings, and their stuffed bodies went thumping onto the floors of their cases in a snowfall of rainbow feathers.

In the passage, the hyenas gave one last shrill whoop and collapsed, their legs snapping beneath them. Sawdust and stuffing lay heaped in every corner, and on top of the walrus cabinet, in a moraine of deteriorated flesh, there came a movement.

A dismembered paw gave a jerk. Then, abruptly, the mound erupted and pieces of spider monkey scattered everywhere as a black shape burst forth, clacking and squawking.

"'Tis said a drowning man doth *clutch* at straws!" a balking voice cried. "Not perish in the same!"

Half-submerged in papery flesh and hairy decay, Quoth sat up and blinked the dust from his eye.

"Squire Neil!" he wailed suddenly, extricating himself from the tangled armatures that still clung to him. "Art thou harmed?"

Lying on the ground, Neil Chapman stared up the corridor, and alighting with a flurry of dust upon his shoulder, Quoth did the same.

There in the gloom, its creamy coat shimmering under the mesh of light that gleamed from the resplendent silver antlers, the giant stag took three steps back and lowered its head. The amber fires of its eyes were orbs of molten gold now, and Edie's face glowed in their radiance as the splendid beast sank to its knees before her.

A gentle lowing vibrated in the passageway as the stag closed its eyes and bowed in reverence.

"I don't believe it," Neil whispered.

Smiling, Edie Dorkins reached out and stroked the dignified creature's muzzle. Then Gogus came scampering to her side. Chattering happily, the wooden imp tugged the girl's coat then waddled around to pat the stag's shoulders.

"Gogus . . ." it gibbered encouragingly. "Gogus . . . Gogus."

The girl looked at the carving, trying to understand what it was saying to her.

"Gogus . . ." it yapped again, motioning with its hooked claws and waving its stunted arms.

Edie giggled. "You want me to climb up?" she asked in joyous surprise.

The imp nodded vigorously, and from the stag's nostrils a hot blast of snorting agreement gusted about the girl's ankles.

Flicking her hair behind her ears, Edie ducked beneath the glittering antlers and reached up to the powerful neck. Scuttling behind, Gogus grasped the girl around the waist and boosted her up over the firm, muscular shoulders. Falling back, Gogus gave a gruff bark, and the stag rose gracefully from its venerating bow.

Catching her breath, Edie leaned forward as that proud head reared up, and she wrapped her arms around the wide neck in a devoted embrace. Pressing her face into the mass of soft, lustrous fur, she sighed dreamily and inhaled the great animal's rich, musky scent.

Then the tribal shields and spears clattered from the walls as the noble head turned and the stag wheeled about. With a shake of its splendid antlers, the beautiful creature began to walk majestically down the corridor, with Edie riding high on its back and Gogus trotting cheerfully behind. Over the crumbled effigies the stag stepped, its hooves crunching into the lifeless corpses.

"Squire Neil," Quoth urged, "arise before the apparition prances over thee."

Flinching from the pain in his side, the boy obeyed and pressed close to the shattered cabinets to get out of the stag's way. Radiant eyes roved briefly over the disheveled pair as the stately beast marched by, and when Neil gazed into those golden fires, the despairing horror he had experienced was diminished and a blissful peace settled over his soul.

"Where . . . where are you going?" he stammered to Edie.

But enthroned on her august steed, the girl merely held her head higher, too grand at that moment to make any answer as they paraded toward the doorway.

Ambling behind, Gogus grunted contentedly to itself. A shred of dandelion-colored cloth was caught in its teeth, and the imp picked at it with its claws. Through the sawdust and stuffing the carving cantered, kicking up smothering clouds and thrashing them with its tail. When it drew level with Neil, Gogus sniffed and approached him warily, its snout sampling the smell of the boy's shoes.

A disagreeable bark snapped from the imp's wide mouth, and turning up its nose dismissively, it scurried off again. Down the corridor Gogus bounded, pausing only when it reached the hyenas' carcasses. Leaping over them it performed a victorious jig, then hopped from their broken backs to a drift of moldering tiger dust.

With a yammering yell the wooden creature plunged its tail in, foraging until it fished out Edie's pixie hat. Flourishing the green hat behind it like the banner of a conquering army, Gogus jumped into the air, then bolted off after the stag and Edie.

Forgotten in the corridor, Neil and Quoth were left speechless and staring.

* * *

Through the door to the landing the mythic beast strode, and the wooden carving scooted out after. Deliriously happy, Edie Dorkins knew she could never describe her elation as she sat atop that momentous guardian of Nirinel. Through the gleaming fence of its antlers, she saw the second-floor landing of the Wyrd Museum open up around them, and the dim dark fled before their luminous grandeur.

Down the stairs her majestic mount strode, and gradually, with every proud step, a change came over the building.

The striping shadows that streaked across the rising treads deepened when the stag passed. Then, from the surface of the worn carpet, the black bars peeled away and rose steadily into the air. Tall and straight the dark pillars grew, thrusting high into the obscured ceiling until they became the trunks of great trees.

Beneath the stag's hooves the steps quivered from sight, and the carpet disappeared into a steeply sloping hillside. The paneled walls of the Wyrd Museum shrank into the surrounding night while, overhead, a dense forest canopy rustled and creaked in the breeze.

Gabbling in excitement, Gogus sprinted forward, bouncing over the snaking tree roots, frantically beckoning the stag and Edie on.

Pricking through the wooded awning, shafts of cold, clear moonlight speckled the plunging path with pale, pearlescent patches. Down into that variegated province the stag bore Edie, and the child was dappled with a field of soft, silver lights. Like glimmering phantoms they descended still further into the enchantment, until Gogus held up one of its claws. Then, with its arms by its sides, the wooden creature bowed so low that its carved mane brushed against the ground.

"Gogus . . ." came a profound, declaring grunt. "Gogus . . . Gogus." Flicking its tail behind it once more, the imp jumped up and capered forward.

The mighty trees grew thickly around them now, and no moonlight penetrated the strangling growth above. Engulfed in the dark, Edie saw ahead of them a wall of blank, gray mist threading through the forest. Shifting and rippling behind and between the night-clad trees, the solid-seeming vapor formed a chill fence that stretched wide around the fringes of the wood.

Pushing past the low, obstructing branches, the imposing stag forged onward. Haring in front, Gogus hesitated on the brink of that screening fog and twisted its head to make certain the others were following. Then, yapping loudly, the carving dashed into the smoke, and its squat figure vanished from sight.

Biting her lower lip uneasily, Edie Dorkins stared at the mist before her. It was not a natural fog; it clung stickily to the snarled twigs, and Gogus's barks were already lost in its clammy depths.

Yet it was too late to turn back now, and as the stag marched forward, the girl took a deep, apprehensive breath. Into the mist their shapes melted as the vapor closed silently behind them.

CHAPTER 15

PSYCHOMETRY

Still standing among the debris that littered the passageway, Neil waited until the sound of the stag's hooves faded before he relaxed and gazed around him.

"Jack Timms is getting stronger," he said. "At first I could only hear him. Now look what he can do."

Quoth clicked his tongue. "The arts of mine former master doth course through his spectral flesh," he croaked miserably.

"But he isn't a ghost," Neil corrected. "The register said that he disappeared one night, and no one knew what happened to him. Well, we know now—Tick-Tock Jack came here, to this time."

The raven whined morosely. "To all times," he uttered. "The Gallows God hath lost none of His ancient guile. Unto His dark service He didst call this crumpet-faced felon. What better scourge to harry the Spinners of the Wood than he, who knoweth this edifice well—was it not a home unto him? Thus doth the Allfather own a foothold in this murksome lair, and with it He shalt turn the abode of the Loom Maidens against them."

"But how can He?"

"This unglad lodging is an untame beast with many heads," Quoth answered darkly. "The Nornir doth not rule it absolute."

Trudging through the rancid rubble, the boy stepped over the shattered baboons and stared at the rusted spearhead that had fallen from the warder's grasp.

"How could Miss Ursula be so careless to leave this out for Jack Timms to find?"

"The Loom harpies feareth yonder blade," Quoth cawed gently. "The very touch pains them. Yet unless their eyes are constant upon it, there is naught to halt the bloated one from thieving and putting it to mine Master's infernal usage."

"Your Master?"

The bird shook itself and in a fluster amended what he had said. "A thousand pardons, Squire Neil," he clucked profusely. "This mud-brained dolt knows not the blather that doth dribble from his tongue. A slip of speech, no more. Thou art my dearest lord, and there shalt ne'er be another."

"All right," Neil said. "I believe you. But what are we going to do with this?" Bending down to pick up the spear, the boy winced and clutched at his ribs.

"Thou art injured!" Quoth cried, fluttering down to peer at Neil's torn uniform.

Tentatively, Neil brushed the moths and dirt from his clothes, then gingerly pulled the ripped material apart. A vivid red gash ran the length of his side, and he dabbed it delicately.

"It's not deep," he said, inspecting the ugly wound. "Looks worse than it is. At least it'll match the one the Valkyrie gave me."

"Valiant and fearless art thou," Quoth praised him. "A true warrior knight. How favored is this worthless esquire to be blessed with such a master."

"Pack it in," Neil told him as he took the spear in his hands and ran his fingers over it thoughtfully. "We can't let Tick-Tock Jack get his paws on this again," he said firmly.

Gazing around the deserted passage, the raven narrowed his eye. "Nay," he rasped. "He who serveth the Captain of Askar shalt make no return this night."

"You sure?"

"In the very core of mine quills I doth know it to be the truth," Quoth replied earnestly. "The argent deer didst put flight to the varlet, and ever shall it return to confound and throw down his dastard plots."

"Well," Neil began. "Just in case, I think I know the best place for this." Calling for Quoth to fly to his shoulder, the boy strode through the corridor and headed for the landing.

Lingering behind, the raven glowered at the shadows. "Speak not thy seducing lures at me," he whispered to the dark.

"Hurry up!" Neil called to him.

Flicking his tail feathers contemptuously, Quoth took to the air and flew swiftly after his young master.

In The Tiring Salon, working by the light of the candles, Austen Pickering sat at the small table, busily writing in his notebook all that he had witnessed so far that evening.

"But would the society believe me?" he wondered aloud, absently chewing the end of his pen. "Why didn't I think to use the camera? Austen, old lad, you're slipping. Keep it in your pocket at all times from now on."

Returning to his notes, he looked up when the door was pushed open and the caretaker's son came bursting inside.

"Spectacular manifestation!" the ghost hunter cried before Neil could utter a word. "I don't know how to explain it in psychical terms, I really don't, but I wouldn't have missed it for the world. A completely perfect glimpse of the past—this entire room was shunted back four hundred years. What do you think of that?"

"Very glad for you," Neil said with no enthusiasm. "We've seen a few things ourselves." At his shoulder Quoth cawed in doleful agreement, and Mr. Pickering regarded them keenly.

"What's happened?" he asked. "You're both covered in muck, and your jacket's ripped to bits. Been in a fight, lad?"

"It's nothing, really. Had an argument with a tiger, that's all."

The old man looked at him blankly, but Neil shrugged the remark away. "This is what I wanted to show you," he said, placing the rusted spear on the table.

Adjusting his glasses, Austen Pickering peered down at the battered and buckled blade. "Interesting," he muttered. "Is this one of the exhibits?"

"I suppose it is now."

"Let's have a closer inspection then." Leaning across the table, the ghost hunter picked up the spearhead. But a violent shudder jarred the old man's body the instant his fingers came in contact with the flaking metal, and he threw it down again as though it had burned him.

"The blade!" Quoth squawked in alarm. "It stingeth with hornet's venom!"

"Are you all right?" Neil cried.

Mr. Pickering jumped from his seat and paced around the table, waving his fingers in the air as if trying to shake the pain out of them. "Caught me out again," he eventually blustered with a dry chortle. "I'll never get used to the tricks of this place."

"How come it hurt you? I didn't feel a thing when I touched it."

The old man sniffed and studied the spear a moment longer before responding. "Not hurt exactly," he tried to explain. "More a type of psychic shock. Took me by surprise, that's all. It won't happen again. Too receptive, that's my trouble. I'm ready for it now."

Returning to his stool, Mr. Pickering took several deep breaths then closed his eyes and reached out his right hand. Keeping his palm a few inches above the corroded weapon he slowly passed his hand up and down its length, murmuring quietly to himself.

"What are you doing?" Neil whispered.

"I'm going to try an experiment in psychometry," the ghost hunter answered without opening his eyes. "Seeing what I can discover about an object merely by touching it."

"But you're not touching it."

Austen Pickering cleared his throat and opened one eye in irritation. "I was just about to," he stated tersely. Neil grinned apologetically and stood back as the old man resumed the experiment.

"Come on," Mr. Pickering breathed. "Tell old Austen."

Fanning his fingers, he gently laid them on the spear, and the high dome of his forehead creased in concentration. Then, very gradually, his head nodded onto his chest.

"The lumpen oaf hath fallen into a doze," Quoth clucked.

"No," Neil murmured. "I think he's gone into a trance."

Suddenly, the old man drew a sharp breath. "There is power in this," he exclaimed, his eyes still firmly shut. "Great power. It's no ordinary weapon, goes back a long way, it does. For many, many years it was hidden in the dark. I can feel aged hands clasped about it, and a covering of gold and gemstones . . . Wait, there is change and disturbance. I see a high green hill and huge black wings."

Abruptly, Austen Pickering let out a ghastly shriek.

"Valkyrie!" he screeched in a cracked voice that was

not his own. "Listen to their blaring voices. Something's going to happen. Oh, Edith—I'm afraid."

"That was Veronica!" Neil whispered incredulously.

The old man gave a terrified yell and arched his back as though struck from behind. "Edith!" Miss Veronica Webster's anguished voice echoed from his lips. "The spear has done its work."

A long silence ensued as the ghost hunter sat on the small seat, his head wrenched back and his mouth stretched horribly wide.

"Methinks the fellow hath expired," Quoth hissed in Neil's ear.

The boy fidgeted, wondering what he ought to do. Then Mr. Pickering stirred and began again. "Deep into the darkened years and over the rolling seas," he uttered in a hoarse murmur. "Back to where the sun burns hot and parches the wilderness. So long, so far, to when it was forged . . . Ah, there, the time when it was one among thousands. I sense an army—no, a legion of soldiers. Wait, there is lamenting all around, the sun has died. I feel violence—pain!"

The old man convulsed. With his free hand he gripped his side, then threw his head back with such jolting force that his glasses were catapulted from his face.

"Why have you forsaken me?" he screamed.

Hearing those words, Neil swallowed nervously, and on his shoulder Quoth clacked his beak in surprise.

Whimpering and spent, Austen Pickering slumped forward onto the table. The old man's stubby fingers fell away from the tapering blade, and his arm swung heavily down to his side. Then he was still, his head resting on the table and all color drained from his face.

"Mr. Pickering?" Neil ventured. "Mr. Pickering— are you all right?"

Quoth tutted sorrowfully. "Like unto a coffin nail," he said.

Dreading what he might discover, Neil worriedly stepped over to the table and gave the ghost hunter a cautious nudge. "Mr. Pickering?"

To Neil's overwhelming relief the old man groaned and his eyelids opened slowly. Lifting his head from the table he pressed his hand to his face and waited until his labored breaths subsided before uttering a word.

"I never expected that, either," he finally said, his speech thick and heavy. "So strong—almost finished me."

Flapping from his perch, Quoth flew to where the glasses had fallen on the floor and plucked them up in his talons.

"Thank you," the ghost hunter mumbled when the raven dropped them by his elbow. "Dear me, what a trauma." Taking the handkerchief from his pocket, Austen Pickering vigorously wiped the sweating hand that had touched the spearhead, as if attempting to clean it, then returned the glasses to his nose.

Puffing and blowing, the old man stared at the weapon before him and drummed his fingers upon the table.

"How are you feeling?" Neil asked.

Mr. Pickering coughed politely. "Been better," he confessed. "Feel as if I've gone three rounds with a tiger myself. Well, lad, this is a nasty little object, no mistake about that."

Leaning back, he eyed the spear a little longer. "I've never come across so hideous a thing," he said gravely. "Death and ruin crawl all over it. Where did you get it?"

"Jack Timms had it," the boy answered. "We . . . we saw him just before."

The ghost hunter raised his eyebrows, then nodded with understanding. "That makes sense," he declared. "The spear has a positive thirst for blood. It would suit that villain down to the ground."

"That's why I brought it to you," Neil told him. "If you could keep it and guard it, then Tick-Tock won't be able to use it again. You're the only one I can trust."

"I'd best put the wretched object out of harm's way, then," Austen Pickering muttered. "Although will anywhere be safe enough?"

"How do you mean?"

The old man shook his head and, in a solemn, warning voice, said, "I learned a great deal from that unholy relic. But the one thing that sticks out strongest in my mind is this one simple, yet awful, fact: I was wrong, that time when I said you had nothing to fear from the departed. I was going by all the other investigations I've done. This building isn't like them. It's unique, and therein lies the danger."

"What are you saying?"

"Before too long," the ghost hunter murmured as

he pointed at the spear, "this profane bit of goods will be used. I know, I felt it. The murderous appetite will be appeased. Pretty soon that blade will kill again."

In the unsettling hush that followed, Quoth squirmed and pulled his head into his shoulders, while Neil could only look at the rusty spear and wonder. "Do you know . . . who?" he finally managed to utter.

Mr. Pickering shook his head. "Only that it's someone under this roof, that's all I could tell. But it's enough, don't you think?"

"Then Dad's right," the boy said. "We should get out. While we still can."

"Amen to that!" Quoth crowed eagerly.

"I'll get going, then," Neil announced, edging toward the door. "I've got to talk to Dad."

The old man waved him away. "You do that," he called. "Probably a good idea to leave this place far behind."

"What about you?"

"A good general doesn't desert the field," Mr. Pickering answered confidently. "There's still too much to do. I'll be careful, don't worry. Remember, if you need me—I'll be right here."

His thoughts churning, Neil took Quoth out of The Tiring Salon, and Austen Pickering covered the spear with his handkerchief. Then, glancing quickly at his tape recorder, the ghost hunter grumbled in annoyance and snapped his fingers. "I didn't catch any of *that*, either!" he rebuked himself. "Come on, Austen, what are you thinking of?"

* * *

Disturbed by what the old man had told him, Neil tramped down the stairs in silence. On his shoulder, Quoth sought for ways to lighten his master's somber mood, but nothing he could say had any effect, and he sighed wistfully, looking forward to the time when the museum would be only a memory. Away from this place there would be no more visits from Woden, no difficult choices to make.

It was only when they reached the main hallway that Neil was shaken from his thoughts. Stumbling from the stairs, he looked up at the empty wall where the watercolors used to hang and cried out in fear.

Startled, Quoth gazed up at the blank space but could not decipher the clumsy, scrawling letters that he saw written over the paneling.

Neil get out
run away
save your brother
let the children live

"It's insane," the boy breathed fearfully. "Who's doing this?" Dragging his eyes from the fresh graffiti, he glanced around nervously, then pelted through the corridor toward the caretaker's apartment.

A still calm reclaimed the entrance hall, and even when a tall, elegant figure came gliding down the stairs, the uncanny peace was not disturbed.

With her hand on the banister, Miss Ursula Webster looked up at the childish scribbling, and a curious, distracted expression flitted across her fine features. Surveying the broken picture frames that littered the hall, an idiotic giggle suddenly sprang from her lips. Clapping her hands, she roughly dragged her fingers through her hair, snapping the fastenings of the jet beads that twined about her curls. In a cascading deluge, the glittering stones rattled and spilled down the staircase.

A foolish smile spread over her finely boned face as she watched their clattering progress. Then her arched brows twitched, and the childish grin was banished from her mouth. Clasping her hands together, Miss Ursula pressed them to her chin, and her slender frame shook uncontrollably, wracked with dreading despair.

"Is it with me already?" she implored the shadows, her eyes wet and glistening. "Is the thief come to burgle my sanity? Give me one more day. That's all I need. One more day—I beg you."

Standing there, her silhouette trembling, the eldest of the Fates shed resentful tears, and the Wyrd Museum eased itself into another long night.

CHAPTER 16

MEMORY RECALLED

True to his word, Brian Chapman had packed all of Neil's belongings into boxes by the time his frightened son returned. The boy readily agreed to their leaving, but only if the raven could accompany them. The discussion was abandoned, however, the moment the caretaker noticed the wound on Neil's side.

Naturally, his son did not want to tell him how it had happened, but Brian was so insistent that in the end he was compelled to. To Neil's amazement, his father believed him. When the shallow gash was cleaned and bandaged, Brian urged the boy to get a decent night's rest, promising that they would decide about Quoth in the morning.

Having elected to remain outside the apartment this night, thereby avoiding any midnight expulsion,

Quoth made himself comfortable in The Fossil Room. Constructing a nest from Austen Pickering's socks, he sat in one of the ghost hunter's suitcases and fluffed out his feathers. Woden could hunt for the raven outside the building all night and he would not find him. The second visitation would not occur, and no forfeit would be paid.

Now, his bald head lolling to the side, his throat making faint piping sighs, Quoth drew his wings a little closer about him and dozed fitfully. Into the exquisite, welcoming embrace of sleep the raven eventually tumbled, sinking far into that voluptuous balm of oblivion where his malformed mind drifted over a sluggish sea.

He was snug within his woolen nest, and the concerns and fears of the day lifted from his face as tootling snores gruntled from his beak.

With creeping stealth, a delicious warmth infiltrated The Fossil Room, encroaching purposefully over the cabinets, until at last it inched over the slumbering Quoth. The bird mumbled with languorous contentment as he became immersed in luscious summer heat.

Basking luxuriantly, he buried his head a little deeper into his wing, for sunlight was beating down on him and excited voices were mingled with the neighing of horses. Brighter the day blazed and Quoth stirred with reluctance. Yawning and stretching his wings, the raven lazily clicked his tongue, then with a great effort of will, he forced his eye open.

The fierce intensity of the noonday sun seared his

sight, and the unexpected shock of it caused him to dive back into his wings once more. But when the impossibility of the situation dawned on him, Quoth made a peculiar gobbling cry and parted his feathers to peep out.

Gone were the cabinets and counters of The Fossil Room—in fact, the entire building had disappeared. A beautiful cerulean sky stretched all the way to the wooded horizon, and before him, Quoth beheld a verdant meadow foaming and frothing with golden buttercups and intense scarlet poppies. Yet this luxuriant Eden, where the seeding grasses swayed in the refreshing, perfumed breeze, was disturbed by a strident clapping.

Turning his head, the raven gave a honk of astonishment. "Yea," he murmured hoarsely, "beauty is soonest blasted."

As far as his eye could see, utterly filling the field behind him, were row upon row of high, round tents. Above each one a dark green banner fluttered, and it was this flapping clamor that had so assailed his hearing.

Doubting his senses, Quoth blinked and shook his head, but the incredible scene was still there when he looked again. It was the encampment of an immense army, and he was sitting just within the defensive ditch and ramparts that had been dug around it.

Rising on his scrawny legs, Quoth discovered that the sock nest and suitcase had also vanished, and he had been sleeping inside an empty saddlebag. Stumbling from the capacious leather bunk, he gaped at the spectacle before him.

All about these canvas shelters tall spears, glaives, and cruel-looking halberds porcupined from the ground, and herds of horses stamped their hooves while esquires and grooms attended them. Every tent was dyed a uniform dark red, but above each entrance, the badge of the lord or knight within was clearly visible on a wide standard. Into the distance the assembled host stretched, and a forgotten memory kindled in the raven's addled brain.

"'Tis said that much abides behind what the fool thinketh," he muttered. "Yet what of thee, Quoth? What gold grains doth glint in the dry bed of thy parched reason? Assuredly this site is known unto thee. Verily, hither thou hast sported awhiles."

Ransacking his wits, the raven endeavored to remember. Surely he had been here before? This was a place he recognized. But, try as he might, he could not recollect either its name or his reason for being here. Aggravated with himself and impatient to learn more, he strutted cautiously through the grass, passing between the outlying defenses, fascinated by everything he encountered.

The preparations for a great battle were certainly under way, for carefully tended weapons were everywhere he looked. Quivers were stuffed with green-feathered arrows, crossbows strung, shields and armor brightly polished, and coats of burnished mail gleamed in the dazzling sun. On all sides voices shouted as foot soldiers were drilled and made ready. From somewhere in the camp the clanging chime of a smithy rang out, tolling like the bell of war, and among the din came the noise of the grinding wheel where long knives were being sharpened. Astonished, Quoth marveled at how familiar and comforting he found the music of those sounds.

Pressing on, he espied countless horses already geared in blood-colored pageantry, and over the tops of the cone-shaped awnings, behind the streaming pennons, reared the forbidding engines of war.

Siege towers, with their high scaffolds stark and black against the pure blue heavens, were coupled with the lofty arms of enormous catapults that cast long, sinister shadows over the crowded field. Seeing those mighty structures, Quoth cooed in delight and almost took to the air to swoop about their beloved shapes.

Abruptly the raven upbraided himself, questioning where these emotions were stemming from. Yet he could not interrogate and examine his thoughts for long, for at that moment a shadow approached, and he scuttled quickly beneath a wagon loaded with supplies.

A stranger dressed in peasant attire strode by, and without realizing he was doing it, Quoth adopted a scornful sneer. "Base-born churl!" he spat as the serf strode by.

As soon as the derisive words were out of his beak, Quoth clamped it shut and staggered farther into the wagon's shade, flabbergasted by his disdainful outburst. Fortunately the man had not heard him, but Quoth's face clouded over.

"What sorceries conspire in thy moribund faculties?" he berated himself. "No vain lordling art thou."

When he was certain the coast was clear, the raven scampered out of hiding and proceeded with the utmost care, winding his way through the encampment.

Ducking under guide ropes and hiding in overturned buckets, he made painful progress, but the wish to see more of this camp had become a consuming desire within him. With every prudent step, images and memories long discarded were dredged from the slurried sump of his mind, and soon he began to predict what lay ahead: what standard he could expect to see waving above the tent around the next corner, and how many horses belonged to which knight.

Intrigued by this singular foreknowledge, Quoth realized that his path was not an aimless wandering, that there was a purpose and direction to his waddling gait. By some instinct foreign to him, he was heading for somewhere in particular, and the deeper he stole into the army's base, the closer he drew toward the place where a pall of oily smoke rose into the sky.

"Yet whither this mooncalf is bound, he knoweth not," he told himself.

Into the very heart of the encampment he now advanced, where the tents were larger than any he had yet encountered and the armor richly embellished with precious metal set with shining gems.

As he skirted around each one, the names of their noble occupiers popped unbidden into his mind, and an indistinct fear began to gnaw at him.

"What gawk's errand be this?" he gabbled faintly. "'Tis said the fool's heart lieth in his tongue. Yea, in thy case, thine feet also." Engrossed in the confusion of his thoughts, the raven neglected to look where he was going, and before he could stop himself, he blundered over a large, steel-clad foot.

With a squawk of dismay, Quoth toppled head over tail. When he glanced upward, he was horrified to see a fierce-looking, red-bearded knight glaring down at him. The imposing, powerfully built man was in the middle of being dressed for battle. His young esquire was fastening his armor about him, and he too stared down at the floundering bird, who quacked and bleated ridiculously as he wriggled to right himself.

At once the knight's countenance grew stern. His gauntleted hand waved to his attendant, who hurriedly passed him his glittering sword. Grasping the weapon tightly, the man raised it, and feeling the shadow fall upon him, Quoth plowed his beak into the soil and covered his head with his wings, expecting to be sliced in two.

"My lord," a gravel voice proclaimed. "What is thy bidding?"

More astonished to find that he was still alive, Quoth lifted his head and spat out the clump of earth he had inadvertently gouged from the ground.

"Command me, Lord Memory," the voice spoke again. "What counsel would you give a loyal subject?"

Rolling backward, the raven suddenly realized that the knight was addressing him, and to his bewilderment, Quoth discovered that the intimidating, half-armored man was now kneeling in subjugation before his prostrate and absurd self.

"My sword is always in your service," the knight

vowed. "Tell me, will our forces win the day? 'Tis rumored that the ravens who die not have the gift of foresight. Speak unto me—will I fight valiantly and with honor?"

Quoth picked himself up and struggled for something to say. But the words never came for, in that one blinding moment, he understood and remembered all. Without a second thought for the knight's concerns, the raven leaped away from him and charged around the tent until his sparkling eye saw that which he had come to find.

There, in the center of the vast encampment, was the wide clearing he knew would be there, and standing before a great bonfire, casting herbs into its heart, was a tall, sable-cloaked man wearing a silver helm over his long, flaxen hair.

"Mine Captain!" the bird cried in exultation. "Mine most honored Master! To thee, mine Lord, to thee!"

Into the air the raven raced, sweeping high above the crowded tents and rippling banners until the clearing appeared as a wide circle below him. Then, with a crowing yell of jubilation, he plummeted down in a whirling spiral.

Through his feathers the hot, funneling air rushed, and as he dived swiftly down, blasting through the climbing column of black smoke that coiled up from the burning wood, a dramatic change transfigured the scraggy-looking bird. All that was Quoth, and all that he would later become, was cast away.

Over his bald scalp, sleek black plumage appeared. The ragged primaries of his wings became elegant and lustrous once more, and in the shriveled socket of his dead eye there now glittered a bright and cunning intelligence.

Below him on the ground, the young figure of Woden, with a second raven perched on his cloaked shoulder, raised his eyes to the dark, invigorated speck that came zooming from the rising reek of the flames and smiled in greeting.

"Hail, Memory!" he called as the raven wheeled above him to alight expertly upon his vacant shoulder. "We did wonder what had become of you, your brother and I."

The other raven gave an acknowledging croak. "Great wast thy carousing this ender night, brother mine," he chided. "Doubtless some ditch didst thou find for thy roosting?"

Regarding him with his restored vision, Memory emitted a scornful cackle. "'Tis better to be envied than pitied, O Thought, most ardent and solemn sibling. What drear revels didst thy stale humor nullify?"

"Thou wouldst make a mock of this day of high import!" his brother rasped accusingly. "Afore the cockcrow I didst rise, and here art thou, come belated and dilatory, past the hour of shortest shadow."

Memory snorted. "Best late ripe and bear, than early bloom and blast," he cawed.

"Peace, my friends," their master intervened. "I will not hear your grudges this day. Come, Thought, forgive your brother. Last night there was cause for the feasting. There are still some hours till dusk, and then to a bitter contest do we ride. Resent not the pleasures of our loyal forces; for many they will prove their last."

Thought hunched his wings and bowed his flat head before Woden's rugged face. "Allfather," he spoke in a less harsh tone, "forgive thy lieutenant. He is beset with doubt and portent this day."

"Is it possible you harbor misgivings as to the outcome of the battle?" his master asked. "Every omen is with us."

The raven shifted uneasily. "And yet," he began, "who hath measured the strength of the witches in yonder wood? 'Tis many years since the daughters of Askar didst ride from the fray when their mother fell before the ogres of the first frost. What forces are theirs to wield now?"

"Only the descendants of those who would not heed my summons," Woden told him. "The rag-taggle company of those still loyal to the Royal House. Have faith in my wisdom, Thought. Did I not hang upon Yggdrasill? Did I not attain godhead? Against me the Nornir will fall and the end of their tyranny will come to pass. Man will be free to choose his own destiny once again and no more will we be compelled to dance to Urdr's tune. Her Loom will be thrown down and the webs of Fate burned in the fires."

Stepping aside, the spurs on his boots jangling with the brisk movement, Woden turned to where an immense wooden framework reared above the clearing.

"You know that our own loom shall be strung when dusk falls," he uttered grimly. "The crimson weft will be made."

Amused at his brother's concerns, Memory hissed with cruel mirth. "In truth, this is no place for old women!" he mocked. "To the slop houses with thee, Thought. Go aid them in their pot washings. Or perchance the picking of daisies is more to thine palate?"

Flinging himself into the air, Memory shot toward the great structure of his master's incomplete loom, and his high, rejoicing laughter could be heard all across the vast camp. "Who couldst withstand the Gallows God?" he boasted, returning to the sable-covered shoulder. "This night the Twelve shalt fly at the vanguard of our army. Against them there is no defense, no salvation."

Woden smiled indulgently and tickled his faithful adviser under his beak. "Be not over harsh with your brother," he said. "It is his lot to consider all chances."

Bowing stiffly, Thought said, "To do otherwise wouldst be to serve thee false."

"I know it. Yet in this you worry over much. Already I have summoned the dread spirits of the *Valkyrja,* and when their unclean shadows sully the gloaming sky, then shall we take up our arms and ride."

Puffing out his chest, Memory let loose a horrible, vaunting laugh. "At the forepart of their number shalt I be!" he bragged. "Much doth I crave to witness the ruin of Urdr and her reviled sisters. What right have they to spin the Cloth of Doom? To the Captain of Askar, the living God, that high office ought have gone. To see the *Valkyrja* claw and rend most bloodily doth my heart yearn. Let the crimson weft be spun with the entrails of the Nornir, and may it flow free with their gore."

"So be it," Thought concluded, contemplating the fierce flames of the bonfire before them. "This night The Cessation is come."

Woden stroked his forked beard and, with a tinge of regret in his voice, added, "No other road is left to us now. The new age of freedom must dawn with the morrow. The burdening yoke of Fate must be lifted, and peace everlasting will stretch over the lands."

"I wilt cavort and jape in the Loom Maidens' gizzards," Memory swore excitedly. "Their bloods shalt I guzzle like unto wine."

His master drew a hand over his dark eyes. "Would that it was not so," he murmured. "There was one amongst those three to whom my heart did turn. A victory this battle will prove, but no triumph."

Thought shot his brother a reproachful glance, then said to their lord, "'Tis time. The flames of war hath been fed and thy warriors await thy commands."

"I know it," Woden said. Drawing his sword from its jewel-encrusted scabbard, he pointed it at the bonfire. A blinding blend of sunlight and flame shone over the gleaming steel until it looked as if the blade of righteousness burned in his hand, and all the knights who stood about the clearing cried out in wonder.

"Hear me now!" he called to the surrounding knights. "Go among your men and spur them to great deeds. I will be with them, and they must know no fear. Though the terror of the Twelve be above, they must not shrink nor cower. The reign of the ruling Fates has ended, and by our valor this night all our futures we will forge anew."

Memory listened to his master's inspiring words with a wicked expression on his sharp, ugly face, and he rocked to and fro on the sable perch, delighting in the rousing oration. His sharp, piercing eyes could see the hope and hunger for victory enliven the faces of the encircling knights, and he dreamed of the glorious moment when the loathsome sisters who lurked in the enchanted wood would be defeated.

With equal rapture, Thought harkened to Woden's intoxicating speech, but his attention was focused on the speaker rather than the assembled host. His darting eyes looked long and penetratingly at this more-than-man who had reared himself and his brother from their flightless infancy and bestowed on them the gift of language.

Toward this one campaign his master had directed all his efforts and squandered much of his power. To summon the *Valkyrja* from the darkness and enslave them to his bidding had cost him dearly, and the raven could not help but ponder on what might happen should this desperate contest fail. What then for the Allfather?

Whatever the consequence, he and Memory would be there in the aftermath to give their counsel and their unfaltering devotion. The Twelve obeyed Woden through black wizardry, but the two ravens were enslaved to him by love alone.

With a resounding cheer from the surrounding nobles the Captain finished his address, and they brandished their swords in salute before leaving to obey his will.

"Now, my friends," Woden began, turning to each of his advisers. "In these remaining hours do what is needed. Though I have faith in their loyalty, my knights might not be able to kindle the hearts of their troops to the same degree that I do in them."

Memory nodded wisely. "A little wind feedeth the flames," he declared. "Too much puts it out."

"Just so," his master said. "Be then my eyes and ears about the camp. Fly among the foot soldiers and common men, and be certain that they are steady in their resolve. No man must shrink from the conflict ahead. Where there is revolt, quell it. Where there is doubt, turn it. Where courage is wanting, inflame with hero's words. Go now, my beloveds, and return ere the sun sets and the first shrieks of the *Valkyrja* split the sky."

From his shoulders the ravens flew, and the sun gleamed over their wings as they climbed high over the camp to look down upon its sprawling vastness. To the eastern rim of the curving landscape an immeasurable forest reached into the horizon, and as one, they turned their glance to that trackless and suffocating realm.

There, in the unbounded, unexplored wildness, the last surviving root of the World-Tree reared from the earth. Beneath its titanic, arching shape the enemies of Woden made their abode and measured the threads of every living thing. But tonight it would change. The Twelve would seek out the Nornir, and Woden would claim his rightful place as Lord of the World.

"Brother!" Thought screeched in the lofty airs. "At the first trumpet of war we shalt meet on the plain and fly together into battle!"

Memory tossed his head and squawked shrilly. "Together, brother mine," he promised, "we shall put an end to the Witches of the Wood."

"Till the horn sounds, then!" Thought cried.

Gliding on the wind, the ravens hovered for a moment, letting the tips of their wings touch. The lights in their eyes spoke more to one another than all their shrewd, artful words ever could. Then down they flew, one taking the southern tip of the encampment while the other raced to the north.

Throughout the rest of the afternoon, Memory flitted among the tents and the men preparing for war. With his vainglorious words he encouraged them, and with the compelling force of his will he instilled his own lust for mastery and conquest in their hearts. The raven's spirit blazed with an infectious excitement. Never had he been so deliriously happy. This would be the crowning day of them all, and henceforth every song would sing of the Nornir's ruin and of intrepid deeds done in his master's name.

From company to company he darted, the power of his skillful speech fueling the murderous cravings and stressing the holy nature of their task. He even spoke to the horses, croaking in their ears, instructing them to race bold and true into the dark and pathless wood.

Into every mind he sowed his malevolent seed of hate and vengeance. By the time he had finished, the central bonfire had fallen in on itself, and the troops were massed on the field outside the earthen ramparts of the camp, facing the dark, forbidding wood.

Never had such an army been assembled. Their spears were like an opposing forest of thorns, and their shields reflected the fiery sunset like a huge, shimmering lake. Looming high over the tall gleaming helms, the siege towers were hitched to horses and the primed catapults strained at their taut, creaking ropes.

A column of mounted knights, four rows deep and two leagues long, was at the forefront of the host. Before them, sitting on a coal-black stallion, his fair hair blowing in the breeze, was Woden. Every face was turned toward the sword he held high over his head. Over its mirrored surface the evening sun sank in a sea of boiling blood, and a deathly calm descended as each man waited. Only the snorting and stamping of the horses disturbed the eerie quiet, while the multitude listened for the ones who would bring about their victory.

Then, high above the twilight world there blasted a chilling screech, and the horses reared, rolling their eyes in terror. A fearful murmur rifled through the troops as they turned their heads, and there, up in the darkening heavens, they beheld twelve abhorrent, winged shapes.

"Now is the moment come!" Woden yelled, brandishing his sword. "The Valkyries are here!"

Over the deserted encampment Memory raced. In the distance he could see the twelve horrors racketing rapidly through the sky, and he cursed himself for lingering too long in search of carrion. Already his brother was circling above their master, looking for him, and soon the heralds would sound their trumpets and the charge would commence.

Beating his wings furiously, the raven tore over the central clearing, then wheeled about and stared down curiously. The bonfire had disappeared, and in its place a tent now stood. Yet, unlike the others, this was dark green in color and from its open entrance a thread of white mist was curling.

"What devilment is this?" he squawked. "No artful threat nor black chance must harry this high moment of renown."

Raging with curiosity and wrath, he dived down— spinning about the tent until finally alighting upon the ground before the entrance. Narrowing his leery eyes, Memory glared into the dark interior from which the pale smoke flowed.

"Who dares hazard the plots of mine Master?" he demanded. "What witchery brings thee hence?"

No answer came from the tent, and the raven hopped a little closer. "No disruption to this grand hour shalt I brook," he announced. "Show thyself. I, Memory, command it!"

Over the clearing, massive wings came gusting, and scale-ribbed talons came reaching from the enfolding night to wrench the framework of the unfinished loom from the ground.

"So goeth Shrieker and Biter!" the raven cried. "Hither I shalt be detained no more. What manner of craven cur lurketh within this weirdsome hut?" Impatient to join his brother at their lord's side, Memory barged furiously into the entrance, and the shrouding mist quickly wrapped itself around him.

Sitting in the middle of the tent, wreathed around with vapor, sat a hooded figure, the deep shadows beneath its cowl making it impossible to see the features within.

"Declare thyself, recreant knave!" Memory demanded. "Or atop the traitor's scaffold thy hidden head shalt be spiked."

Only a silken laugh issued from the hood, and this enraged the raven even more. From outside the tent there came a tremendous tumult of trumpets, and Memory whisked about.

"The charge begins!" he shrieked. "I durst not tarry. When the feasting and revels are over this night, I vow to return and make a settlement of this. Look to thine neck!"

Unfurling his wings, the bird prepared to fly out of the tent, but the hooded figure raised a withered hand, and in a voice like cream, he called, "Hold, my friend."

At once Memory fell back into the curdling fog and stared at the stranger intently. Outside, the clearing faded into the growing dark, and the uproar of the storming army dwindled into silence.

"You did not miss the battle, dearest of counselors," the figure told him. "You were there before all others and you were the first to fall. Do you not know me?"

Confused and afraid, Memory edged through the smoke. "Master?" he called.

The Woden of the later years nodded and reached out to caress his cherished pet.

"Explain unto me, O Lord!" the raven begged. "Unravel this riddle!"

The faint laughter sounded again. "It is but a dream, my love," the Gallows God murmured. "The remembrance of this day has been my gift to you as you lay sleeping. It is an insight into all that you were, so you may recall the fealty and trust we shared. I do not believe that you have forgotten that which you once held so dear."

"But I hath not!" Memory protested. "Where is mine brother—he will tell thee!"

The bony fingers stroked the bird beneath the beak. When he next spoke, his tone was grave. "Alas, yes," Woden muttered. "Your future self has spurned me. This will be the second time I ask you to rejoin with me. Now that you know the import of my ambition— to depose the ruling Fates—will you not aid me in their destruction? Much do I ache for your company once more."

"And most willing shalt it be given!" the raven crowed, flinging himself on his master's mercy. "To thee only doth my allegiance lie."

"You speak as the fledgling I once reared," Woden said sadly. "But when this dream is done and you awake, then must you choose. Will it be Quoth of the garbled brain, or my lieutenant?"

Reaching up with his wings, Memory answered in a firm and resolute voice that sent the smoke scattering before him. "To the one who fed me, to the one who taught me, to the one who inspired me—I shalt be loyal. To this life he wert reared. Memory will be reborn, and when he sits at the shoulder of the

Allfather the daughters of Askar shall fall! This is my judgment, so mote it be!"

"Then return to your waking," Woden told him. "And decide well, for this time if you reject my offer the forfeit must be paid. You will not go unpunished. What I once gave to you freely I shall most certainly snatch away."

Lifting into the air, Memory threw back his sleek head and cackled with murderous laughter. "Fear not, my Master!" he hooted. "The choice is ready made! Ever thy creature shalt I be."

"Go then," the cloaked figure instructed. "Prove to me your unbounded love. Awaken!"

* * *

In the darkness of The Fossil Room, a black shape stirred within the nest of socks, and a feathery head reared over the edge of the suitcase. Shaking himself, the raven gazed groggily about him, recalling all that had happened during the vivid, conjured dream.

And in that rousing instant, his heart was determined.

Brushing his wings over his scalp, the bird discovered it to be bald once more, and his left eye was again shriveled and blind in the socket. But Quoth did not care. This was the life he had resolved upon. To be the faithful companion of Squire Neil was all he desired to be, and that prospect filled him with rejoicing.

As Memory did before him, Quoth cast back his comical head and hooted with mirth. Then he sighed deeply, wondering what their new life together away from the museum would be like. Yet, when he voiced his thoughts, only a harsh, croaking caw blared from his beak.

Alarmed and distraught, the raven squawked and crowed again. But it was no use—he could not form the words. Collapsing into a dismal heap, he bleated sorrowfully and hung his head as he finally understood.

With large tears streaming down his face and trickling into his scraggy plumage, Quoth knew then that this was his penance. To punish him for rejection a second time, Woden had taken away the raven's gift of speech.

Sobbing wretchedly, his voice a cacophony of ugly, braying cries, Quoth wept well into the night.

CHAPTER 17

WITHIN THE GIRDLING MIST

The candles in The Tiring Salon had all burned themselves out. With his copy of *Billy Bunter* lying open on the table, his head drooped over his chest, Austen Pickering was fast asleep. The miniature spools of the cassette in the tape recorder revolved idly, nearly winding to the end of their allotted length.

Through the spacious expanse of that long gallery a darkened figure moved, and only the headless mannequins were witness to its shambling presence. Icy vapor steamed from chill lips, and wheezing sighs turned the already wintry air even colder. Over the bare floorboards, where once the Webster sisters had danced, heavy footsteps dragged, shuffling close to where the ghost hunter sat slumbering peacefully.

A bleak shadow fell over Mr. Pickering's face, and his flesh crawled in the supreme cold as the slow, stumbling figure crept nearer to stand over him. The old man's glasses, askew on his nose, misted over when the intruder's reflection appeared in the lenses.

From pallid blue lips a hollow moan issued, and Austen Pickering grumbled in his sleep. "No such thing as ectoplasm," he burbled through chattering teeth. "All muslin and mummery."

With a loud click, the tape machine came to the end of the cassette and snapped itself off. Suddenly the ghost hunter jolted awake and he shivered, huffing on his freezing hands.

Reaching for the flashlight, he flashed it around the room, but his glasses were frosted over, and he spent a couple of minutes breathing hard on them before he could see.

On edge, he swept the bright beam about the gallery, the playful attitudes of the mannequins alarming in the swiftly moving spotlight. But The Tiring Salon was now empty.

The old man shone the light on his watch and scribbled down the time. "Twenty to five," he said aloud. "Hell's bells, it's cold."

Bringing the light to bear on the thermometer, Mr. Pickering gave an exclamation of surprise. "Minus four!" he breathed. "Time for another coffee, I reckon."

Unscrewing the lid of the thermos, the old man absently rewound the tape machine several minutes and replayed what had been recorded. The hiss of an empty room blasted out into the gallery, but when he was sipping his coffee and warming his hands on the plastic cup, Mr. Pickering heard those labored, trawling footsteps as they first came into the room.

Looking up from his steaming beverage, he shone the flashlight over to where the noises on the tape suggested the mysterious person had entered. Holding his breath, he listened as the machine continued. Closer the painful-sounding, hobbling footfalls had come, and in spite of the bitter cold, a speckling perspiration glistened over the old man's forehead.

The recorded sounds came over to where he was sitting, and he flashed the light about the room once more, just to double-check he was alone. Then, over the speaker he heard a deathly murmur, and the steps dragged away toward the nearby door.

Again the machine ran out of tape, and the button clicked off.

Rising from the seat, the ghost hunter hurried across the room and looked out onto the landing. He shone the flashlight into the darkness, but there was no one out there, and he quickly pointed the beam down the stairwell.

"In the name of all that is good, can I help you?" he called to the emptiness below. "I only want to help, you know that."

But no answer came, and after several minutes the old man returned to The Tiring Salon to finish his coffee, for the cold was unbearable. Picking up his cup once more, he raised it to his lips, then spluttered and spat out the contents.

"Freezing!" he cried.

With the flashlight trembling in his hand, Mr. Pickering left the table and wandered through the room, hastening toward the other doorways. Crouching before them, he inspected the ghost strings he had stretched across the entrances. The cords were snapped and lying in brittle, rigid strands upon the ground, like raw and shattered spaghetti.

Taking a fragment of the broken string in his fingers, he examined it, muttering in disbelief, "Frozen solid. How on earth? . . ."

His breath escaping in great clouds from his mouth, the old man rose and his brow knotted with concern. "There's got to be a reason," he said. "But what?"

* * *

Edie Dorkins huddled into her grubby coat. The cold of the blanketing fog permeated right into the marrow of her bones. Her hair hung wet and limp about her shoulders, and dewdrops of moisture dangled from her small, pointed nose.

Seated astride the majestic stag, she pushed deeper into the confounding gray nothingness around them. In that colorless void, the girl could see only the beast's silver antlers glimmering before her. When she turned her head, her eyes ached as they searched the mist, so now she concentrated on the way ahead and held tightly onto her steed's neck.

Into her lungs the dampness seeped, and Edie coughed, burying her face into the collar of her coat as she wondered how far they had journeyed. Then, very slowly, the obliterating fog was diluted. Vague images of trees could be glimpsed on either side, and from somewhere in front she heard the muted chattering of Gogus.

"Gotta be nearly there," she told herself.

The mist became thinner, shredding and parting until only flimsy, floating skeins were snagged within the twisted twigs of the surrounding wood. From that shadowy realm the milk-white stag emerged, and Edie leaned forward and peered between its antlers, glad that the choking vapor had been left behind.

A beautiful, cloudless summer's night was upon the forest, filling the hollows with deep midnight blues. Still leading the way was the squat, bow-legged figure of Gogus. Trundling happily along, the pixie hat waving on its tail, the wooden carving glanced back and nodded frenetically, pointing with its claws through the trees ahead.

Lifting her gaze, Edie followed the imp's excited directions and clapped her hands in wonder. There, through the breaking trees, was a wide clearing where the figures of three women stood waiting for them.

Rearing its head, the stag lowed a bass greeting that Edie could feel trembling through its immense frame. In answer, the tallest of the three figures raised a hand in welcome.

Gogus hopped from the last vestige of the screening wood, lingering on the grassy slopes beyond until Edie and her mount were also free of the trees. High on the stag's back, Edie Dorkins opened her eyes wide in marveling amazement.

Fringed by the dark, fog-filled forest, they were standing on a gently dipping, bowl-shaped bank. Moonlight and starfire danced in the air, and the myriad lights glittered and shone over the calm, still surface of the wide pool that filled the center of that great open space.

Yet over that sparkling water, rising high into the crystal night and straddling the breadth of the clearing, was a colossal shape. Casting its delicious shade across the encircling woodland was a vast, arching bulk, the fallen trunk of an impossibly gigantic ash tree.

"Nirinel," Edie mouthed.

Here, then, was the last surviving root of Yggdrasill, as it had been in the first ages of the world, before time and drought had withered its supreme form. Mightier in every respect did this earlier incarnation appear to the young girl's worshipping eyes. The diseased and rotting mass she had seen in the underground chamber of the Wyrd Museum, that staled the air with sweet stagnation and putrid decay, was but a wraith of its former splendor. That future aspect of this heavenly spectacle was black and blighted, with bark flaking from its ulcerous, atrophied size in wasted, withered cankers.

But the consummate creation that towered over that paradise was unsurpassed in its vigor and sylvan beauty. The smooth rind of its callow bark shimmered with a pale light of its own, and across its broad, spanning length, green glowing shoots were clothed in a lush, verdant foliage.

An intoxicating aroma of perfumed blossoms and fragrant flowers infused the clean, sumptuous air with their heady scents, and Edie inhaled it greedily.

The idyllic place revived and restored her. In that blessed glade, where the immortals dwelt, she could feel the forces of vibrant life pulsing and quickening in her own blood. The young girl was aware of the movement in every leaf, of the sap coursing through each stem, even the slow increase of the stretching grasses. Yet uppermost in her thoughts and perceptions, impressing itself absolutely above all else, was the constant surge of divine existence that flourished throughout the incredible length and girth of Nirinel.

It would have taken a lifetime for Edie to grow bored with that peerless sight, but a cheering voice was calling her, and she forced herself to look away.

"Edith," came the warm, hailing cry. "We have waited long for you."

Dressed in simple, flowing robes, the three women beckoned to her, and down upon the sloping ground Gogus bowed until its snout was buried in the grass.

"Norn . . . Norn . . ." he growled reverently.

With a dignified gait, the regal stag held its head high and sauntered around the edge of the pool.

Chuckling in elation, Edie stared at the figures as she drew close. Just like Nirinel, so too were they, the Webster sisters, the younger versions of themselves.

Clad in a garment of the deepest black was a youthful Miss Ursula—Urdr, as she was known in that time. The silvery-white curls that Edie knew had been replaced with chestnut tresses, covered by a filmy, web-patterned veil that was bound onto her head by a circlet of gold.

The woman possessed all of her later elegance. The delicate modeling of the features was the same, but the stern lines, so bitterly etched into that older face, were nowhere to be found in this smiling countenance. Only a controlled determination and resolve could be discerned in her lovely eyes, and when she put out her hand to the stag's velvety muzzle, the creature sank to its knees in obeisance before her.

"We thank you, Durath," she said, and the amber jewels of the stag's eyes burned adoringly at her.

At Urdr's side, the one clad in a modest gown of plain red cloth stepped forward and held out her hands to help the child down.

"Come, daughter," Skuld beamed, but with none of the toothy grin that would one day be hers. "My joy at your visit is the greatest. Let me aid you."

With her strong arms the woman lifted Edie from the stag's back and set her on the grass. Laughing, the child stared up at the figure who would one day turn into Celandine. Surely that ruddy, wrinkled face that always resembled a goofy walnut could never have belonged to this striking and beautiful woman. Only the braids that dangled down her back gave Edie any clue. But instead of scorched corn, this maiden's hair was the color of the spring sun on early flowers, and the starlight that brimmed in the clearing was caught and meshed within its brilliant luster.

"There is so much I want to show and share with you, my little one," she sighed, clasping her arms about the girl in an aching embrace. "I thought you would never get here."

Squeezed tightly, Edie threw her arms around Skuld's neck, then looked over her shoulder to where the third sister stood.

Hanging back from the others, shy of the great stag, was the loveliest of all the daughters of Askar.

She appeared just as Edie remembered her upon Glastonbury Tor. A slender, white-robed woman with eyes of delicate cornflower blue set in an ivory complexion. Pulling away from Skuld, the child walked haltingly over to her.

"Veronica!" she cried, her eyes stinging with the tears that threatened to appear. "Veronica!"

The youngest of the Fates shook her head gravely, and the locks of her long raven-black hair rippled behind her. "I am Verdandi," she corrected in a gentle voice.

Sobbing, Edie threw herself into the woman's arms and hugged her desperately. Watching them, a look of disapproval appeared on Urdr's face.

"Edith!" she called. "You must not bring your grief with you into this place. That is for the future alone to hear."

The girl sniffed and dragged her sleeve across her nose as she untangled herself from Verdandi's arms.

"You do understand?" Urdr asked. "This is a different age, where there are sorrows enough without you fetching in the burden of others as yet untold."

Swallowing the uncomfortable lump in her throat, Edie nodded but clasped Verdandi's hand and gripped it earnestly. "I won't say nothin'," she promised.

Urdr smiled, then returned her attention to the stag that was still kneeling upon the ground. "Arise, Durath. What would we do without you to guard us?"

Kissing Verdandi's hand, Edie left her side as the Lord of the Wild Wood snorted and reared up, its antlers gleaming in the night like forks of frozen lightning.

"Twice he done saved me now," the girl declared as she stroked the powerful flanks.

"Durath is one of the four sentinels of Nirinel," Urdr told her. "The noblest blood that ever flowed courses through his veins and those of his three brothers. Long before the city of Askar was built about the World-Tree they were here, guarding and waiting. It was they who took the Loom from the palace courtyard, and they who led we three from the battle with the Frost Giants when our mother was slain."

Gazing up into the beast's amber eyes she rested her head against its neck, and the stag breathed gently upon her. "In your time, Edith," she began softly, "the four guardians have been dead for many years. But Durath will always return when called upon, to protect Nirinel and those who tend it."

"Were it Gogus what called him?" the girl asked.

Pricking its ears up at the mention of its name, the imp came scampering through Durath's legs. "Gogus . . . Gogus . . ." it jabbered.

"It was," Urdr replied, stooping to pat the carving's head. "You know how the Loom of Destiny came to be created, don't you, Edith?"

The girl laced her fingers behind her back and rocked on her toes, as if preparing to recite a lesson at school. "Frost Giant chopped a branch off the World-Tree," she proclaimed. "The Loom was made out of it."

"Just so," Urdr assented, removing the pixie hat from the imp's tail and placing it back on the child's head. "Yet from the same timbers of that bough our mother, the queen, commanded the woodwrights of Askar to fashion a figure within the decoration of the Loom. When it was complete, she spoke words of enchantment over it."

"So Gogus is part of the Loom!" the girl cried.

"It is the Pedagogus," Urdr instructed her. "Our tutor. It was the wood urchin who taught us how to string the Loom of Destiny and weave the mists to keep out our enemies. It is the slave and spirit of the tapestry, our companion—the Fates' familiar."

Hearing this, the imp danced dementedly around them, with its claws in the air and yammering at the top of its gurgling voice. "Gogus . . . Loom . . . Gogus . . . Spin . . . Gogus . . . Gogus . . . Gogus! . . ."

Capering up to each of the sisters, the carving took their hands and whirled a wild jig about them, tumbling over the grass and leaping into the air until it stood before Urdr once more and made another deep bow.

"There will come a time," Urdr said, and now her voice was grave and solemn, "a point of torment and conflict, when the last surviving remnant of Yggdrasill and those who tend it face their direst threat and peril. In that hour the Pedagogus will come forth to give what aid it may. This the Queen of Askar foretold."

"That's why it kept turnin' up!" the girl exclaimed. "It were warnin' us about that Tick-Tock. It tried to stop us goin' through the doors. It knew what was behind 'em. Clever Gogus!"

Still doubled over in the low bow, the carving humbly wrung its claws and gave a bashful gurgle.

Urdr inclined her head. "Yes," she agreed. "The

prophecy tells us that the Pedagogus shall be the saving of us. At the final hour it is the wood urchin who will defeat the lords of the ice and dark, though all that we hold dear may lie in ruin about it."

Gogus hid its large face in the hooked claws and gabbled to itself in embarrassment.

"But that is yet many, many ages hence from this blessed time," Urdr said. "Come, Edith, the moment you have yearned for, since you first heard of its existence, has arrived at last. Let us show you that which chains us all to this place, the harp upon which the tune of our lives is played, wherein all our fates and fortunes are strung—the Loom of Destiny."

With Gogus leading them, Urdr and her sisters turned to skirt around the edge of the pool. Unable to stop the grin flashing across her face, Edie followed. Over the grassy banks they made their way, while Skuld told the girl of the eagles that roosted high upon Nirinel's curving summit and of the undine who dwelt in the deep regions of the sacred spring.

Devouring each word, Edie listened voraciously, but although the magnitude of the last root reared in grandeur before her, the child's eyes were drawn more often to the silent figure of Verdandi who walked beside them.

Gogus scampered into the luminous shade that shone beneath the immense, bridging structure, barking eagerly, and Edie soon noticed that a different light was flickering ahead. As they rounded Nirinel's obscuring bulk, a livid emerald and silver gleam welled up to flood out over the flower-freckled sward.

Upon Edie's head, the tinsel strands knitted into her pixie hat crackled with white flame in response. Seeing the girl's excitement, Skuld put her arms around her shoulders.

"It's the light of the tapestry that shines," she told her. "When we reach it, you shall see an ever-moving vision of life and loveliness. The tale of the world thus far is woven into its fabric. The Cloth of Doom is a ravishing, ensnaring sight, Edith."

Her heart in her mouth, Edie Dorkins bit her lip as they traversed the remaining distance. The captivating rays were brighter now, and where she walked, the land was steeped in their resplendent beams. The grass beneath her feet glowed with a scintillating viridity, and the nearby water was like a vessel of turquoise glass through which a beryl sun was bursting.

Not far now, Gogus was already somersaulting impatiently in front, its stunted form caught in the fulminating glare. Holding her breath, Edie stepped forward and raised her eyes as the glory of the Loom blasted upon her.

The sight was blinding. Throwing her hand to her face, the girl squinted, glimpsing only a vague, tall shape. Then, before her vision could adjust and without warning, the ground shook under her.

At once Gogus growled and sprang back along the bank, yapping fearfully. A tremendous bellow erupted across the pool, and Edie whirled around.

"What's happening?" Skuld cried. "Urdr!"

Again the earth shuddered, and the surface of the water was whipped into foam-capped waves that rode up the grassy slopes and sloshed over Edie's feet.

"Durath!" Urdr shouted. "Look—Durath!"

All eyes turned to the stag at the far side of the clearing, and each caught her breath at what she saw. Rearing up on its hind legs, the largest of the four guardians of Nirinel pawed the empty air, as though attempting to fend off some invisible threat. Hideous, baying shrieks trumpeted from its jaws, and even at that distance they could see its amber eyes blazing and rolling in terror.

"He is in pain!" Verdandi yelled. "We are attacked!"

"We must go to him!" Urdr called, running over the bank. "Quickly, my sisters. Hurry, Edith!"

The beast's terrible cries were shrill with fear. When its mighty hooves pounded the ground, even the immeasurable height of Nirinel quivered, and the birds who nested over its huge dimensions sent up a distressed screeching. Yet, in the midst of that discord, above the dreadful call of the tormented stag, Edie could hear the dull chiming of metal upon stone.

Splashing through the crashing waves, the girl could see that Gogus had already reached Durath and was darting under the trouncing hooves, yammering and barking, trying to calm the beast. But the stag could not be appeased and tossed its great, silver-crowned head, recoiling as though unseen forces struck and battered against it.

Into this horrible scene Urdr and her sisters ran, and they too raised their hands to calm the god of the forest. Over the buckling slopes the suffering creature stumbled, kicking its legs in the air as it whinnied and screamed.

The Fates were powerless to help, and Durath blundered into them, driven down the bank by the hidden, hammering blows.

"How can this be?" Skuld wept. "Who can do this?"

"Is it Jack?" Edie wailed. "Is it him?"

Above her, the stag's face was streaked with panic, and agonized tears poured from the blazing eyes that flicked hopelessly from side to side. "Help him!" Edie shouted, staring up into that tortured visage.

Trying to avoid the heedless, shielding kicks, Urdr dashed forward. But in the anguish of its madness, Durath threw her down and the antlers raked and tore the turbulent night.

The ominous, ringing clangs were louder now, and the discordant, metallic din drowned out the high, skirling cries. Rolling from under the glancing hooves, Urdr rounded on Edie and gripped her arms urgently.

"Something awful is happening in your time, Edith!" she told her. "This danger—it comes from the museum. Return at once. Whatever it is must be stopped. Quickly—before it is too late! For Durath's sake!"

With the stag's thunderous shrieks and the unrelenting, jarring riot knifing into her mind, Edie felt Gogus's wooden claws grip her hands, and she was dragged toward the forest.

"Go!" Urdr demanded.

Snatching one brief glance behind her, Edie's last sight of that hallowed place was filled with the image of the stag as it reared and bucked.

"Veronica!" the child bawled in confusion. "Come

with me!" But the scene was torn from her eyes as the wooden imp spurred her on into the waiting trees.

"Gogus! . . ." it jabbered at her. "Go . . . Save . . . Stop!"

Through the forest fringe the carving hastily pulled and propelled her until the wall of mist reared before them. With a final anxious yelp, Gogus pushed Edie into the fog. Stumbling forward, unable to stop herself, the girl was engulfed by the cold, cloying vapor, and the stag's horrific bellowing was stifled from her ears. Yet even in the supernatural mist, that strident noise of striking metal could still be heard echoing through the midnight woodland.

"Urdr!" Edie called in vain. "Urdr!"

But there was nothing. Alone in the dense blindness, Edie Dorkins tore between the trees as fast as her young legs could carry her. Back to her own time and the Wyrd Museum she raced, and every lurching step brought that clanging menace ever closer.

CHAPTER 18

DESECRATION

Neil Chapman was awakened by the cold and by the unhappy moans of his younger brother, who shivered at his side. Clambering from the bed, the boy swiftly slipped into his clothes, dragging on as many layers as possible before venturing into the living room.

"What's happened to the heating?" he asked.

Sitting on the sofa, with stubble bristling and darkening his face, Neil's father was staring out the window. He made no answer.

Sighing, the boy made his way to the kitchen and picked up the kettle. However, when he turned on the tap, no water gushed out.

"Dad?" he called. "I think the pipes are frozen."

Slotting a couple of slices of bread into the toaster, he waited for an answer.

"Did you hear me?" he called again. "I said there's

no water. Have you packed all of Josh's clean clothes? He'll need some today."

Brian stirred lethargically. "It's freezing out there," he muttered.

"It's freezing in here!" Neil said, returning to the living room with his breakfast.

"Look at the icicles," his father told him. "They're hanging over the window like bars. There must be nearly an inch of ice covering the glass."

Neil looked at his father instead. "Are you all right?" he asked in concern.

"I'm cold, son."

Crunching his toast, the boy eyed him crossly. "Well, if we're going to drive up to Scotland today you'd best get changed. Did you sleep in those clothes? Dad—you're starting to smell."

His father cleared his throat and ran his gaze over the cardboard boxes crowded on the sofa. "Josh's things are in one of these," he said abstractedly. "I'll get him dressed and we can start loading the van."

Finishing his gobbled breakfast, Neil moved to the door. "I'm just going to check on Quoth," he began. "He is coming with us, isn't he?"

A vacant expression had established itself on Brian's face. "Quoth?" he asked.

"The raven."

"I don't know what your auntie will say."

"I'm not leaving without him," Neil stated firmly.

The caretaker ran his fingers through his unkempt, greasy hair. "All right, " he relented. "The mangy bird can come too, but if we catch anything from it . . ."

"If you don't wash soon, it'll be Quoth who'll have

to worry about catching something from you."

Disturbed by his father's appearance but leaving him to attend to Josh, Neil hurried out of the apartment. His father had always looked rather like a startled scarecrow, but over the past few days he had become extremely seedy. Perhaps the stress and the pressure of the Wyrd Museum had been too much for him, thought Neil, but one thing was certain—Brian Chapman was not himself.

In The Fossil Room, Quoth was still roosting in the suitcase when the boy entered. "Morning," Neil greeted him.

Not raising his head, the raven cawed miserably.

"How was it out here?" Neil asked. "You didn't see anything else, did you? I didn't, and no more creepy messages, thank goodness."

Another faint, dejected croak came from the bird's beak, and Neil stroked him affectionately. "Hey," he muttered, "you're not sulking because you couldn't stay with me again last night, are you? Don't worry, we're leaving here this morning. You're coming to Auntie Marion's with us."

With his finger under the bird's beak, Neil gently tilted Quoth's head until he could see the one bead-like eye.

"Quoth?" he began. "What's the matter? I thought you wanted to get out of here. Have you changed your mind?"

The raven shook his head.

"Then what is it?"

Quoth sniffed, then rose from the sock nest upon wobbling legs. Taking a hesitant breath, he stared up at his master and let loose a dissonant, clacking squawk.

Neil drew away in surprise. "What's happened?" he cried. "Why don't you say something?"

Giving one last, inconsolable croak, the raven threw himself down and buried his face in his wings, weeping loudly.

"Hush," Neil told him. He slid his fingers underneath the bird's sobbing body to lift him from the suitcase and hold him to his chest. "You . . . you can't talk, can you?" he guessed.

Pressed into the warm wool of the boy's sweater, Quoth shuddered, and Neil cuddled him all the more.

"But how?" Neil asked. "Are you ill? Is there anything I can do?"

The raven could only weep in reply, and his wings dangled limply from his shoulders.

Neil didn't know what to say or how to comfort him. "There, now," he uttered, feeling completely inadequate. "It doesn't matter. I'll help you, you know I will."

A loud tapping suddenly came echoing through the galleries, and Neil looked up quickly.

"Jack Timms!" he whispered.

In his arms Quoth cocked his head, then shook it vehemently. The noise was different from the deliberate taunting of Tick-Tock's Tormentor. This was an intense and hurried hammering, and Neil felt the tension that had cramped his insides relax.

"It's not him," he said gratefully. "But what is it?"

Still cradling Quoth in his arms, the boy wandered through the collections, and the fierce hammering gradually grew louder.

It was only when they came to the main entrance hall that they discovered the answer. There, with the large oaken door swung wide, was Austen Pickering. He was kneeling before the steps outside, a hammer and chisel in his gloved hands.

The base of the tiled steps was already shattered, and the old man was so absorbed in hacking away at the stone beneath that he wasn't aware of the boy's presence for several minutes.

"What are you doing?" Neil eventually shouted above the racket.

Giving the chisel one more whack, the ghost hunter glanced up and waved the hammer at him.

"Ah!" he cried. "Hope I didn't disturb you. It is rather early, I know, but I simply had to put this theory to the test. I found your father's tool bag in one of the galleries and didn't think he'd mind me borrowing it."

"What theory?" Neil asked, placing Quoth upon the ledge of the ticket window.

Austen Pickering lumbered to his feet, flexing first his legs and then his back. "Never known it to be so cold," he declared. "Dropped to minus seven inside the museum, you know. Makes holding a metal chisel difficult work. Tried it without my gloves at first and nearly lost the top layer of skin."

Breathing hard, he leaned against the bronze statue at the side of the entrance, which had grown a beard of ice overnight, and wearily wiped his face.

"You've made a mess there," Neil remarked, looking at the steps. "They're wrecked. The Websters'll freak out."

"I don't see why," the old man replied defensively. "That cantankerous woman said I could more or less do what I wanted."

"She didn't mean this, though."

Mr. Pickering looked appealingly at Quoth. "Haven't you got anything pithy to add?" he asked.

The raven gave a mournful cheep. "He can't talk," Neil explained sadly. "I don't know how or why. He just can't."

"Then the cat did get his tongue," the ghost hunter lamented. "What a tragedy. Perhaps it'll mend."

Quoth made a peculiar mewing sound and Neil hurriedly changed the subject. "So why are you smashing the steps up?"

Austen Pickering polished his spectacles. "Ever seen a horseshoe nailed above a door?" he began.

"For luck, isn't it?"

"Not exactly. A horseshoe is made of iron, and that keeps the witches and other sundry evils at bay. You'll often find them over doorways in remote country areas where old superstitions still linger."

"But there aren't any horseshoes here," Neil countered, "and the only witches are inside."

The old man held up a silencing hand. "But it wasn't always horseshoes," he continued. "And it wasn't always *over* the door where the talisman or charm was kept. In many cases, some unfortunate animal, most commonly a cat, was buried alive under the threshold, or stuffed up the chimney so that its spirit would keep the night-roaming demons away."

"You think there's a dead cat under there?" Neil asked.

Clearing the chipped rubble from the fissure he had already made around the steps, Austen Pickering began to hack away at them once more. "It would make sense for there to be something," he shouted above the din. "This is a very old building, and it might solve all our problems."

"How do you mean?"

"Well," the old man said, "what if there were the remains of some poor creature under here, and what if, just like everything else in this cockeyed place, they're not doing what they should be? What if, instead of stopping things from coming in, they're preventing things from escaping? No wonder this building's jammed full to the rafters—the souls of the poor departed can't get out."

Neil and Quoth watched him for a while longer, until the cement that held the steps in place was completely chiseled away. Mr. Pickering clapped his gloves together in satisfaction.

"Will you give me a hand here, lad?" he asked. "If we could just shift this block out of the way, I'll be that much closer."

Jumping out of the museum to help him, Neil knelt on the freezing pavement of the alleyway. Fluttering from the ticket counter, Quoth alighted on the topmost step.

"When I count to three," the ghost hunter said, "you put your shoulder against that side there and shove, while I heave and pull at this end. Now—one, two, *three!*"

There was a grinding of stone as the steps grated over the ground. Quoth hopped up and down, cawing his encouragement to both his master and Austen Pickering. It was arduous work, but at last the three-tiered block was shifted, and a blank rectangle of sandstone was revealed in the space where the steps had been.

"More chiseling," Mr. Pickering declared.

"I'll help if you like," Neil offered. "But I can't be long. Dad'll be wondering where I am."

The old man handed him the tools. "Of course," he said. "You're going today, and who can blame you? Still, if this works I might be going sooner than I thought myself."

Wrapping his hands in the sleeves of his sweater to protect his fingers from the intense cold of the chisel, Neil started striking the stone. The early morning rang to his incessant blows.

Upon the steps, Quoth turned his gaze from his young master and looked up at the grim fortress of the Wyrd Museum. A sparse scattering of snow drifted from the cold sky, and against the bright, speckled heavens, the jagged outline of that ancient building was stark and bleak. Locked within a wintry grasp, the museum was trimmed with huge icicles that stabbed from the gutters like crystal stalactites, spiking from every ledge and sill. Hoary frost peppered and painted the bricks, while thick barriers of ice obscured the windows. Above the entrance, the gilded, scrolling sign was encrusted with a serrated, glacial shell.

Scratching his beak against the wall, Quoth thought that the entrance to the museum resembled a huge, screaming mouth, with the sign a white and drooping mustache above it.

"Done!" Neil said abruptly, and the raven regarded him with pride. The sandstone had been fairly easy to splinter, and clearing the chunks away, the boy and Mr. Pickering uncovered the black earth beneath.

"Got to be down there," the ghost hunter breathed. "I know it." He foraged inside the tool bag and brought out a builder's trowel—the most suitable implement he could find—then sliced at the soil with its triangular blade.

"Frozen solid," he grumbled. "No matter, I'll manage."

Grunting at the effort, he chopped and clawed, but after five minutes' back-aching toil he had only created a shallow scrape in the ground.

"Is there another one of those?" Neil wondered, rummaging in the bag. "I'll give you a hand."

Making do with a paint scraper, the boy drove it into the soil and the work progressed. "What are you going to do with the cat's bones if you find any?" Neil asked.

"Disturbing them will be enough," Mr. Pickering replied confidently. "All we have to do is move them, and their power over this place is extinguished forever. I'll be able to do my work without hindrance, and the poor wretches trapped in this museum might stand a chance of peace at long last."

Listening to their words, Quoth clicked his beak thoughtfully as a growing sense of unease arose within him. His master and the old man had succeeded in turning the scrape into a trench, and the more the raven considered their actions, the more uncertain he became. A forbidding doubt had surfaced in his mind and, shaking his wings, he gave a warning croak.

Neither Neil nor the ghost hunter heard, so Quoth cawed a little louder.

"You hungry?" Neil asked, turning his head to the squawking bird. "Won't be much longer, I promise."

Quoth stamped his scaly feet, maddened at the frustration of not being able to make himself understood.

"Wait!" Mr. Pickering cried excitedly. "I think . . . yes! I've found something."

As the trowel tore through the soil, there came a hollow knock where the blade struck against bone, and Quoth took to the air to fly about their heads.

"What's got into you?" Neil cried.

The raven landed on his shoulder and stared anxiously down the hole, into which Mr. Pickering's hands were already reaching.

"It's a skull!" the old man announced. "Far too big for a cat—or a dog either, for that matter . . . Horse or a cow, maybe? If I can just get it out . . ."

Within the Wyrd Museum, Miss Ursula Webster came hastening down the stairs, her gaunt face a picture of anger and fear.

"Stop that!" she called, plunging toward the hall. "How dare you! You have no conception of the damage you're causing!"

Immediately, Neil jumped to his feet. "Mr. Pickering!" he said urgently. "Wait a minute!"

But the ghost hunter was far too engrossed in fishing his discovery from the hole to pay any attention.

"*Please!*" the boy insisted.

"Leave it alone!" Miss Ursula screamed, fleeing the stairs and running toward the entrance. "You will bring ruin on us all, you stupid, stupid man!"

Dashing to the doorway, she stood upon the threshold and glared down, but it was too late.

From the trench, Austen Pickering lifted his newfound treasure. Shaking in her distress, the old woman clutched the sculpted bronze figure at her side.

"Simpleminded fool!" she raged in a broken voice. "What have you done to us all?"

Behind her, the hidden mechanism that opened the way to the subterranean chambers whirred and clicked. Up from the depths and out of the past Edie Dorkins came racing.

"Ursula!" the girl called feverishly. "All that clangin'—did you hear it? Poor Durath, he was hurtin' real bad! . . ."

The eldest of the Fates revolved slowly to look at her and, with a shake of her head, moved aside. Shocked at the sight that met her eyes, Edie covered her mouth with her hands and gasped. For there, looking up at them in consternation and bewildered at their reaction, was Austen Pickering. In his hands he held the skull of a large and mighty stag.

"Durath!" Edie choked, her voice smothered by her fingers. "I weren't fast enough."

Turning a face of stone upon the ghost hunter, Miss Ursula glowered at him in contempt and took the skull from his grasp. Her lips pressed white, she placed a trembling hand on the splintered bones where, in ages past, she had stroked a warm, velvet muzzle. Her eyes glistened wetly.

"You have desecrated the grave of the museum's greatest protector!" she told Mr. Pickering with terrible solemnity. "You have violated his memory and rendered his power useless. Never can he return now to defend us. If you had set out with our destruction in mind, you could not have afflicted us with a more grievous injury. What madness is in you?"

Abashed by her words, Austen Pickering swallowed and stammered an apology. "I . . . I thought I was . . . I had a theory, you see."

"Thanks to you we are left without our principal guardian," Miss Ursula stormed. "Do you comprehend what that means? The forces awakening in this place are growing beyond my control—and now there is nothing we can do to halt them."

"You mean Jack Timms?" Neil ventured.

"I mean everything!" the old woman snapped. "We are all at risk—each one. Any aspect of the museum may be turned against us without fear of challenge."

Returning to the hallway, Miss Ursula caressed the skull in her hands and glanced fearfully around her. "My plans are now awry," she muttered to Edie. "What hope can there be? Woden has wormed His way in, and through His agent He will do all He can to destroy us. The game has turned more deadly than I anticipated. Against Durath none could stand, but we are without his protection now."

Her young face scrunched with sorrow, the girl stared into the soil-filled holes of Durath's eye sockets as Miss Ursula set the skull upon the table.

"We must prepare ourselves," the old woman said sternly. "Before night falls we must be ready."

Pointing a damning finger at the ghost hunter, she summoned him and Neil Chapman back indoors. "There is much to be done!" she commanded. "Because of your incompetent, bungling interference you have made this place perilous to all. I say to you now, abandon your amateurish investigations and concentrate your efforts in The Separate Collection."

The oaken door closed behind him.

Mr. Pickering frowned and shook his head. "Can't," he declined. "I'm not ready for that room yet. Besides, it would spoil my schedule. I've mapped out a careful timetable of . . ."

"Your schedule!" Miss Ursula retaliated. "Can it be you still do not understand? By this profane act, you have granted the very worst elements of my museum a liberty that places us all in jeopardy. There is no governing them now. The only arsenal we possess, with which we may hope to defend ourselves, lies within The Separate Collection."

"But my work!" the old man spluttered.

"Your work be hanged!" she retorted, her eyes shining in her temper. "It is irrelevant. Would you tinker and toy with the dead while the living are slaughtered?"

"Don't exaggerate. So far—"

Snatching up a gauntlet from the broken armor that littered the floor, Miss Ursula cast it across the room, where it hit the paneling with a tremendous crash.

"Are you being deliberately obtuse?" she shrieked. "How can I make it any plainer? This evening, when darkness falls, this building will become a battlefield—

a treacherous, evil place. No one must walk alone in its galleries and corridors. Whatever any of you have experienced thus far will be nothing compared with the horrors that we will all undoubtedly be compelled to face."

Austen Pickering fumbled with his fingers. "Very well," he said. "I'll do what I can."

"Miss Webster!" Neil interrupted. "We won't be staying. Dad, Josh, Quoth, and me—we're leaving today."

The old woman turned on him. "Then you had best depart at once," she snorted, the suggestion of a smile lifting the corners of her mouth. "Go now, while you are able, while the museum still permits it."

"You don't mind?"

"Go, stay—it matters not," she replied archly. "Your petty family is unimportant. What care I if you remain or run?"

Stung by her harsh words the boy spun around, and with the raven cawing faintly in his ear, he made his way back to the caretaker's apartment.

"You're a cruel old woman," Austen Pickering berated her.

Miss Ursula crossed back to the stairs. "I am what my fortune made me," she answered gravely. "I have no time for delicacies of feeling and the etiquette of the outside world. There is too much at stake here to indulge in such ephemeral refinement—far too much."

And, sweeping her gown behind her, she ascended the stairs, with Edie and the ghost hunter following in her wake.

* * *

"Right," said Brian Chapman when his son returned. "Josh is all wrapped up and ready to go. Take some of these things and we'll start loading the van."

From the stack of boxes and garbage bags piled in the living room, Brian passed the smallest carrier to Josh while Neil grabbed a large cardboard box.

"Won't be happy till we're on the highway and this awful hole is way behind us," their father ranted. "I'll open the back door, and we can leave through the yard."

Stomping into the kitchen, the gawky man twisted the handle, but the door wouldn't open.

"It's not locked," he mumbled in puzzlement, giving it another tug. "What's the matter with it?"

Scowling and pinching the bridge of his nose, Brian Chapman gripped the handle fiercely and heaved with all his strength. But it was as if the door had been nailed into the frame. Though it juddered and rattled when he kicked and beat his fists against it, the barrier would not budge.

"What's wrong?" Neil asked.

"Can't move the ruddy thing," his father replied in disbelief. "Like it's glued or something."

Putting the box down, Neil ran to help him, but their exertions were in vain.

"Don't understand it," Brian murmured. "Think it's iced up?"

"I'm not sure," Neil answered, and a horrible dread clutched at his stomach. "Let's go through the front. That door's all right."

Through the collections they went, with Quoth flying after them, until they reached the deserted hallway. Brian Chapman pulled impatiently at the oaken entrance door.

"It won't budge, either," he marveled. "What's going on here?"

Nothing they could do would open the door even a chink, and watching them wrestle, Quoth let out an unhappy, rattling moan. But his master was not defeated yet.

"The windows!" Neil cried, running into The Roman Gallery. "They're big enough to climb through!"

Frantically, he tested the latches on each of the square Georgian windows, but they too were frozen to their frames. "They're jammed shut!" the boy exclaimed, a note of desperation creeping into his voice.

Brian and Neil tried every window without success, then they hurried into The Neolithic Collection and tried there.

"We can't get out," Neil breathed in a horrified whisper, the truth of their predicament sinking in. "We're trapped. The museum won't let us go."

"Nonsense!" his father declared quickly, rejecting the alarming notion. "Well, there's only one thing to do."

"What?"

"I'm going to smash the glass," Brian announced. Removing one of his shoes, the caretaker tapped the heel against the nearest pane.

"You'll have to do it harder than that," Neil told him.

Brian cast him a harassed glance, then swung his arm back and brought the shoe crashing into the window. There was a shattering of impacted glass, but no glittering shards fell to the floor. Only a fractured white star radiated out over the window. Brian darted forward, incredulous.

Gingerly, he ran his fingers over the cracked square, but every piece of ruptured glass was held firmly in place by the thick ice that smothered the outside. Incensed and afraid, the man pounded the window, but no amount of hammering could break through.

"It's sealed us in," Neil murmured again, shuffling backward. "Dad, we can't get out."

With a thud, the shoe fell from his father's hand, and Brian Chapman staggered from the window, his bristled face ashen and scared. "I won't believe it," he warbled. "I can't."

"The sooner you do, the better it will be for us all," a terse voice broke in. "You are needed elsewhere. There is no time for this."

Standing in the entrance to The Roman Gallery, Miss Ursula Webster watched them, her features set and severe.

"You knew this would happen!" Neil accused her. "Haven't we done enough for you already? When are you going to leave us alone?"

"I suspected this might occur," she conceded, "but it is not of my ordering. The museum can be a jealous and covetous creature. Yet I do wish you would make up your mind, Maggot. One moment you cannot bear the prospect of returning to your former, monotonous existence. Then, as soon as the first flags of danger unfurl, you protest."

Entering the room's unforgiving wintry light, Miss

Ursula considered them with glittering eyes. When she resumed speaking, her voice was darker and threatening.

"I warned you, this has become a dangerous place. It has been reigned and shackled for millennia, and the hazards can only increase now that it is unfettered and the sentinel is no longer capable of patrolling the corridors. That is why tonight we must all assemble in The Separate Collection."

Brian waved his arms emphatically. "Not a chance!" he exploded. "We're going to get out of here."

"The enemy of my sisters and me is the guiding will behind this rebellion," Miss Ursula declaimed, "and through His agent the museum is being controlled. Once this building has set its mind upon what it wants, there are few powers in this world capable of denying it. Certainly nothing you possess. Though you try all day, you will not be able to escape, and only then, when the dark descends, shall you realize how foolish you have been. The time you ought to have spent preparing and arming yourself you will have squandered."

"You don't frighten me!" the caretaker warned her.

"Then you are more ignorant and idiotic than I ever envisaged," she replied. "Listen to your son, Mr. Chapman; he will tell you. There is no secure haven down here. Only in The Separate Collection with us will you be safe, and even that is not guaranteed. Should you retreat into your apartment, you will discover to your cost that it is no refuge. The untame, ravaging hosts will come and seek you out, and in the morning, you will all be dead."

"I think we should listen to her," Neil advised his father. Standing on the windowsill, staring at the impenetrable ice that coated the glass, Quoth nodded his bald head, croaking in ready agreement.

"How long for?" Brian muttered. "How long are we to be prisoners in here?"

Miss Ursula showed her discolored teeth in a grim smile. "One night only," she answered. "This shall be the final contest between the Spinners of the Wood and the Gallows God. If we can survive tonight and the dangers Woden hurls against us, I am certain that, come tomorrow, we shall all be free."

Brian Chapman squeezed his eyes shut and surrendered to her. "Nothing else we can do, is there?" he said in resentful resignation.

"Not if you wish to live. This is your only chance. For good or ill we are all trapped here together, and the darkest hours shall be the testing time for each of us."

And, with those fateful words hanging in the air, she swished from The Neolithic Collection.

"Blood and sand . . ." the caretaker said feebly. "I'll . . . I'll go get Josh." Slipping his shoe back on, the man shambled off to the apartment, and Neil turned a worried face to Quoth.

"We should have left last night," he murmured, and the raven cawed in desolation.

"Make haste," Miss Ursula's voice called from The Roman Gallery. "There is much to make ready before the comforting day is stolen from us."

Quoth stepped onto Neil's proffered wrist, and the boy moved away from the windows.

Through the ground floor they trailed, their minds

not daring to speculate what new terrors the night would bring. "Do you think Mr. Pickering knew what was under those steps?" Neil asked the raven. "He was so determined to dig up that skull he wouldn't listen to anyone. But what could be his reason for doing it?"

Quoth could only lift his wings in reply.

"Maybe the museum itself made him," the boy continued. "Possessed him so that it could get rid of the stag. Oh, I don't know what I'm say—"

They had reached the entrance hall once more, and Neil stumbled to a standstill.

"No!" he cried. "Make it stop!"

Miss Ursula was ascending to the second-floor landing when she heard the boy's frightened outburst and the raucous shrieks of the raven that ensued. Her eyebrows raised in questioning surprise, she turned and retraced her steps until the hall was in view below her.

Neil had pressed himself against the wall. Distraught and shivering, he had fixed his eyes on the firmly closed entrance. At his shoulder, Quoth too was ogling into the gloom, and intrigued, Miss Ursula descended.

Crossing the parquet floor, she strode to the door. Then the look of fear that flashed across her face at what she saw there was instantly replaced by a desperate and censorious frown.

"More vandalism!" she remonstrated. "This I will not tolerate. When you first arrived, did I not say how much I loathed schoolboy pranks?"

"It wasn't me and you know it," Neil replied hotly.

"Who else?" she demanded, wringing her hands. "I will know the truth, Maggot!"

"What about your precious museum?"

"That cannot be," she said quickly.

"I don't see why not. It's capable of everything else."

The old woman pressed her clasped hands to her breast. "No," she uttered, "the museum would use weapons far worse than words, believe me."

"Well, what about your sister? She's crazy enough—for all I know it might even have been you!"

Unexpectedly, the old woman winced at the suggestion that it could have been herself, and she whirled away to conceal the doubt that crept across her face. "I am not so unhinged as to go scribbling on the walls and doors," she snarled, although the possibility alarmed and frightened her. "Remember to whom you speak, Child!"

And with a rustle of her gown, Miss Ursula Webster hastened away up the staircase.

Neil glanced at the oaken door one last time, and goosebumps rumpled his skin when he read the three terrifying words that had been freshly scrawled there. The writing was no longer wavering and uncertain. Now the crayoned letters were firm and effected with a determined, resolute hand, which in itself was sinister and more menacing than before. Yet this time the message was no desperate plea, and the malice behind it was staggering.

KILL THEM ALL

CHAPTER 19

BESIEGED BY DEATH

Austen Pickering stared up at the brass plaque that gleamed above the doorway to The Separate Collection and steadied his nerves with a nip of brandy from his hip flask.

"Don't let it get the better of you, Austen, old lad," he buoyed his sagging spirits. "Think of the article you'll get out of it. You could fill a book with this stuff."

Standing in the heavy shadows of The Egyptian Suite, he clicked his fingers to set his thoughts in order, then he closed his eyes and stepped cautiously forward. A violent shudder rifled down his body.

"Like walking into a minefield!" the ghost hunter hissed through clenched and grinding teeth.

His face flushed with strain, he tentatively made his way between the shattered cabinets and broken statuary, hands outstretched to grope the empty air.

"I don't know where to begin," he uttered breathlessly. "So many powers, so many different forces, but all dormant—all waiting."

"They are waiting for you, Mr. Pickering," Miss Ursula told him, following the old man from The Egyptian Suite. "The artifacts assembled here are the cream of my collections. One of the principal reasons the museum was founded was that it should be a repository of those items too dangerous to be kept in the world outside. Here you will find objects and devices best unnamed and forgotten. To this place the torments of myth and ancient memory were brought, and safely have my sisters and I harbored them down the endless years."

Lightly brushing the glass cases with her fingertips, the old woman inhaled the aged must that saturated the oppressive atmosphere, and her eyes gleamed with a gentle pride.

"In our custody these objects have remained for many centuries, Mr. Pickering, and mankind has been unburdened with the knowledge of their existence. Yet now we must call them into our service. They must be roused and compelled to defend us. This, then, shall be your task. Before evening falls, use what gifts are yours to awaken the exhibits. They are our only chance in the trial that awaits."

Opening his eyes, the ghost hunter straightened his back and considered her through the thick lenses of his glasses.

"You never had the slightest intention of allowing me to conduct my proper work, did you?" he asked indignantly. "This is the real reason you called me in. I've been playing your game right along, just so I could be here now to do exactly what you wanted."

Miss Ursula turned away. "I have granted you insights to more than you ever dreamed was possible," she answered dryly. "It is too late and rather ungracious to play the curmudgeon now. However, since our association commenced, events have taken a more drastic turn than I anticipated. If you fail this day, then we shall all join the ranks of those wretched phantoms you were so anxious to save."

Haughtily lifting her sharp nose, she headed back to the doorway. "I must bring Celandine and instruct the others in what they must do," she declared abruptly. "Familiarize yourself with the exhibits, Mr. Pickering. It is going to be one of the longest days of your life."

Watching her depart, the old man shifted his glance to the surrounding room and cleared his throat.

"All right, then," he told himself. "Come on, Austen, old lad. Take no notice of that spiteful cat and just do your best. Rise to the challenge, that's the thing to do. It's all you can do."

*　*　*

While the ghost hunter examined the bizarre artifacts stored in The Separate Collection, Miss Ursula Webster appointed tasks to the others. Neil and Edie were ordered to fetch as many weapons from the other galleries as they could.

"Swords and shields may be as vital in this contest as any of the less tangible defenses," she told them. "But do not stray too far from one another. I do not feel there is much to fear before nightfall, although the museum may trick you with its old deceits and lead you through the maze of its being. Keep your wits sharp and your minds upon your duties. If you do not return within two hours, I shall come searching."

Grudging the company of Neil and Quoth, Edie Dorkins set off at a run and the boy hurried after.

Directing her gaze at Brian Chapman, the old woman charged him with the gathering of wood to build a fire in The Separate Collection.

"This unnatural cold will only become more intense," she predicted. "Bring anything that will burn. Tables, chairs—anything!"

"And what'll you be doing?" the caretaker demanded.

"Seeking for ways to ensure we outlive the night," she replied.

Throughout the morning the preparations were made. Neil and Edie ransacked the other galleries, taking swords and knives and removing helmets from suits of armor. They returned to The Separate Collection dragging heavy shields behind them.

Having cleared the cabinets and cases from the center of the room, Brian Chapman surveyed the space he had made. He had lifted the flagstones from the kitchen floor of the caretaker's apartment and dragged them all the way upstairs to form a resistant base for the fire.

"Just hope the boards underneath don't catch," he murmured dubiously.

At his side, Josh was peering into the case that contained a row of dangling, shrunken heads. He pulled a succession of mimicking faces until his father called him away to assist in the hunt for wood.

"You come and help your dad," he said. "No, put that knife down. Josh, will you stop messing around!"

"Don't shout," Neil told their father. "You'll scare him."

Brian snorted. "I wish that's all he had to be frightened of," he said, leading his youngest son from the room.

By the time Edie and Neil had lugged in their third haul and dumped it by the doorway, the girl was already weary of her foraging partner. When he went to speak with the ghost hunter, she seized her opportunity and scampered off alone.

In the corner, where his suitcases and equipment were now assembled, Austen Pickering glanced at his watch and made a note of the time.

"What do you think will happen tonight?" Neil asked him.

The old man shrugged. "How can I know the answer to that?" he replied. "But one thing's for certain. That Webster woman is terrified."

"If Miss Ursula's afraid," Neil murmured, "I dread to think . . ."

"Quite right. I reckon she's expecting all hell to break loose—literally."

Looking back into the room, Neil suddenly noticed Edie was missing, and he cursed under his breath.

"The little nuisance! Why doesn't she ever listen?"

With the raven flying after him, he ran out of The Separate Collection, but the girl had given them the slip.

"Idiot," the boy fumed. Quoth waggled his beak in accord.

Behind them, Austen Pickering stared out of the windows and whispered nervously to himself, "Four hours till dark."

* * *

Through The Tiring Salon Edie Dorkins dashed, her pockets jingling with the extra trifling treasures she had acquired while gathering weapons. Straight to the door that led to the Websters' quarters she raced and flung herself through it.

"Ursula!" she exclaimed.

Standing on the narrow stairway, her gaze fixed intently on the great oil painting that hung there, her delicate fingers stroking the canvas, the eldest of the Fates stirred as though emerging from a heavy slumber.

"Edith," she uttered huskily.

"What you doin'?" the girl demanded.

"I . . . I was about to fetch Celandine."

"You been ages."

Miss Ursula moved away from the painting, and the countenance she turned to Edie was pale and drawn.

"Have I?" she breathed. "I had not realized. What was it Baudelaire said? 'I felt the wing of imbecility brush against me.' I too know what it is to feel the poisonous draft of approaching madness. My own personal doom is stalking me, Edith. I cannot elude it very much longer. I am at the brink, and my mind is collapsing into the abyss. There is little time left to me—the sure ground of reason is already crumbling."

"You don't know that!"

"Indeed I do. I have seen it."

"Where?" the girl cried. "Where have you seen it?"

But Miss Ursula ignored her and strode up the steps. "Celandine!" she called. "You must accompany us to The Separate Collection."

Pouting peevishly, Edie Dorkins watched her push through the damask curtain that hung over the entrance to the cramped attic room, and the girl kicked the green stair carpet in annoyance.

Then, a half smile crinkling her young face, Edie looked up as a wild thought dawned on her, and she studied the great oil painting with renewed interest.

* * *

When four o'clock came, they were all gathered in The Separate Collection. A small fire was burning on the flagstones, and a stack of chair legs, splintered tables, yellowing newspapers, and broken cabinets was heaped nearby in readiness for the night. Crackling and spluttering in the flames, the varnish that coated the shattered furniture gave off a black, acrid smoke that set the eyes watering, but it was an inconvenience none of them minded. To have heat was all that mattered.

With Quoth perched on his knee, Neil Chapman sat

before the fire, staring at the faces of those around him. His father and brother were huddled close by. Josh was wearing an air-raid warden's tin hat and his hands toyed with a small scabbard. But he was restive, and wanting to go running about the room, he complained when Brian forbade him.

On Neil's other side, Austen Pickering watched the creeping light fail outside the windows and readied himself for the approaching night. Opposite, beyond the flames, Miss Celandine and Miss Ursula Webster sat with Edie squeezed between them.

Twisting her braided hair in her fingers, Miss Celandine hummed snatches of tunes to herself, but extreme tiredness made her overripe face haggard, and her eyelids drooped as she yielded to the profound fatigue that ached in her old bones.

With a long dagger glinting in her hands, Edie Dorkins chewed the inside of her cheek and glared back at the boy who was peering through the flames at her. Averting his eyes to the stiff form of Miss Ursula, Neil tried to guess what she was thinking. But that face was flinty and impassive, betraying none of the turmoil that steamed within her as she counted out the remaining minutes.

Throughout the afternoon the temperature had fallen steadily, and the drifting snow specks had become a monotonous movement of white flecks behind the frozen windows. Now, even in the fire glow, they were all shivering in spite of the many warm garments they wore.

A lethal clutter of weapons leaned against the woodpile, within easy reach. Neil and Edie had collected far more swords, maces, shields, and knives than they could possibly use, and Miss Ursula had enigmatically insisted that the surplus be left by the entrance of The Egyptian Suite.

Mr. Pickering had lit his remaining candles and every oil lamp he could find, placing them on the counters. Although the electric lights were switched on, he did not trust them, and at his side he kept his flashlight and Bible.

"Where's Veronica?" Miss Celandine's weary voice abruptly cut through the pressing silence. "She should be here. Shall I fetch her, Ursula—shall I?"

Her sister placed a hand upon her arm. "No, dear," she said firmly. "We will join Veronica later."

Miss Celandine hung her head and muttered into her lap. "She'd better not start the dancing without me."

Nestled between them, Edie swiveled around on her bottom and peered up at the old woman dressed in the high-collared black taffeta gown. "Why ain't Gogus 'ere?" she asked. "Won't we need him?"

"I take heart from his absence," Miss Ursula informed her. "The Pedagogus appears only at the most perilous of times. When he is here, then we shall know how deadly our plight has become. The wood urchin will show himself only when the threat reaches its pinnacle."

"Where is he, then?" the girl demanded.

Miss Ursula gave a leaden smile. "You know the answer to that already, Edith," she answered evasively.

Turning from Edie, the eldest of the Fates glanced at the blank gray squares of the windows, then focused her attention on the entrance to The Egyptian Suite. In that enclosed room the shadows were black and obliterating. Then, sensing the brooding, resentful atmosphere mount within the other rooms of the museum, she knew that it was time.

"Mr. Pickering," her clipped voice began. "We dare not wait any longer. The instant is upon us."

Arrested by her penetrating gaze, the ghost hunter found himself nodding dumbly, then he coughed and closed his eyes.

"This is crazy," Brian Chapman murmured.

An expectant quiet followed, broken only by the crackling flames and Mr. Pickering's deep breaths as he attuned himself to the indolent forces contained inside that room.

Then, very softly, he began to speak.

"In the name of all that is good," the old man whispered, "I ask you to hear me. I am a friend. Listen to my words. There are those of us here who need your help and assistance. The time of your sleeping is over. Come to us now—please."

Crouched into his wings, Quoth let his eye rove about the assembled circle. With the exception of Miss Celandine and Josh, they were all looking at the ghost hunter, their faces blank and expectant.

"Come to us!" Mr. Pickering repeated, raising his voice to a resonating demand that awakened echoes from every corner of The Separate Collection. "Give us your protection this night. There are those whose intent is to harm us. We commend our safety to your care. Keep the evils at bay, I beg you."

Sucking the air between his teeth, his eyes still firmly closed, the old man lifted his face to the ceiling and became as still as stone. A quiet, more intense and onerous than before, penetrated the room. Even Josh ceased his fidgeting and shifted uncomfortably, sensing the overwhelming tension that prickled and tingled about him.

In the center of the nervous group, the sizzling flames sputtered and dwindled inside the charred framework of the fire. Brian Chapman reached for a sword with which to stoke the embers.

Shaking her head, Miss Ursula stopped him. "Not yet," she hissed. "You might douse the fire completely and it will never be relit."

Neil's palms were sweating with anxiety, and wiping them on his coat, he glanced fearfully at the windows, where a funereal dark now pressed against the icy panes.

Then, overhead, the electric lights started to flicker. One by one, the bulbs shrank into shadow. Swiftly darkness flooded into The Separate Collection. From The Egyptian Suite it gushed, sluicing in around the boundering walls like a torrent of Stygian waters, dammed only by the oil lamps and candles, beyond whose tapering flames the room became a cavern of night.

"It begins," Miss Ursula breathed.

With a sharp gasp, Austen Pickering shuddered and looked feverishly about him.

"I did what I could," he muttered quickly. "But all the while I sensed a resistance. It was another force—outside this room—fighting against me. "

"It is the rest of the museum," Miss Ursula told him. "It is waking and aware of what we do. The mind that controls it this night wishes only our destruction. This room has become an island and we are besieged by death."

"But has it worked?" Neil asked Mr. Pickering. "Are we safe?"

The ghost hunter dabbed his handkerchief over his high forehead. "I'm not sure," he answered feebly. "I can only prod and jab with my humble gift. I don't know if the powers in here will respond."

"If they do not," Miss Ursula announced in a melancholic whisper, "then the strands of all our lives will be cut."

An unhappy croak issued from Quoth's beak, and he waddled backward to press his head against Neil's coat.

"Quiet," Edie snapped, leaping to her feet. "Can't you hear?"

From some remote region, deep within the museum, there came the distant sound of a rhythmic knocking. From the ground floor it vibrated dully through the building, beating like the pulse of some forbidding timepiece. On the walls of the caretaker's living quarters the ominous tap-tap-tap originated— the place where the warders of the Wyrd Infirmary had once made their common room.

"It's him!" Neil murmured, the hair on his neck rising. "It's Jack Timms!"

"The agent of Woden," Miss Ursula commented. "It is through him the Gallows God assails us."

Edie Dorkins gripped the hilt of her dagger and glared at the entrance to The Egyptian Suite where the shadows swirled with a substance all their own, and she bared her teeth in a feral growl. Straining to hear that dismal, taunting noise, they fell into a breathless silence, until Quoth ruffled his feathers and cawed wretchedly.

"I know," Neil said, understanding what the raven was trying to tell him. "The sound's moving—Tick-Tock's making his way through the galleries."

"Of course he is," Austen Pickering declared. "He's headed for the hallway and the stairs. He'll be coming up here."

"Dad!" Josh began to wail. "I doesn't like it. I scared."

Brian Chapman gathered his youngest son into his overcoat, but the four-year-old would not be comforted.

"It's cold!" he whined. "You're cold."

"Quiet, Josh," his father told him. "Keep still."

Gradually, other noises were given voice in the corridors and chambers of the Wyrd Museum as, under Jack Timms's dominating influence, the building lapsed back into its former incarnations and history. Through the passages and halls the evil man prowled, his Tormentor rapping out his measured progress. In his wake the binding years were shed, and a chaotic jumble of identities scrambled over the creaking walls.

The shrieks of the madhouse mingled with the drone of plainsong, until the blast of an air-raid siren abruptly drowned all other sounds. No, not all; even above that blaring horn the steady thumping report of Tick-Tock Jack could still be heard.

"He's on the stairs," Neil said.

Up to the second-floor landing the staccato beat reverberated, and still the museum imploded into its past. Floating through the ether, a babble of young voices suddenly entered The Separate Collection, and the company sitting around the smoldering fire turned their heads in consternation.

"Who saw him die?
I, said the Fly,
With my little eye,
I saw him die."

"What's that?" Brian Chapman cried. "Who is it?"

It was Miss Celandine who answered him. Swaying to the music and meter of the old rhyme, she grinned her goofy smile and twittered dreamily.

"The children, Ursula." She sighed. "All the sweet little darlings. Do you remember—do you? They used to recite their lessons and chant the words so prettily—they did, they did."

Miss Ursula clenched her sister's large hand as the haunting voices continued.

"Who caught his blood?
I, said the Fish,
In my little dish,
I caught his blood."

"The children of the Well Lane Orphanage," she explained to the others seated around the fire. "It is the morning instruction we are hearing."

"It's horrible," Neil whispered.

"Who'll make the shroud?
I, said the Beetle,
With my thread and needle,
I'll make the shroud."

Echoing through the freezing room, the unnerving singing flowed, and like a diabolic metronome the Tormentor of Jack Timms tapped incessantly to the old nursery rhyme tune.

"Those children . . ." Mr. Pickering began in an uncertain murmur. "Are they in the museum now? With that vile killer?"

The expression upon Miss Ursula's face was answer enough.

"Oh, no!" he spluttered.

Confused and nonplussed by what was happening around him, Brian Chapman pressed his fingers to the bridge of his nose, and he spoke in an agitated fluster. "Wait, wait!" he stammered. "I don't understand. All right, so this place is crammed with spooks and stuff. But are you trying to say that one ghost can hurt another? It doesn't make sense—I just don't—"

"Dad!" Neil said impatiently. "It's never been about ghosts. It's the past itself that comes back. Those kids are in this place now, and they're as real and alive as you and me."

"Who'll dig his grave?
I, said the— "

Suddenly the rhyme came to a brusque end, and the orphans' voices faded upon the chill air.

Without the childrens' chanting, the building was horribly hushed. Only the enduring throb of Jack Timms's cane continued to drum out the dragging seconds.

"What happened?" Edie demanded. "Why'd they stop?"

"There is no cause for concern," Miss Ursula assured her. "The children have returned to their correct place in the museum's history. It is weaving in and out of the years; no harm came to them."

At Edie's side, Miss Celandine twirled a forefinger through her braided hair and, in a singsong voice, completed the morbid rhyme: "All the birds of the air/Fell a-sighing and a-sobbing/When they heard the bell toll . . ."

The old woman's words were unexpectedly swamped by a squawking cry from Quoth, who, flying to Neil's shoulder, honked for quiet, then cupped a wing to the side of his head.

Inside The Separate Collection a new sound had begun. Very faint and barely audible at first, it tinkled beneath the tap-tap-tap that hammered from the landing. Presently it grew in strength until they could all hear a delicate jingling of tiny bells.

"The frog skeletons!" Miss Celandine cooed delightedly.

"My congratulations, Mr. Pickering," Miss Ursula complimented him, allowing herself a slight chuckle. "Your gifts are not so humble as you pretend. They are indeed rare and efficacious."

"What does it mean?" Neil asked.

In the somber darkness beyond the lamps and candles, indistinct shapes and shadows were moving, and Edie's eyes glittered as a broad grin lit her face.

"The Separate Collection," the girl whispered joyously. "It's comin' to life."

CHAPTER 20

THE FIRST WAVE

"Now you may stoke the embers, Mr. Chapman," Miss Ursula commanded. "And feed the flames well." But the caretaker barely heard her for he, like the others, was staring into that murky realm outside the influence of the candles.

Dark masses that only moments ago had been rigid and immovable were now shifting furtively through the gloom. Stiff and awkward at first, tall shapes stretched awake and left their bases in jerking, jolting motions until the shadows were alive and creeping with hidden activity. Ponderous weights strode inexpertly across the floor, and the boards groaned and juddered beneath them.

"I don't believe it," Neil's father uttered in a choked voice. At the man's side, his son was just as stupefied, and Quoth chirruped in amazement.

Around the cleared space, the silent figures moved between the crowded cabinets. Although the imposing outlines kept clear of the lamp and candle glow, the group caught glimpses of powerful, stone-colored limbs as the granite-clad torsos wove through the enshrouding shade.

"The statues," Neil marveled. "They're moving!"

Every sculpture that had graced The Separate Collection was infused with supernatural life. Even those fragmented remnants of forgotten figures had returned to their original, complete condition, and their crunching steps strode about the darkened room as each hewn form headed for the entrance to The Egyptian Suite.

There the concealed troop congregated. Effigies of kings, satyrs, warriors, and forgotten gods gathered close about the heap of weapons Miss Ursula had instructed Neil and Edie to deposit by the doorway.

"What are they doing?" Brian asked in a wavering voice when the night started to chime and scrape with ringing metal.

Rising to her feet, Miss Ursula Webster walked to the edge of the circle and selected a heavy broadsword from the array that leaned against the woodpile.

"They are arming themselves," she said, choosing a round bronze shield to accompany the sword.

"Where you off to?" Edie called as the old woman sidled past one of the glass cases. "Lemme come!"

But Miss Ursula was not venturing far. Threading her way through the flickering lights, she halted by a gilded pedestal and raised her eyes to the figure it supported.

Upon that plinth, where golden ferns curled and scrolled, the shapely female foot that had stood there for thousands of years, carved from ivory and broken off at the ankle, was now part of a much larger whole.

Two dainty feet now pointed their gleaming toes on the crest of that pillar, and the slender ankles were connected to graceful calves that disappeared into the skillfully sculpted folds of an alabaster Ionic shift. Over lovingly modeled thighs and hips the exquisite, cunningly crafted chiton was draped, rising to a narrowing waist and belted beneath the bosom by a simple carved cord.

Where the low neck of the classical garment joined the budding ivory once more, the hinted musculature spoke of a seductive suppleness, and lithe arms that tapered from elegant shoulders were held open in a welcoming embrace.

Captivated by the loveliness of the regenerated figure, Neil moved forward to see the face of that beautiful statue. But the head was cloaked in shadow, and he could only wonder what fair features the sculptor had bestowed upon his creation.

"Too many ages of the world have wheeled by," Miss Ursula began as she looked up into that concealed countenance. "Too many years have seeped into oblivion since the day Pumiyathon first fashioned you, little knowing the scourge he had made to inspire terror in the streets of Paphos. Unto me your broken form was delivered, lest Ashtoroth return and command you once more. But now the term of your incarceration is over. The debt has been paid, yet still

I, Urdr, will not release you till one further penance is undertaken."

A hissing breath caused the alabaster breast to rise gently, and the ivory fingers twitched with life.

Holding up the weapons, Miss Ursula respectfully bowed her head, then named her request.

"Be now the new protector of this place. For this night only, I appoint you commander of my stone legion. In this desperate hour, guard we who sit in this room from the hazards without, and let none break in upon us."

Ivory hands reached out to take the sword and shield from her grasp, and the blade cleaved through the gloom as the statue signaled its assent.

"Then lead the others," the eldest of the Fates ordered, taking a brisk step back. "Suffer no opposition, and cut down the enemy who approaches. Let it be done!"

Clutching the bronze shield to its chest, the statue stirred. The lapping candlelight glimmered through the translucent alabaster of its shift as the feet moved and it stepped down from the pedestal.

Into the glowing radiance the sculpture's head finally emerged, and around the small fire, Neil and his father cried out in fear. Josh buried his face in Brian's coat, and Austen Pickering swore under his breath.

Cawing in fright, Quoth hopped from his master's shoulder and went scurrying across the floor to dive into a medieval helmet, the grilled visor clanging shut behind him.

At once the ivory hands clenched the broadsword

all the more tightly, and the blade sliced the air in a death-dealing arc.

"Be silent," Miss Ursula warned them quickly. "Remain calm. You have nothing to fear."

Inside the steel helmet, Quoth timorously pressed his eye to one of the visor's slits and quailed at the spectacle that loomed beyond the nearby cabinets.

Made from the same smooth ivory as the lovely form, there was, where the enchanting head should have been, only a grinning human skull.

From his bolt-hole, Quoth stared up at that twisted ugliness and shook himself uneasily.

The contrast to that perfect, shapely figure was monstrous and horrific. Wearing a crown of carved laurel leaves, the skull twisted aside to glare at the people seated around the fire, its hollow sockets seeming to bore right into them.

Neil shriveled inside as those deep spaces fixed on him and the jaw snapped wide to issue a threatening, serpentlike hiss.

Her mouth falling open in fascinated imitation, Edie adored the wondrous creation and longed to run over to it. But Miss Ursula was already pointing the statue toward the entrance where the other shadowy sculptures were waiting, and the figure strode from the lights that danced about its lustrous form, shimmering off into the darkness.

Through The Separate Collection it stalked, brandishing the sword before it. At the doorway of The Egyptian Suite the statue halted, while the rest of the stone infantry closed in behind.

Long blades gleamed dully in the gloom as marble

fists upraised their weapons; at a commanding hiss, the silent crowd went lumbering through the entrance and out into the museum.

"So march our principal defenses," Miss Ursula remarked, listening to the heavy footfalls rumble through the dark. "The deciding battle is about to commence."

Edie Dorkins rushed to her side and stabbed her dagger into the empty air. "I want to go fight!" she exclaimed. "Lemme go with 'em."

"No, Edith, dear," Miss Ursula admonished kindly. "I will have more need of you here. Let us return to the fireside."

Reluctant, the girl lingered by the cabinets. "Can't I just go an' see?" she implored.

"Obey me in this," Miss Ursula cautioned. "If any should set foot beyond this room, it will be the end of them. Outside this collection, Jack Timms now rules the building. We must stay here and weather the coming storm."

As she said those words, the pounding of Tick-Tock's Tormentor, which had been beating along the connecting corridor, suddenly ceased, and everyone looked up sharply.

"He is aware of them," Miss Ursula uttered. "The contest begins."

A loud, braying shout erupted from the passage, and the sound of that repellent, familiar voice caused Neil and Edie to glance nervously at one another.

Still shut inside the helmet, Quoth also heard the malignant curses of that evil man. Unable to open the visor, the bird lifted the steel headgear on his back and waddled over to his master's side, his scrawny legs poking from underneath.

Behind the paneled walls, the malicious warder of the Wyrd Infirmary gave a defiant yell, but his cries were overwhelmed by a tremendous clamor that came charging from The Dissolution Gallery as the alabaster statue led her army to battle.

Resounding crashes boomed through the museum as the marble soldiers burst into the corridor, their unstoppable might smashing through all obstacles. The night was slashed with a furious clanging as steel clashed against steel, and to Neil's relief, he heard Jack Timms's bawling voice retreat toward the landing.

"They're forcing him back," he murmured.

"He doesn't stand a chance against armed statues," Mr. Pickering joined in. "What person would?"

"One who has the power of our enemy burning within him," Miss Ursula remarked grimly. "Do not celebrate our victory just yet."

"Are we having a party, Ursula?" Miss Celandine piped up unexpectedly. "How adorable!" No one answered her.

The echoing tumult was fainter now.

"They're on the stairs," Edie breathed in bloodthirsty excitement. "Hark at them swords a-bashin' and a-duelin'. Wish I could see the look on that fat dog's face when they stick it to 'im. Chop his ugly head off, that's what I says!"

The bitter conflict continued to rage below, and Neil chewed his lip uneasily. "It's taking too long," he said, speaking his fears aloud. "They should have won by now."

Miss Ursula agreed, clenching her fists till her

knuckles shone white as the bone beneath. "It is, indeed," she whispered.

* * *

His pitted face distorted with murderous fury, Jack Timms roared with the full force of his rattling lungs as he confronted the stone sortie that assailed him. Stumbling backward down the stairs, his beaten top hat knocked from his head, the burly man glowered at the sculpted figures that pursued him, swiping their swords through the surrounding shadows.

The wooden steps splintered and cracked beneath the thundering weight of those marble feet, while the banisters buckled as impervious limbs crashed against them. At the forefront of the company, Pumiyathon's statue came savaging, her jawbone clacking and snapping atop that lovely neck.

Tick-Tock Jack staggered away from her. In his left hand he held his cane firmly, but his right fist gripped a Roman sword snatched from the wall, and with its blade he clumsily fended off the lunging thrusts of the statue as best he could.

Stabbing wildly, he chipped a sliver of ivory from one of the sculpture's beautiful arms. Then the bronze shield swung around to knock his fat body aside. Down the steps he was driven, his great black coat flapping madly about his corpulent bulk, and after him the sculptures came stomping.

"You blowsy headstones!" he shouted. "Get old Tick-Tock if you think you can. He ain't afrighted o' the likes o' your churchyard mugs."

Dodging awkwardly, Jack Timms dropped his weapon and tumbled down the remaining stairs and into the main hall. Defenseless without his sword, the vile braggart blundered backward, but still he was not afraid and a vain guffaw spilled from his thick lips.

The architecture of the entrance hall was a confusion of centuries. Patches of wattled walls flickered beneath the paneling, and the large window on the stairs was a tortured mongrel of conflicting periods.

"Now we'll see," he mocked. "Takes more'n you to knock off Tick-Tock!"

Before the words had left his mouth, there came a belching "plop," swiftly followed by another. From the ground around him, bubbling up through the parquet tiles, muddy water started to squelch and squeeze. Out of the cracks a brackish ooze frothed, and the interlocking segments of wood that formed the floor bulged and quivered, lifted upon an undulating, marshy bog.

Leaving the stairs, the animated statues trampled unerringly toward Woden's agent, but the burden of their relentless advance was too great for the wood-crusted swamp that the hallway had become. Into soft, sucking mud the sculptures sank, dragged down until the filthy fen reached their waists, and Jack Timms sniggered to see the mighty limbs toil and flounder.

Yet not all were helpless in that turgid marsh. A defiant hiss issued from the commander's grinning jaws, and the empty hollows of her eye sockets stared with a hideous intent at the warder. Though the thick quagmire clung to the finely crafted folds of her shift, the living sculpture waded forward, the broadsword poised and ready.

Faltering momentarily in his boastful laughter, his ratty eyes trained on that alabaster figure already stepping from the unnatural swamp, Tick-Tock Jack edged toward The Roman Gallery. The exhibits had vanished, and in their place stood row upon row of desks. Darting his sly gaze to the large chalkboard at the end of the room, the warder's black confidence was restored, and he gloated with unholy mirth.

"You'll not gut me," he slobbered foully.

*   *   *

Up in The Separate Collection, they could no longer hear what was happening downstairs. The clashing of steel had ceased; so too had the rumor of crunching footfalls. Only Jack Timms's hellish laughter came to them, and they waited fearfully.

"Never have I felt so powerless!" Miss Ursula snapped in frustration.

From the darkness that smothered the nearby wall, there came a gasping cough, and everyone turned quickly.

"Who's there?" Mr. Pickering demanded.

Inside the helmet, Quoth warbled worriedly as the dry, wheezing cough sounded again.

"Gogus?" Edie called doubtfully. "That you?"

"Gorgeous Gogus!" Miss Celandine crooned. "It likes its ears tickled, you know—it does, it does."

With furrows creasing her brow, Miss Ursula picked up an oil lamp and strode into the shadows, the gentle flame lighting the interiors of the cabinets she swept past. "Where are you?" she demanded, peering into the crowded recesses. "Speak!"

To her right, the small voice spluttered a third time, and the old woman's eyes flashed exultantly when she dispelled the masking gloom.

"Not the Pedagogus," she addressed the others. "Yet perhaps something even more serviceable."

Turning up the flame that burned in the lamp's fluted glass, Miss Ursula smiled widely. Over tiny, shriveled faces the generous light now played, and watching from behind, Edie saw that the old woman was looking at a row of shrunken heads.

Suspended on braided cords, the seven macabre exhibits looked like apples at a Halloween party. They were each the size of a baseball, but long hanks of thick dark hair hung from the constricted scalps. Fine stitches sealed the sunken eyelids and wizened mouths, and an assortment of primitive yet beautiful jewelry dangled from the ears.

All were male. Two of them had long, wiry beards, while another was covered in tribal tattoos that coiled over the wrinkled skin in an intricate and magical design. A serene but solemn expression was set into every one of those toylike faces. They looked as if their straw-stuffed heads were filled with contented dreaming, but Miss Ursula scanned her keen gaze across them with irritation.

"Which of you is it?" she inquired, scratching at the glass with her fingernail. "Speak up."

There, the fourth in from the left of those ghoulish objects was swaying slightly on his thread, and Miss

Ursula brought the lamp as close to him as the intervening glass permitted. Saturated by the warm radiance, every detail of that diminutive face was set in stark relief, and the spirals of his tattoos obligingly displayed their still-fresh colors.

In the middle of that gruesome exhibit, a perfect miniature nose suddenly twitched and wriggled as though suppressing a sneeze. Then the stitches that bound the lips together strained and grew taut as the mouth began to squirm. From one corner, where the sewing had slackened, the head gave another cough and a fine rain of dust was expelled out into the case.

"There is little time," Miss Ursula declared. "Can you hear me?"

Within that small face the eyebrows trembled, and behind the concave cheeks, a motion like the chewing of a particularly sticky toffee began. The untidy seam that held the mouth shut started to unravel, and when the stitches had been loosened sufficiently the shrunken head spoke.

A thin, rasping voice sounded within the glass case as the ghastly object acknowledged Miss Ursula's presence and greeted her in a language that neither Neil nor anyone else recognized or understood.

Yet it was plain that the old woman comprehended every word, even though the voice was further impaired by the fact that there was no tongue behind those parchmentlike lips, and the speech leaked out in a pinched and breathless whine.

"No, my friend," she responded. "The hour of your deliverance is not upon us. My apologies for awakening you prematurely. It was necessary, I'm afraid. Will you aid us? We are encompassed by the forces of the Gallows God, and I must know what is occurring outside this room. Use those skills you were favored with, set your thought a-hunting, and relate all that it spies to me."

The crinkled face bobbed upon the string as the head attempted to nod, and the nasal voice dwindled to a concentrated whisper.

"What's it doing?" Mr. Pickering asked, joining Neil and Quoth to stare in astonishment at the outlandish discourse.

Miss Ursula glanced at them in distraction, her face divulging a chain of emotions as the wizened head of the long-dead shaman sent his mind flying through the museum, revealing to her all that he saw.

"They are down in the hall," she recounted to the others. "He sees devastation and destruction all around. The floor has regressed to an evil age when a stinking quagmire crept through the land to consume the forest in which Nirinel was hidden."

A volley of harsh words spattered abruptly from the withered lips, and Miss Ursula clicked her tongue in dismay. "Into this marsh many of the statues have fallen and cannot free themselves. Yet five have accomplished it and even now are striding through what should be The Roman Gallery. Aha—Jack Timms is in there, and they are hurling the furniture out of their path to reach him . . . but he is laughing . . ."

Without warning, the head let out a compressed scream and Miss Ursula recoiled, visibly shaken.

"What?" Neil cried. "What's happened?"

The old woman looked across at Edie, then

swallowed and turned toward The Egyptian Suite. "Jack Timms is mustering a force to protect himself from them," she whimpered.

"What kind of force?" Mr. Pickering murmured.

Miss Ursula made no answer—she did not have to.

In that same instant the Wyrd Museum rang with the shrieks and screams of young children.

"Ursula!" Miss Celandine wailed unhappily. "The infants—someone is hurting them!"

The children's panic-filled screams were horrendous to hear, and Austen Pickering slammed his fist upon one of the cabinets. "Explain that!" he demanded angrily, snatching up his flashlight and almost running from the room.

"The orphans," Miss Ursula said quickly, with a disgusted, fearful tremor in her voice. "That man has summoned their schoolroom back; he is going to use the children as a shield. If the statues are to get to him, they must first cut down the children."

Mr. Pickering shook his head. "Then he's got away," he murmured.

"No!" Miss Ursula cried, when the shrunken head gasped and rattled further grisly intelligence. "The sculptures were commanded to let nothing stand in their path. They are advancing. The children are herded between them and the warder—the swords are raised—"

"Stop it!" the ghost hunter yelled.

Anguished and appalled at the abhorrent screams echoing through the building, the eldest of the Fates readily conceded. Thrusting the oil lamp into Edie's small hands, she darted to the doorway to throw up her arms.

"Enough!" she shouted into the thickly swirling dark. "Let not one drop of innocent blood be shed. Put down your weapons and be as stone once more—I, Urdr, command it!"

The children's screams climbed to a harrowing crescendo and then—there was nothing.

From The Egyptian Suite a frightened whimpering came floating on the freezing air. By the fire, Neil's young brother stifled his cries, and the voices of the Wyrd Orphanage were cast back into the chaos of the building's past.

A heavy silence descended.

No one dared to make a sound. They were all waiting for the noise they knew must come.

Tap-tap-tap.

It was almost a relief to hear that dreaded drumming, and Neil let out a huffing breath. "The children," he began. "None of them? . . ."

Miss Ursula returned to the case that housed the shrunken head, and the little face whispered to her once more.

"No," she told them. "The statues were stilled in time, and the infants faded with the schoolroom."

Through the ground floor they could hear Jack Timms striking out the seconds as he swaggered back toward the hallway. Then a grievous, discordant crash ricocheted through the building, followed by another and another.

"What's he doing down there?" Mr. Pickering asked.

"Sounds like he's smashing the place up," Neil muttered.

The line of Miss Ursula's jaw tightened. She did not

need the shrunken head to tell her what was taking place in The Roman Gallery. Moistening her lips, the old woman said, "The statues are being destroyed."

"Then we've got nothing," Brian Chapman blurted. "There's no hope for us!"

Now freed from the helmet and perched once more on Neil's wrist, Quoth cawed in misery. They all stared across to where the black mouth of The Egyptian Suite gaped high and wide. A mocking laugh soared up the stairwell, and leaving The Roman Gallery and the entrance hall behind, Jack Timms ascended.

"Tick-Tock!" his snickering voice taunted. "Can you hear it up there? I'm countin' out the time what's left to you. Tick-Tock, Tick-Tock. There's a lot of learnin' to be done up there in that poxy hole where you're skulkin'."

Swilling the spit around his mouth, the repugnant man cackled with infernal glee. "It's the worse for you now, it is. You can't escape from old Tick-Tock, oh, no. He's wantin' his jamboree, an' he'll have a real grand one tonight, with no nasty stag to put a spoil on his jolly. Tick-Tock, Tick-Tock."

Higher the awful man climbed, and all the while his cane rapped out his menacing journey. The horror of his metered approach had cast a hopeless paralysis over the group gathered in The Separate Collection, but when the Tormentor began pounding on the second-floor landing, Quoth roused everyone with a bleating alarm.

Immediately the others stirred and looked to Miss Ursula. "What can we do?" Neil cried. "He'll be here any minute."

Striding between the cabinets, the old woman turned a troubled face on them. "This moment has come earlier than I anticipated," she confessed. "The first wave of our defenses has proven worthless. Therefore, we must rely on the second."

"And what's that?" Mr. Pickering asked.

Miss Ursula spread her arms wide and gestured toward the surrounding displays. "We must take what exhibits we can from their cases and keep them with us about the fire. From that point on, no one must rise or leave the group. We must enmesh ourselves within as powerful a boundary as can be forged."

Neil frowned. "That's madness," the boy snorted. "It's not going to keep him out. There must be something more we can do."

"No, Child!" she uttered gravely. "Nothing."

Whisking around to face Austen Pickering, Miss Ursula said, "The Spear of Longinus—I know it is in your keeping. Bring it here."

The endless beat of Jack Timms's cane had now entered The Dissolution Gallery, and the old woman clapped her hands urgently. To the displays they hastened, and where the cabinets were locked, they smashed the glass to break inside.

"Take all you can carry!" Miss Ursula told them. "There is so little time!"

From their cases the exhibits were torn: small, sealed boxes inscribed with runic symbols, iron bottles, a fetish stuck with countless nails, mirrors of black glass. There were forbidden books, tall jars in which pale serpents entwined, demon masks, dice carved from animal bone, volumes of alchemical lore—even the shrunken heads were tugged from their hanger in the frantic scramble.

Driven by panic, they all threw themselves into the ferrying of artifacts to the fireside. So absorbed were they that none of them noticed Miss Celandine twirl stealthily out of the candle glow, humming faintly to herself.

Lifting the lid of the case that housed the large golden locket, Miss Ursula allowed herself a moment's pause as she considered the import of what she was about to do. Then her meditation faltered, and she saw that Edie was staring into the cabinet where the Eye of Balor resided.

"No, Edith," she directed. "Do not think to shatter that glass."

"Why not?" the girl cried. "We could open the eye and make it look right at Tick-Tock Jack. That'd get 'im good an' proper, that would. Lemme do it!"

Slipping the golden chain over her head so that the heavy locket, glittering brightly against the deep black of her gown, dragged against her neck, Miss Ursula hurried to the child's side.

"It will not avail us!" she insisted. "Do you not think I have considered it? The eyelid's flesh has dried to an adamantine rigidity, and the special salve that makes it supple has been lost for centuries. No other power in this world can raise that petrified skin now. It is useless to us."

Guiding her back toward the fire, Miss Ursula laid her hand on the girl's head and in a solemn whisper told her, "If all else fails, there is only one other hope left. You must be ready to sacrifice the gift of the Fates."

"My pixie hat?" Edie murmured.

"Yes, dear. Within its stitches the forces of Destiny are woven, and if it looks as though the agent of Woden might prove victorious, we must unpick the threads and cast them in a protective circle around us."

"Would we be safe then?"

"Should that final barricade yield to the will of the Gallows God," Miss Ursula said in a hoarse whisper, "then our lives are truly doomed. If He has grown that strong, perhaps we do not deserve to survive."

Edie removed the woolen hat from her head and set it down among the exhibits that had been wrenched from the cabinets. Lit lurid by the flames, Austen Pickering's grizzle-haired figure stood trembling in their jumbled midst, the rusted spear in one hand and his Bible clutched tightly in the other. Winding their way back to the littered space, the others returned with the last hoard of plunder they could manage. The cluttered disarray they had already gathered constituted only a third of the pieces that made up The Separate Collection, but it was now too late to retrieve any more.

Tap-tap-tap.

The fatal knocking had finally reached The Egyptian Suite, and a scoffing snicker sounded within that prodigious dark. At once Quoth sent up an earnest squawking and flapped his wings hysterically.

"Quiet!" Neil hissed, hurrying back between the empty displays. But the raven would not stop; though the boy covered Quoth's black beak with his hand, still the bird protested.

From the night-filled entrance, Jack Timms's gruff and loathsome voice called out to them. "Time's done now," he proclaimed.

In that shadow-cloaked room, the pulse of the Tormentor was suddenly stilled.

"You gonna be good and peaceable?" the warder chuckled hideously. "Come take your learnin' like sweet little lambs? Or are you gonna make Jack work up his sweat?"

With one hand clasped about the golden locket, Miss Ursula raised her outraged voice in answer. "How dare you plague and harry us!" she cried. "Begone, you base-born creature, before she who cuts the strands of life severs your revolting thread."

The man cackled in reply. "You don't have no sway over Tick-Tock!" he grunted. "Got just as much right to be 'ere as you. Many's the life he's cut short in these walls, so don't think you're anythin' special."

"Prince of fools!" she railed back. "What injury do you think you or your despotic Master can inflict upon the Spinners of the Wood? His Valkyries were consumed by righteous flame, and in our keeping we hold the spear He would use against us. Your paltry threats are empty and vaunting. Return to the death that should have been yours in the filth-strewn gutters of the past."

A gust of fetid air blasted through the doorway, and the candle flames shivered and died before it. Only the oil lamps remained burning in The Separate Collection, and upon Neil's shoulder, Quoth continued to croak and cry.

"You don't see, does you?" Jack Timms spat. "All them high and mighty words—when you've already lost."

Neil glanced at Miss Ursula. "What does he mean?" he breathed.

Suddenly, from the Egyptian gloom, a large white boulder came hurtling. For an instant its irregular round form spun in the shadows before crashing to the floor, bouncing violently against a cabinet that toppled on its side under the force of the impact.

"He's lobbin' stones at us!" Edie exclaimed.

Snapping on the ghost hunter's flashlight, Neil pointed the beam through the murk, and its circle of brilliant light blazed upon the heavy missile that was now rocking on the floor. In the shining light they saw the splintered ivory of a finely carved skull. The harsh radiance glared in the empty eye sockets and gleamed across the broken and shattered jaw.

"The lovely lady," Edie murmured sadly.

A disgusting snigger issued from the entrance. "Looks a lot better now, she do," the warder drawled. "Pity I had to hack off one of them pretty arms as well, but there's no stoppin' Jack at times when he's havin' his fun."

"The Loom Maidens have other forces at their command," Miss Ursula said coldly.

"Have they now?" the insidious voice hissed with a disdaining archness. "It's a cryin' shame that you'll not get a chance to use 'em. A real weepin' c'lamity."

Horrendous gurgling laughter exploded in The Egyptian Suite, a chilling barrage of monstrous mirth that unexpectedly diminished as the man swaggered back into The Dissolution Gallery.

"Where's he goin'?" Edie spouted.

"I do not know," Miss Ursula replied, the puzzlement revealed on her face. "Why did he not enter?"

"Perhaps he can't," Mr. Pickering suggested. "Maybe he could sense the accumulated powers stashed in here."

"No," the old woman said sharply. "There is some other devilment he means to do."

Switching the flashlight off, Neil winced and swore when Quoth nipped him hard on the ear to finally get the boy's full attention. "What was that for?" Neil demanded. "What is it?"

Fluttering from his perch, the raven flew once around the group before alighting on one of the counters, where he hopped up and down and screeched, shaking his feathers.

Staring at him in irritation, Miss Ursula suddenly glanced about her, and a strangled breath choked in her throat.

"Where is she?" the old woman cried. "Where is Celandine?"

Only then did the others realize that Miss Celandine Webster was no longer among them, and their hearts quailed.

* * *

While the others were so busily engaged in raiding the collection, Miss Celandine wandered bemused through the room, playfully waving her fingers over the candles and giggling at the shapes the shadows made on the ceiling.

As she absently meandered away from her sister and Edith, who were both so serious and cross with her the whole time, her crabbed lips mouthed the words to a half-remembered tune.

Celandine adored the romance of candlelight, but the darkness was even more enticing. There she could be young and beautiful again and simper at the compliments her imagined suitors paid her. What a delicious evening it was; she barely noticed the supreme cold, and the carriage of her thoughts was already traveling a different road. She had quite forgotten about the orphans and was engrossed in practicing her curtsies when a low, lilting refrain reached her ears.

Consumed with violent curiosity, she tossed her braids behind her bare shoulders and rested her prominent teeth on her lower lip as she listened intently to that tantalizing melody.

The rapturous music was drifting from behind the closed door that led out into the passage. Tripping lightly around the displays like a scurrying mouse, Miss Celandine capered forward. A warm and sumptuous light was shining under the door, broken by many shadows as a crowd of people seemed to pass by on the other side.

The delightful music was clearer now. Somewhere a quintet was playing, and mingled with that blissful harmony came the buzz of merry voices.

"Is it a party?" she breathed deliriously. "How precious—it is, it is."

With a wave of sudden remembrance, a childish guilt washed over her as she shot a cautious glance at Miss Ursula and the others.

"They'd be so angry," Miss Celandine debated with herself. "But they're so busy they shan't even notice. Oh, but what if they did! Ursula would be so cruel and mean."

As she stood there, dithering about whether to slip from the room, a shadow darker than the rest blocked the light that poured beneath the door. Gazing down, the muddled old woman saw a piece of card being slid under the crack. Vastly intrigued, she stooped to claim it and gasped with pleasure.

The card she held in her large, leathery hands was an invitation printed with shining silver ink. She gazed at it in enchanted wonderment.

Miss Celandine Webster

*cordially invites you to
a celebration banquet
to be held in honor of our noble Lord Nelson's
victory over the French.*

*Wyrd Place
Well Lane*

There will be dancing

A pitiful whimper escaped her lips as she lovingly traced the elaborate, flowing letters. "My party," she lamented, her nutty face falling as she recalled only too clearly the uproar that had ensued when her sister had discovered her fanciful intent all those years ago.

"The darling party Ursula wouldn't permit me to have," she murmured, crumpling the card in her hands and crushing it to her bosom. "When she burned all my pretty dresses to punish me."

Behind the door the jaunty tune continued, and Miss Celandine's agonized vacillating was over. "It's happening at last," she marveled. "That's my lovely party out there. It's really happening, and they're waiting for me—they are, they are!"

Without another thought for her sister or anyone else, Miss Celandine grasped the doorknob and slipped silently out into the corridor—oblivious to the terror that awaited.

CHAPTER 21

MORTAL DREADS

"Celandine!" Miss Ursula called in anguish. "This is no time for your games—Celandine!"

Neil swept the flashlight beam around the room, but they could not see her anywhere. Searching under the empty cases, Edie Dorkins scrabbled over the ground on her knees, but Miss Celandine could not be found.

"Where can she have gone?" Mr. Pickering asked. "Why didn't she stay in here?"

Glaring at Quoth, Miss Ursula slapped her hand on the counter where he stood, and the bird jumped in alarm. "Tell me!" she snapped. "What did you see? Where did my sister go? What has befallen her?"

The raven cawed dejectedly.

"He can't speak!" Neil defended him. "Quoth, did you see Miss Celandine leave?"

The raven waggled his bald head energetically and flew to the passage door.

"Celandine!" Edie shrieked. "Come back—Celandine!" Reaching it first, the girl yanked it open, but the winding corridor outside had plunged back into the darkness, and there was no sign of the missing woman.

"Where is she?" Edie cried, stepping out into that tunnel of engulfing night, the dagger still clenched in her hand. Swiftly, Miss Ursula came after her and held an oil lamp high over their heads to push back the pressing shadows.

The stretch of corridor was deserted in both directions. Only the crumbled remains of the taxidermied menagerie littered the ravaged route before the path turned the obscuring corners.

"Celandine!" Miss Ursula shouted.

Abruptly, the flashlight beam shone into the narrow passage, flaring in the scattering of fractured glass as Neil and the others joined them.

"Which way did she go?" Brian Chapman asked, remaining with Josh in the doorway of The Separate Collection.

"I do not know," Miss Ursula answered, aghast. "She could be anywhere within the museum by now."

"No!" Edie sobbed. "We got to find her! Bring her back!"

"Yes," Miss Ursula agreed. "Before it is too late. We must search for her."

"But Tick-Tock's out there," Neil whispered.

"She knows that, lad," Mr. Pickering assured him. "She knows."

"Edith," Miss Ursula said quickly, "you come with me—we shall look this way."

But the girl shook her head stubbornly. "I wanna go down here." Before Neil could stop her, Edie wrenched the light from his fingers and pelted into the dark.

"Edith!" Miss Ursula cried. "You must not go alone!" But the girl had already rounded the corner, and the old woman turned anxiously to Neil. "Run after her," she pleaded. "I beg you."

Barely realizing what he was doing, Neil found himself running down the passage, and crowing behind him flew Quoth.

"That's a brave boy you have there," Austen Pickering told the caretaker. "I'll try and keep up with him."

"No," Miss Ursula commanded decisively. "Come with me, if you will. Celandine must be found, and the more who search the better. Mr. Chapman, stay in The Separate Collection with your young son, and call if Edith and the boy return."

In a moment, she and the ghost hunter had hurried off in the opposite direction from Neil and Edie. Closing the door behind them, Brian Chapman drew Josh back to the fireside.

"I want Neil!" the toddler wept. "Dad, I'm scared and the cold hurts."

The caretaker pushed another piece of wood into the flames and sat beside his son, his eyes staring spellbound at the bright, leaping colors. "It can only get colder," he whispered softly.

* * *

With the beam of light bouncing feverishly before her like an insane will-o'-the-wisp, Edie Dorkins hared down the corridor, calling for Miss Celandine. Over fragments of disintegrated spider monkey and crippled hyena the wildly waving white glare leaped, glittering in the staring, lifeless eyes. The girl's shoes crunched through the stuffed carcasses and fractured glass splintered under her stamping heels.

Behind, she could hear Quoth gaining as the raven rushed through the moldy air, squawking loudly, and she was forced to a staggering halt when he beat his feathers against her face.

"Get off!" she yelled. "I've got to find her!"

Quoth ducked and darted away from her flaying hands, but the delay had been enough, for his master had caught up with them.

"Stop right there!" Neil panted, grabbing hold of the girl's coat.

Edie growled at him. "Let go!" she raged. "I know she's down this way—I can feel it!"

A twittering giggle suddenly sailed from the darkness in front, and the girl pointed the flashlight at the twisting corner ahead of them.

"Hear that?" she cried. "That were Celandine right enough—she's just around there!"

"Give me that," Neil said firmly, taking the flashlight from her and moving forward in the direction of that childlike voice.

"Run," Edie told him, sprinting away like a rabbit from its hole.

"Wait!" the boy called. "Edie, not so fast—don't you see? The hallway was never this long before. We should be at the landing by now. Edie, come back!"

Cursing her under his breath, Neil dashed down the passage, and together they turned the corner. Through the long expanse of darkness that lay beyond, the intense ray of the flashlight pierced and stabbed, and there, at the far end of this unfamiliar corridor, they saw her.

"Celandine!" Edie shouted.

The powerful beam shone over the faded ruby velvet of her gown. Around and around Miss Celandine Webster whirled, the ample folds of her mildewed dress wrapping and furling about her as she waltzed dreamily down the passage.

Yet Miss Celandine was not dancing alone.

Her partner was a tall, burly man dressed in Regency finery. A frock coat of bottle green adorned with rows of gleaming brass buttons covered his broad back. Tucked into a pair of highly polished calf-length boots were white pantaloons, and wedged on his head he wore a black bicorne hat.

Holding her firmly about the waist, he waltzed her farther down the stretching corridor, and Miss Celandine laughed giddily. Quoth gave a feeble caw, and Edie spluttered as Neil trained the flashlight on the man's scarred and pockmarked face.

"Tick-Tock," he uttered.

"Let her go!" Edie bawled, brandishing her dagger and springing after them, her hair flying wildly. "Celandine, get away from him!"

With a snarling cackle, Jack Timms swiveled his rodent eyes cruelly around, glaring and gloating at the children who were rushing toward them.

"Jack told you it were too late!" he gargled. "You done lost her now—lost her fer good!" And with that he laughed horribly, throwing the whole of his awful strength into the dance.

Around and around Miss Celandine was spun. Faster and faster Jack Timms flung her. Tighter he wrapped his arm around her waist, crushing her against the barrel of his fat self. In his iron grasp her hands were smothered, and the waltz became a berserking reel.

"Too boisterous, sir!" the old woman protested, trying to resist and pull away. "I cannot keep up. Slow down—please!"

But the warder laughed in her face, and the demented dance degenerated into a violent tussle.

"Unhand me!" Miss Celandine cried, stumbling over the fleeting ground, her long braids flicking out around her, whisking and smacking the walls. Into the gloom of the ever-receding corridor she went wheeling, her feet no longer touching the floor as Jack Timms lifted her in his viselike arms.

Running after them, Neil and Edie saw a melting change alter the foul man's fine garments. The frock coat darkened and grew in volume to become his regular black greatcoat, and the bicorne hat acquired a battered brim in which the crown swelled and rumpled. Dressed now in his usual warder's clothes, he twisted Miss Celandine's arm behind her back, and she squealed in fear.

About her faded red dress the shadows shimmered. Then the color bled away until only the crisp white linen of a starched nightgown remained.

"No!" Neil howled, suddenly feeling sick and lurching to a standstill. "Quoth!" he called in distress. "Go back. Find Ursula, bring her here as fast you can. Quick! I . . . I think I know what he's doing!"

Not wasting an instant the raven cawed, and with a mighty sweep of his wings he shot back up the passageway, disappearing into the shrouding distance.

Miss Celandine shrieked as all semblance of the dance was abandoned. Tick-Tock Jack seized her roughly by the waist and throat, dragging the old woman toward one of the waiting doors. Ominously, it creaked open at his guffawing approach.

A sickly radiance abruptly flared in the corridor as gas lamps glimmered into being on the walls, and Neil's skin prickled as his suspicion mounted. Through the door Jack Timms trawled the struggling Miss Celandine, who scrabbled at the wall and kicked out with her naked feet.

"Ursula!" she yowled, her eyes an unpleasant, rolling white. "Save me—oh, Ursula! Help me, Edith!"

Into the room the woman was hauled, and the door slammed back in its frame just as Edie came dashing up to it. Frenetically the girl wrenched the handle, but the door wouldn't budge, and behind it she could hear Miss Celandine's piteous screeches growing ever fainter.

"Open up!" Edie demanded, throwing her small body against it, hammering the panels with her fists and the pommel of the dagger. "Celandine! Celandine!"

* * *

Rocketing through the corridor, Quoth thrashed his wings faster than he had ever done before, crying at the top of his raucous voice. Around him the swirling shadows shifted as the passageway switched in and out of the past. Dim gaslight flickered briefly, only to be blasted by a buzzing electric glare, and then the darkness sprang back to reclaim its ghastly realm.

With his one eye straining to see the dim, winding way ahead, the raven hooted and honked for Miss Ursula, but there was no sign of her. As Quoth swooped recklessly around the sharp corners, his fear and distress soared. The museum was playing its old tricks and deceits on him. Already the corridor was twisting far more than it had on the outward journey, and on either side, doorways appeared where there surely had never been any before.

The raven started to panic—he had failed his young master. The museum would not let him find Miss Ursula, and he wondered if he should race back to Neil's side.

Circling in retreat he plunged backward but immediately skidded in midair. He stared hopelessly about him and came to the horrible realization that he was completely lost.

Cheeping forlornly, Quoth flipped over in the moldering atmosphere, wondering what to do. All was silent and still, and he was alone in the threatening dark.

Feeling small and totally vulnerable, Quoth jabbered to himself. He was on the verge of despairing tears when he remembered that his master was in danger, and that awful knowledge rekindled his spirits.

No longer afraid for his own scraggy skin, Quoth resumed his urgent errand. Let the museum perform its treacherous chicanery, he thought. Let it torment him with false lures and lead him around in circles. He would never give in while his young master was in peril.

Swiftly the raven tore into the swallowing gloom, banking and pitching to clear the black barring obstacles that leaned out from the walls and into his path. Through unknown doorways he rushed, surging blindly into empty rooms, only to emerge where other unfamiliar entrances yawned open.

But Quoth was dogged and determined. He did not permit the bewildering labyrinth to confound him—he knew that he had to keep going. Like a feathered dart he bolted through the dust-swirling galleries that tried to snare him with their mazing exits. In that forbidding pitch, the raven's eye shone bold and resolute within his grim face.

Diving through another foreign doorway, Quoth unexpectedly found himself back in the passageway, and in the distance, he could see a faint, glimmering light. Hope blazed like a beacon in his breast, for there—cupping the flame of his cigarette lighter in his hand and searching the darkness—was Austen Pickering.

Squawking gratefully, Quoth beat his wings all the faster, and the ghost hunter looked up sharply at the sound of his frantic, clamoring voice.

"Quoth?" he called as the raven hurtled down the corridor. "Is that you?" Swiftly the anguished bird flew to the old man's wrist and gibbered wildly.

"Hold on, old son!" Mr. Pickering exclaimed. "Calm down."

The raven gulped down beakfuls of air as his bald head darted from side to side, seeking for Miss Ursula.

"Have Neil and Edie found Celandine?" the ghost hunter asked. "Is that what you're trying to say?"

Quoth nodded beseechingly and stared up into the old man's face. The reflection of the lighter's flame played brightly over the thick lenses of Mr. Pickering's glasses, and the raven felt oddly disconcerted at not being able to see the man's eyes.

"A good thing you found me, then," Mr. Pickering said with an unaccountable calmness in his voice. "But it's Ursula I 'spect you'll be wanting. She's just around that corner."

A halo of flickering light swept over the wall behind, and Quoth spread his wings again. There was something about the old man that disturbed and unsettled him, and in agitation, he hopped from his wrist to fetch Miss Ursula.

"Oh no," the ghost hunter said mildly, "you can't leave—not yet." And, to the raven's astonishment, Mr. Pickering grabbed hold of his legs, plucking him roughly from the air.

Struggling furiously against this unexpected attack, Quoth shrieked in alarm. But the old man continued to cling to him, and an unpleasant smile parted his craggy face.

"Mr. Pickering?" Miss Ursula's angst-ridden voice called in the near distance. "Is that the boy's raven? Mr. Pickering, where are you?"

Screeching, Quoth pecked at the hand that gripped him, but the stubby fingers would not let go, and suddenly the darkness snapped about them both as the lighter was extinguished.

"We'll just stop that racket now, shall we?" Mr. Pickering muttered, and Quoth felt the other hand come reaching for his face.

Unable to free himself, the raven was suddenly silenced when his beak was seized and clamped firmly shut. "Can't have you warning anyone now, can I?" the ghost hunter hissed. "Not after all the trouble I've gone to."

"Mr. Pickering!" Miss Ursula cried again. "Where are you? What has occurred?"

The old man glanced at the bobbing light behind. Any moment now she would come around that corner and find them. Squeezing his fingers even tighter about Quoth's beak, Austen Pickering ducked into the nearest doorway and pressed himself against the wall.

Floundering in his grasp, Quoth made as much struggling, flapping commotion as possible, until the old man pulled him so close that the bird was almost smothered and could no longer move his wings.

In the corridor outside, the light welled up as Miss Ursula Webster turned into the passage, calling to the oppressive dark.

"Why do you not answer when I call?" her distraught voice rang out. "Where has the man gone?"

Helpless, Quoth could only watch as the space beyond the open doorway glimmered brightly and the oil lamp held by Miss Ursula appeared. Pressed against Mr. Pickering's chest, the raven could hear his heart thumping rapidly as the old man held his breath when the eldest of the Fates cast a cursory glance into the room before hastening off down the corridor. Swiftly, the radiance dwindled. That part of the Wyrd Museum was swamped by the inky night once more, and Miss Ursula's desperate cries faded into the remote background.

Without releasing him, Austen Pickering loosened his grip on the raven and lifted the bird to stare into his goggling face. "Did you really think I'd let you squeak your scabby head off and give the game away?" the old man chortled. "Oh, no, my little friend. What a shame you lost the power of speech. You might have been able to save the day—even at this, the bitter end."

Quoth wriggled in his grasp, snorting through his stifled nostrils. His eye glittered with the inflamed anger that raged inside him. How dare this madman hold him captive while his young master was facing untold hazards?

"I've waited far too long for my designs to be ruined by anyone." A chilling edge had crept into the old man's voice. "Especially not you. This is a moment to savor and I shall, most gladly."

The raven ceased his squirming resistance as the truth finally trumpeted inside his decayed mind. All his innocent, harmless dreams came clattering in ruins around him as he looked up into that shadowy face.

"Very soon it will be over," the ghost hunter murmured. "The Cessation will be complete."

Gazing at those dark, bespectacled eyes, Quoth whimpered in Mr. Pickering's fists as he penetrated that unassuming persona and knew his hour had come.

The old man chuckled softly, his voice dropping to a seditious whisper as he said, "Did you think I would forget our last appointment, my dear, beloved Memory? I told you we would meet three times. This is your last and final chance."

Here then, wearing the crusty disguise he had created to inveigle his way into the Wyrd Museum, was the raven's former master—Woden.

"Even now, at the very brink of the Nornir's destruction, it is not too late to reconsider," the compelling voice told him. "Though that fat oaf Timms has served me well thus far, I still have need of your fond companionship, Memory."

Quoth's apoplectic terror was beyond anything he had ever experienced before. His entire frame trembled violently. He wanted to scream, but even if he had been able to open his beak, he doubted if he could find his cringing voice.

"The choice is yours," Woden hissed. "Return and serve me loyally or remain this ignoble, absurd apology of a creature. Only know that if you spurn me this time, you will pay the ultimate price for your insolence and ingratitude. Which is it to be? Make your final answer."

The raven shuddered. A great tear streamed down his face and his soul cowered inside him. How could he reject Neil and go back to being that cruel monster of his malignant youth? The prospect horrified and repelled him. Yet, if he did not become Memory and fly at Woden's side once more, then he would most certainly perish.

What alternative did he have? Staring at the fraudulent face of Austen Pickering through his watering eye, the raven knew that there was no denying the Captain of Askar.

Swallowing a bitter breath, Quoth went limp and he hung his head despondently.

"The decision is made?" Woden demanded.

The raven gave one mournful nod, defeated and crushed.

An insidious laugh rippled from his captor's mouth. "You have selected with your old wisdom, my friend," Woden congratulated. "Come, Memory, let us watch the ultimate humiliation of the Witches of the Wood together."

Quoth felt the tenacious fingers unfasten from around his beak, and his hunched shoulders sagged with dejection. "Do not grieve," Woden ordered him. "In a moment you will scorn this pitiful existence."

Into the corridor the Gallows God carried the raven. Then, snatching this one chance he had been praying for, Quoth threw back his head and valiantly let loose a piercing, clarion scream.

Throughout the Wyrd Museum that shrill warning echoed as Quoth screeched for his life and hoped that, somewhere, Neil could hear him. Into that last, sacrificing shriek he propelled all that he would never again say to his beloved young master.

Then his discordant, dolorous cry was silenced.

"Faithless crow!" Woden snapped, catching hold of

the raven by the throat and twisting his hands savagely. "I'll waste no more time on you!"

And in that throttling darkness, Quoth's earnest little life was ended.

* * *

In the glimmering gaslit passageway, Neil Chapman threw himself against the door. But before his shoulder slammed into the panels, the barrier swung treacherously inward, and the boy went sprawling into the room beyond.

Edie Dorkins leaped after him. Miss Celandine's pitiful screams were several rooms away, and not waiting for the boy to pick himself up from the floor, she scampered off, waving her dagger.

Scrambling to his feet, Neil looked quickly around him. The room was crowded with empty hospital beds. A pungent reek of chemicals and damp bed linen soured the air of that ghastly place, and the acrid stench burned into his nostrils.

A pang of recognition pulled at the corners of Neil's mind—he had been here before. This was how the Wyrd Infirmary had looked long after it had closed its doors, having lain empty and neglected for many years. During the time of World War II the boy had wandered through these deserted wards, and now he knew exactly where Miss Celandine Webster had been taken.

Racing in Edie's wake, he plunged through ward after ward while the old woman's fevered shrieks grew steadily closer. Finally he caught up with the girl outside a windowless, boxed-in room, and although Miss Celandine's weeping cries were very close now, they both hesitated before entering.

"The Egyptian Suite," Neil murmured.

"Will be," Edie corrected him.

"I know what's through there."

The girl gripped her dagger in readiness. "An' so will I!" she answered gravely.

Into that dim place the children pressed. Two meager gas flames made a soft popping noise about their mantles, and Neil stole a glance at the barbaric dentist's chair that dominated that room before hurrying out into what would one day become The Separate Collection.

There was the horrendous surgical chamber he remembered from his previous exploration, and Edie spluttered in distress when she entered. A raised platform of tiered wooden benches clustered around three of the walls, forming a rudimentary amphitheater. A number of well-dressed people sat waiting, their idle chatter dying when the children burst in.

Yet neither Edie nor Neil paid any attention to them for, in the middle of the sunken stage, Jack Timms and two other warders were dragging Miss Celandine across the sawdust-strewn floor to where a long table, fitted with sinister-looking buckled straps, was waiting.

"Stop it!" Edie squealed, barging forward, dagger in hand. "Let her go! Celandine—Celandine!"

"Edith!" the old woman squealed in despairing confusion. "Help me!"

Lunging at Tick-Tock Jack, Neil cannoned into him; the odious man reeled aside, only to flash out with his mighty arms and crack the boy against the side of his head. Even as Neil crumpled to the floor, Edie pounced and stabbed at the warder with the dagger. But the burly man spun around as the striking blow ripped harmlessly through his coat.

"Drop that, you savage little 'eathen!" he growled, seizing the girl by the wrist and shaking her brutally until the blade clattered from her fingers. Then, with a disdainful grunt, Jack Timms hurled her aside, and Edie went flying into one of the three carts that bore primitive surgical instruments.

"Timms!" a stern, highly strung voice cried. "What is the meaning of this? How did those urchins get in here?"

Tick-Tock assumed a guileless expression that looked ridiculous upon that iniquitous sinner's face. "Don't rightly know, sir," he gargled piously. "I'll get Mr. Naggers to chuck 'em out straight'way, sir."

"Do so!" the stranger's voice commanded.

At once, a lean, weasel-featured man with a long nose let go of Miss Celandine and grabbed Neil by the collar. Hoisted from the sawdust where he had fallen, the boy spluttered, licking the lip that had split where Tick-Tock had struck him.

Dazed, Neil shook his head and gazed fearfully around the auditorium as Harry Naggers marched over to Edie, pulling both their madly kicking figures from the room.

Jack Timms threw the children a filthy, gloating

glance. "Put 'em next door, 'Arry," he cackled to his confederate. "I'll see to 'em meself, after."

"As you say, Mr. Timms," the warder's whining voice replied.

With a wicked grin splitting his pitted face, Tick-Tock returned to the evil business at hand.

By the long table, a pallid, nervous-looking young man wearing a leather apron tersely barked an instruction and impatiently waved to the warders to bring Miss Celandine over. "Be certain you restrain her correctly," he ordered. "I don't want any accidents."

"Don't you worry none, sir," Jack Timms's oily black voice promised. "She won't be able to wiggle so much as a little toe when I've done."

The jittery young surgeon turned to the distinguished group assembled on the benches, raising his voice above Miss Celandine's cries as the warders lugged her onto the table and set to with the buckles.

"My good Lord Darnling," he called, smiling ingratiatingly. "I am honored that you could accept my invitation at such short notice."

An aristocratic-looking man wearing a neatly pointed gray beard and full evening dress tapped his pocket watch irritably. "This procedure going to take long, Lawrence?" he asked with consummate arrogance. "There are two hansoms waiting outside to take us back to town for the opera. Not expecting any more interruptions, I trust?"

"No, of course not," the zealous doctor answered. "I can commence immediately."

Seated beside the bearded man, a plump woman wearing a preposterously wide hat trimmed with black ostrich feathers waved a perfumed handkerchief under her upturned nose and playfully wagged a lace-gloved hand at the surgeon.

"Who is your patient?" she inquired, peering over his shoulder through her opera glasses. "One of your mental deficients?"

"Indeed, Lady Darnling," he replied respectfully, "but a murderess—one Mary-Anne Brindle. She killed a warder several nights ago. She is of no consequence—a hanging case, merely."

Towed harshly to the anteroom containing the dentist's chair, Neil cried out in horror as he heard those doom-laden words. "No!" he yelled. "You've got the wrong person. It's not her—can't you see that?"

"Pipe down!" Harry Naggers threatened.

But Neil was not intimidated. "That isn't Mary-Anne Brindle!" he shouted. "You're the mad one—you don't know what you're doing! Listen to me!"

Bundled roughly into the dim windowless room, Neil caught a momentary glimpse of a large tray on one of the carts, and an abhorrent dread constricted his throat.

"They can't hurt her!" Edie boasted, shrieking so that Miss Celandine could hear. "Don't worry, you'll be all right! They can't touch yer!"

Heedless of Mr. Naggers's bruising grasp, Neil turned a drained face toward the girl, and when he spoke, his voice was tight and faltering.

"D . . . Didn't you see it?" he stammered.

Touched with his terror, Edie's eyes widened and her blood streamed cold in her veins. "What?" she uttered.

"On that tray," the boy replied, "with the knives and saws. It was there—I saw it!"

Instinctively, Edie knew what Neil had seen, and she shook her head in fierce defiance, lashing out with renewed vigor and desperation at the man who held her.

"Celandine!" she screeched. "Celandine!"

But she could not escape from Harry Naggers's cruel arrest, and the girl screamed as she clawed and bit him.

"Edith!" the old woman's voice squealed. "I'm frightened. Where are Ursula and Veronica? Help me! Save me!"

"Gogus!" Edie cried at the surrounding walls. "Where are you? Gogus, we need you. Celandine needs you!"

In the operating room, Doctor Samuel Lawrence blithely took the Spear of Longinus from the tray in his trembling hands. And at that same moment, Quoth's dying screech resounded throughout the building.

* * *

With the oil lamp lighting her way, Miss Ursula Webster hastened through the strangling gloom of the corridor, calling out her sister's name. Behind her, the raven's death call was suddenly silenced, and she whirled around, terrorized and mortally afraid.

• 383 •

"No," she breathed desolately. "Too late—too late!"

A barbed pain ripped into her stomach, and she fell to her knees. "Celandine!" she shrieked. "No! Celandine!"

A revolting guffaw boomed out through the passageway as Jack Timms rejoiced in his jamboree, and Miss Ursula buried her face in her hands.

Deep below the foundations of the Wyrd Museum, the withered vastness of Nirinel quaked and shivered, and from its arching magnitude a cascade of blackened, stinking bark rained down into the chamber.

Outside, in the frozen night, the Victorian entrance to the museum shuddered within the thick layer of ice that sealed it. Upon its plinth, the bronze figure by the door quivered and shook as, over its graceful form, an ugly, jagged crack ruptured and split.

With a splintering crash the sculpture exploded.

Miss Celandine Webster, she who as Skuld had woven the tapestry of so many destinies, was dead.

CHAPTER 22

THE JOURNEY TO THE STAIR

Edie Dorkins's horrified screams cut through the gaslit gloom, and present time surged in around her once more. With a final pop, the gas lamps slipped back to the past and the dentist's chair dissolved into the dim dust. Filling the antechamber, three Egyptian sarcophagi congealed into solid existence. Then Harry Naggers's pinching grip disintegrated from her arms, and both she and Neil were free.

Storming from that cramped room, Edie fled into The Separate Collection, but Neil wavered before following. "Quoth?" he called, certain he had heard the raven's echoing cries. "Where are you? Quoth?"

In the adjoining room, the caretaker stood as still as the broken statues down on the first floor.

"Celandine!" Edie wept, sweeping the hair from her eyes as she searched. "Celandine!" It was then that she turned to Brian, and the gray-faced, stricken man managed the slightest of nods.

"She . . . she just turned up," he mumbled faintly. "Out of thin air. No, stay where you are—I don't think you should . . ."

Beyond the large screening case that contained the Eye of Balor, Edie Dorkins's shrinking gaze saw Miss Celandine Webster lying on a long glass counter, her arms hanging over the sides. The wrinkled, ruddy face that had lived with such sprightly animation was now forever stilled. She was wearing her favorite velvet gown once more, but now the color was stained more intensely ruby than it had been for many years.

With faltering steps, Edie approached, then took the gnarled brown spade of the old woman's hand and kissed it, resting her cheek in its already cold palm. Tears drove clean tracks through the grime on her young, devastated face.

"In God's name, what happened?" Brian gasped. "Where's Neil? Is he . . ."

Emerging from the shadows of The Egyptian Suite, his elder son assuaged the caretaker's fears. "I'm okay, Dad," he said bleakly. Joining him, Neil wiped his eyes. He could see the velvet-robed figure lying upon the counter, and he sorrowfully hung his head.

"There was nothing we could do," he breathed. "He had it all worked out. She didn't stand a chance."

A grotesque silence descended, in which the caretaker and his sons watched Edie stroke Miss Celandine's face and arrange her braided hair about her shoulders. "There," she murmured softly in her ear. "You'll be with Veronica now, 'aving jam an' pancakes, and you can dance as much as you want."

Walking up behind her, Neil gently touched the girl's arm. "Come over to the fire," he said. "Till the others get back."

Edie shook her head obstinately. "No," she refused. "I can't leave Celandine on her own."

A purposeful tread chimed on the floorboards behind them, and Miss Ursula strode in from The Egyptian Suite, her eyes glinting and her thin lips pressed bloodlessly tight.

Miss Ursula Webster was now the last surviving member of the three ancient Fates, and Neil hardly dared look at her for fear of what he might see in that gaunt, finely boned face. Yet the monumental grief he had expected was not there. A dispassionate and rigid composure controlled the old woman's bearing, and her expression was as hard and unfathomable as the jet beads that adorned her evening dress.

Stepping aside to make way for her, Neil could not understand how she was able to maintain that outward aloof detachment, and the absurd thought struck him that perhaps she did not yet realize Celandine was dead.

But no, as she advanced, there could be no doubt. Behind that impassive façade, Miss Ursula's eyes were as windows to a torment that she could not begin to mask or deny.

"So," she said in a level, mastered monotone, "she is departed. I knew it would be so—I felt it. Our old foe has claimed another of the Royal House. A second defenseless victim has fallen in this madness."

Running her fingers through her dirty hair, Edie sniffed and said miserably, "If I'd still've had my hat on I could've stopped 'em. Why didn't I take it with me?"

"Apportion no blame to yourself, Edith," Miss Ursula consoled her. "From the moment she stepped outside this room, Celandine was doomed. Have no doubt about that."

"What . . . what should we do now?" Brian Chapman asked uncertainly.

The old woman's head reared, and she pierced him with her spiking glance. "Do you really desire me to answer that?" she demanded. "Or would you rather have me respond to the true meaning so clumsily veiled behind your stumbling words? What you wish to learn is whether it is over and are you safe. Is that not correct?"

The caretaker fidgeted uncomfortably. "Partly, I suppose," he confessed. "Are we?"

Casting her gaze about The Separate Collection, Miss Ursula waited before giving her reply. The impenetrable ice that obliterated the exterior of the windows was now forming on the inside of the glass, and long icicles were already tapering down from the sills. Around the perimeter of the room, on the surfaces of those cabinets that stood farthest from the fire, stellular frost was sparkling, and a ghostly whiteness covered the paneled walls.

"No, Mr. Chapman," she eventually said. "We are not safe—none of us. Do you not understand? By murdering my sister in here, albeit in the past, the agent of Woden has claimed this room as his own.

There is also a new consideration which we must not forget."

"What's that?"

It was Neil who answered. "Jack Timms has the spear, Dad," he said flatly.

"With that accursed blade he is able to cut through all our defenses," Miss Ursula admitted. "He will not rest until he has slain us all, Edith and myself in particular."

"But how did he get his scummy paws on it?" Edie demanded. "It were in 'ere with us."

Miss Ursula raised her eyebrows. "How indeed?" she echoed. "Did Mr. Pickering not have it in his keeping?"

"Why isn't he back yet?" Neil murmured uneasily. "He and Quoth should have turned up by now. You don't think something's happened to them as well, do you?"

"Who can say?" Miss Ursula replied.

From the corridor outside, they suddenly heard the ghost hunter's anxious voice calling, and Neil hurried to the doorway. In the absolute blackness beyond, Austen Pickering cried out in relief.

"Thank goodness!" he shouted. "I thought I was permanently lost in this blind warren. I didn't have a clue where I was. The passage seemed to go on for miles, and I couldn't get my dratted lighter to work."

Out of the shadows, Woden's prosaic disguise came ambling, a delighted but weary look established upon his face.

"I couldn't find her," he puffed, resting his hand on the boy's shoulder. "And after I lost the other one, I never heard or saw a soul. Did you and the girl fare any better?"

Neil stared at him for a moment, fumbling for the right words, then drew him inside The Separate Collection.

"Miss Celandine's dead," he told him squarely. "Jack Timms got her. He made her take the place of Mary-Anne Brindle on the operating table and . . . well, you know how she died."

An utterly convincing, mortified horror flashed across the ghost hunter's face as he lumbered into the room and surveyed the wretched scene.

"I never really thought it would go this far," he muttered. "Even tonight I didn't believe . . . I'm so very sorry."

Miss Ursula waved his condolences aside. "My sister was killed by the spear that was in your charge, Mr. Pickering," she said archly. "Would you inform me as to how the agent of Woden came by it?"

"The spear?" Austen Pickering blustered with accomplished surprise. "But I left it by the fire, with the other exhibits!"

"Then our enemy's power is greater than my vanity believed," Miss Ursula said. "This room is no longer secure. We must abandon it immediately, before we are attacked again."

"Where is there to go?" Brian Chapman asked. "You told us nowhere in the building was safe and that this was our only hope."

"So it was," she answered severely, "and see where that groundless hope has led us. My immortal sister is dead, cut open and butchered! Within this museum there can be no haven now—through His agent, Woden governs it completely."

"But we can't get outside," Neil interrupted.

"Did I say that is where we are going?" Miss Ursula snapped. "Did I?"

"Then where?"

"To the one place where no one, save the Spinners of the Wood and Edith, our adopted daughter, has ever set foot."

Leaving Miss Celandine's side, Edie Dorkins traipsed to the fireside and retrieved her pixie hat. Pulling it down over her head, the girl glowered around at the confused faces of the others and with a haughty declaration announced, "We're goin' deep under the ground."

"Are there cellars?" Brian asked. "How will they be any safer than in here?"

Miss Ursula ignored him and clapped her hands urgently. "We must go at once," she commanded. "Before Jack Timms returns. Hurry, let us depart, while we are still able."

"But isn't it dangerous in that corridor?" the caretaker demanded.

"It is just as deadly in here," she informed him. "Maybe more so, now that the room has tasted blood. At the very least we shall not be waiting for Woden's creature when he returns to murder us."

"Stop a minute!" Neil objected. "What about Quoth? He isn't back yet. You didn't hear him, did you, Mr. Pickering?"

The old man blinked mildly behind the thick lenses of his glasses, and opening the same hands that had wrung the life from the faithful raven, he lied. "No. Like I said, I heard nothing and no one."

Neil frowned, his disquiet rising.

"I sent Quoth to fetch you," he told Miss Ursula, "and I haven't seen him since. I'm not going anywhere without him."

The old woman regarded him strangely. "I heard your raven calling when I was out in the passageway," she said. "But there is no time for you to linger here. If he is still alive, there is a chance we shall encounter him on our journey."

"That's not good enough!" the boy protested. "I'm not moving!"

"Mr. Chapman!" Miss Ursula ordered. "Make that maggot obey you. We must all leave at once! Those who remain will die!"

Brian turned to his son. "You heard that!" he said. "No more nonsense."

Holding on to their father's sleeve, Josh reached out to his older brother and implored, "Please, Neil, come with us."

The boy closed his eyes in resignation. "All right," he whispered, despising himself.

Casting his gaze upon the gathered artifacts, Austen Pickering asked, "What should we bring with us?"

"There is nothing here to counter and withstand the power of the spear," Miss Ursula answered. "Choose a sword if it will make you feel easier, but do it swiftly, we must be gone. Edith, lead the way!"

Remembering how useless the dagger had been against Jack Timms, Edie would not take another weapon. "What about Celandine?" the girl cried. "We can't leave her 'ere."

Miss Ursula clasped her fingers about the golden locket she still wore and said, "We must look to the living, Edith. When this night is done and the evil spent, then we may surrender to our bereavement and bewail her death. If I were to yield to it now and reap in full the harvest of my grief, then I should not be capable of moving from this place, and the Spear of Longinus would find me swiftly."

Edie pouted unhappily, but she knew that Miss Ursula was right.

"Hurry!" the old woman told everyone. "We must dare the perils that await outside if we are to gain the stairway. To the entrance hall we must flee, at all costs!"

Edie ran through the door first, and Miss Ursula ushered the others into the passage. Before joining them, she looked one last time upon the body of her dead sister.

"Good-bye, Celandine," her brittle voice called faintly. "Forgive me, our merry little Skuld. This is the only way."

With that, she strode from the room, and The Separate Collection, with its most recent and grisly acquisition, was left behind.

* * *

Down the dark corridor the group hastened, with Edie at the forefront, holding the ghost hunter's flashlight to illuminate the narrow way. Keeping close to one another, they hurried along, two abreast.

Apprehensive and aching with concern for Quoth, Neil kept his eyes fixed firmly upon that bright, bobbing circle in front, searching and scanning the moldering debris that littered the route in case a ragged black feather was caught in the glare. At each new turn he expected them to come across the raven's injured body. Perhaps Quoth had flown headlong into a wall and was lying sprawled and stunned somewhere.

That was the only hopeful explanation he could cling to, for if Quoth was unharmed then surely he would have returned or they would have heard him cawing. Neil did not dwell on the only other forbidding possibility.

Edie's thoughts were blighted by a different dread. Her fear was that the flashlight's beam would shine suddenly over Jack Timms's obstructing figure, and she listened vigilantly for any rumor of his bloated breaths ahead. At least the corridor appeared to be behaving itself. There were no unexpected corners, no elongating paths or misleading entrances to dupe and beguile the senses.

"Look!" Neil hissed when a splintered doorway glimmered at the far end. "That's the exit to the landing."

"It all seems okay so far," his father observed in a dubious whisper.

"Yes, it does," Mr. Pickering agreed. "Let's just hope it stays that way."

The instant he had uttered those words, they each became aware of a change in the hemming blackness.

Hastening toward that exit, they felt the floor begin to pucker and swell under their feet, and a draft of biting air funneled about them. The oppressive, heavy shadows lifted over their heads, and the corridor's walls seemed to retreat into the dark.

Craving to know what was happening, but not permitting her gaze to wander from the flashlight beam, Edie cried out abruptly.

"Edith, dear," Miss Ursula called to her, "what is amiss?"

The girl breathed an allaying breath and reproached herself for succumbing to her raw, jangled nerves. Rearing before them, rising up from the center of the passage and ripping through the fusty carpet, was a tall beech tree.

Over its trunk the light swept, to incredulous gasps from Brian Chapman. Then, higher still, the girl directed the light, and they all saw the tree's sturdy branches reach up into a starry sky.

"The museum!" Neil spluttered. "Where is it? Where are we?"

Drinking in the keen air, Miss Ursula stared about them. "Where we have always been," she replied.

They were standing on a sparsely wooded rise over which a muted radiance was moving, for beyond the extreme rim of the world a pallid dawn was about to edge into the night. On their left, the land sloped steeply downward into a dense and immeasurable forest, the clumped, crowded trees resembling a cumulus expanse of thick black thundercloud.

"I do not understand why Woden has sent us back to this age," she said. "Let us resume at a brisker pace.

We must gain the security of the wood. Only then will we truly be safe."

Skirting around the beech tree, they discovered that some elements of the Wyrd Museum had not completely disappeared. The threadbare carpet was still in evidence, appearing in patches between the grass and fallen leaves. It continued to run in a straight line, right to where the timber frame of the landing doorway rose incongruously out of the ground.

"Do not deviate from the path," Miss Ursula told them when Brian Chapman showed signs of descending the ridge before the abstract entrance had been reached. "We must not be confounded by this place. Where there are doors we must use them, or our goal may never be attained."

Through the frame she herded them, then down the slope. Even there, fragments of the museum's fabric could be found. A slanting length of banister guided them on their descent, and protruding sporadically from the earth like steps under a thawing drift of snow was the staircase itself.

Clambering down the declining track, Edie Dorkins gradually came to a halt, and as the others brushed by her, she lifted her head to gaze back up the hill.

"Edith," Miss Ursula asked, seeing her pondering face. "What fascinates you so?"

The girl put a finger to her lips. "Heard somethin'," she whispered. "Come from way up there, it did."

Miss Ursula put her arm about the child's shoulders as she too strained to listen. "Now I comprehend!" she said a moment later. "That is why we are here."

Whisking sharply around, she took hold of Edie's hand and vigorously hurried down the submerged steps to catch up with the others. Neil, his father, and Josh were waiting for them a little way below but, clutching the banister rail and seemingly unaware that the old woman and the girl had lingered behind, Mr. Pickering trotted on regardless. It was only when the noise that Edie had heard grew a degree louder that the impostor paused and, with great aplomb, showed his surprise.

From over the crest of that ridge arose the rumor of many voices raised in anger and challenge. Vague and indistinct at first, the sound swelled swiftly, and among those defiant yells and doughty shrieks rang the clashing of sword against sword.

"Our plight is very great!" Miss Ursula cried, the urgency chiming in her voice. "If we do not fly from this place we shall be overridden by battle."

"What is that up there?" Mr. Pickering asked.

"This is a time of bloody conflict," she answered quickly. "Woden has delivered us into the path of two opposing armies. Over this site a cruel and bitter conflict was waged. The forces of Caesar were met on this field by the descendants of Askar, and so fierce was the fray that it raged even to the eaves of the enchanted wood. Within the circling mists, my sisters and I heard the ferocity of that contention. Fear for your lives! The storm will burst down upon us and you will be caught within its midst."

The distant uproar had mounted to a tremendous

clamor. In that stentorian struggle, horses were screaming and the ground echoed with the pounding charge of countless foot soldiers. Death cries rent the fading night, and not waiting for the first of those legions to come swarming over the hill, the refugees of the Wyrd Museum plunged the rest of the way down the sheer slope, their legs buckling and galloping under them.

Josh's chin bounced on his father's shoulder, and his voice juddered and shook as he stared back up that steep rise. He saw a volley of arrows leap up into the starry heavens before speeding back down to earth. One of the green-feathered shafts went stabbing into the grass only a few feet behind them, then another embedded into the banister.

"They're shooting at us!" the boy wailed.

"No," Miss Ursula shouted. "The attack was blind."

"Still hurt though, wouldn't it?" Brian cried. "If one of them hit us."

The old woman threw him a stony glance. "They would injure you and your sons, Mr. Chapman, yes."

Louder now the battle blared, but the fleeing group had almost reached the bottom of the high hill, and the eaves of the pathless forest were only a sprint away. Descending that lower slope in lunging leaps, Neil suddenly saw an impossible sight sail from the gloom before him, and he slithered to the ground to avoid crashing into it.

There, above the banking grass, hanging impossibly in midair and supported by nothing more than its position in future time, was the large Georgian window that lit the entrance hall of the Wyrd Museum.

Edie moved the flashlight beam over it momentarily. Gleaming through that ice-smothered glass was the orange glare of Bethnal Green, yet ducking under the floating sill she could see only the shadowy mass of forest behind.

"Into the wood!" Miss Ursula impelled them.

With a fearsome roar, the murderous conflict above broke over the brow of the hill, and all eyes turned to see the combating forces rampage down the slope, their swords sparking in the dark. The gloom-laden countryside boomed and resounded with that desperate tumult, and as Miss Ursula stared at that racketing advance, her expression changed.

With uncharacteristic theatricality, her features contorted in a look of horror. Emitting a juvenile shriek, she threw her hands up over her head. "Run!" she squealed, her normally level voice high and frantic. "Fly and flee!"

Then, hitching her taffeta skirts up to her knees, she scurried toward the trees.

"Ursula!" Edie called, as the others looked curiously after her. But that was not the time to stand and wonder, and leaving the great floating window behind, they set off in pursuit.

Haring swiftly in the bounding woman's wake, Edie caught up, checking her pace in order to run at her side. The girl was disturbed to see that Miss Ursula's eyes were abnormally wide and staring. Tossing and shaking her head, the last of the Fates giggled in a deranged manner, and her meticulously coifed white curls wagged in an unruly tangle about her ears.

Running with his father and Josh, Neil called back to Austen Pickering, who was obviously too old to keep up with them. "Not far now!" the boy encouraged him.

Huffing behind, the ghost hunter gave a returning wave. "Don't you worry about me, lad," he answered.

To the outlying trees the group ran, over to where sections of oak paneling stretched tall between the thickets. On the ground, the fragments of broken statues could be seen; limbless torsos, a satyr's head cloven in two, marble drapery lying in jagged pieces, and shattered fists still holding on to the hilts of splintered, twisted swords.

Many of the sculptures were partially buried in the earth, and their top halves projected from the parquet tiles that peppered the grass in attitudes of struggle and toil. Allowing her gaze to fall from Miss Ursula's idiotic face, Edie saw, in the jiggling light, a woman's arm fashioned from ivory lying across the path in front.

Swinging the beam around, she hunted through the crowding forest. There, standing a little distance away, virtually hidden within a snarling growth of holly, was the alabaster image made by Pumiyathon.

The statue was no longer beautiful. Marring clefts and cracks had been viciously hacked into its form, and above the once seductive neckline of the draped shift only one arm remained.

Edie scowled sorrowfully, but at that moment Miss Ursula also beheld the sculpture and she hooted with imbecilic laughter. From the granite-and-marble-strewn path she bolted, and mindless of the holly's sharp leaves, the old woman plowed through to where the statue stood. Her black gown was ripped by the needling barbs, and the tiny spikes cut red lines over Miss Ursula's skin as she plunged still further into the thicket until she reached the mangled figure.

Running up behind, Neil and the others stared in confusion, but Edie was already wading in after.

"What's going on?" the caretaker called. "What's the old bat doing? Is this where we're supposed to be safe? Doesn't look it to me."

"Quiet, Dad," Neil muttered. "There's something wrong."

Panting for breath, Austen Pickering viewed the commotion with a look of genuine disappointment on his face. "She's ill," he observed with concern. "Look at her."

"Just like Celandine and Veronica were," Neil added.

"Ursula," Edie Dorkins said sternly.

With her arms wrapped tightly around the alabaster sculpture, the last survivor of the Royal House of Askar hid her face when the girl approached, still tittering inanely.

"We don't 'ave time fer this," Edie told her.

Miss Ursula moved behind the statue and propped her chin on the severed ivory neck.

"Am I young and pretty now?" she asked foolishly. "Verdandi and Skuld were always the popular ones, never Urdr. They had all the admirers. Verdandi even lied to Mother about where she went, so she could be with her Captain. But I did a bad thing. I took Him away from her—wasn't that wicked? He chose me, instead, coldhearted Urdr. Oh no, she was always too grand for any of them. Too virtuous and holy—and so alone."

Laying her cheek upon the damaged shoulders she ran her fingers over the lustrous alabaster, and her eyes grew moist.

"As hard as this stone, that's how I was—everyone said so. They thought I didn't know, but I did. I heard what they all whispered about me at court. That's why I took Him away from her. I thought He wanted me. I thought He could see that I wasn't really cold—I wasn't, truly. He said that I was the one He really desired—me! And I believed Him. I loved Him and told Him what He wanted to know. Then it was over; He nailed Himself to the World-Tree and became a god. Where did that leave me? Where?"

Listening to her lamenting words, Austen Pickering lowered his eyes and stared silently at the ground.

"That's why!" she continued with a snivel. "That's why I came to this place and brought my sisters with me. He'd be sorry! If He couldn't love me I'd make Him hate me, and I did, I did! No passion, no ardor is greater than hatred. It eats and dominates without mercy. Always would I be in the Captain's thoughts, and in His dreams would I thwart and defeat His lust for conquest and control. Such is the obsessive might of loathing. So you see, I got what I wanted in the end. He was wholly mine, and no other could compete due to His enmity of me."

Beyond the trees the horrific battle had reached the

suspended window, and those terrible death screams bellowed ever closer.

"Ursula!" Edie shouted fiercely. "Stop this—come back."

The old woman's holly-pricked forehead twitched, and she raised her eyebrows meekly. "You don't want me back," she whispered with a mournful shake of her unraveled curls. "I've been such a naughty girl, done nasty, hateful things. No one knows what I've done."

Edie leaned forward to take Miss Ursula's elegant hands in hers and drew her from the statue. Then she gazed up into the old woman's face, and such was the force behind her almond-shaped eyes that Miss Ursula could not look away but was held captive by the solemn power that beat out from that young stare.

"Come back to us!" Edie commanded. "It's too soon for you to go."

For a moment they were locked in a grim yet silent struggle, as the girl endeavored to wrest and invoke Miss Ursula's eroding intellect back from the chasm of madness into which it had tumbled.

Then, slowly, the old woman straightened. The vacant, witless expression left her scratched face, and her usual sobriety was restored.

"Thank you, Edith," she uttered huskily. "I was lost and you found me. You have deferred the moment of my complete dotage and lent me the time to do what I must."

The girl gave her a brilliant smile, then led her back to the path.

Pulling a holly leaf from her hair, Miss Ursula glared imperiously at the others. "Why do you stand there like Celandine's mannequins?" she declared as if nothing had happened. "Harken to the battle noise. In minutes it will sweep over this place and you shall be slaughtered. Quickly, to the secret stairway!"

Still clutching Edie's hand, she rushed on to where the oaks grew thickly, and in their midst a stone archway reared from the undergrowth. It framed a heavy, iron-studded door, held in place by large, ornate hinges.

There was the entrance that lay behind the paneling of the Wyrd Museum. Once through that portal, they would descend the winding stair that led to the Chamber of Nirinel, and all would be well.

"Almost there!" she called. "Almost at the end of our travails."

The magnificent oak trees towered around them as they plunged deeper into the forest, and Miss Ursula fished up the fine chain that jingled from her waist to separate the keys she kept there. But before she could stretch out to grasp the bronze handle of the stout door, a tall figure stepped from the close darkness, and its imposing bulk blocked the arch entirely.

Stumbling to a standstill, Edie and Miss Ursula uttered cries of dismay. For there, revealed in the beam of Edie's flashlight, was Jack Timms.

Dressed in the uniform of a Roman legionnaire, the agent of Woden looked faintly ridiculous. The helmet was too small for his big-boned head, and the metal bands of the cuirass that encircled his stomach strained and squeaked in the girdling of his rolling paunch.

In one hand he held the standard of the legion,

which, judging from the violent din behind, had reached the edge of the forest. Above their heads, the silver eagle that topped the standard glinted in the shadows. To Edie's distress, she saw that the warder clutched a long lance, whose spear was covered with rust, in his other hand.

"Quite fittin', ain't it?" he sniggered repulsively. "For this 'ere to be back to what it were—a jabber of old Julius's. Full circle, as you might say."

Having caught up with Miss Ursula and Edie, Neil and the others looked at the odious man fearfully as his gloating smirk widened to reveal his black and rotten teeth.

"Jus' the job to spike an end to the last of them what the guv'nor told me to. The oldest and the very youngest—what jolly that'll be." Reveling in their woeful faces, the warder regarded his victims with his ratty eyes and gave a pernicious cackle.

"Will they make as much cat-curdlin' row as that other one, we asks ourselves?"

"Shut your stinkin' gob!" Edie bawled.

Tick-Tock snarled and his small eyes glittered at her. "It's the rare ripe end I'll be saving you fer," he swore. "Made it difficult for old Jack, you 'ave. Extra special care he'll take when it's your turn."

Swaggering forward, he lowered the spear and prodded its tip menacingly against the girl's throat. Edie recoiled from its tingling sting, falling backward into the leaf mold. From her hand the flashlight went flying, and its intense beam whipped dizzily over the oaks before it smacked into a wide trunk. With a loud crack and a rattle of batteries, the glare was quenched.

"Like I said afore," Tick-Tock growled, switching his attention to the rest, especially Neil, "there's a deal of learnin' to be done with you sorry lot, and it's real glad I'll be to do the schoolin'."

Neil returned the man's degenerate stare, but against Jack Timms he felt small and powerless. At his side, his father was strangely hushed and Josh whimpered fretfully. Austen Pickering had also remained unusually silent throughout this encounter, the boy thought. Yet there was no one among them who could stand up to that dissolute warder of the Wyrd Infirmary, for the might of Woden flowed through him and he wielded the Spear of Longinus.

Lying in the mulch, Edie turned away from that horrendous man and looked back along the way they had come, scrunching up her face in concentration, while the strands of silver tinsel glittered dully in her pixie hat.

Standing stiff and erect, Miss Ursula looked down her nose at the vile man. "If you are going to despatch us," she said, undaunted by his repelling menace, "you had best do it forthwith. The forces of the Roman army will be stampeding over this ground all too soon, and not even you will be able to withstand their swords or the fury of those they fight against."

"I like a woman who knows what she wants," Tick-Tock gurgled. "But you'll pardon me if'n I change to my normal clothes. These 'ere armors might be 'istorical, but they pinch an' restrict the arms somethin' cruel. Got to be comfortable when settin' to your fun, or it takes all the pleasure out."

In the gray shadows the Roman costume faded to

be replaced by his usual shabby clothes. The spear remained exactly as it was, while in his other hand the standard dwindled but did not completely disappear.

Instead, the silver eagle became a mocking parody of itself, and Jack Timms honked with malice, watching the expression on Neil's face as the boy saw what it had transformed into.

The tall pole had shriveled in size and the stick in Tick-Tock's fist was now the dreaded Tormentor. But impaled on top of that bullying cane, instead of the proud Roman eagle, was a large black bird whose head hung limply from a broken neck, and whose one eye was open in a fixed and sightless stare.

"Quoth!" the boy screamed, and the warder guffawed all the more.

Incensed, Neil flung himself forward, his fists plunging ineffectively into the fat assassin's gut. Jack Timms barely stopped laughing. One callous swipe with the back of his hand sent the boy crashing to the ground, and he contemptuously threw the dead raven on top of him.

Now his taunting was complete, and he pointed the spear's blade at Miss Ursula's breast. Upon that regal, dignified face not a flicker of fear or anxiety registered, and Tick-Tock hesitated momentarily.

"Listen to me, vassal of the Gallows God," she pronounced in a chilling voice that dripped with doom. "Before you strike me down, know this—for the one who takes the life of the Fates, a special Destiny has been set aside in the tapestry of life. Though Celandine, my sister, suffered untold agonies, your own will be three times more extreme. A horrific demise awaits you,

Jack Timms, and in that knowledge I find a sweetness that I will take to my grave."

Disturbed by her fatal words, Tick-Tock sneaked a glance at Austen Pickering, but his confidence was at once restored by the assured glint he saw behind those thick glasses.

"That's enough!" he snapped, darting his eyes back to the old woman. "Takes more'n words to fright old Jack. You've had your say, but I've got a sharper tongue than yours—a lovely rusty one, and it's time you were licked."

With that, he drew his arm back, and as the uproar of the rampaging armies blistered through the wood, the spear hurtled from his unholy hands.

At that same instant, an astonished yowl galed from his slobbering mouth. A dainty white fist came shooting from the darkness, slamming into the side of his flabby face, and Woden's corpulent agent went toppling sideways. Like a great tree he was felled, his heavy, barreled weight striking the forest floor with a reverberating crash.

High over Miss Ursula's head the spear went whistling, and setting Josh down on the ground, Brian Chapman immediately went scooting off to fetch it.

Jumping up, Edie Dorkins looked on the warder's prostrate figure. His florid face was a blank expanse of pitted flesh. No movement agitated those ugly, scarred features, and the detestable pricking eyes were firmly closed, squeezed in a fold of excess skin. A dark, bloody bruise was already forming on the side of his head, and the girl clapped her hands triumphantly.

"Spark out!" she declared with an impish grin. "He won't 'urt us no more." Then, lifting her eyes, she gazed up at the one she had summoned to aid them. With its remaining ivory hand still clenched, the alabaster statue stood over Jack Timms's unconscious body, swaying slightly from side to side.

"Thank you," the girl said.

The headless sculpture lifted its foot in response and planted it firmly on Tick-Tock's back.

Brandishing the key in her hand once more, Miss Ursula stepped over the comatose man and turned it in the lock of the iron-studded door.

"Excellently done, Edith, dear," she said proudly. "How very great you have become in the short while you have been with us. But we are not clear of danger yet."

The surging nightmare stormed ever closer to the oaks where Miss Ursula and the others stood. Roman soldiers crashed through the trees, swinging their swords and hollering Latin oaths, while their enemies harried them at every turn. In that sea of war, scarlet-striped horses reared in pain and terror. Most of their riders were slumped, lifeless, with arrows in their necks.

"All of you," the old woman ordered as she pushed the stout door inward, "hurry inside before the battle claims you."

Staring down at his agent, Austen Pickering suppressed a disdainful sneer, then turned to see Brian Chapman holding the spear.

"I'll take that if you want, old son," the ghost hunter offered, wearing his most affecting smile. But Brian simply shook his head, and picking up Josh with his free hand, he ducked under the stone arch to enter the darkness beyond.

Edie Dorkins strode to Neil Chapman's side and held out her hand to help him up. The boy declined and, cradling Quoth's body in his arms, picked himself up from the floor.

"He didn't ought to 'ave been killed," Edie stated.

"Leave us alone," Neil said hollowly, and clutching the raven close to his chest, he followed his father and brother, his head bowed in grief.

Wiping her nose, Edie hurried after, and Miss Ursula called impatiently to the ghost hunter as she too plunged under the arch.

"I'll be right behind you," Mr. Pickering promised, lingering by Jack Timms to give him a parting kick.

"Dolt!" he cursed with crackling scorn. "Now another way will have to be found. I have wasted enough of my power in nourishing your clumsy misadventures. Be thankful there is not time to deal with you in the manner you deserve!"

With a curt wave of his hand, the strident clamor suddenly ceased, and the battle melted from the forest. The Captain of Askar shot a withering glare at the alabaster figure that pinned his acolyte to the ground. Then he strode through the entrance that led to the secret stairway.

CHAPTER 23

THE GLISTERING GRAINS OF TRUTH

Deep into the devouring dark the straggly group trudged. The blackness in that spiraling stairway was absolute and their progress painfully slow as they fumbled down the treacherous, unseen steps. Aching and weary after the flight from The Separate Collection, they focused their attention on the plunging descent to keep themselves from slipping.

Lost in that winding night, they heard the echo of their own breathing hum in their ears, and the scuff of heels over smooth stone was the only noise to break the despondent silence. Isolated by the secluding gloom, each of them became wrapped in their individual thoughts.

Leading the way, Brian Chapman tapped out his descent like a blind man, using the shaft of the spear as a cane. With his arms holding tightly to his father's neck, Josh closed his eyes to shut out that horrible, helter-skeltering dark. To his child's mind it was safer not to look, and he colored his thoughts with the brightness of his imagination.

No illuminating hues cheered Neil's grief. For him it was just as dark inside as without. A barren emptiness that would never again hear Quoth's heartening hails was all he knew, and he plodded down mechanically.

Running her fingers along the wall as she trod those still unfamiliar stairs, Edie Dorkins was thinking of many things. Memories of Miss Veronica and Miss Celandine were shouldered aside by images of Miss Ursula laughing idiotically, which in turn were supplanted by thoughts of Jack Timms.

Behind her came Miss Ursula Webster. Of all the group, her brain burned the most fiercely. In that vast darkness it was almost impossible to keep a rein on her sanity—how it longed to drift into that delicious oblivion and never return. With gritted teeth, the old woman strove to control and be ever vigilant. If she were to surrender now, even Edie would not be able to call her back. If she could just hold on a little while longer, to complete that which she had begun.

Bringing up the rear, the disguised Captain of Askar came, the complex compartments of his subtle faculties calculating his stratagems. Yet, rising above all his designs and murderous schemes, the knowledge of where they were headed continuously surfaced. In spite of himself, he could not repress the excitement that he felt as the scent of sweet decay grew ever more powerful.

After what seemed an eternity, the steps came to an end. Prodding the spear shaft before him, Brian Chapman discovered that the floor abruptly became level, and the noise of their footsteps was suddenly lifted up into a vaulting blackness as a spacious cavern opened around them.

"Now our destination is almost reached," Miss Ursula's voice rang from all sides. "I shall lead the way—I need no guiding light to steer me through these catacombs, not to that blessed place where my beloved sisters and I dwelt in ages past."

Through the vast cave Miss Ursula strode, as surely as if the noonday sun were shining upon her path. Trailing after, groping their way in the supreme dark, the others followed. After several minutes of stumbling and tripping over invisible stones they were called to a halt, and Miss Ursula charged them to prepare themselves.

"Beyond the gates that lie before us," she said with exalted reverence, "is a sight no mortal eye has ever witnessed. You have come to the abode of the three Fates of the ancient world, where the seed of all legend still lives. For here is the final surviving root of Yggdrasill, mightiest of all the three that delved and flourished in the deep beginning of time, before there was day, and before the frost flowers were cast into the eternal night. Behold—Nirinel!"

At that, she touched her gnarled hand upon the gates and they swung silently open. Immediately, the blazing glare of the countless torches that flamed endlessly in the chamber beyond burst through the oppressive dark. The people covered their faces as the intense flickering dazzled and seared their weary eyes.

Only Miss Ursula was unaffected by that brilliant eruption, and she strode determinedly forward. Into the Chamber of Nirinel the old woman advanced, and the torches flared as if in greeting.

Edie was the first to follow her, and she rushed to her side. To the wellhead Miss Ursula swept, and spinning on her heel, she discovered that the others had still not entered.

"Why do you hesitate?" she demanded. "Come—look on the most precious jewel of the world, and let your fears be eased."

Through the great metal gates Neil came, staggering as he shifted his disbelieving gaze around him. It was as if he had stepped back into an age of forgotten myth. Despite his mourning for the raven he nursed in his arms, the boy could not help but gasp and be awed.

In the center of the huge space, where Miss Ursula and Edie were standing, was a circular dais of stone. As Neil drew closer, he saw that it was smothered in a velvety layer of soft, sooty ash.

Beyond them, a mighty treelike shape thrust up from the cavern floor. Then he became aware of the blackened chunks of wood and bark that littered the ground, and realizing they could only have fallen from the tree, he raised his gaze to see how high that wide trunk reared.

Slowly he moved his head around, and in the distance he saw the massive form reaching down to drive into the furthest part of the wall. "Nirinel!" he breathed. "I never dreamed . . ."

Shuffling in behind him, his father placed a shivering Josh down upon the ground and wandered through this astounding chamber, the spear trailing across the earth in his wake.

"I'm cold!" Josh whimpered, unimpressed by the marvelous sight. "Dad, I'm cold." But Brian had already moved away, toward the stupendous shape of Nirinel.

Into this fantastical place the Gallows God came, his shambling disguise savoring the momentous grandeur. Even blighted and withered with age, the root possessed an unequaled majesty, and he dragged the glasses from his nose to stare upward.

Since that ominous day when the daughters of the Royal House had ridden into the enchanted wood, he had desired to look on this final vestige of the World-Tree. Now, as he stood transfixed beneath its diseased glory, it dredged up a profusion of memories and emotions that he thought he had expunged long ago.

Snatches of forgotten moments glimmered fleetingly in the barren regions of his mind—of the dappled emerald light that shone beneath Yggdrasill, and the delicious sapphire shades of a tranquil evening. Through those vibrant blues he had walked the high ground, his faithful ravens soaring and swooping above as he looked down on the citadel of Askar, its towers gleaming in the ravishing twilight. And in that trysting place of his memory, he recalled the slender figure who had hastened to meet him.

Woden passed a hand over his eyes and shook his head sadly. Those blissful days had died with the World-Tree, and there was no returning.

"Now we may set aside our cares, for a while at least," Miss Ursula began, breaking into his reverie.

With a sonorous clang, the metal gates swung shut of their own accord, and the ghost hunter glanced at them suspiciously. Here he was, in the very heart of his enemy's domain, and there was no escape.

Walking over to the wellhead, Neil gently laid Quoth on the ashes, folding those limp, lifeless wings about the raven's body.

"Yes," Miss Ursula addressed the boy with a tenderness in her voice he had not heard before. "To lie in peace beneath Nirinel—that has long been my wish. Your loyal friend has rightfully earned his place on the brink of the sacred well. There let him remain until the final end comes."

"Seems the proper spot for him, somehow," Neil answered.

The old woman smiled benignly. "It shames me to admit that I never trusted him," she said. "When Memory was restored, I suspected his previous nature would assert itself once more; how mistaken I was. Never was there a more faithful companion. We were fortunate to have him among us, even for such a little while. Would that I could call back the harsh words I spoke unto his gallant heart."

"Too late for that now," Neil mumbled. "And his name was Quoth."

Miss Ursula inclined her head in apology, then sighed with a sudden, overwhelming fatigue.

"You must remember, Child," she told him, the strain evident in her voice, "I am not as you are—of a different, older race am I. Many years have I guarded and tended the last root of Yggdrasill—too many. Unto it I am irrevocably bound, as were my sisters. Like theirs before me, my wits are failing as it, too, fails. I am sick in heart and mind, and the weight of endless ages crushes me down."

With dragging footsteps, she crossed to the wall where a small niche was hewn amid the carved animals. "Two aims only have sustained me throughout the palling years," she murmured, taking from the recess an earthenware beaker imprinted with the image of a white stag. "To find a successor to our custodianship was my primary concern. But the waiting for the true heir was interminable, and when the strand of her life finally shimmered within the web, I missed her. Eventually, however, and with your assistance, Edith was delivered to us."

As Edie Dorkins watched the old woman saunter back to the wellhead with the double-handled drinking vessel in her grasp, a puzzled frown crinkled her forehead.

"What you doin?" the girl asked.

"I am tired, Edith, dear," Miss Ursula replied, avoiding the question. "More tired than I have ever been. Long have I anticipated this moment, and of all the sensations I envisaged I might feel, drained and weary were not among them. I am just relieved that it is finally over, and all the perils are past."

"You sure?" Neil said doubtfully. "What's to stop Tick-Tock coming down here, or Woden trying to get at us again?"

"As for the factotum warder, I do not think he will trouble us—Edith's alabaster friend will see to that.

And with regard to the Gallows God, He must be weakened, as am I. We are both too ancient and spent to vie with one another beyond this night, and already the dawn is waking."

"You said there were two things," Neil reminded her. "If Edie was the first, what's the other?"

Setting the beaker down in the soot, Miss Ursula peered into the clear water it contained. "Matters unfinished," she replied simply. "Something I would have done long, long ago if Edith had been born in an earlier age. As it is, I only barely managed to achieve it. The creeping madness stalked me, but I evaded it in the end. There is just enough time to accomplish what must be done."

Edie's frown deepened. "What you sayin'?" she demanded.

"You must forgive me if candor does not come naturally," Miss Ursula answered, "but after the countless, dissembling years, one cannot be surprised. Yet, in this hallowed place, at the instant of Doom, all veils of deceit and mendacity should indeed be torn away, and the glistering grains of truth laid bare."

Toying with the golden chain that hung around her neck, she looked over to where Austen Pickering was regarding her cautiously. "Do you not agree, Mr. Pickering?" she asked.

The ghost hunter shrugged with feigned confusion. "I'm afraid I didn't hear," he prevaricated. "This is . . . it's all so incredible. I was aware of the great ash myth . . . but you don't expect . . . I mean, how can I ever go back to my ordinary investigations after this?"

"Your investigations," Miss Ursula repeated with a

wry smile. "Yes, of course, all those morose and tragic specters you so diligently release from their torment. I'm afraid your few days here have been a trial in themselves, have they not, Mr. Pickering? Still, I trust your experiences inside the museum were worth your patient waiting."

"More than I can possibly say!" he exclaimed. "Although I'll never be able to write them up, not if I want to be believed."

Lifting the chain from around her neck, the old woman gave an understanding nod. "And it is so important to be convincing, do you not agree, Edith?"

The girl made no response. She did not comprehend what Miss Ursula was doing and began to wonder if her reason had wandered again.

"You agree with me, don't you, Child?" she appealed to Neil.

"I don't really know what you mean," he muttered with growing unease.

Miss Ursula unclasped the large, glittering locket and inspected the nugget-shaped, chalky substance it contained. "Why, to inspire faith and trust," she enthused. "Throughout the slow ticking of eternity I have been compelled to assume new guises, for the building above was always evolving. Those different roles were a taxing responsibility—one had to immerse oneself wholly into each character and age. Did I not tell you as much at the festivities we held to celebrate the birth of the Princess Elizabeth, Mr. Pickering, where you danced the Horse's Bransle?"

The old man studied her warily. "I think you might

have said something along those lines," he responded. "I'm not sure."

"Not sure?" Miss Ursula exclaimed. "Can this be the fastidious psychic detective speaking? The one who jots down everything in his little notebook? The man from the north with his meticulously arranged ghost strings, and his tape measure and thermometer always at the ready?"

"I really don't know what game you're playing," he bluffed. "But after everything we've just gone through—"

"Games!" she cried. The sudden, stinging force of her voice lashed violently from her tongue, and the hairs on Neil's neck prickled as he glimpsed for the first time the full might of Miss Ursula's divine and dreadful power.

"There have been enough games played already!" she shrieked. "And here—at the font of all things—is where this last charade will cease!"

Dumbfounded at the intensity of Miss Ursula's outburst, Edie glanced from her to Austen Pickering.

The ghost hunter was glowering at the old woman. His cheeks flushed as he puffed and blustered, preparing to deny any accusation she hurled at him. Then, even as Edie stared, a change occurred. An inexplicable calm descended over Mr. Pickering, and all traces of that righteous anger and injured dignity dissolved completely.

He returned Miss Ursula's condemning gaze, and a look of resignation stole over that craggy, grizzle-haired mask. "I thought the part had been played well," he uttered in an arrogant voice that did not belong to the retiring Austen Pickering. "When did you suspect?"

Neil and Edie stared at him with round eyes, and the girl's face crinkled in loathing as she understood.

Miss Ursula laughed bitterly. "Suspect?" she declared. "Vanity was always your weakness, and that unbridled conceit inflates you still! Are you so enamored of yourself and your squalid plots that you imagine I was *ever* deceived?"

"You knew?" he murmured, that vaunting voice shaken by the revelation.

"I have *always* known!" she proclaimed fiercely. "From the very beginning when first you returned, long after the rout that destroyed your forces. When your wounds had been licked and part of your strength renewed, I was aware of you. Do you still not perceive the overreaching folly of your actions? Are you still so blind?"

Inflamed with anger, Edie Dorkins darted forward to claw and bite the old man, but Miss Ursula seized her arm and held the girl back before she could reach him. "Let go!" she yelled. "It's Him—He killed Veronica and Celandine!"

Neil turned a ghastly, blanched face to him. "I don't . . . what does she mean?" he stammered. "Mr. Pickering, answer me!"

"He's Woden!" Edie bawled. "It were always Him!"

The boy edged backward. "No," he muttered, not wanting to believe it. "Tell them it isn't true—tell them!"

Consigning his glasses into the pocket of his raincoat, the figure of Austen Pickering had nothing to say to him.

"All those lies," Neil whispered, numbed by the awful realization. "From the start, everything you ever said, it was all lies. Tick-Tock Jack, that disgusting . . . that killer—he was working for you all along . . ."

Tears suddenly sprang to the boy's eyes, and his face was wrung with anguish and resentment as the full bitterness of the inhuman betrayal smote him. "You . . . you murdered Quoth!" he wept. "Why? What sort of monster are you?"

"Keep a hold on your tongue, boy," the Gallows God spat, angrily pointing a threatening finger, "before you join that treasonous bird in death!"

Neil lunged at him in furious outrage, but the eyes of Woden blazed out of the old man's face, and the boy's temper was utterly extinguished. He recoiled as though struck by an invisible fist. Against the Captain of Askar, he who had hung from the World-Tree and rode into battle against the Frost Giants, the caretaker's eldest son was as nothing; his young, defiant spirit was utterly cowed.

This was a matter far beyond the reach of Neil's mortal comprehension. Here was the final confrontation between the Mistress of Destiny and the Allfather—and the feelings of an eleven-year-old boy meant nothing.

Dismissing the boy's insignificant presence, the outward aspect of Austen Pickering shimmered with shadow. The figure rippled as Woden brought an end to the masquerade of the ghost hunter, and the façade was torn from him. About his shoulders the color of the raincoat deepened, and the fabric reached to the ground as the old man's sharpening, wizened features retreated into the concealing darkness of a heavy cowl.

There stood the true appearance of the Gallows God, and he turned his hidden face on the woman he had waited so long to overthrow and destroy. In her grasp Edie Dorkins still squirmed, longing to let fly at him. Seeing her fierce loathing, the enemy laughed coldly.

"Your adopted daughter has not yet discerned the truth," he observed in a disdainful whisper. "How very like you she is. Headstrong and hearing only what she wishes. Did you not mark the import of Urdr's words, Child? From the very beginning she was aware of me, long before I entered her precious museum. It was to her tune alone that I danced."

Edie growled at him, and then, all at once, she grasped his meaning and stopped her wrathful struggles. "Ursula . . ." she breathed in horror.

Woden chuckled darkly. "Now you see," he told her. "Now you know the iniquitous depths to which she has fallen."

"Let go of me!" Edie screamed, recommencing her wriggling efforts. But this time she was desperate to escape from Miss Ursula.

An expression as blighted as Nirinel took possession of Miss Ursula's face, and avoiding the girl's eyes, she released her.

Edie bolted as though scalded, and she raced around the wellhead until the broad ring of scorched stone stood between them.

"You knew!" she denounced the old woman. "You

did this—all of it. You knew what He was up to and you let Him! You let Him kill Veronica and Celandine! I hate you—I hate you!"

Like a pillar of rock beset by a squalling tempest, the last of the ruling Fates, those Three of Mortal Destiny, endured Edie Dorkins's blistering abuse until the overwrought child could no longer continue and threw herself down into the ashes, where she sobbed wretchedly.

"Yes, Edith, I knew." Miss Ursula's unrepentant confession cut through Edie's consuming grief and shock. "I admit all and regret nothing. The Gallows God had returned, as I knew one day He would, and already He was hatching His schemes, summoning the Valkyries back from the darkness. I could not allow the possibility of His victory."

"But Celandine and Veronica!" Edie wept, lifting her face from the soot. "Why?"

The old woman reared her head. "Need you ask that?" she demanded archly. "My sisters were mindless, and I, Urdr, was soon to accompany them into the detritus of their dementia. When the time came for Him to assail us, our enemy would discover that the Loom Maidens were no more than three senile, gibbering hags!"

"And so you used me," Woden's voice rang out, "as you always used everyone."

Taking the heel bone of Achilles from the locket, Miss Ursula dropped it into the earthenware beaker. At once the water began to fizz and foam.

"Toward this end, everything was planned," she said with pride. "When I saw in my sisters the Doom that awaited me, I set about the weaving of all that has since transpired. Do not think I undertook the task lightly, for I did not. Into that web I spun a terrible Destiny, cutting the strands of my poor sisters' undying lives, but there was no other way—none. If The Cessation was to come, then it would be of my contrivance, not yours."

The voice of the Gallows God bristled with revulsion. "You manipulated me in order to bring about the deaths of Verdandi and Skuld," he cursed. "In your hated web you entangled me, and your sisters you sent like cattle to be slaughtered. Was there ever a harder or a colder heart? It was true what they whispered in the palace court."

Miss Ursula winced at that, then steeled herself and brought the brimming beaker over to him. "Your time is ended," she told him. "This day your immortality is severed; so it is woven in the Cloth of Doom, and from that you know there is no escaping. One drink of this and your godhead will be revoked, and the spells that knit your undying flesh will fail."

The shadows beneath the hood stared at the frothing liquid she offered him, and he raised his hand to dash the vessel from her grasp.

"Accept your Doom!" she commanded. "The death you have cheated these thousands of years will claim you at last. It is the hour set down and here, in the place you so ached to conquer, you will die by my hand!"

Slowly, the cloaked figure lowered his arm.

"So," his rancorous voice hissed, "here at the very end, you have beaten me. Though armies have battled on both sides, and warriors unnumbered perished in our names, we face each other here, and the outcome has been decided by your woven strands. To rid the world of Fate's binding shackles and free mankind from the threads of your fatal cloth was all I craved. Yet now, after everything, Destiny and Fortune will prevail. Greedily will I put that cup to my lips. The contest is done, and you may spin what dooms you can—I will be a part of them no longer."

A grave smile lightened Miss Ursula's face. "You are mistaken," she said. "There will be no more decrees of Fate. Only madness awaits me here. By this evening my sanity will have gone to dust. In that dread tapestry that was woven in secret, my own Doom was spun. This day my life also is severed. When you have supped of your mortality, then I shall die like a princess of the Royal House, and join my sisters on their journey."

Turning to Edie, the last of the Fates looked at her adoringly. "Forgive me," she entreated. "The way had to be made clear for you to succeed us. You will grow to understand. Into your care I entrust the guardianship of Nirinel and the exhibits of the museum."

"What are you going to do?" the girl asked fearfully.

"When the Gallows God has drunk the water of death, and I am certain He is no more, then shall I take up the Spear of Longinus—and plunge it into my breast."

Edie staggered back aghast. "No, Ursula!" she protested.

"I must."

From the hooded figure a sorrowful breath sighed. "Then this is, in truth, The Cessation," he murmured. "Of the daughters of Askar and the Captain of the palace guard."

"Our time is over," she answered wearily. "The world needs us no more."

"Then at the final moment of Doom, know this," he said. "When we were together in the gardens beneath Yggdrasill, my heart was yours." Taking the beaker from her, the cloaked figure of Woden lifted a hand in salute, then bowed.

"I know," Miss Ursula whispered.

His glittering eyes trained upon her, the Gallows God brought the vessel to his lips. Watching him, the old woman suddenly realized that she could not bear to look and turned quickly away.

"The spear!" she cried bitterly. "Bring me the spear!"

Forgotten by everyone, including his sons, Brian Chapman was standing before Nirinel, engrossed in running the fingers of one hand over the rotten surface of the bark—as though he were insensible to all else around him. In his other hand he still held the blade of Longinus.

"Hurry!" Miss Ursula demanded.

Yet the caretaker made no answer. He did not turn around but continued to stroke the diseased and gnarled expanse before him.

Even as the lethal liquid wet his lips, Woden hesitated, and his resolve waned when his glance flew to where Neil's father persisted in ignoring her.

"Do you hear me?" the old woman called. "The spear!"

An empty, biting laugh like the howl of a winter gale resounded in the chamber. At Neil's side, Josh's mouth fell open, but the boy was too afraid to cry. His brother's arms wrapped swiftly around him, and Neil spluttered as his despair was finally made complete.

From the decayed root Brian Chapman turned to look at the others, and a strangled shriek sprang from Miss Ursula Webster's throat. Instinctively, Edie Dorkins ran to her, while out of Woden's fingers the beaker slipped to go crashing and shattering upon the ground at his feet.

An abhorrent transformation had stolen over the caretaker of the Wyrd Museum. The eyes that stared out at the horrified group were hideously white and glinted with bright, bitter frost. The grubby unwashed skin that covered his gawky features had turned deathly pale and was mottled a ghastly gray. Around his mouth and nose, where the breath blasted out into the stagnant air in clouds of Arctic vapor, crystals of ice had formed to beard his unshaven stubble, and the lank hair that fringed his brow was now dripping with rime.

Out of some vast region of barren, glacial cold that baneful laugh raged again, ringing chill in every heart.

"Ancient fools!" a hollow, echoing voice blistered from cracked blue lips. *"So closeted in thine petty feud wert thee, casting thy nets and steeped in the embroiling of thy layered deceits, thou didst not recognize the true threat when it came!"*

"Dad!" Neil howled desolately, and he lurched forward, only to be restrained by Woden's powerful hands.

"That is no longer your father," the hooded figure hissed in an anguished murmur. "And we are all lost."

Her clasped hands pressed to her mouth, Miss Ursula realized then the full enormity of her folly. It was she who had opened the way for the true foes of the world to enter her domain. Finally, here at the end of her reign, Urdr herself had been manipulated, and the damning torment of what she, in her blind stupidity, had brought about petrified her.

Those sparkling, ice-crusted eyes pierced into her cringing, terrified soul, and high into the shadows the discordant laugh blistered with a supreme malevolence.

"*Now dost thou see how thine sordid wrangling hath brought about the ruin of all thou holdest dear?*" the entity within Brian Chapman mocked. "*Long hath the rightful lords of the world endured their exile, biding their time for this one chance. When the first of thine sisters didst taste of this sweet blade, we who strode from the boundless oceans in the first darkness and didst clad ourselves in frozen flesh espied thy weakness and made of it full use.*"

The hands that gripped the Spear of Longinus were now more like claws. Even as the others watched, long knives of ice stretched from beneath the fingernails, and Edie pressed close to Miss Ursula.

"What's happening to him?" Neil demanded woefully.

In the deep shade of Woden's cowl the Allfather's eyes narrowed, and the voice with which he replied trembled with dread. "He is possessed. The lords of the ice and dark have been roused from their everlasting waste—it is one of their voices that speaks."

"Frost Giants," Edie Dorkins breathed, shivering from the intense cold beating out from the apparition that was Neil's father.

"*Ages uncounted hath my kind waited on this moment,*" the rancorous voice blasted. "*Now is our forbearance rewarded and the victory complete. The age of light is done, and that which stands betwixt us and our rightful sovereignty must perish!*"

"You cannot!" Miss Ursula cried. "No!"

But there was nothing she or anyone could do. Already weakened by the struggle of their dueling conflict, the last of the Nornir and the Gallows God were no match for the might of the Frost Giants.

The unholy fiend that inhabited the caretaker threw back the man's hoary head and laughed triumphantly, as the arms were raised and the rusted blade of the fatal spear was thrust forward with inhuman strength.

"Stop!" Miss Ursula screamed, rushing forward. But her protests were in vain. Before she could attempt to drag Neil's father away from Nirinel, a blizzard of hail stormed from the creature's mouth, and she was driven, battered and beaten, back against the wellhead.

Through that tempest Woden battled, the folds of his great cloak whipping wildly about his tall, wizened figure. But against the ice lord there was no contesting, and he too was catapulted back.

Deep into the blackened, flaking bark of Nirinel the Spear of Longinus stabbed, and the gloating mirth of that hideous presence was terrible to hear. "*Now is the prophecy fulfilled!*" it trumpeted. "*The last drop of living juice shalt cease its trickling flow, and the lingering vestige of the hated Yggdrasill wilt die. The reign of everlasting dark is come again!"*

In that viciously riven hole, the Frost Giant twisted and ripped the rusted blade—tearing and chopping through decomposing timber until a wide, ugly gash had been hacked. Then, dredging the spear free, it lifted one hand clear, and the glittering spikes that scissored from the man's fingers raked and sliced the air as the ice lord relished this doom-filled moment to its utmost malignant degree.

"Die now, accursed usurper of the first ones!" it bellowed, and with irresistible force, it rammed the caretaker's arm deep into that repulsive wound.

In the pale, ice-brindled face, the muscles convulsed. Freezing white vapor gusted from his sleet-drizzling nostrils as the foul cold of the lords of the ice and dark flooded out through his being. Up into the veins of Nirinel it pushed its murderous, mordant way. Into the innermost depths, where the sacred sap of life yet coursed in the hale heart of the titanic root, that corroding cold went slicing.

"Nirinel!" Miss Ursula gasped, hot tears streaking down her cheeks as she felt the agony of that lethal force pushing and killing up through the gargantuan, arching structure. "What have I done?"

Edie Dorkins wrapped her arms around the old woman as the last moments of that majestic wonder came. The nightmare vision of Brian Chapman drove the virulent winter into the remaining fibers, rupturing and dealing its venomous death throughout the length of that mammoth, worshipful bulk.

"It's dying!" Miss Ursula sobbed, racked with pain. "The jewel of the world is dying!"

"Behold the commencement of the new age!" the Frost Giant's voice exulted. *"Yggdrasill hath met its deserved end—eternal night is here!"*

Suddenly, within the cavern, a frightful groan reverberated above their heads as the maleficent frost invaded the root's hallowed core, and the immensity of its prehistoric existence was finally ravaged and destroyed.

Beneath their feet the ground shuddered, and a jagged crack fractured the breadth of the chamber, cleaving the encircling walls and splitting the carved animals with a wide, forking fissure, through which rained a torrent of rubble.

Within the frozen, devastated center of Nirinel the fibers of its polluted timbers exploded, and the rumble of its death thundered through the deepest regions of the earth. From the enormous, arching mass, huge flaking sheets of stinking bark toppled. Out of the darkness they came tumbling to crash into reeking fragments on the quaking floor.

Pulling Josh away from the wellhead, where chunks of diseased wood and cascading rubble deluged down, Neil dragged the four-year-old back to the metal gates and stared at the cataclysmic scene before them.

The evil vision of their father tore his arm free of the mortal wound the ice lord had slashed in the root's decayed grandeur. From those cruel fingers there now splashed a phosphorescent lymph that swiftly congealed and fell, shivering, to the juddering ground, where it smashed into sparkling diamond dust.

Flinching before the ominous creaks that traveled through the surrounding stone, Neil saw the caretaker hiss with laughter. But the dying throes of Nirinel drowned out any other noise.

Shaking violently, the scorched stone dais of the well tilted and shook. Over its surface the body of Quoth went lurching through the ashes, plummeting down into the chasm of the central shaft until it disappeared into the fathomless, empty dark.

Staggering to her feet, Ursula Webster lumbered over the buckling floor, staring with unbelieving horror up into the impenetrable shadows from which the avalanche of fetid debris came falling.

"Nirinel!" she screamed bleakly. "Forgive me. I did this! Through the obsession of my hatred, this evil bore its malevolent fruit. I have failed you—I am sorry!"

"Ursula!" Edie squealed, darting through the tumultuous downpour of rock and ulcerous timber. "We gotta get out! It's goin' to smash on top of us! It'll kill us!" But the old woman stumbled further into the crashing cataract, where vast segments of bark dropped perilously from the gloom.

"Quick!" the girl screeched, tugging at her arm.

Swaying unsteadily as the entire chamber shook around them, Miss Ursula glanced down at her, then through the teeming dirt and disease to where Woden clung to the wellhead.

In the desert of her grief a spark of hope was fanned

into flame and she gripped Edie tightly. "There is still a chance!" she yelled above the din. "The end is not upon us—not yet!"

At that moment, a tremendous splintering tore through the destructing turmoil above, and they both gazed up to the black space directly over their heads, where a colossal tonnage of festering timber came spinning into view. There was no time to think; if they remained where they stood, it would crush them utterly.

With a ruinous crash, the mighty fragments of Nirinel collided with the ground, and a choking cloud of dirt was hurled into the churning atmosphere.

Coughing and wiping her eyes, Edie hobbled back to the well and glanced around her for Miss Ursula. But in jumping to safety they had leaped in opposite directions, and the old woman was now on the far side of the mountainous section of cancerous bark.

Edie called to her, but even as the last of the Fates tottered over the crumbling mass, there came a sound more terrible than anything she had ever heard. It was more than sound; that catastrophic, upheaving din possessed an almost solid substance, and everyone present felt it slamming into them.

Through the very essence of the girl's existence the ghastly tidal wave of noise vibrated, jarring her bones and ripping into her mind as the harrowing force threw her to the pitching ground.

Utterly consumed by penetrating, slaughterous frost, the primeval fibers of Yggdrasill's last surviving root snapped and shredded, and the rolling uproar screamed in Edie's soul.

No longer able to support the monumental glory of Yggdrasill's straddling size, the putrid, ancient timbers ripped and sundered, and the full, awful might of Nirinel finally came collapsing down.

"Ursula!" Edie cried, but it was too late. A black, engulfing shade hurtled over the mistress of the Wyrd Museum, and there was nothing the girl could do.

At her side, Woden glared up at the cataclysm that descended. "Flee, Child!" he commanded fiercely, and the Gallows God rushed forward, his cloak billowing about him.

Across the dividing gulf the age-old enemy of the Fates ran, his strident voice yelling defiantly. In that same instant, recognizing her doom, Miss Ursula shouted.

"The Loom, Edith! The Loom! Nothing else can save you!"

Through that tumbling chaos, Edie Dorkins caught a last glimpse of Ursula Webster as Woden reached out to her, and when they were united in that final moment, their resentments were completely renounced.

Before the ending came, Edie thought she saw the Captain of Askar as he was in the vigor of his youth. A tall silver helm gleamed on his head, and his mail-clad frame was wrapped in a sable mantle. Before him, a beautiful serene-faced woman, whose auburn tresses were banded by a circlet of gold, gathered him into her arms as the pulverizing, obliterating blow came.

Down to the floor of the chamber the tortured magnitude of Nirinel went thundering. The world tipped in revolt, and Edie was flung across the cavern.

Then the metal gates were thrown down, and Neil and Joshua Chapman were sent reeling.

In that disharmony of despair, the voice of the Frost Giant blared his loathsome victory because, at last, the end of all that was good had come.

CHAPTER 24

THREE TIMES MORE EXTREME

Outside the Wyrd Museum, the bronze figure that surmounted the Victorian entrance quivered within the mantle of ice that smothered it. Splitting thunderously, that third image fractured above the scrolling sign, and out over the frozen alleyway a thousand splintered fragments of metal exploded.

Deep below the foundations, lying across the mangled gates, Neil Chapman warily raised his pounding head. The air was a choking maelstrom of seething soil and spores of rotten wood. Into his eyes and mouth the swirling filth blasted as he desperately called to his brother, searching the rioting gloom with his fumbling fingers.

"Josh!" he croaked, spitting the stale dust from his tongue. "Where are you?" A timid whimper answered him, and Neil crawled anxiously toward that meek, fretful noise, until his blindly seeking hands touched the younger boy's shoulder.

"You hurt?" he cried.

Josh mumbled wretchedly in response.

"Can you stand?" Neil pressed.

"Think so."

Taking his brother's hand, Neil Chapman hauled himself to his feet and stared back into the cloying cloud. Nearly all of the torches had been quenched in Nirinel's plunging ruin, but here and there, around the broken walls, a meager few still guttered and flared in the perdition of that terror-filled chamber.

Among the whirling reek of glacial death haloes of dun light glowed in the suffocating, swarthy murk, and gradually Neil perceived the complete devastation that had been wrought. Within that broken world he could just make out the round dais of the wellhead, surrounded by a sea of splintered destruction. Beyond that, and rising like a hill of darkness, was the toppled wreckage of Nirinel.

It was as if a mountain had fallen into the cavern. Neil could not begin to see the extent of that stupefying devastation. The immense, crippled shadow rose like a ruptured wall into the gloom, stretching as far as the light allowed, and he nervously swallowed the gritty, soil-clogged spit in his mouth.

"Where's Dad?" Josh asked feebly, voicing his own and Neil's fears.

Neil squeezed his hand. "I don't know," he murmured, hopeless and afraid.

Then, from that curdling, umber effluvium a shape came staggering, a burning torch held high above its head. Out under the fractured entrance, clambering over the twisted gates, Edie Dorkins emerged, her face black with grime and glistening with tears.

"They're dead!" she sobbed, stumbling over to where Neil and his brother stood. "Ursula's gone. They're both back there—under all that . . ."

Straining his eyes, Neil tried to pierce the turbulent, dirt-ridden ether.

"It's settling," he whispered as the heavier particles started to float downward. Gradually the drifting, obscuring veils were lifted, and further into that catastrophic vision the boy peered.

Then he saw him.

Knee-deep in rubble and blackened splinters, the shape of a tall, awkward man was floundering through the chamber—a long spear clenched in his hand.

"It's Dad!" Neil cried. "He's all right, Josh!"

His shoulders bowed and his head slumped forward, Brian Chapman waded with difficulty through the tide of debris that swamped that ruined cavern.

"DAD!" the boy yelled, waving his arms wildly. "DAD!"

Raising his head, the caretaker looked over to where the warped gates lay buckled below the entrance, but even across that sundering distance, Neil could see the glitter of his wintry eyes.

"The Frost Giant's still in him!" Edie exclaimed.

"Oh, no," Neil breathed. "I thought it was over."

The bitter smile that contorted Brian Chapman's pallid face disappeared as the white ice of his eyes, blazing with intense and deadly cold, stabbed through the curtaining swathes of dust.

"*Why are my brethren not released from their wasteland stronghold?*" its hideous, scathing voice demanded. "*The third and final root hath been destroyed. No trace of Yggdrasill remains to forbid our return, no sap bleedest through vein or stem. Why hath the darkness not yet descended aboveground? Answer me! Answer!*"

Dragging his host's human feet from the heaped destruction, the ice lord clambered onto the larger fragments of withered wood that sat like rafts upon that solid ocean. Leaping from piece to piece, it snarled in murderous rage through its frost-bearded mouth.

"He's coming after us!" Neil uttered anxiously. "What should we do?"

Holding the flaming torch above her, Edie darted into the dark of the connecting cavern. "Don't be stupid!" she cried. "Leg it!"

Dragging Josh with him, Neil pelted after. The unclean abomination that bounded toward the broken gates called after them, and the sound of that supreme malice was a whip to his heels. Through the caves and grottoes that led to the spiraling stairs Edie Dorkins fled, the fiery torchlight streaming behind her in a ribbon of flame.

"*Can it be that a piece of the World-Tree yet exists?*" The Frost Giant's dreadful shrieks resounded in the caverns they had just raced through. "*Where is the Loom fashioned from the first hewn bough? Doth the fluid of life flow through the timber of its accursed* frame? *It must be discovered—it, too, must be destroyed!*"

At last, the children reached the steps, and not pausing to catch their breath, they instantly commenced the arduous climb. With the aid of the torchlight, their ascent was much swifter than the blind journey down had been, and they took the treacherously worn stairs two and three at a time. As they climbed, however, Neil realized that the echoing snarls that drifted up the ponderous shaft were growing fainter.

"That foul thing's not chasing us anymore," he declared in astonished relief.

Not pausing in her stretching stride, Edie grunted. "It's huntin' through the caves," she said incisively.

"For the Loom?"

"Yes. Ursula always said it'd got broke, but I never believed her and she knew it. It's our only hope now—she said it were. But that fright'll never find it down there; it's lookin' in all the wrong places."

"You know where it is?"

"'Course I does." And with that, she quickened her pace, and Neil had to carry Josh to keep up with her.

Ever upward they rushed until, eventually, the studded door appeared above them. Onto that last step they labored, puffing to ease their spent lungs while their legs cramped and burned with fatigue.

Wrapping her grubby fingers about the bronze handle, Edie gave it a sharp twist, and the stout oaken door was pulled open. Over the threshold, out of the claustrophobic dark, all three children barged. But they were not prepared for the sight that met their eyes, and they blinked like small owls brought into the sun.

Inside the Wyrd Museum all was chaos and confusion. At their feet, the unconscious body of Jack Timms still lay stretched across the floor, the ivory foot of the headless statue pressed firmly on his back. But they were the only recognizable features of this insane and disoriented world.

Flicking in and out of existence, the paneled walls pulsed and trembled, their outlines fading and melting then jolting back into solid reality once more. About the stone archway that led to the secret stairs, an ever-shifting patchwork of the building's history careered. The great hall of a Norman manor, with its small, slitted windows and impressive oriel, crackled momentarily before them, only to be replaced by the painted plaster of a Roman temple in which a large golden urn stood. The livid green stream of smoke that coiled from its smoldering incense lingered on the air long after that aspect was snatched away.

Staring beyond the inconstant, wraithlike walls, the children saw the surrounding landscape quiver through the fluxing centuries. Dark, intractable forests switched into neatly trimmed pleasure gardens with manicured lawns and brooding yews, clipped to form geometrical symmetry. Then devouring marsh consumed all, and in the sky, where the sun and the stars vied for supremacy, the towering beams of wartime searchlights blazed.

Into this cauldron of bubbling ages indistinct shadow figures darted between the folding years, ripped from their rightful times to invade and rampage throughout tormented generations. Saxon warriors went charging over blacktopped roads; knights in gleaming armor did battle with Roman legionnaires; a plague cart toiled toward the infirmary doors as children from the orphanage played around the wheels.

Eventually wresting his gaze from that jumbled anarchy, Neil turned to the girl at his side. "Why's it like this?" he cried. "Woden's dead. Why isn't it back the way it should be?"

Edie nibbled her bottom lip as she considered the bloated figure of Tick-Tock Jack, who lay before the archway. "That's the reason," she announced, nudging the warder with the toe of her shoe. "Woden put his power into 'im—the museum's still feedin' off it."

An eruption of flame abruptly blossomed behind the Jacobean garden's high screening wall, and a searing stream of antiaircraft fire spouted up into the beleaguered heavens. Edie's eyes sparkled as she reveled in that familiar sight, and it seemed to inspire courage and hope within her.

"We've got to get upstairs," she said with grim determination. "*That's* where the Loom is!"

Neil stared across the bewildering, unraveled ages to where the carpeted stairs rose to the landing. But, even as he looked, the steps vanished and a great slab of granite, supported by three smaller, roughly hewn blocks, took their place. Beneath that dolmen, the floor became sprinkled with tiny tiles as a mosaic depicting a flowering tree tessellated into being, and the boy knew they would never be able to find their way through that galloping madness.

"The stairs'll disappear under us," he told Edie. "The museum's out of control. If we don't wind up lost in the past, we'll probably get an arrow in our backs."

"But we've got to get up there!" she insisted.

"How?"

A frustrated scowl crinkled the girl's filthy face as she concentrated, trying to force the stairs to return and solidify. The silver threads glinted in her pixie hat, and she ground her teeth together as her compelling will summoned and conjured.

Another bomb erupted, this time in the immeasurable forest, which was suddenly hidden from view by the cloistered walkway of a convent. It was no use; all her efforts were futile, and the pandemonium continued to rage around her. The glittering strands within the gift of the Fates dimmed, and she looked in dejection at the alabaster figure that stood close by.

All at once, the disappointment fell from her face, and Edie let out an excited squeal. "There's a way!" she cried. "We can do it—we can!"

Shooing the boys back into the darkness beneath the archway, Edie gave Neil the burning torch and held out her hand toward the statue. "Come with us," she implored. "I needs you."

The sculpture stirred and outstretched its one ivory arm, placing the delicate-looking fingers upon the girl's open palm.

"In 'ere," Edie invited.

To the stone portal the mutilated figure strode, its dainty feet pulverizing the grass that had sprung up through the now flagstoned floor of the entrance hall.

Under the arch the statue stepped, to where the flame-lit gloom of the secret stairway delved down into the earth.

Displaced from the topmost step, Neil and his brother looked up at the lustrous alabaster that glimmered in the torchlight, its hacked, towering frame dwarfing the small eight-year-old girl who guided it further inside.

"What are you doing?" he demanded. "That thing won't be any use against the Frost Giant—you saw what it did to Ursula and Woden."

"I don't want to go down there again!" Josh wailed miserably. "Dad scares me."

Edie growled at them. "We won't be ploddin' back all the way."

"Hope you know what you're doing," Neil muttered.

"You got yerself a plan then, have you?" she replied. "Right, so shut it and get movin'." Down the plunging stairway the children picked their path, and the sculpture made by Pumiyathon followed.

With his cratered face pressed into the tufting grass, Jack Timms uttered a dismal groan. The crushing weight of the statue was finally lifted from his back, but the cracked cheekbone caused by its punch sang an agonizing dirge inside his head. From his red-lipped mouth, a frothing string of bloody saliva trickled out, and sucking the air through his rotten teeth, he blearily opened one ratty eye.

* * *

Into the black depths below the foundations of the Wyrd Museum the children retraced their steps, with the statue stomping after them. All the while, Edie Dorkins peered at the rocky wall around her, anxiously hunting for the signs and clues that she remembered.

Holding on to Josh with one hand and lifting the torch with the other, Neil tentatively led the way. For the life of him, he could not understand what the capricious girl was thinking of, for there was no escape down here.

When they had descended barely a fifth of the distance, suddenly, without warning, Neil heard a sound that made his heart beat frantically against his ribs. Far below them, dragging footsteps began to echo up the stairs.

"It's him!" Neil murmured. "The Frost Giant—it's coming up the steps."

Glaring past him to where a moldering pipe projected above their heads, Edie nodded. "'Course it is," she declared. "The Loom ain't down there. That thing knows it now."

To the boys' alarm, the rumor of those pounding footfalls grew rapidly louder as their possessed father ascended with frightening speed. "We've got to turn back!" Neil blurted. "At the rate that monster's climbing, it'll be up here any minute."

Lurching about-face in that winding tunnel, Neil tried to take Josh back to the chaos of the entrance hall, but Edie Dorkins would not let them pass.

"This is crazy!" Neil snapped. "You'll get us all killed, Edie!"

In that deep shaft the air had grown much colder, and they could hear the hiss of the ice lord's glacial breathing gusting up from the unlit regions.

"Edie!" he begged. *"Please!"*

Ignoring him, the girl looked up at the encrusted pipe. She swept her hands over the curving rocky wall that reared up on their left and pressed her ear against it. "This is it!" she exclaimed. "Just 'ere should do."

Grabbing the torch from Neil, Edie brought the leaping flames close to that blank stretch of stone, and the alabaster figure planted its feet firmly apart on the steps.

"Now!" the girl commanded.

At that, the ivory arm was raised, but before its delicate-looking fist could be brought smashing down upon the rock, from the entrance high above them they heard an all-too-familiar, fearful sound.

Tap-tap-tap.

"Tick-Tock Jack!" Neil breathed in despair. "He's come around."

Edie's eyes opened wide. The repulsive warder was much closer to them than the fiend that stormed up from below, and she hoped there was enough time.

Tap-tap-tap.

"Does you hear me down there?" that gargling voice came threatening. "Old Tick-Tock's hot on your track. He's got bruises to repay, and he'll do it all right. You can't have got far down this stinkin' rat hole. Ain't no use hidin' from old Jack, he'll be on you soon—Tick-Tock, Tick-Tock."

Glancing nervously up the twisting stairs, Edie gave

the statue a desperate pat, and the ivory fist came flashing through the light. Into the wall that graceful hand crashed, and a tremendous crack went booming throughout the deep shaft as the solid stone splintered under the ferocious impact.

A disgusting guffaw burst from above. "Sounded nasty, that did!" the warder laughed. "I does hope no one's gone and got themselves damaged. You don't want to spoil Tick-Tock's jamboree now, does you?"

Into the cracked rock the sculpture's ivory fingers went gouging, tearing aside the fragmented chunks of wall.

"Quicker!" Edie urged as the steady knock of the warder's Tormentor bore down toward them.

"Many's the jolly old Jack's had in coal cellars like this," that detestable voice boasted. "Ain't no better throttlin' or batterin' ground."

With a sharp snap, one of the statue's slender fingers broke off, but the ivory hand had already scraped and excavated a prodigious hole in the wall. Down the smooth stairs the quarried rock went rattling, and Neil wondered if it would continue to roll and bounce all the way to where the Frost Giant was clambering.

The echoes of that nightmare were howling in the ether, ricocheting around the coiling walls and instilling a horrendous dread into them, while above, Tick-Tock Jack's cumbersome steps trudged ever closer.

"We're trapped," Neil mumbled fitfully. "Stuck between a killer up there and a devil underneath."

He thought his spirits could sink no lower until the

ivory fist suddenly struck a curving expanse of metal concealed behind the rock. A thunderous clang, like the tolling of a vast, discordant bell, vibrated through the darkness.

"That's it, then," Neil uttered, abandoning all hope when the flickering torchlight revealed rusting, riveted plates. "We can't get through that."

Craning her head around, Edie saw the cudgel-end of a cruel-looking cane come thumping from the turning above, followed by a pair of black-booted feet. "We ain't got no choice," she said flatly.

Squaring itself up to the corroded iron, the alabaster figure drew back its four-fingered fist and sent it hurtling forward, crunching and hammering against the flaking metal. With a shrill, piercing squeal, a great dent formed in the barrier. Then the sculpture drove blow after blow into its yielding surface, the exquisitely modeled knuckles chipping and shattering as the punches became more violent and fierce. Soon there came a loud, rending snap when one of the rivets was shorn from its anchor, and part of the wide, ribbed plate juddered loose.

A grinding squawk signaled a second rivet torn free, then a third and a fourth. Into that mass of buckled metal the scratched and splintered arm reached. The remaining fingers closed tightly over the iron seams to pull and rip with monumental force, until a large hole with twisting, girdered edges had been pried open.

"That's fer the skull-cracker!" Jack Timms's bawling voice burst in on them.

Down the remaining steps Tick-Tock Jack came rushing, ramming the Tormentor into the alabaster sculpture's side with his powerful arms.

There was a horrible thud, and the statue wheeled around, pitched off balance. For a desperate moment the elegant feet teetered upon the worn steps, and the milk-white arm flailed through the flames, knocking the torch out of Edie's hand as the scrambling fingers clutched at the wall.

Neil pulled Josh against the rock as the tumbling fire went sizzling past their heads to gutter and flare down the steps, until its light was doused around the turning below. Then, with an almost balletlike grace, the statue tipped and toppled from its footing.

A bleak cry rang from Edie's mouth as the great, glimmering figure lurched into the shadows, and with a tremendous crash, the sculpture fell. Onto the stone stairs the ivory shoulders pounded, instantly losing the arm with a shattering smash. Over and over it somersaulted, the feet swinging up to crack against the wall, and the Ionic shift with its translucent folds shivering in two.

Following the extinguished, smoking torch, the largest fragments were lost from sight as they careered uncontrollably down the stairs. All the while, Jack Timms brayed his disgusting laughter. Then he turned his murderous attention upon the children and slapped his palm with his cane.

A dim radiance filtered from the great opening the statue had made, and its pale light poured over the warder's repugnant, bruised face as he came prowling toward them. The resounding crashes of the sculpture's destroying descent still thumped and shattered down the shaft below.

"Not so brave now, is we?" he slurred, those bloodshot rodent's eyes twinkling with menace in the dingy glow. "Tick-Tock's got to work up a real soakin' sweat to take his mind off the smarting grief where that statue whacked him."

But Edie was already clambering through the hole, and springing between that and the burly warder, Neil urged Josh to hurry after her. "Your master's dead!" he shouted. "Go back to when you belong!"

Jack Timms leered at him. "Oh, I knows that a'ready," he answered with a gurgling chuckle. "I felt the guv'nor get what for, but the way I sees matters— that leaves me in charge now, don't it?"

Shoving the boy aside, Tick-Tock lunged at the opening through which Edie had already disappeared and where Josh was now dithering mournfully.

"Get you back 'ere!" the evil man snarled, seizing the child in his dirty mitts and shaking him brutally. "You'll not put the spoil on old Jack's fun. The little witch can scarper if she wants; I ain't got the jabber no more, but there's plenty of learnin' I can give to the likes of you!"

Squealing in Jack Timms's grasp, Josh saw the Tormentor rise purposefully above his head. But before it could strike him, a streak of milky stone went crunching against the foul man's temple, and the boy was dropped from those fat fingers as Tick-Tock staggered against the wall.

Breathing hard, Neil Chapman lifted the chunk of alabaster he had plucked from the stairs over his head once more and prepared to hit the warder a second time. But Jack Timms would not be caught that way again. Whisking through the air, the Tormentor smacked the stone from the boy's fingers, and Neil howled at the stinging pain.

"You got to whack harder than that to split old Jack's head!" Tick-Tock spat. He lumbered forward to catch hold of Neil's hair and wrench him to the ground.

"Josh—get out of here!" the boy screeched before the killer's fingers wrapped around his throat and strong, flat thumbs pressed against his windpipe.

"Bigger pups'n you have tried bestin' me!" the warder rumbled. "Ain't none ever so much as bit, but I did fer 'em, anyways. You've a right jollification due—feed you to the sparrows, that's what Jack'll do when he's minced yer!"

Neil choked and balked as those strangling hands squeezed tighter, but Jack Timms was far too strong. All Neil could do was kick feebly with his legs and thrash the steps with his arms. Crouched halfway in the opening, Josh stared in terror as Tick-Tock's obese bulk stooped over his brother, pinching the life out of him.

* * *

Down the steep stairway the shattered statue continued to thunder. Now an avalanche of broken alabaster, it trounced an unstoppable, winding course all the way to the bottom.

Suddenly, a ferocious din blasted up from the

depths, as the crashing, thudding tide plunged about the possessed Brian Chapman and the fearsome force within him shrieked out in fury. Up the spiraling stairway that horrendous voice blared, and the steps shook under the might of the Frost Giant's wrath.

His hands still clenched about the boy's neck, Jack Timms faltered as the atrocious power of that echoing scream blasted around them. "What were that?" he muttered, turning his florid face to glower down the dark passage.

Again the ghastly voice blared out, and the warder's fingers slipped from his victim's throat. "Jack don't like it," he hissed, spitting into the gloom. "Not another o' them hateful stags?"

Sprawled beneath him, Neil coughed and retched as the man drew himself up to listen. The ice lord was very close to them now. They could both hear the leaping footsteps come chiming over the stretch of stair that wound almost directly below them. Through the twisting tunnel a wintry gale went ravaging, freezing the dripping water that trickled down the rock. Flurries of ice crystals blew into the bitter air before the Frost Giant's frightening approach.

"That's something even you can't fight against," Neil cried hoarsely. "I hope it kills you!" With that, he wriggled clear of Jack Timms's bloated size and flung himself toward the opening, pushing a startled Josh through the jagged hole before him, not caring what was on the other side.

Alone in that Arctic murk, Tick-Tock Jack listened a moment longer to the unseen fiend's threatening calls before reeling around, just as Neil dropped out of sight.

"Don't you leave me 'ere!" he bawled. "Don't leave old Jack in this perishin' chill with that!"

But Neil was gone, and the Frost Giant came bounding ever closer.

* * *

Neil Chapman fell into a dimly lit space, then his shoes crunched onto concrete and his collapsing knees struck him in the chest. At his side, Josh was already being helped off the ground by Edie Dorkins.

"Took yer time!" the girl chided them.

Neil eyed her ruefully, but his attention was instantly caught by the place he now found himself in. A wide tunnel arched high over them, and turning his head from left to right, he saw that it stretched far in either direction. At regular intervals, along the thick, grime-covered cables, electric lamps shone in the sooty shadows. Their monotonous glare was reflected in the parallel metals that coursed through the length of that immense, subterranean thoroughfare.

"We're in the Underground!" Neil breathed, the shock of breaking back into the modern world stupefying his senses. "Somewhere between the stations. I don't—"

A harsh, cursing voice suddenly broke into his amazement as, above them, Jack Timms came squeezing through the opening. Fearfully, the children stared upward to where the curving wall seemed to be delivering a grotesque, breached monster into their unhappy world. From the ruptured girders the odious man's boots came dangling, swiftly followed by his struggling legs.

"Didn't Jack say there was no escapin' him?" his wheezing voice called, straining with a squirming effort as that broad, barrel-shaped body became temporarily wedged in the gap.

On the ground below, Neil leaped to his feet and scooped his brother up in his arms. "This way!" Edie cried, plunging alongside the tunnel wall, kicking up a trail of black dirt with her heels.

With a string of sickening oaths, Tick-Tock Jack finally fought his way through the hole, and his great, blubbery weight plunged down onto the track behind them. Above him, a blast of glacial breath erupted from the opening as, beyond those few feet of wall and rock, the possessed caretaker stampeded up the stairway and on into the Wyrd Museum.

A white, squalling vapor tore into the tunnel, eddying in fitful gusts beneath the curved ceiling. It settled as a light sprinkling of snow on the bull-sized shoulders of Jack's greatcoat, and he hammered a gleeful tattoo on the wall with his cane.

"Got the charmed life of the devil 'imself," he cackled smugly, until his eyes flicked along the gleaming tracks to where the children ran into the distance. "Some folks just won't never be learned," he said viciously. "Well, they been spared the rod fer way too long."

In between the rails the warder leaped, his powerful legs carrying him with unexpected speed. As he ran, he stretched his thick lips as far back over his brown gums as it was possible without them splitting, letting loose a caterwauling, vengeful shriek that ignited a despairing terror in the children's hearts.

Through the endless tunnel Neil and Edie ran, with Josh a dead weight in his brother's arms. Glancing over her shoulder, Edie saw that Neil was finding it increasingly difficult to keep up. The pockfaced killer was gaining steadily on the boys, the folds of his black coat flapping like the wings of Woden's Valkyries.

Laughing foully, Tick-Tock began using the Tormentor to smash each lightbulb he passed. The dark pounced in behind him, seeming to gather about his charging figure, making him appear even larger and more menacing than ever. Cloaked in this swathe of shadow, Jack Timms bore down on the hapless Neil, who was puffing along like an old steam engine.

Another lamp exploded as the cudgel-end of the cane drove into it, and Neil felt a shard of glass graze his neck. The murderous warder was almost upon them, and in a last, desperate attempt to elude him, the boy jumped across the rails, taking consummate care not to touch them.

If there was any justice, or if the Fates had indeed woven a terrible end for Tick-Tock Jack, then Neil prayed it would find him now. If that hateful assassin could only make contact with the lethal current that flowed through that track, then all his swaggering savagery would be purged from the world by an arc of blinding blue light. It was a spectacle that Neil longed to witness, but no blissful crackle of deadly voltage illuminated the tunnel behind, and he felt his legs weakening under him.

This time there was no escape. There was nowhere left to run and no one to save them.

Haring across to the opposite side of the tunnel, the boy flung himself back, to give his one hope another chance, but even as he turned, the Tormentor came lashing against the backs of his legs. With a howl, Neil went tumbling headlong over the rails and Josh flew from his arms.

Onto the hard concrete that lay in the center of the track the boys fell, cracking their knees and elbows, while Jack Timms loomed over them, snickering vilely.

"You won't be running nowhere!" he gloated. "Tick-Tock's gonna do fer you 'ere an' now."

"No!" Edie yelled, rushing at Woden's heinous servant to stay his hand. "You were told to get me."

Snarling so that the crescent-shaped scar puckered in his face, the warder shrugged her off, just as he had done on their first meeting when he had assumed the role of the workhouse overseer.

"You know there's nowt I can do to 'urt you without that flamin' spear," he snapped. "But it'll do me no end of good to see your face as I knock an' dash the daylights outta these two."

Pushing her roughly against the wall, the braggart strode over the rails and raised a booted foot to stamp on Neil's legs. Staring up at him, the boy scrambled backward as the crushing blow descended. Onto the concrete Jack's foot went pounding, but the sadistic man merely laughed the louder and swung his

Tormentor behind his back to bring it thrashing down upon Neil's head. Feverishly, the boy tried to dodge aside but blundered into Josh, and Edie screamed when she saw that the blow could not miss.

Suddenly, her voice seemed to fill the whole tunnel, and Tick-Tock hesitated, staring suspiciously at her, but the girl had already closed her mouth. Yet still the noise blared in the gloom.

Too late, Jack Timms whirled around to see the bright lights of a Central Line train come hurtling along the track. A riot of expressions flashed across his repulsive face as he realized the danger and leaped clear of the rails.

With only an instant to spare, he sprang to safety. But it was his own cherished Tormentor that was to be the instrument of his destruction. Gripped tightly in his hand, the barbaric, bullying cane that had been the terror of untold inmates of the Wyrd Infirmary still projected back into the path of that speeding engine. With undeniable force, the train cannoned into it.

Before he knew it was happening, Jack Timms's burly figure was levered back against the traveling carriages and sent smacking and crashing into them, his ugly, breaking face bouncing against the racketing windows.

Then out across the tunnel the warder was hurled, his now splintered cane waggling in his fist. With a grisly crunch of shattering bone, Tick-Tock Jack hit the opposite track, and the yowl that gargled from his raw mouth was a sound that Neil would never forget.

Both of Jack Timms's legs were broken, and from

the impossible way it bent in the sleeve of his great-coat, it looked as though his left arm now had two elbows.

Only Edie contemplated his piteous screams with a detached coldness. "Good," she said severely. "You deserves that, an' more."

Blasting its horn, the train thundered on through the tunnel, but the sound did not fade. Instead it grew louder again, and Neil turned to see a second engine come racing the other way, along the track where he and Josh were crouched.

Yelling for his life, Neil bolted from inside those deadly lines, hoisting his brother after him. To the arching wall he raced, to Edie's side. "Flatten yourselves against the tunnel!" he shouted.

But as Neil did the same, he saw that Tick-Tock was still stuck on the rails, screeching and shrieking for help.

"Get me offa this!" his high, petrified voice pleaded. "You can't let me die! Not me! Please! Please!"

Tears of pain and panic gushed from his tiny eyes to mingle with the scarlet juices flowing from his countless wounds. Faced with his imminent demise, the torturer of the Wyrd Infirmary was like a terrified child. "Help me!" he begged again, stretching his one good arm toward those he had wanted to kill.

Neil shuddered and even jerked forward, but Edie grabbed him and pulled him back. "There's nowt you can do!" she told him.

In agony, Tick-Tock Jack tried to drag himself out of the oncoming train's path. From the rail he heaved himself, but that was as much as he could manage. At that moment, the engine came bursting through the dim dark. The warder flung himself back to lie in the center of the lines, hoping that the engine and carriages would rumble harmlessly over him.

Yet, even as the back of his broad head struck the concrete, he caught sight of the person behind the driver's window of that rushing train, and he knew he was done for.

For the briefest of moments, Jack Timms thought he saw in that cabin an elderly, gaunt-faced woman, whose fine white hair curled out from under the cap of her uniform. A solemn smile was traced over her thin lips, and she looked him full in the eyes before the engine rode over his head.

So was the horrendous Destiny that Miss Ursula Webster had woven for the abhorrent warder fulfilled, for he was caught under the train. Such was the scourging decree of Fate, the man did not die until three whole circuits of the line had been completed. Only then was his unequaled suffering ended.

Over the children's faces the squares of light from the carriage windows swept swiftly, and then it was gone, shooting off into the distance. Down the tunnel the warder's tormented howls echoed as the train tore over the track, with him ensnarled beneath.

Only when no whisper of those awful cries could be heard did Neil and the others stir. The enemy they had learned to fear, the agent of Woden, could no longer do them any harm. Now, at the end, Neil felt only pity for Jack Timms.

Seeing how shaken Neil was, Edie took charge of

Josh. "This way," she said, and in silence they resumed the journey down the tunnel.

There were still more dangers to face.

look. "This way," she said, and it was
through the curtain dawn that they
rushed now, still more anxious to find

Chapter 25

Reunion and Confrontation

It was only when four more trains had rocketed by that Neil finally spoke. "There's a station ahead."

Some way in front, the arched gloom became much brighter as a long platform curved into view like an oasis in that desolation of gleaming rails.

One more train hurtled by, and when it had passed the children hastened toward the slope that ascended to that orange-and-cream-tiled expanse. Up onto the platform they clambered, exhausted and drained by everything that had happened, and Neil wondered how they must appear to the rest of the world. Begrimed from head to toe, they looked as though they had scaled the inside of every chimney in London. Fortunately, when Neil glanced up and down the platform, he saw that it was deserted, and he peered curiously at his watch.

"Quarter to six in the morning," he murmured. "Not surprised there's no one here. We've been up all night."

Traipsing to the nearest row of seats, he sat Josh down and threw himself beside him under the sign that announced their location as Bethnal Green.

Having paced a little way up the eerily empty platform, Edie Dorkins turned and a deep frown marked her forehead. "Don't stop!" she ordered. "There ain't time!"

Supporting his head in his hands, Neil stared at her. "We can't go on," he groaned. "I'm not going back to that museum, and there's no way I'm letting Josh anywhere near it."

"You must!" the girl cried, stamping her foot. "It's the only chance we've got—all of us. The Frost Giant'll find the Loom sometime. He might've already. That's more important than anythin'!"

Neil's fingers pinched the bridge of his nose. It was his father's habitual gesture, and the boy shivered when he realized he had done it. "Don't you see?" he declared. "That's our dad back there. I can't face him again, not the horror he's become. If everything's going to end, then it might as well, because Josh and me have got absolutely nothing left. I'd rather the darkness came while I was out here in the ordinary world than back in that madhouse."

Edie ran to him. "You don't mean that!" she exclaimed.

The boy gazed at her, then shook his head. "It's all right for you," he said. "You're Edie Dorkins, the Websters' heir. Well, I'm only human. You might've forgotten about your real parents, but I haven't."

"Then I'll go on my own," she responded.

"You'll have to," Neil said hollowly. "I'm sorry—I just haven't got anything left to give."

It was then, when they were at their lowest, that they heard a shuffling footstep descend onto the platform from the station above. The well-wrapped figure of an old woman pattered into view, looking eagerly around her.

For a moment she seemed to sag with disappointment. Then, when she noticed the children, the newcomer gave a slight gasp and ambled toward them, the tartan shopping bag in her gloved hands swinging jauntily at her side.

Neil and Edie stared at her as she raised her hand in greeting, but neither of them recognized this early-rising stranger. "Well!" she called out to them. "Who'd have thought it, eh?"

The kindly mother of Gloria Rosina, that slovenly landlady of The Bella Vista guest house, came shambling over the platform, a delighted smile upon her aged face.

"I never did!" her warm, sweet voice proclaimed. "Just look at the pair of you—not a day different."

Edie and Neil exchanged baffled glances, and the old woman laughed merrily at the blank expressions on their faces.

"You don't remember me, do you?" she chuckled. "But I know you right enough. Neil—Neil Chapman, how are you, love? And if this isn't little Edie Dorkins—I weren't expectin' you, dear. Didn't make the connection! What a turn up, an' no mistake!"

The children could only stare back, dumbfounded.

"Looks like the message were right after all." The elderly woman sighed. "Always thought it were. Wouldn't have stayed 'round here otherwise, not with our sour-faced Glor. Could've gone to live in Canada with Danny. Always asks, and soon as this is done I'll pack my few things and take him up on it."

Neil shook himself. "Message?" he prompted. "What message? How . . . how do you know us?"

The old woman's faded green eyes sparkled at them both as she lifted her shopping bag and reached inside. "Mustn't forget," she said, becoming serious. "There's no time for anything in between; it's now what counts. Deadly urgent, ain't it?"

"What do you know about it?" Edie asked, suspiciously scrutinizing the newcomer and noticing that her fur-lined boots were covered with snow.

The elderly stranger tutted solemnly and brought out a rolled-up piece of pale-blue fabric printed with small pink roses. It was tied in the middle with a lock of corn-colored hair.

"Well," she said, passing it to Neil, "Doom is hanging by a thread, ain't it? Only you can stop it, that's what it says. You've got to get a move on, ain't you?"

Taking the scrap of cloth from her, Neil handed the binding curl to Edie, who took it in trembling fingers, recognizing it at once. Taking a deep breath, the boy unfurled the material and there, in a wavering, underlined script that had bled slightly into the pale rosy buds, was written that day's date, the exact time—even the place: Bethnal Green Underground Station, Platform Two. Then, beneath those directions, he read aloud for Edie's benefit:

To Neil Chapman

The Doom of the world is hanging by the slenderest of threads. (I always wanted to say that, but Ursula beat me to it every time!)

Firstly, I should say that this is very naughty, but Edward made me do it—he did. He said if I knew, then I should tell, but I daren't tell Ursula because she'd be so cross with me, she would. Not supposed to do any knitting on my own, to have a peep and see what'll happen, but I can't help it if Veronica casts on for me. That's how I know—I saw it all! Well, bits of it, and that's as good as!

If you don't go back into the museum, then chaos and darkness will reign and it will be too, too terrible. Edith really does need you, she can't do it by herself.

Edward's saying for me to get on with it, and I'd better before I have to leave. I was just about to sew up the nice new version of him when I let slip about what I had seen. He got so angry when I said I couldn't tell anyone and that he mustn't either, so that's why he made me write this note. Go back to our museum. Do what needs to be done. Help Edith. Your presence is vital to the Destiny of everything!

Good luck, dear—to both of you.

C.

Neil looked up from the pale-patterned fabric. His voice had fallen to a murmur. "Where did you get this?" he asked.

The elderly messenger gave him a gentle smile, and Neil found that there was indeed something familiar about that aged mouth. Although the eyes had dimmed with the passing years, he felt certain that he had seen the light that shone there before.

"Found it in among his kapok," she said. "There it was, written on a piece of cloth cut from the best comforter."

Returning her attention to the bag, she reached inside, and a sublime grin flashed across her face. "There were times when I thought I must be off my rocker for believin' it at all, but somethin' told me I was right to. Always knew there was more to what happened back then, too many things that couldn't be explained. Anyway, I waited all these years and now here you are. I suppose on this occasion it was me who traveled through time, although I did it the usual way. But you did it back then to save me, so I could do no less."

"Save you? . . ." the boy repeated.

The elderly woman laughed. "There's someone 'ere you'll want to see again," she said.

Out of the shopping bag she brought an old, shabby-looking object, and when Neil saw it, a cry burst from his mouth. "It can't be!"

There, dangling in her hand, was a one-armed teddy bear. Tears welled up in the boy's eyes as he reached out to the toy that had once accompanied him back to the London of World War II.

"Ted!" he gasped.

Although the wooly fur was dustier than when he had last seen it, the teddy bear was exactly as he remembered. Within that assortment of sheepskin and wadding, the soul of the American airman Angelo Signorelli had been imprisoned. Together, they had defeated Belial, the demon that had escaped from The Separate Collection, and on the toy's fur there were still frazzled patches to show where he had been singed in that desperate conflict.

Now, looking at that slightly mournful expression sewn into the bear's face, Neil could almost hear the GI's voice again. *"I got faith in ya, kid—hang on in there!"*

The boy looked up sharply. Was that brash American accent really only inside his head?

"You and that teddy," the old woman remarked, breaking in on his thoughts. "Always was mad about it. Over fifty years I've waited for that boy my dad found in the bomb site to return. Been a long time, Neil."

Raising his eyes from Ted, Neil regarded the stranger again, and at last he knew her. "Jean!" he breathed. "Jean Evans!"

The older version of the lovely woman whom Neil and Ted had journeyed into the past to save grinned back at him. The intervening years had left their mark, but the spirit of that young, beautiful creature still burned within her.

"Like I said," she began, "we don't have the time it'd take to explain what's happened in between. Have you decided what you're going to do, Neil?"

"What did you mean when you said you were now saving me?" he asked her.

"Isn't it obvious? If you don't go back to that museum then you'll die, Neil. We all will."

The boy stared back at the teddy bear and, for an instant, imagined he saw that old, sparkling intelligence glimmer deep within those glass eyes.

"What else can I do?" he announced with fresh determination. "Edie and me are going back—right now."

"Then let's get ourselves outside," Jean said. "By the looks of things, I don't think there's hardly any time left."

Wondering at her words, the children roused Josh and followed her up to the concourse of the station before climbing up the same stairs where Jean's vindictive and spiteful grandmother had died in the war.

"The year after Sandy, my husband, came back from the prison camp, I had our Gloria," she told Neil. "Turned out just like that mean old baggage, she did. Took after Ma Stokes in everything, 'ceptin' Glor's a lot fatter. I'll be glad to go and live with Daniel now and get out of her way."

Mounting those steps, Neil and Edie swiftly discovered that the winter that raged about the Wyrd Museum had spread to the whole of the East End. A scouring wind filled with swirling snow blasted into the stairwell from the entrance above, and emerging onto the pavement, the children could hardly believe the transformation.

Wherever they looked, their gaze was dazzled by a blank, glaring whiteness. Bethnal Green was in the merciless grip of severe Arctic weather. The roads were devoid of traffic, submerged beneath frozen dunes, and the doorways of snow-swaddled buildings were blockaded by high, sweeping drifts. Into this desolation the small group surfaced, where the howl of the abrasive gale was the only sound.

Edie Dorkins glanced up at the slate-colored sky. "The lords of the ice an' dark," she muttered. "With Nirinel gone, their power's stronger than ever. If the Loom's smashed and they get free, it'll be 'undred times worse than this."

Neil looked at her worriedly. "Do we stand any chance at all?" he asked.

The girl pushed her hand into the plunder-filled pocket of her coat, where her fingers met with something small and round, and her eyes glittered when she answered him. "I reckon so," she said. "A small 'un, if I'm right."

Neil considered her doubtfully, then turned to Jean and shouted above the battering wind. "Will you look after Josh until . . . well . . ."

The elderly woman took the little boy's hand in hers. "You just go and do what you have to," she replied. "He'll be safe with me."

"You'd better take this, too," the boy called, handing Ted back to her.

Jean leaned forward and planted a kiss upon Neil's forehead.

"How did you know?" he asked.

"Know what, love?"

"About me and Ted, going back to save you."

The lovely smile creased her face again, but she did not answer the question. "I'll see you again when all this is over," she promised. "Now, hurry along and remember what he said. 'Hang on in there.' You can do this."

Neil could only gape at the woman. Then, giving his brother a final hug, he took a resolute breath and hastened after Edie, who was already trudging her way over the thickly layered roads, commencing the journey back toward the Wyrd Museum.

Standing by the entrance of the station, Jean Evans and Josh waited a moment longer, then the old woman turned and led the four-year-old to her daughter's bed-and-breakfast.

His head sticking out of the shopping bag, Ted's glass eyes stared back at the glaring scene until the figures of Neil and Edie were hidden from sight by the obscuring snowfall. Where the frozen flakes landed on the bear's cheeks, they melted to form two trickles of water down his wooly fur.

Over Bethnal Green the glacial winter deepened.

* * *

Through the white, deserted streets Edie and Neil labored, their legs aching and their faces numb with the hideous cold. Down every narrow way the blizzard blew, but fighting against it, they eventually saw the turrets and spires of the Wyrd Museum rearing behind the rooftops and rising up into the freezing mists.

Locked within a covering of thick, impenetrable ice, the ancient building bore the full brunt of that lashing, frost-fueled tempest. Whirling the weather vanes, the gales tore around the roof to go raging about the solid, square walls and scream in the rear courtyard. The icicles that thrust from the building's gutters now stretched all the way to the ground and had become mighty pillars. The museum looked like a palace of cold, wherein the Frost Giants had already made their formidable stronghold.

Down Well Lane the children battled, the storm wailing in their ears. They slithered over the rippled banks of ice to turn into the alleyway at the front of the museum, then halted abruptly. Filling that cramped path was a gathering of nearly thirty people. All were well wrapped in warm winter clothing, and every scarf-bound face was turned to the doorway as though they were aware that something of the utmost importance was occurring inside that forbidding place. It was as if they were keeping a silent vigil outside the building, waiting upon the momentous events that were about to befall.

Stumbling forward, Neil and Edie stared at them curiously, astonished by their presence. They were a strange assembly and, by the looks of them, from all walks of life. The only factor that linked them, as far as Neil could see, was that they had chosen to congregate outside the Wyrd Museum at this the critical hour of Doom.

Then he understood. "The well wishers," he muttered.

These were the people he had seen when he had first moved into the museum, those few descendants of the race of Askar over whom the mother of the Webster sisters had ruled as queen. In this time, Aidan had been their leader, and to this place every year they came in pilgrimage to lay flowers around the broken drinking fountain.

Searching those frostbitten faces, Neil quickly found the one he knew would be there. "Chief Inspector!" he yelled.

In the center of the large group, a tall figure stirred and glanced up the alleyway to where the children stood. With a shout, he hastened over to greet them. His uniform concealed beneath several layers of clothing, Chief Inspector Hargreaves met Neil and Edie with a somber expression graven in his hollow-cheeked face.

"I took it upon myself to summon the others," he addressed Edie with solemn reverence. "At this, the time of judgment, it is fitting that we stand and wait for the outcome. But what has happened? I thought you were inside the museum."

The girl eyed him sternly. "Nirinel has been destroyed," she proclaimed for him and the others to hear. "The last root of the World-Tree is dead, and so are Urdr and Skuld."

Despondent cries issued from the gathering, and the police officer took a horrified step backward. "The Fates are no more?" he murmured incredulously. "We saw that the three figures about the entrance were broken, but we did not dare to think . . . Then the eternal dark must surely take us."

Edie snorted and barged past him. "Keep yer beard on," she declared. "It's not finished yet."

Hargreaves stared at her, but it was Neil who answered. "We're going back inside," the boy said.

"But the doorway is sealed!" the chief inspector exclaimed. "The ice has got to be a foot thick."

"Getting in is the least of our problems," Neil told

him. "You don't know what's loose in there."

Reaching the entrance, Edie found that the fragments of the bronze sculpture that had represented Miss Ursula had been cemented to the ground by the frost. Gazing at that imposing Victorian façade, the girl saw that it was indeed embedded within a solid curtain of ice. In those bleak, frozen depths, the oaken door was almost impossible to see. There was no way anyone could break through.

A superior smile curved over Edie's mouth as she raised her eyes to the gilded sign above the arched doorway.

"You have to let me in," she said with sudden authority. "I belong here. You can't keep me out. I'm the daughter of the Three."

Upon her head the silver strands of her hat shone coldly as a deep furrow creased her brow. Then, within the ice, beneath those bronze letters, the one remaining feature of the ornate entrance was lit with a green, pulsing glow. There, the molded face of a cherub gleamed under her commanding glare. Suddenly, the alley chimed with a brittle, crackling din as the ice that smothered the door shattered and collapsed in great, glittering fractures that spilled out onto the frozen ground.

Over the children's feet the glacial splinters tumbled, until at last the way to the door was clear. With a prolonged squeak of its hinges, the stout oak barrier yawned open.

Edie tossed her head, snapping out of her fierce concentration. "This is it," she told Neil. "You ready?"

Staring into the main hallway, the boy gave a

resolute nod. "Let's get it over with," he said.

Turning to the well wishers, Edie told them to wait a little longer.

"You sure you want to go back in there, just the two of you?" the chief inspector asked uncertainly. "Wouldn't it be safer if we all . . ."

"No!" she snapped. "This is our Destiny, not yours. You must stay out here. If what we're gonna try don't work, you'll know soon enough."

Hargreaves bowed. "Then all our hopes go with you," he said respectfully.

Yet Edie Dorkins was already stepping over the fallen ice to the doorway, and with a final glance at the chief inspector and the descendants of Askar, Neil followed.

*   *   *

Inside the Wyrd Museum, the chaos of the churning centuries had ceased completely. The familiar, paneled entrance hall met the children's gaze when they clambered inside, but here, too, the horrendous winter had invaded.

Knives of jagged ice stabbed viciously from the ceiling, and the shadowy corners were heaped with snow. The statues that Jack Timms had disfigured and defaced dripped with glass-like needles. Looking at the stairs, the children saw that the banisters were painted white with the extreme, hoary cold.

"Your dad's been this way," Edie whispered.

"That thing's not my father!" Neil denied angrily.

The girl peered into The Roman Gallery and the

connecting corridor. Devastation was everywhere. All the exhibits had been thrown down and the walls had suffered a dreadful, hacking violence. Every frost-sparkling surface had been smashed by the berserking ice lord, and they both knew the reason why.

"It's searchin' for the Loom," Edie said. "Tearin' the museum apart bit by bit till it's found."

From somewhere upstairs there suddenly came a frantic crashing, and they both started in alarm.

"Least we know it hasn't been discovered yet," Neil breathed.

"Can't be long, though," the girl added. "We've got to get there first."

"Upstairs, where that thing is?"

Edie nodded and moved toward the steps, pausing to plunge her hand into the pocket of her coat once more, praying she had guessed correctly.

Without warning, the entrance abruptly slammed shut behind them, and outside, the ice seeped back over the door, locking them within.

"I won't be able to open that again," Edie murmured. "Not from in 'ere—the head won't hear me."

Neil glanced warily up the stairs. "Let's just get to the Loom as fast as we can," he urged.

"Not yet," the girl told him. "First, I've got to get somethin' from The Separate Collection."

"We haven't got time!"

"If we don't, then we might as well give up now!"

Neil groaned. "All right," he relented. "If you're sure."

Up the slippery, ice-covered stairs they ventured, and all the while those terrible sounds of destruction grew steadily closer. No expanse of wall had been left unscathed in the Frost Giant's furious hunt for the device made from the first branch hewn from Yggdrasill. Savage gashes ran the length of the stairs to the second-floor landing, where a whole section of paneling had been torn down and the plaster beneath ravaged by a frenzied assault.

Standing there, looking at the wreckage, with that awful clamor thundering endlessly about them, Neil stared at the landing door and in a small, anguished voice said, "Edie, it's on this floor. The Frost Giant's in there somewhere."

The girl's eyes opened wide. "We've got to reach The Separate Collection," she breathed. "We must."

Cautiously they edged toward the door, fearfully moving into the passageway, where they held their breath and listened to that constant hammering turmoil.

"That noise is coming from either The Egyptian Suite . . ." Neil muttered.

"Or The Separate Collection," the girl agreed.

Neil shivered. "Which way should we go?" he asked.

Edie pointed down the corridor. "This way'll take us straight there," she said. "Better than runnin' through the rooms and bumpin' smack bang into him."

They raced through the passageway where the remains of Mr. Jamrach's stuffed menagerie still cluttered the floor, leaping over broken display cases and crumbling corpses.

More loudly now the dreadful riot boomed, and reaching the far entrance of The Separate Collection,

Neil hesitated as he grasped the doorknob. The entire second floor was shaking under that terrible, pounding fury. Even the air trembled under the severity of the Frost Giant's belligerent attacks, and the boy tried to quell the terror that steamed within him.

"What if it's already in here?" he whimpered.

Edie gripped his arm. "Then we'll have to make a run for it," she said flatly. "Go on—open it."

Inside the room, the calamitous uproar intensified. With a quailing heart, Neil inched the door open and peered inside. Gusts of squalling frost were charging between the display cabinets. All was glittering white, and on the counter at the far side, the body of Miss Celandine Webster was interred within a high drift of snow. But it was the entrance to The Egyptian Suite that commanded the children's attention, for it was in there that the possessed Brian Chapman rampaged.

Out from that windowless room the deafening commotion came blasting as the unclean fiend inhabiting the caretaker's body clawed and smote the hieroglyph-covered walls, hurling the sarcophagi out of his way as though they were no more than empty shoe boxes.

As Neil and Edie watched, great holes were smashed in the panels of The Separate Collection as the ice lord roared with fury and hatred on the other side.

Biting her top lip, Edie Dorkins pushed the door open a little wider. The object she wanted resided in one of the large cases, and with her eyes fixed on the storm that blasted from the ruined Egyptian Suite, she stole inside.

At once Neil dragged her back into the corridor. "You're crazy!" he hissed. "That thing'll come barging out any second. You'll be caught and killed!"

Edie glared at him, but she knew he was right. "Only one thing to do, then," she decided. "You'll have to distract it for me."

"What?"

"I'll run back through the other rooms, and while you lure it away, I can run in, get what I need, and dash out again."

Neil shook his head. "It'll never work!" he objected. "And if you think I'm going to stick my head in there and be a sitting duck for that . . . that monster, you're even madder than—"

But Edie had pulled away from him and was already haring back up the passageway. "Meet me upstairs!" she called. "The Websters' room in the attic! And don't let it catch you!"

"Edie!" the boy cried desperately. "No! Come back."

Laughing grimly, the fey Dorkins girl raced around the twisting corner, and Neil knew that there was no dissuading her. He had to act as a decoy. The time had come for him to confront that abhorrent apparition of his father, and he battled to master the terror that surged within him at that harrowing prospect.

Allowing Edie as much time as he thought she would need to run from the corridor and into The Dissolution Gallery, Neil waited. Each slow second was an agony to bear. Then he returned to the door and spied through the crack.

Brian Chapman had lumbered from the demolished Egyptian Suite and was now destroying the room that housed the exhibits too perilous for the outside world. The boy stared through the blitzing tempest that howled around the displays to where the figure of his father vented the full fury of the malevolent spirit within him against the shivering walls.

The sight that met his eyes was more horrible than anything he had imagined, and it was then that he discovered he had no more tears left to cry.

Neil's father was now a misshapen parody of a human being. The weakest link in the chain of those who dwelt within the Wyrd Museum, he was the ideal host for the obscene forces of those who had waited an eternity for their chance.

Over the caretaker's body an even greater, more grotesque transformation had taken place. The ice lord who controlled him had swollen and burgeoned in strength. From the fastness of the frozen northern wastes the Frost Giant projected its pitiless malice, invading and infecting every cell of the man it had made its creature.

"This can't be!" the boy spluttered.

The clothes hung from its bulging, buckled back in tattered shreds, and the hands that clenched the Spear of Longinus were distended talons of ice. Into the juddering walls that rusted blade went striking, and those unclean claws ripped and lashed against the breached and quivering surfaces.

For the moment the face of that abomination was turned away, but Neil knew as soon as he called out he would be compelled to look on those altered features, and he wondered how much longer his courage could endure. Yet Edie must have reached the wreckage of The Egyptian Suite by now, and steeling himself, the boy pushed the door fully open to brave the blasting tempest that scourged the benighted room.

The Frost Giant gouged the plaster away from the underlying bricks, splintering the oaken panels with an unhallowed frenzy. It was so intent on this destruction that it did not observe Neil's scared figure when he entered.

Neil opened his mouth to call out, but even his voice was too afraid to make itself known to that lamentable horror, and he stood there, stricken and silent, just like one of the statues that had once been part of the collection. Then his cringing fear was broken as, in the decimation of The Egyptian Suite, Edie Dorkins's small face appeared over the mounded rubble.

The caretaker's son glanced from her to the distorted vision of his father, and in a warbling cry, he called out, "Hey! Over here!"

At once the violent, hammering blows were stilled as the Frost Giant finally became aware of him. With torrents of hail raging about its humped form, the monstrous shape turned its malignant head, and Neil stumbled against the doorway, too distraught to utter another sound. As an ogre that figure now appeared, but it was that repellent countenance from which Neil's sight recoiled.

Brian Chapman's face had warped and blistered out of all recognition. A huge, ridged forehead bulged over his thin nose, where branching forks of ice erupted from his nostrils. Across that ballooning skull, the once-lank hair spiked in razor-sharp spines. Under that bone-bursting brow, the Frost Giant's eyes were clustered ice crystals that looked as though they belonged to some gargantuan, glacier-dwelling insect. Within the rime-locked beard blue lips had peeled back to the ears, revealing a pernicious expanse of bloodless gums from which countless jags and thorns of ice protruded, and out of that ghastly maw the atrocious, evil winter came fulminating.

Nothing remotely human remained in that loathsome burlesque of a face, and the fragmented eyes shone a deathly light upon the boy who cowered by the door.

Then from the awful, howling throat, the Frost Giant's chilling voice spoke. *"Where is the Loom?"* it demanded with a rumbling shriek. *"Where is the last remnant of Yggdrasill?"*

Neil fumbled for the door, the inextinguishable might of that grievous aberration swallowing his nerve.

"Where is the Loom?" it thundered, taking an intimidating step closer. *"Thou shalt answer!"*

The boy saw Edie Dorkins creep out from the ruined entrance of The Egyptian Suite, behind that horrendous apparition. Choked and stammering, he finally managed to cry, "Where you'll never find it!"

"Show it unto me!" the ogre of the first cold commanded.

Lingering as long as his daunted valor could bear, Neil saw the creature come stomping forward, brandishing the spear in its deadly grasp and casting the cabinets aside.

"*I wilt find it!*" the cruel voice screeched. "*My brethren shalt be freed.*"

That was all the boy could withstand, and throwing himself from the room, he pelted up the corridor as fast as his shivering legs would carry him.

A vicious crash suddenly exploded only inches from his head. In a bombarding barrage of plaster, the passage wall erupted as the Frost Giant smashed its massive fists against the panels of the room beyond, and Neil was hurled to the floor. Underneath him, he felt the jarring thud of the ogre's stampede as it lurched toward the door. The boy scrambled to his feet, then charged toward the landing.

"That had better've been enough time, Edie!" he bawled. "It's after me now!"

From The Separate Collection the ice lord burst, its eyes blazing in the gloom, the hail-teeming gale stinging from the bellowing mouth. Up the corridor that scathing, hunched horror lunged, the spines of its hair raking the ceiling. Neil Chapman fled before it, racing for his life.

CHAPTER 26

AN ETERNAL EMPIRE
OF COLD AND NIGHT

Out onto the landing the boy flew, skidding over the ice-brindled wreckage that was strewn everywhere. Close behind him, the trumpeting rage of the Frost Giant came booming out into the stairwell, and the churning air was sullied by scoring, scratching snow.

Up the stairs Neil catapulted, not pausing for breath until he reached the third floor. Below, the ogre that his father had become stomped over the splintering steps, and a whirling white storm tore before its ominous approach.

Panting furiously, Neil charged over that topmost landing, flew across the dim passage, and dived into The Tiring Salon. The obliterating cold had not yet reached that spacious gallery, but as he sped through it, the boy knew that it would be only a matter of moments before the finery of Miss Celandine's thronging mannequins would be stained and speckled with ice.

Leaping over the headless dummies, Neil finally attained the small door bearing the image of a flowering tree. In his panicking flight, he kicked it open. In the narrow space beyond, where the green-carpeted steps rose to the Websters' attic apartment, he slammed it shut behind him and saw that Edie Dorkins was waiting there.

Standing on the middle stair with her back to him, the girl was staring at the large oil painting. She had removed the sweater she wore under her coat and now held the gathered welt in her hand, with the empty arms trailing down the step. The grubby garment was strangely filled with a spherical bulk, and Neil guessed that whatever she had taken from The Separate Collection was stuffed inside.

Before he had time to ask, The Tiring Salon abruptly resounded with the terrible roaring of the Frost Giant as the ogre thundered onto the third floor, and Neil hurried over to the stairway. Up the steps he bounded, heading for the curtain-covered door at the top while, outside, the long gallery rang with the ice lord's wrath.

Dragging the damask drape aside, Neil stared desperately into the Websters' cramped little room, then turned back to Edie. The girl was still gazing at the painting.

"Edie!" Neil called. "Where now?"

Over the polished floorboards where once the Fates had danced, the distorted vision of Neil's father crashed, and beneath the small ornate door, the first grains of snow came flurrying.

"Edie!"

Tilting her head to one side, Edie Dorkins narrowed her almond-shaped eyes. "This is a poky attic for such a big buildin'," she reflected. "What's under the rest of its roof?"

Stretching out her free hand, she touched that part of the painting where the forgotten artist had portrayed his indistinct version of the Loom and curtly commanded, "Lemme see!"

With that, the entire painting, including its baroque gilded frame, slid silently to one side. There, revealed behind its hanging space, was a low opening where three steps led up into a hidden, secret room.

"Knew it!" The girl grinned, glancing at Neil. "Don't stand there like a daft lemon! Quick—inside!"

Into the secret opening Edie jumped, and with the tremendous clamor of the ogre's echoing shrieks reverberating just outside the small door, Neil hastened down the stairs and hurried after her.

Immediately the painting glided back behind them. Yet the moment its well-oiled mechanism purred into place, the door outside was thrown from its hinges as the abhorrent enemy smashed its way within.

On the other side of that large, shuddering canvas, the voice of the Frost Giant came screaming, and the children heard the foul creature clamber up the stairs. Inches away it trampled past, with only the thin partition of the painting to screen them from its mordant malice.

Holding his breath, Neil heard the apparition

ascend the steps. Then came a shrill, squeaking jangle as the curtain outside was wrenched from its brass rings, and the monster heaved its tall, ungainly bulk into the Websters' room.

"Thou canst not conceal thyself!" it shrieked. *"Thine shielding cloak shalt be torn from thee! Where is the Loom? Where?"*

Throughout the attic the dreadful violence of the ice lord's anger went shuddering. In that cramped and dusty space, furniture was flung aside and the walls crunched and split under those immense fists.

With that riotous tumult rattling the roof slates, Neil slowly backed up the three steps and bumped into Edie. "Lor!" she breathed in a marveling, awestruck murmur. "It's beautiful!"

Only then did Neil turn around and a blissful, silvery-green light blazed onto his face. In that secret room beneath the gabled rafters, steeped in the glimmering glow, they both stared at the dramatic and ravishing spectacle that captivated their astounded vision.

"Amazing!" Neil breathed, and for a brief moment his terror was forgotten. Rearing before them, rising up into the sloping roof, was undoubtedly the most glorious and splendid object he had ever beheld.

There, in the place where Miss Ursula Webster had kept it hidden for centuries, was a towering framework of sturdy, richly carved timbers—the Loom of Destiny.

It was a magnificent, elegant structure that possessed all of Nirinel's regal majesty, being made of that same divine substance. Here was the first wood chopped from Yggdrasill, the World-Tree, and Neil could feel the might of its enchantment throbbing through its fibers.

Around the two main supporting pillars images of leaves and flowers had been skillfully crafted. But where the monumental frame stood on the ground, actual living shoots had sprouted and pushed out from the wood grain. Over the surrounding floorboards these tendril-like, foraging roots had snaked, fanning out into the attic, to go delving down inside the walls of the Wyrd Museum.

Upon those timbers, stretched within the Loom's stately, unparalleled framework, was the Cloth of Doom itself. The wool of Edie's pixie hat gleamed and sparkled in response to the glistering glare that pulsed and flickered from that shimmering tapestry. Within the taut expanse of woven threads a vibrant web of shifting light flared with lustrous colors that neither of them had ever witnessed before.

It was impossible to see exactly what designs were spun there, for they moved and changed constantly: one moment they were portraits of faces; the next, scenes of distant and remote lands, which were in turn replaced by patterns of dazzling brightness. In many areas, however, the endlessly fluid weave was marred by ugly holes and rents, around which the resplendent effulgence was dimmed. Edie knew that in the rippling tale of the world those flaws were the blemishes of war, and through one of those she herself had been plucked.

"All those years Ursula lied," the girl whispered. "She told Celandine and Veronica the Loom had broke, when really she'd brought it here to work at in secret. The Doomcloth was finished after all, and in it she put the deaths of Woden, her sisters, and herself."

Stepping forward, hesitant in case the fabulous, dreamlike vision might be snatched away, Edie Dorkins studied those intricate, shining depths and bent the fluctuating images to her controlling will. The fatal strands of the tapestry were suddenly lapped with an emerald flame, and then she saw what she had yearned to see.

In the center of the web the lambent threads disclosed a sprawling, verdant landscape dominated by a colossal, but supremely graceful, mountainous tree. Up into the heavens that miracle soared, its leaf-covered branches mingling with the clouds, and in one distant region beneath the momentous trunk she saw the glittering silver towers of a fair city.

"Askar," she murmured. "Under Yggdrasill when it were young."

Standing behind her, Neil was enthralled, but then the clangorous racket in the Websters' apartment restored his thoughts to the dangers of their predicament. How long would it be before the Frost Giant finally discovered them?

The delicious scene within the tapestry melted as Edie sighed, lifting her face up to where an arch of carved decoration linked the Loom's two supporting columns. In the middle of the curling fronds and interweaving vines, she looked on the central figure amid that sculpted adornment and clapped her hands when she saw that it was already stirring.

Neil could not help laughing grimly when he, too,

noticed the wooden effigy that had so terrified Quoth and himself in the darkness of The Roman Gallery only three nights previously. Compared with what had happened since, and their present plight, those fears seemed ridiculous and childish.

With an agitated splintering of wood, the outlandish shape of the Pedagogus worked itself free of its position on the Loom of Destiny. Using its monkey-like tail, it swung down from the arching ornamentation to land, with a slap of its splayed claws and a wheezing, piggy grunt, at Edie's feet.

"Gogus!" it barked, executing a low bow before her and waiting obediently. "Gogus . . . Gogus!"

The girl beamed at it, patting the wood urchin's large head. "Yes," she admitted, "this is the time when you're needed most, what was foretold by the Queen of Askar. The others are gone, Gogus— Nirinel, Ursula, all of 'em. There's just us left."

With a forlorn whimper the imp slapped its head and jabbered woefully before waggling its ears and gnashing its teeth at the din that echoed throughout the attic.

"The Loom . . ." Neil began. "Can you make it show us what we're supposed to do? Can we see what's going to happen?"

Edie laid her hands upon one of the intricately carved pillars, wherein the sap of the World-Tree still flowed. "Yes," she answered. "Then we'll know."

Concentrating upon the tapestry once more, Edie frowned, and the tinsel in her pixie hat crackled and sparked as she compelled the cloth to reveal what the future would hold for them.

Without warning, the commotion in the Websters' apartment suddenly ceased, and the silence that ensued was more frightening than any amount of thunderous crashes.

"What's it doing now?" Neil whispered.

Gogus grunted and pattered softly down the three steps to listen behind the oil painting.

At the Loom, beneath the flickering, emerald flame, an image was forming within the Doomcloth. Staring intently at the gleaming threads, Edie saw a desolate wasteland shimmer into view. There was the realm of the lords of the ice and dark—an empty, tortured domain of winter, devoid of all life and hope. This, then, was what the immediate future held, and the girl staggered back, aghast.

"It's no use!" she cried. "We're done fer! The end of everythin' really will 'appen!"

Covering her eyes in anguish, the girl recoiled from the bleak vision. At once, the icy wilderness disappeared back into the ever-switching patterns.

Neil looked at her in consternation. He had never seen Edie so crushed. "There *is* a way out of this mess!" he spat. "There must be! Can't you make the tapestry work for you? Can't you cut out the life of the Frost Giants?"

Edie shook her head. "Nothin' will be any good," she wept. "We can't change it! It's Fate—don't you understand that by now?"

"Well, I won't believe it!" he fumed, glaring around the attic. "There has to be something we can do. Come on, Edie, you can't give up now!"

Tearing through swathes of ancient cobwebs, Neil

ran the length of that dusty space, then darted around the far corner to where the rafters angled sharply, forming a high gable end. There the boy saw a rickety-looking ladder stretching up to the inside of one of the many turrets that crowned the Wyrd Museum. Testing the rungs, he found that it was sturdy enough to support his weight, and a desperate plan flashed into his mind.

Before the Loom, Edie Dorkins drew the back of a hand across her nose and considered the sweater that held the object she had set such store in. She must have been wrong; that was not the answer after all.

The eerie, unsettling hush deepened. Not a sound came from outside that hidden room. Wherever it was, the ice lord was keeping absolutely silent.

Questing the air with its snout, Gogus grimaced and pressed one of its large pointed ears against the canvas.

"Gogus, " it hissed. "Where . . . Gogus . . . Cold?"

Suddenly, with a hideous rending tear, the Spear of Longinus came stabbing through the oil painting. Behind, the rancorous shrieks of the Frost Giant bellowed in triumph. Yammering wildly, Gogus tumbled head over tail as the monstrous deformity of Neil's father ripped the canvas aside and pushed its way into that secret room.

Up into its glimmering space the nightmare lumbered. The bitter despair of the deathly light that beat from those malignant, clustered eyes contested with the heavenly radiance emanating from the Doomcloth. Under the steepled roof beams the whirling winter went storming. Over the caretaker's disfigured features, an arrogant snarl twisted those blue, repellent lips within the ice spikes of the branching beard.

"The Loom!" that ghastly voice proclaimed. *"Now shalt the rightful rulers of the world be freed of their shackles."*

Shrieking with blaspheming laughter, the Frost Giant surged forward, the spear raised above its malformed skull. Squealing, Edie Dorkins rushed in front of the Loom to protect it, but the unstoppable force of the ice lord knocked her aside, and the girl was sent reeling.

At once Gogus snapped and barked, pouncing onto one of the monster's legs and scampering up over the distorted back to claw and bite, thrashing the horror's face with its long tail. But the fiend was oblivious to that insignificant onslaught. Consumed with hate and malice, the great inhuman figure lifted the rusted spear high over its ice-crested head, then plunged it down.

Edie screamed, and a searing flash of silver light blasted out across the attic. Dashing back to the girl's side, Gogus somersaulted and gibbered in a feverish panic. Returning from the far reaches of the attic, Neil Chapman was just in time to witness the end of the Fates' dominion over the world.

Into the Cloth of Doom the Spear of Longinus went tearing. With bursts of blinding fire, each of the glittering, fate-filled threads was severed and snapped. Up through the riven fabric tongues of devouring flame shot out, licking over the rusted blade, traveling along its shaft. When they touched the Frost Giant's ice-clawed hands, the ogre screeched in agony.

Yet nothing could prevent that savage creature from executing that reviled and heinous deed. From the Loom's towering framework, the omnipotent Web of Destiny was finally ripped, its glorious splendor diminished as the power of Fate failed within its woven strands. Emerald flames roared fiercely, and the tapestry withered and was utterly consumed in their devouring heat.

A horrendous shout of evil mirth gusted from the ogre's throat, but in its grasp, the Spear of Longinus was also destroyed, and blackened fragments of that hallowed blade fell as charred, flaking cinders from those cruel claws.

To accomplish its true purpose, the fell spirit needed no weapon other than its own unquenchable malignance. Bellowing furiously, the monstrous figure lashed with its talons and gouged deep wounds into the Loom's supporting timbers. From those vicious gashes a luminous lymph oozed out over the ornate carving, and the hellish laughter trumpeted into every corner of the Wyrd Museum.

Shrinking away from that awful spectacle, Edie watched in hopeless dread as those raking claws hacked and slashed their way into the Loom's living wood. Then, into that bleeding mutilation, the Frost Giant breathed its glacial breath. Just as Nirinel had suffered and perished before, so the timbers of the Loom were killed by the thrusting ice that murdered its corrosive way through the sacred fibers of its grain. From the top of the arching decoration down into the magical, serpentine roots that spread through every part of the Wyrd Museum, the slaughtering cold coursed, and the building was seized by a violent shuddering.

"Die now, last vestige of Yggdrasill!" the terrifying voice howled on the snow-seething gale. *"The last drop of thy sovereign blood is stilled and blighted at last and evermore!"*

With a ruinous crash the stately frame of the Loom ruptured, and the mighty timbers split asunder, collapsing and toppling onto the floorboards, which smashed and shattered. Down through the shriveling roots the fractured remains of that device that once governed and controlled the lives of all mankind went tumbling, cannoning into The Tiring Salon below.

The malevolent force that dwelt within Brian Chapman threw back its grotesque head. *"The age of darkness and despair hath come at last!"* the discordant voice exulted. *"Now doth our rightful reign commence."*

While Neil and Edie stared at that repulsive figure, the might of the Frost Giants flowed more fiercely within it, and the caretaker's form became even more distorted and monstrous.

"Edie," Neil whispered, with one eye trained upon the terror that had once been his father, "what's your plan?"

But the girl could not wrest her eyes from that ghastly apparition which, with a horrible cracking of bones, was growing before them and cackling foully. "Edie!" Neil persisted, shaking her. "You must have had something in mind. What did you take from The Separate Collection?"

"No point," she muttered flatly. "We've lost. This is the end."

Mewling morosely, Gogus buried its face in the girl's arms. Then, as Edie absently ran her hands over that pugnacious head, her eyes suddenly kindled with her former fire. "Maybe not!" she cried, the faith in herself soaring once more. "That's what the prophecy meant—'course it did!"

Snatching up her bulging sweater, she clutched Gogus by its claws and turned a resolute face on Neil. "We got to get out in the open!" she urged. "Quickly!"

Even with the biting hail squalling about him, Neil chuckled. "This way!"

Through the snow-lashed attic they ran to where the ramshackle ladder reached up into the empty turret. Edie stared up at the wooden slats that shuttered that lofty enclosure and nodded vigorously.

"Get up there!" she ordered. "An' climb out onto the roof."

"What are you going to do?" Neil demanded.

"Tell your dad just what I think of 'im," she answered with a mischievous grin.

With that, she hared back under the rafters to where the disfigurement of Brian Chapman was now complete.

Any semblance of the man he had once been was completely erased. The ice lord had total dominion. The flesh that covered his warped and crooked skeleton shone cold and gray, and from those hunched shoulders long, powerful arms stretched down to the ground. In that giant, gruesome head the glaring, ice-covered eyes cast a cadaverous pallor over everything. The mouth, now a harrowing blue-lipped slit that divided the swollen skull in half, was enmeshed within the thicket of a white and rigid briar-like beard.

About its immense repugnance, the infernal cold tempested furiously. Striding into that battering gale, Edie Dorkins glowered and snapped her fingers at that inhuman obscenity.

"Hey!" she yelled, swinging her bulky sweater behind her. "You ain't won yet, you know, and yer won't, neither!"

The corpse glow of those frozen clusters gleamed at her across the attic. *Little fool!* the ogre scorned. *"Canst thou not feel the everlasting dark descending? Death shalt come swiftly unto thee."*

"You're the fool!" Edie bawled back, and her voice rang with a challenging disdain reminiscent of Miss Ursula Webster at her most imperious and condescending. "You think you've got rid of every drop of sap what flowed through the World-Tree—well, you ain't!"

"Thou liest!" the Frost Giant roared.

The girl tossed her head and laughed. "You might've killed Nirinel and the Loom," she cried mockingly, "but you forgot about the Pedagogus, dintcha? He were made from that same bit of Yggdrasill, an' in his veins the sap still runs. Your rotten old crew's stuck out in the cold, where you all belong!"

An ear-splitting shriek blared from the ogre's dark throat as it leaped forward, spitting icy death and scything the air with the slashing knives of its claws.

"Come on, you dirty old snowman!" Edie called impudently, and she scurried off toward the ladder.

* * *

Having climbed up into the turret, Neil Chapman squirmed around in the cramped confinement of its walls, then kicked out at the wooden shutters that hemmed him in. Perched upon the rungs directly beneath, Gogus yapped and barked impatiently and the boy growled right back.

"I'm doing the best I can!" he snapped. "It's not easy, you know!"

With that, he gave the boarded slats another shove with his heel and at last they yielded. Out over the tiles of the sloping roof the broken shutters went slithering, and Neil crawled through the opening.

Scampering up behind, the Pedagogus paused at the summit of the ladder, wrapping its tail about the topmost rung to peer down at the attic floor where Edie Dorkins came running into view.

"Gogus!" the wood urchin yammered. "Gogus . . . Climb . . . Gogus!"

Glancing over her shoulder, Edie let out a squeal of fright as the Frost Giant tore after her. She threw herself at the ladder, scuttling up as fast as possible, her bulging sweater dangling madly in her grasp.

"Don't wait fer me!" the girl shouted up at the imp. "Get out, quick!"

Wagging its head dutifully, Gogus swung across to the new gap in the turret's side. Higher Edie toiled, shrieking in alarm when the ogre came raging below and seized hold of the rungs. For an instant she thought that it was going to tear the ladder from the turret, but instead the misshapen horror began to clamber after her.

"Hoped you would," the girl mumbled under her breath as she reached the top and scrambled outside.

Neil Chapman was shaking his head in disbelief when she emerged. "Where are we?" he murmured.

The blizzard that had so beleaguered the building was raging still, but the surrounding, snow-shrouded sprawl of Bethnal Green had disappeared completely. Not a brick or a lamppost remained to show that the district had ever existed, and beyond that immediate emptiness the whole of London had also vanished. In every direction, wherever they stared, all they could see was a desolate winter landscape, and overhead was a canopy of absolute night.

"This is what I saw in the tapestry!" Edie exclaimed.

"But what's happened to everything?" Neil cried.

The girl smiled gravely. "You don't understand. It ain't gone nowhere—it's us what's moved. Right now, them lords of the ice an' dark are almost as strong as they ever was. It's them what's done this. The whole museum's been shifted—slap bang in the middle of their territory, that's where we is now."

A baying shout issued up out of the turret behind them, and the children stared back fearfully. "This really is the last hope," Edie declared. "We'd best run before that 'orror breaks out."

"Where to?" Neil cried, but Edie and Gogus were already hurrying over the ice-smothered slates.

"You'll see!" the girl yelled.

Up that tiled slope of the gabled roof they clambered, to escape from the pursuing ogre that had now reached the top of the ladder.

The roofscape of the Wyrd Museum was a disordered, graceless clutter of historical periods like the rest of the building. Tudor chimneys of flat red bricks pointed like sandstone fingers up into the freezing dark, while less elaborate but stouter structures were topped by tall, crown-capped pots. Toward the center a large verdigris bump, too irregular and pinched in shape to be termed a dome, peeped up over the high, containing ridges.

Around those rearing columns and squat towers many pieces of spearing ironwork rose like naked hedges of barbed bramble. Weather vanes adorned almost every chimney, and rows of railings ran like fences along every apex. Finials of all shapes and dimensions presided over the leaded junctions, and below them the clogged gutters meandered as rivers through that geometric gray mountainside.

From the attic, the ferocious call of the Frost Giant blasted out, and the turret shuddered as the ogre heaved its great size up after the children.

Scaling the roof, Neil and Edie squeezed through the railing at the top, then slid down the other side as Gogus bounded and hopped before them, chattering excitedly. Behind, there came a fearsome splitting as the turret burst open, and the four shuttered sides, together with the scalloped copperwork of its tented lid, went careering down the building to plummet into the blanketing ice below.

Out of the attic the ice lord came, and a reviling laugh was hurled up into the gale. *"So shalt the world be ours!"* it gloated. *"An eternal empire of cold and night. Bring me the carving, so I might crush and destroy!"*

Up from the lead-ripped wreckage the swollen creature dragged itself, the long, hoary arms reaching over the rails as it hoisted that vile, inhuman shape onto the roof. With a trouncing crash the heavy, bloated feet crunched down into the slates, and the ogre went striding over the buckling roof in pursuit of the Pedagogus, in which the last sap of Yggdrasill coursed.

In a feverish scramble, the children fled between the snow-wrapped chimneys, then down the steep, treacherous ravines beyond. Bellowing shrieks of hate thundered after them, and to their dismay they felt the rafters of the museum quail under the Frost Giant's rampaging approach.

Hearing that malice-fueled voice, Neil looked back through the stacks and spikes and saw the awful, deformed shape of the ice lord stomping in their wake. Carelessly it brushed aside the wrought-iron rails as if they were no more than waving grasses.

"How long canst thou evade me?" that damning voice menaced. *"Surrender unto those of the first flesh. Deliver up that trifling contrivance which standeth in our way."*

Turning from that disgusting sight, Neil hastened after Edie and Gogus, and the boy could not help asking himself how much longer they could continue this murderous chase.

"Abandon this folly! Let the embrace of the dark ones take thee."

Darting under an iron archway, Neil suddenly lost his footing and almost went slithering to his death. Upon that whipping wind a new sound pummeled its way into his despair.

In the dark, remote distance of this pernicious wasteland, the hosts of the Frost Giants were calling, answering the booming shrieks of their brother atop the Wyrd Museum. Under that accursed, eclipsed firmament the empty, echoing shouts traveled. With his heart leaping into his mouth, Neil realized that they were quickly growing louder.

"The lords of the ice and dark are headed right for us!" he spluttered.

Clinging to the nearest spire, the boy whirled about and saw that Edie, too, had heard that atrocious uproar. "Don't stand there ditherin'!" she yelled. "Not far now!"

"Gogus!" the wooden imp barked across the tiled valley that divided them. "Gogus . . . Haste . . . Gogus!"

Lurching from the projecting spire, Neil teetered along the tortuous route, while the ogre that came striding after mocked and taunted them.

"Harken to the approach of mine brethren! Soon shalt they converge upon this place and agonies undreamed of wilt they bring. Yield to me and thou shalt suffer but fleetingly. Give me the carving!"

Over the rooftops Edie Dorkins capered nimbly, her assured steps protracting the distance between herself and Neil. A little way in front, Gogus danced along the jabbing rails, yammering at the rising clamor that mounted steadily under the sky.

"This way," Edie told it, turning sharply to hare toward the tallest of the chimney stacks. With a last, defiant yap directed at the veiled horizon, the imp flicked its long tail and obeyed.

At the rear of that confused roofscape, the greatest of those lofty structures was a high Victorian chimney that soared up into the blind heavens, dwarfing the lesser vents and pot-peaked funnels that congregated about its wide base. Ever upward that towering pillar of bricks seemed to rise. Even when the masonry could ascend no more, a sun-shaped weather vane continued above it, the sharp tip of its topmost pinnacle threatening to puncture the cavernous underbelly of that grim darkness.

Hurrying between the smaller chimneys Edie Dorkins finally reached their superior, and tying the empty sleeves of her bulging sweater around a jutting post the girl glared out into the night. The resounding calls of the other Frost Giants were much closer now, and when she peered into the black rim of that horrible emptiness, indistinct monstrous shapes were moving.

"Not much time," she breathed. Dragging the pixie hat from her head, the girl snapped one of the woolen threads with her teeth. Perched on the slate slope at her feet, Gogus coiled its tail about one of the spearing spikes. It grunted softly as she took the gift of the Fates in her fingers and rapidly started to unravel the glittering green and silver stitches.

Trumpeting challenges now filled the plucking

gale. From all sides the frightful calls blasted, and Neil Chapman shivered uncontrollably as he pushed between the encircling chimneys to join Edie and Gogus. Glancing back, the boy saw the distorted apparition of his possessed father lumbering toward them.

"What are you doing?" Neil demanded, mystified by Edie's actions. "It'll be here any minute!"

"I'm buyin' us a bit more time!" she answered curtly as the last of the knitted stitches untangled in her hand. Then, like lightning, she leaped away to tie the end about one of the chimneys. With the thread trailing from her fingers, she scurried in between the posts and funnels that clustered around the tallest stack, weaving in and out, forming the flimsiest of fences around it.

Speechless, Neil watched the fey girl go, twining that ludicrous barricade about them. At his side, Gogus regarded its young mistress keenly, yipping and nodding its eager encouragement.

When she had used up all of the unraveled thread, Edie stood back and surveyed her work proudly. Like the untidy web of some inept and drunken spider those strands appeared, yet in that chill darkness, the clumsy, enclosing net glimmered and sparkled.

Neil stared at it doubtfully. Was there any power in that peculiar, makeshift mesh?

At that moment the grotesque, crooked figure of the caretaker came crashing toward them. With a sweep of those horrendous talons, the pots of the outlying chimneys exploded as the rending claws went gouging into the bricks of their stacks. A torrent of hail seethed around the children, and Neil looked once more upon the atrocity that his father had become.

The ogre was now twice as tall as Brian Chapman had been, and the thorns of ice that crowned its deformed head reared high into the turbulent night. From the hideous death lamps of its frozen eyes that scathing, unclean glare shone, and the children and Gogus were steeped in its defiling light.

Barking madly, the wood urchin bared its teeth and slapped the slates with its own hooked claws.

Brighter and more intent became the unholy glow from its frozen eyes as the blue lips of that abhorrent mouth parted and a merciless laugh was let loose.

"Now the age of Yggdrasill is ended indeed."

Through the remaining chimneys the ogre's odious bulk came savaging, until a flash of silver flame suddenly spat and sizzled across the stacks. A brilliant, burning light flared up into the monster's vile face, and it shrieked in pain. The stretch of Edie's straggly web that it had raged into was now shining fiercely, and searing fires were dripping from the crackling strands.

Lifting its enormous, scorched fist into the air, the Frost Giant yowled, and the violence of that dreadful din shook the surrounding spires. Incensed with wrath, the ogre lunged forward a second time, but the barring cords pulsed with the might of Fate, and the roofscape of the Wyrd Museum flickered and flared as the nightmare battled in vain to breach them. But the supreme forces of Destiny traveled through the net, and every woolen strand was like a ribbon of heavenly flame.

Consumed with wrath, its skin burned and bubbling, the ghastly apparition blundered back, incensed and dismayed.

"It's working!" Neil exclaimed. "Edie, it's working!"

"There!" the girl shouted. "You can't get Gogus now!"

Prowling around that threaded area, the repugnant enemy snarled and tested the strands with its talons. But every time its cruel claws touched the wool, a shower of blazing sparks erupted and those burning stars bit deep into its cold flesh. The ogre hissed with fury.

"Daughter of the three Fates," it growled with consummate menace. *"Remove thy snares before my brethren reach thee. Against their combined might thy traps and games are as nought. This trick they shalt brush aside, and for daring to oppose them, thou shalt be made sensible of the true cold and perceive the full measure of despair."*

Edie snorted and turned away from that malevolent face. Crouching beside Gogus, she cupped her hand to one of its pointed ears and whispered quickly. The imp's eyes swiveled in their wooden sockets, then the carving wagged its large head in ready agreement.

"Yes . . . Gogus . . . Yes!"

"From the fastness of their stronghold they storm!" the puppet of the Frost Giants cried. *"To me, my brethren! To me!"*

Staring out beyond the taut, shimmering strings, Neil felt his heart thump fiercely when he beheld the gargantuan forms thundering across that ice-covered plain. The true lords of the ice and dark were immense and mountainous. Through the whirling white storm they charged, their frigid eyes cutting through the blizzard to beat upon the quailing walls of the Wyrd Museum with the full vehemence of their enmity.

On every side those vast, dark shapes came rushing from the enclosing night, and Neil knew that there was no way Edie's little web could withstand them. Just one of those horrors could easily crush the museum, and the boy shrank against the brickwork of the chimney, trembling at the futility of any battle against such a powerful enemy.

Here, on this rooftop, he and Edie would die. The sap within the carving would be staunched and poisoned with the unstoppable cold, and the final dark would descend. In shallow, anxious breaths, he gulped and swallowed the biting, hail-ridden air. Then he turned to that loathsome abhorrence that dwelt within his father's body.

"Listen to me!" he implored. "I know it now—we've lost. But please, let my dad go. You don't need to use him anymore—you've won!"

The fiend that had twisted the caretaker out of all recognition cackled callously. *"Now at the end dost thou understand!"* it brayed. *"Sip to thy fill the brimming cup of thy terror!"*

"I'm begging you!" the boy yelled. "Let us be together."

"Release unto me the Pedagogus and I might consider it," came the foul reply.

Neil turned beseechingly to Edie, but the girl was

busily untying the sleeves of her sweater from around the post.

"Which is it to be?" that mocking, repellent voice demanded, relishing the boy's torment. *"Wouldst thou choose the petty life of thy weak and irresolute father—he whose own feebleness of mind made it so much the easier to obtain? Such is thy dilemma—the frailest of men or the Doom of thy entire world?"*

"Stop it!" Neil shouted across the fencing threads. "I can't do that. Just let my dad come back!"

The ogre jeered at him, and the mordant sound chilled the boy's blood more than the intense cold ever could.

"Another weak-minded fool!" the apparition hissed. *"Didst thou really believe thy father still lived within this impotent shell? Upon that instant when the first of the Fates didst perish and I claimed this vessel, thy parent was killed. 'Twas I who played his mundane part all times since."*

Neil clenched his fists and drove his fingernails into the palms of his hands. "No!" he screeched.

Even as Neil endured those hellish taunts, Edie Dorkins placed her bulging sweater on the sloping tiles at her feet and gazed out at the shadowy tempest. The blizzard was at its height now, and the vast shapes of the evil host would shortly be upon them. It was time to see if her guess had been correct.

Taking a deep breath, she peeled back the gathered welt and reverently took out that object she had removed from The Separate Collection.

"Chapman!" she hollered. "Get back 'ere, now!"

But the boy ignored her. All he could think of was

his father. "He isn't dead!" he yelled. "You're lying!"

Behind the restraining web, the corpse light of the ogre's ice-clustered eyes glared at him.

"My dad is still in there somewhere!" the boy insisted. "He has to be. It was him who scribbled those messages on the walls of the museum, wasn't it? Before you stopped him. You couldn't control him completely. He's in there—I know it!"

With her back to the chimney, Edie lifted the exhibit in her hands. Gazing up at it, Gogus bowed low.

"Chapman!" the girl shouted again. "If you don't get over 'ere right now, you're done fer!"

The boy glanced at her, distracted. But when he saw what she held in her hands he turned back to the crooked abhorrence of the Frost Giant with even greater urgency and impassioned dread.

"Dad!" he called. "Dad! I know you're in that thing somewhere. Please—it's me—it's Neil! Listen to me! You can fight it—you can!"

Throwing back its ice-crowned head, the nightmare bellowed with pitiless scorn.

"Dad!" Neil pleaded. "For once in your life, be strong—you must!"

Running her fingers over the dry, crackled surface of the large, leathery globe in her grasp, Edie Dorkins placed the Eye of Balor on her knees, then reached deep into her pocket. From her hoard of plundered treasures the girl brought out a small, unglazed ceramic jar and hastily removed the lid.

"Chapman!" she shrieked a third time, but her voice was snatched by the gale, and that battering wind bellowed with other, fiercer calls. The ancient forces of death and darkness were almost upon them. Their enormous sweeping shadows obliterated the surrounding desolation, and the destroying clamor of their bane-filled wrath shook the foundations of the world.

Oblivious to all this, Neil Chapman pleaded with the abomination one last time. "Dad! Answer me—please!"

The hideous slit of that blue-lipped mouth gaped ever wider as the ogre ridiculed his puling efforts. But then, in the midst of that detestable, vainglorious derision, Neil thought he heard a tiny, far-off cry.

"Neil!" that distant voice called desperately. "Neil, it's me! Son, it's me!"

Behind him, Edie stared into the jar she had taken from Miss Veronica's cupboard the day she had returned from Glastonbury. Then she dipped her fingers into the ochre-colored ointment it contained. Not wasting a second more, the girl larded the greasy salve over the parched and rigid leather of the Eye of Balor, rubbing it well into that adamantine skin.

"Please be the right one," she prayed.

To her relief, the shriveled vellum softened and became supple under her fingertips. With a final, anguished glance at Neil, the girl passed the lumpy sphere to Gogus.

"You know what to do," she cried above the squall.

Jabbering, the wood urchin nodded wildly. Wedging the great globe in place under one of its stunted arms, it leaped away.

Edie Dorkins watched the Fates' familiar swarm

expertly up the towering chimney stack. All around the Wyrd Museum huge, malevolent forms reared from the darkness, and she clapped her hands over her ears to blot out their rioting uproar.

Within the harrowing laughter of the ogre that mocked him, Neil could hear his father's shouts growing steadily louder, but time had nearly run out. Up around the chimney Gogus climbed, its bowed legs scrabbling furiously. Swiftly, the imp of the Loom raced heavenward, its yammering barks shredded and scattered by the storm.

"Dad!" Neil cried far below.

Within the disfigured apparition, Brian Chapman's will grappled to reassert itself. As Neil watched, a change came over the Frost Giant's creation. The evil glee died in the ghastly throat, and as the hail lashed about that distended form, its grotesque dimensions seemed to decrease in size, dwindling like wax in a flame.

"Edie!" the boy called frantically. "Look!"

Edie Dorkins stared through the howling snow. As she watched, the ogre's shape blurred and shrank, withering and melting as the rightful owner of that body seized control once more.

A deep, freezing blackness suddenly engulfed the Wyrd Museum. It was a darkness blacker and more stifling than anything Edie had ever known. High above the rooftop, torn and buffeted by the ravaging gale, Gogus had already reached the end of his brick-runged ascent. Then, twirling his tail about the iron pole of the weather vane, the imp shinnied speedily higher.

With the Eye of Balor still wedged firmly in its grasp, the wood urchin clambered on. Past the planished metal sunburst it scrambled, over the compass points where Quoth had once roosted and listened to the unwelcome words of Woden, his former master.

"Gogus!" the imp gibbered. "Gogus . . . Gogus!"

It did not pause to glower at those titanic shapes looming up out of the dark. The wooden eyes were fixed only upon the topmost pinnacle, and with a snorting grunt, the urchin reached it.

Down on the rooftop, with an overwhelming effort of will, Brian Chapman finally succeeded in his internal battle.

"This weakling is restored unto thee!" the departing, vanquished spirit spat as it fled howling out of Brian's mouth with a spiraling rush of hail. *"We hath no further need!"*

From the man's hands the ice talons fell away, the cadaverous pallor drained from his flesh, and the infernal glare perished in those hideous eyes. Then the hoary thicket of the frozen beard cracked and snapped off his face, shattering in a million fragments. Exhausted and spent, the caretaker slumped sideways. But his mind was returned and his gangly body restored—free at last of the Frost Giant's dominion.

"Neil . . ." he gasped, holding out a quivering arm. "I . . . I . . . can't . . ." The caretaker's legs collapsed under him and he fell awkwardly onto the tiles, then went slithering down the steep, slippery roof.

"Dad!" Neil shrieked, rushing forward, thrashing his way through the woolen strands that snapped and twanged around him. The magical light was at once extinguished, and the severed threads of the unraveled pixie hat were torn from the chimneys by the screaming gale, whipping out into the terrifying night.

Clinging to the base of the stack, her hair streaming in her face, Edie watched the boy break through her enchanted barrier.

"Come back!" she yelled to Neil, who was already clambering down the roof. "It's too late—you'll both be killed!"

But Neil was not listening. Edging his way cautiously downward, he peered over the roof's perilous brink and saw that his father was clinging haplessly to the lead gutter. Beneath him, the ground dropped in the distance, and beyond, the darkness was consumed with the fury of the Frost Giants.

Those mountainous shapes were horribly near now. The boy could feel their icy breath battering against him, and he gripped the slates anxiously as he crawled toward that part of the guttering where Brian's knuckles shone white. The lead was bowing under the man's weight.

"Give me your hand!" Neil bawled, reaching out as far as he dared.

His legs kicking the empty air below, the caretaker wailed, trying not to look down at the remote ground or at the vast shadow shapes that were closing about the Wyrd Museum.

With the blizzard tearing at him, Neil recklessly stretched out a little further and took hold of Brian's wrist, then struggled to haul him back onto the roof.

But the man was too heavy for his son to lift by himself.

Then, abruptly, the guttering buckled and snapped away from its fixings. Brian Chapman felt himself drop and lurch, but he was saved from falling by one last bolt that kept the gutter hanging precariously to the roof edge. Almost wrenched from his treacherous position, Neil was blanched with despair as he tried to drag his father up one last time. But it was no use.

"I can't do it!" he cried. "Help me!"

Perched aloft in that slaughterous night, Gogus wrapped its squat legs around the highest spire. Taking the Eye of Balor securely in its wooden claws, the imp lifted the leathery globe above its large head.

In the bellowing dark, countless frost-flaring eyes glared and Arctic gales blasted down from cavernous maws. This was indeed the final instant, and the fate of the world was held in the balance.

"Gogus!" the imp shrieked into the snatching wind, the hail drumming savagely against its outlandish figure. "Gogus . . . Spike . . . Eye!"

And, with that, the Pedagogus thrust the Eye of Balor down onto the topmost point, skewering it adroitly on the spearlike tip. Hugging the back of the impaled sphere, the wood urchin reached over and curled its hooked claws under that fleshy lid that had not been raised for three thousand years.

At that same moment, down on the roof, Edie Dorkins darted out to help Neil drag his father back from the brink. With the caretaker's arms hoisted about their necks, the children lugged him back to the towering chimney.

"Keep in, close as you can!" Edie told them. "Don't move or look up, whatever you do!"

Brian and the children pressed themselves against the rearing stack. A violent tremor shook the roofscape as finally the full, venomous fury of the lords of the ice and dark fell upon the Wyrd Museum.

Into its walls the calamitous, harrowing might of the Frost Giants went pounding, and every window shattered and exploded in its frame. With a tremendous crash, one of the remaining turrets was hurled down, and the roof ruptured and split as monstrous forces smote it. From breached, cloven walls a deluge of crumbling bricks cascaded, and the violated building was beset by a seething maelstrom of clangorous wrath.

Besieged by the cauldron of chaos and hatred, the Pedagogus yammered its loudest and pulled the eyelid open. "Doom . . . Gogus . . . Doom!" it barked.

In that fate-filled instant, the Eye of Balor was finally uncovered.

At first the ancient globe was dark, its curving surface wondrously smooth, glistening with countless, unwept tears. Then, in those dim depths, the many blood vessels and threading veins suddenly shone with a scarlet light. Into the central black pupil it coursed, and then the terrible, destroying power was roused and unleashed.

Out into the fearful night a flickering red glow shone, stabbing through the thundering storm, cutting a scathing, killing course into the darkness.

This was the fulfilling moment of Destiny, when the wood urchin performed the task first prophesied by the Queen of Askar. This was his high-appointed Fate, to be the one who would rid the world of the Frost Giants for all time.

From the Eye of Balor the venomous glare blasted, slicing a deadly beam of light at the malignant host that assailed the Wyrd Museum. Nothing could withstand its lethal force, and the inhuman voices that filled the tempest roared with terror.

Huddled against the base of the chimney, Neil and his father screwed up their faces as the annihilating glance of legend swept through the discordant shadows high above them. Beside them, Edie Dorkins gazed defiantly out across the roof to witness the final end.

Up in the squalling sky, looming over the spires and chimneys, were the dark shadow shapes of the lords of the ice and dark; she saw them writhe in fear as the baleful stare came crackling toward them. Into that foulness the fiery red beams went shooting, and Edie caught her breath as she beheld the immense, monumentally evil faces.

Like nightmare visions of blackened ice were those horrendous countenances. Their gargantuan heads were crowned with a forest of glittering, fang-shaped pinnacles, and their eyes were as frozen stars. Over the rocks and jags of their massive brows the unerring stream of light traveled, burning a crimson line across the crevices of those heinous, twisted features. Into the glacial throats of winter the searing glance shone, and along those piercing rays streaks of slaughterous flame went scorching.

Screams of rage ripped through the blizzard as the

ice lords encountered at last a power as virulent and mighty in the dealing of death as themselves.

Laughing at their torment, Edie mocked the ghastly horrors revealed in that ruby glare. Every illuminated visage was distorted with agony, and their howls quaked the Wyrd Museum to its foundation.

Far above her, seated behind that legendary instrument of carnage, Gogus crowed triumphantly. Then, using its tail to propel itself, it began to spin on the axis of the weather vane.

Around and around the Eye of Balor whirled madly, and in every direction its lethal glance went blasting. Like a beacon of death, the red, fire-raking glare evolved, slaying all in its blistering sight.

The screeches of the dying Frost Giants were terrible to hear, and Neil buried his head in his arms. All around, those malignant creatures withered before the exterminating light that streamed from the murdering eye.

The eternity that had passed since the first of the undines had chosen to assume frozen flesh and stride the land that was never meant for them had finally come to a close. Here, in the heart of their frozen domain, the mountainous contours of the lords of the ice and dark began to shrivel. As that scarlet ray continued to shoot out over the museum's roof, nothing could withstand its devouring might. All perished before it.

Gradually, the hideous clamor was replaced by the sounds of devastation as the huge, surrounding shadows split asunder. Enormous, hail-wreathed heads went toppling down rocky shoulders to explode on the ground beneath. Everywhere the sound of death and destruction thundered as the staggering heights of the Frost Giants came tumbling down, the towering cliffs of their being crumbling and crunching.

From the Wyrd Museum the slates went sliding, and under the shivering rafters the oak beams shifted alarmingly as each wall quivered and trembled. Throughout the world, the disruption of this ultimate, eradicating moment was felt, juddering and quaking into every continent.

Crouched against the chimney, Neil and his father felt the bricks shudder and lift. Then dislodged mortar went rattling over them, and they clung to one another as the final, blaring screeches tore over them.

Then it was over.

The last of the Frost Giants was slain. At once the raging blizzard ceased, and the Wyrd Museum was utterly becalmed.

Sitting on that battered, blasted roof, Edie Dorkins suddenly squealed with joy. Shaking with delighted laughter, Neil Chapman raised his face, while his father wept and rejoiced. The evil cold had been banished from the world forever, and from the already glimmering sky, a soft, warm rain was pattering.

Wheeling wildly on the highest pinnacle, the Pedagogus yapped and barked as the sweet rain splashed over its broad head and trickled over its tongue. Then, solemnly, the imp of the Loom lowered the Fomorian's great eyelid. The destroying glance was covered for the last time, and its unequaled power was never wielded again.

About the wreckage of the museum a gray light was

welling. Edie Dorkins held up her hands to the mizzling heavens to let the falling water wash her sorrow-stained soul clean. The lords of the ice and dark were utterly defeated, and Brian Chapman hugged his eldest son fiercely.

From its vantage point, Gogus looked down on them and grinned. Then, using its tail as a brake, it stilled the weather vane's wild revolutions. Out across the roof the imp stared, to where the dark hills of the Frost Giants' remains were already changing. Streaked by the glad downpour, the vast rockscape of their exposed glacial bones melted behind the rain. Regular shapes took their place as the familiar buildings of Bethnal Green glimmered into view all around. The ancient building of the Wyrd Museum was returned to its proper age-old location, and Gogus's ears jiggled excitedly when they caught the sound of voices floating up through the cloudburst.

Far below in the alleyway, in front of the entrance, the descendants of Askar, led by Chief Inspector Hargreaves, were cheering and applauding. Binding its tail securely about the spindling spire, the wood urchin drew itself up to its full, stunted height and waved dementedly at them.

"Gogus!" it gibbered. "Danger . . . Gogus . . . Gone . . . Gogus . . . Gogus!"

Within the timbers from which the Pedagogus was carved, the last drops of the divine sap that had once nourished the wondrous Yggdrasill in the dawn of the world were still flowing. Upon that high place, the familiar of the Fates threw back its head to give vent to a glorious and grunting pig-like chuckle.

In the Chamber of Nirinel

Edie Dorkins stood in the wreckage that filled the cavernous space, a flickering torch held above her head. It had been two days since the Eye of Balor destroyed the lords of the ice and dark, and there had been much rejoicing. Yet now, here she was, back beneath the museum's foundations, the first time she had dared to return to this place since that most evil of hours when the Doom of the world had hung by the slenderest of threads.

Sadly, she remembered those who had brought her out of the war-torn past and adopted her as their daughter. Now the three Fates of the world, they who had ruled since the fall of Yggdrasill, were gone forever.

Verdandi's charred remains were lost in the bottomless reaches of the well. Skuld had been consumed by the intense cold of The Separate Collection—when the drifting snow had thawed, her body was nowhere to be found.

As for Urdr . . . Edie stared through the murk at the colossal hills of rotted timbers that filled half of the chamber with their dark magnitude, and she knew that no power would ever move the gigantic ruin of Nirinel. Beneath it, the bodies of Urdr and Woden would stay until the tale of the world was ended.

The ancient enmities were over; the Fates and the Gallows God were reconciled in death, yet Edie Dorkins doubted if she was fit to assume their mantle.

"Them's all lost," she murmured sorrowfully. "Now there's just me."

A gruff bark at her side roused the girl from her mournful recollections. Gogus gazed up at her, and Edie smiled.

"An' you, too," she added.

Sniffing the stale air, Gogus turned its head to whimper at the spectacle of the fallen root. Then its wooden ears pricked up, and it jumped up and down in excitement.

"Gogus!" it gibbered, leaping about Edie and dancing before her.

The girl shook her head in bewilderment. "What's the matter?" she asked.

But the wood urchin was too agitated to tell her. Scampering forward over the sea of splintered timber, it yammered and yipped, then turned and scowled to find that she was not following. Bounding back, Gogus took hold of her hand and led Edie deeper into the chamber, to where the wellhead jutted from the debris.

"Gogus . . . Gogus!" it cried, leaping up and prancing wildly about the stone dais. Bemused, Edie clambered onto the well and peered down into the gaping gulf at its center.

Then she heard it. A faint rushing sound was rising from the black depths. Down in the furthest reaches of the immense shaft, water was flooding into the ancient well. As she listened, it surged higher and higher, and the girl began to giggle uncontrollably.

Bright was the gurgling surface of that wondrous sight. Like a glimmering, bubbling disc it drew ever closer to the brink, and beneath the surface, Edie saw a pair of large, fishlike eyes.

"He's here!" she sang through happy tears. "He's finally here!"

Halting his hopping jig, Gogus stared into the clear swishing water and barked in welcome.

"Undine . . . Undine!" it called, somersaulting and flipping itself over around the well.

Edie Dorkins gazed into those same luminous eyes that she had encountered deep beneath the streets of Glastonbury and cried with joy at the object in the undine's webbed and scale-covered hands.

*   *   *

In the hallway of the Wyrd Museum, the Chapman family was waiting to say good-bye. Everything they owned was packed into the van outside, where Chief Inspector Hargreaves and the elderly Jean Evans were waiting. All that remained was for them to take their leave of Edie.

"You sure you want us to do this?" Brian Chapman asked.

Neil looked around them at the devastation that had been wrought on the building. The parquet floor was wrecked and ruined, and the oak panels were ripped and shattered. Everywhere there was chaos, but that was not what had made up his mind.

"What I mean, Neil," his father began, "is . . . I really don't mind it here now. I suppose I've finally found the place where I fit in. This museum knows me, and there's so much repair work to be done. Even Josh is used to it here. The dangers are over, forever."

Neil turned to his young brother and Josh gave him a forlorn look. "Don't wanna go," the boy muttered.

"Can't you see?" Neil said quietly. "I have to leave. There's no way I can stay here—none."

Their father nodded his understanding. "Okay," he sighed. "We can be at Auntie Marion's by tonight."

Then, from the blank emptiness of the open wall, where once the secret panel had concealed the hidden entrance to the stairway, there came the sound of happy laughter. The Chapmans stared at each other in surprise. Edie had been morose and silent for the past two days.

Now, out of the darkness the girl came, calling over her shoulder for Gogus to keep up with her. Then, looking at the caretaker and his family, she folded her arms and pouted peevishly.

"You off?" she demanded, the suggestion of a smile tweaking the corners of her mouth.

"We have to," Brian told her. "Neil can't live here anymore. We just wanted to see you before we went."

Narrowing her almond-shaped eyes, Edie looked at Neil and grudgingly admitted, "I reckon this place needs more lookin' after than I can give it an' . . . well, I s'pose I needs it an' all. Wish you'd stay."

"Can't." The boy shook his head. "There are too many unhappy memories in here."

The slow smirk on Edie's face burst into a grin, and

as the chattering grunts of the Pedagogus came drifting from the dark opening, she told Neil, "Well, it's up to you to make better memories then, ain't it?"

With that, Gogus came scampering into the hall and greeted them, yapping at each of their feet, until it came to rest before Neil.

It pawed him fretfully. "Gogus . . ." it growled. "Gogus . . . Stay . . . Gogus."

The boy frowned quizzically, for the wood urchin was jabbing one of its claws back toward the steep stairway. Then, suddenly, Neil heard the most wonderful sound he could ever have wished for.

"The undine's come to live under 'ere now," Edie explained, "and just look what he's done! Just look!"

From the darkness a familiar, rasping voice was calling, and out into the hallway a creature came swooping, circling about their heads to cast off the last drops of sacred water until finally he alighted upon Neil's shoulder.

"Zooks hurrah!" Quoth squawked. "Zooks hurroosh!"

"Raven!" the imp gargled. "Gogus . . . Raven . . . Gogus!"

"Now will you stay?" Edie asked gently.

It was some moments before Neil could answer. Then, in a choked and sobbing voice, he laughed out loud. Tickling Quoth under his beak, he said, "Of course I will. This is the Wyrd Museum—our home."

THE END